NOT EVEN THE
BLACK SEA...

NOT EVEN THE BLACK SEA...

MILAN VIGNEVICH

To order additional copies of this book, contact:
Xlibris
AU TFN: 1 800 844 927 (Toll Free inside Australia)
AU Local: (02) 8310 8187 (+61 2 8310 8187 from outside Australia)
www.Xlibris.com.au
Orders@Xlibris.com.au
835596

CONTENTS

My special thanks to Rona Hulbert, who helped me with the final English version and who helped me to believe that this book deserves publishing.

Part 1

Reluctantly Klara opened her eyes and looked around the dark room where she slept along with her mother and older brother, Simeon. Her mother's bed was already empty; she had gone to prepare for Klara's departure. Simeon was still sleeping, a sweet smile on his lips. Klara carefully moved past him, trying not to wake him, as she made her way into the kitchen. When her mother saw her, she spread her arms.

'Come here, my dear. See how big you are already, leaving us today. You're not scared, are you?'

'I am scared,' Klara confessed, hugging her mother back.

'Don't be scared, silly girl. Your uncle Naum is a good man, and he will not hurt you. After all, he is your father's brother.' Mother was calming Klara down. 'They will feed you at his house, and you will put on some weight. Look how skinny you are now, just skin and bones.'

'And what about you and Simeon?' Klara asked.

'Well, we can't all go and drape ourselves around your uncle's neck. You go, and it will be easier for us to survive here. Now, go wash your face and get dressed. Uncle Naum will be here soon.'

The toilet was outside, located in the corner of a small courtyard. In Klara's house, there were four more apartments, none of them with a toilet. In the mornings and evenings, it was hard to get to, almost impossible to stay for long. It was still early morning now, and no one else was about. Nearby on the wall, there was a washstand and a small mirror. Klara could only see herself if she stood on a stool.

It was a beautiful morning. The sky was blue and cloudless. Sunlight filled the usually drab-looking courtyard. Quickly Klara used the toilet and washed her face, the freezing water quickly waking her up. On a day as wonderful as this, she thought and smiled, *Everything will be all right.* The smile seldom left her face. Klara loved to laugh, though there were not many reasons to laugh lately.

They lived in poverty, like all their neighbours in the shabby house on Fairground Square. Klara hardly remembered her father, who had died when she was a little over two years old. Her mother, Zelda, was born in 1893 into a Jewish family, the Podvisotsky family, and there were many children. Her parents were not wealthy people, but neither were they desperately poor.

When Zelda was still very young, something almost unbelievable had happened to her. One day, the Russian Tsar stopped at the train station in their village, and everyone had poured onto the platform to see him. Little Zelda stood with her mother and looked into the distance from where they expected the train to arrive. Soon, they saw smoke, and everyone cheered in expectation and excitement. Police began to push people away from the edge of the platform, and there suddenly was the steam engine with all the cars attached rolling into the station, stopping with a creak of the brakes.

The orchestra began to play the Russian anthem, the car doors opened, and an impressive man with a beard, wearing a smart uniform with medals covering his chest, stepped onto the platform. The crowd began to chant, 'The Tsar, the Tsar,' as the bearded man walked along the platform, the police holding back the crowd. Suddenly, the Tsar stopped right in front of Zelda, stretched out his hand, decorated with rings, and stroked her head. Frightened, Zelda didn't move, and soon the Tsar moved back to his carriage, the whistle blew, and the steam engine moved off. Many of the people crowded around Zelda and talked loudly about what had just happened. 'Girl, you don't know how lucky you are. If you are touched by the Tsar, you will be successful all your life. He is like God, a divine sovereign on earth. This means that God will watch over you all your life!' Zelda herself began to believe this and waited for happiness to fill her life. But happiness was still far away. Life was still hard and grey.

The years passed. At this time, the Jewish pogroms were frequent, and Zelda's family decided to immigrate to America, where, according to whispers, everyone was free and it was possible to become rich for those who were willing to work hard. So Zelda's family sold all their property and moved to the port of Odessa, where they would be able to buy tickets for the steamship that would take them to America. It was quite a long wait for this to happen, and, in the meanwhile, Zelda had met a handsome young man, David. David worked in a chocolate factory as a master chocolate maker; he had a good salary and looked very self-confident. It seemed silly for him to go to the still-unknown America, so after courting for a very short time, Zelda and David were married in a modest wedding ceremony, and soon after, the family moved to David's apartment. It seemed to Zelda that finally fortune was smiling on her and that things were only going to get better.

At last, Zelda's family were able to buy their tickets to America. They bought a ticket for Zelda too, but she had to choose between love and America, and she chose love. The steamship left, and she stayed. If she had known then what lay ahead of her in her life, she would have jumped into the sea and swum after the boat that was taking her family to America.

Almost straightaway, the country broke into war. While for many this time was very hard, David had work, good wages, and, of course, the most important thing—he and Zelda were in love. In 1916, their first son was born, and they named him Simeon. The revolution then started, followed by civil war. Odessa was falling into the hands of either the 'white' or 'red' forces, the Japonchik or the Kotovsky, but it was impossible to guess what would happen next.

Although David continued to work in the chocolate factory, now it was very hard to make ends meet. David was providing for Zelda and his small son as best he could, and between them, there was love and friendship. Then in 1918, Klara was born. The following year, a great famine hit the country. David collected everything that was valuable in the house and went around trying to exchange it for food. He travelled in carriages filled with people, sometimes on the roofs of the trains, sleeping at stations with other tramps like himself, all trying to get food for their families.

One day, he caught typhus and returned home with a high temperature, almost delirious, without money or food. He fell into the house, and Zelda was sure that he would die. She stayed with him day and night, never leaving his side, and she saved his life. Although he was weak, he again started to try to find ways to feed his family. But, again, things got worse. This time, it was cholera that raged through Odessa, and David caught it. It didn't matter how hard Zelda tried; she was not able to save her husband, and he died four days later. It was absolutely forbidden to bury the bodies of those who had died of cholera; kerosene was poured over the corpses, and they were burnt. Zelda could not think of her husband being burnt like a sheet of paper. She paid a lot of money to the yard keeper to bury David secretly. She washed her husband's corpse herself, not thinking that she might herself get sick and her two children become orphans.

So, at the age of twenty-eight, she had become a widow with two small children to look after. She had no money at all; she tried to earn money any way she could. She washed and ironed other people's linen, darned old clothes, and cleaned apartments. This money was just enough to keep the family from starving to death. But letters arrived from America, full of hope and optimism. Her relatives were earning good money, and each year it got better. They called for Zelda and her children to go to America too, but by this time the borders had closed and she couldn't find the money for the tickets. The cage door had slammed shut, and life was gloomy.

But even in this hopeless situation, new hope appeared. David's brother, Naum, came and suggested that he take Klara to his house for a couple of months. He was knocking at the door just as Klara finished changing into her dress. When he came into their small room, he seemed so big that there was hardly any place left. Bearded, healthy looking in a worn caftan, he frightened Klara, and she almost burst into tears. Her mother noticed and stroked her head. 'Foolish girl, why are you so frightened? This is your uncle Naum.'

Naum looked at her and smiled, and his brown eyes sparkled. Klara saw the change in his face and calmed down and smiled back at him. Uncle Naum gave Klara a lolly, and at once their relationship was established. Then Klara said goodbye to her mother and Simeon, and she went with Uncle Naum by tram to the train station. At the station, they boarded the train that was packed with other passengers and travelled for about two hours in the smoke-filled carriage. The smell was so bad that Klara thought she would choke, and when they got off the train at the 'Vesely Kut' (Cheerful) platform, it was a delight for her to breathe in the hot steppe air.

'Well, are you hot?' Uncle Naum asked her.

3

'No,' she answered.

'Do you want to eat?' he asked.

Klara shrugged her shoulders. Then Naum took out a small backpack and pulled out a paper bag. Inside was a piece of bread and a sausage. He carefully broke the bread, and with the help of a penknife, he cut off a piece of sausage and gave them to Klara. She smiled as she took it and bit off a piece. The bread was grey but very tasty, and the sausage smelled so good that Klara could not remember anything like it. Trying not to look greedy, she ate slowly and then shook off the crumbs.

'Now, are you ready to go?' her uncle asked. Klara nodded, and she followed in his steps.

They travelled for about an hour to the village of Tsebrikovo and then another half hour to the Freiberg farm, where all the Germans lived. The sun was already on the horizon when they arrived at the courtyard where all of Uncle Naum's family were waiting: his wife, Sima; their two daughters of Klara's age; and a small but very active boy, Mishka. Aunt Sima stretched out her arms in welcome, but Klara stopped in shock. Her aunt's face was covered in a terrible red scar, making Sima's face ugly. But Klara was a bright girl, and she tried to pretend that she didn't notice the scar. She came closer to her aunt, and Sima said as she hugged her, 'You are a poor little orphan girl! It's good that you are here with us. Look at you, just skin and bone! Well, we will try to fatten you a little. Let's all go the table,' she said in a most commanding voice, and everyone followed her obediently.

Although Uncle Naum's house didn't look new or particularly big, inside there was room for everyone. In one corner of the front room, which also served as the kitchen, there was a furnace, and on the opposite side, there was a big wooden table surrounded by benches and stools. In the middle of the table was a plate where cut bread was waiting. Uncle Naum took his place at the head of the table, and everyone else quickly took their seats. Only Klara remained standing, not knowing where to sit. But Uncle Naum put a stool near him and said, 'Sit here, next to me. You are our guest after all.'

Klara sat down, and Aunt Sima pulled a pan from the oven, put it on the table, and took off the lid. The room filled with the smell of chicken broth, waking in Klara an unbelievable hunger. Aunt Sima put a small piece of bread pompushki, and then poured over some of the broth. Klara filled her spoon, wanting to start as quickly as possible, but her aunt warned her, 'Take your time, dear. Blow on the broth to cool it first, or you will burn your mouth.' Klara blew a few times onto the spoon and quickly put it into her mouth. The broth burnt her throat pleasantly and then into her stomach, giving Klara real pleasure. She did not want to appear greedy by eating too quickly, but it was difficult. She looked at her cousins and noticed that they were eating quickly too. It seemed that chicken broth was not a daily food.

Only little Mishka ate nothing. He sat and stared at Klara. 'Why are sitting with your mouth open but eating nothing? Is it Klara that has affected you? But you must remember that if you do not eat, you will never grow up big and strong, and girls will never look at you!' his mother said. Mishka blushed but picked up his spoon and began to eat his broth. Then Aunt Sima pulled out from the broth a stuffed chicken neck. She put it on a plate with a bowl of boiled potatoes and put it on the table. She carefully cut the neck and put each of the pieces on everyone's plate. Everyone helped themselves to their potatoes. It was so quiet while they were eating that the only sound was the rattle of the forks against the plates. Klara, too, was quiet. She had only known these people for about an hour, but already she felt that they were real family members, and she liked them.

After dinner, they all sat for some time around the table, asking Klara about her life in the city. Klara was happy to answer their questions, though again it seemed that Mishka was her best listener . . . he couldn't take his eyes from her face. Only when it got dark did people move, and everyone went to bed. Klara was sleeping in the same room as her cousins, and being exhausted after her long trip and all the new things that had happened to her this day, she fell asleep very quickly, lulled by the songs of the crickets.

When she woke the next morning, she saw her aunt standing next to her bed. She handed Klara a glass of fresh milk and said, 'Here, our little orphan girl, drink this on your empty stomach.' Klara was not used to drinking fresh milk, and she found the taste a little unpleasant, but remembering that it would do her good, she drank to the end of the glass and smiled as she gave the empty glass back to her aunt. Aunt Sima smiled back, and the awful scar on her face twisted. She tried not to stare at the aunt's face and looked away.

Uncle Naum had noticed Klara's reaction to her aunt's face, and during supper that night, he asked Klara, 'Why are you so afraid to look at your aunt, little Klarochka?' And not waiting for a reply, he went on. 'Are you afraid of her scars?' Klara nodded. 'You know, these scars saved my life. It was in 1919, when the authority in our city changed every week, one week white, the next red, or Mahno's gang, or any other gang. All of them took anything that they could and often took men as recruits. One day, it happened to me. I was forced to leave with the reds, and I served with them for about half a year. They let me visit my wife, who was about to give birth to Rita.

'In our village at that time, there was no authority—it was anarchy. I stayed for a couple of days, but, unexpectedly, Mahno's gang arrived. I don't know who had informed them that I had served with the reds. They broke into our house while I was sleeping and pulled me out into the courtyard. They were going to shoot me. Sima started to shout and begged them to spare me. It was not possible to change their minds, though, and the tallest fighter trained his gun on me. Just at that moment, Sima jumped on the gun and blocked me from the shot. But the bullet hit her in the face! Bloodstained, she fell to the ground, and I rushed to help her and tried to close the wound. The bandits were all in shock themselves, unnecessarily shooting a pregnant woman! The big fellow understood the change of mood among his fighters and angrily thrust his pistol back in its holster. He spat on the ground and said, "To hell with you. Say thanks to this woman, only because of her bravery are you still alive!" Now I am in her debt for life, and she, poor creature, could barely eat for a whole year and will have that scar for the rest of her life!'

Klara was silent for some time after Uncle Naum had finished his story. Then she turned to Aunt Sima and said, 'Aunt Sima, what a courageous person you are. A real heroine!'

'Nonsense,' answered Aunt Sima. 'I simply knew that I could not survive without Naum with two small children on my hands. And I was frightened,' she said with a smile.

But Naum interrupted her. 'Scared people hide in corners, but you jumped on his gun!' After that, Klara was no longer afraid of Aunt Sima, and on the contrary, she now thought the scar made Sima's face kinder. Now she felt like a loved member of the family, especially by little Mishka, who followed her around everywhere and was completely captivated by Klara.

Klara stayed in Freiburg for about a month. Then one day, her mother arrived. During her stay there, Klara had managed to put on some weight so that her bones no longer showed through her dresses. Mother was amazed and kept thanking Sima and Naum. While it was not ideal to go back to Odessa, where everyone was still starving, this year, Klara was supposed to go to school. On the train going home, her mother told Klara a secret. As it happened, Zelda had met a widower, Aron Sirota (this word meant 'orphan' in Russian). She had met him in the house of a woman for whom she washed clothes. Aron mostly sewed fur caps, but on the money he earned, it was hard to support three children, and there was no one at home to look after them. So when he met Zelda, he asked her to marry him, suggesting that it would be easier to share the burden of the children.

By the end of that summer, Zelda had moved with her two children into Aron's house. There was not very much space in the house, and everyone had to sleep on the floor, and they were always hungry. Klara went off to school with her two new sisters, Zina and Katya, and at school everyone called them 'the three orphans', not just because they were poor—practically everyone in the district lived the same way—but because of their surname.

The best part about their new home was that the back gate of the house faced the sea. In the summertime, Klara spent practically all of her free time on the beach, seldom coming out of the water. The sea became a big part of her life, and she felt like a fish in the water. She quickly learnt to swim and wasn't afraid to go into the deeper water to catch crabs with the boys. Sometimes it was very easy to catch fish. It was well known that the Black Sea contains a lot of nitrogen sulphide, and occasionally it rose to the top of the water. The fish would then jump out of the water! On these days, people rushed to the beach carrying pots, bowls, and big jars. People were even catching fish in their bare hands. And what fish there were . . . mackerel, flounder, jack mackerel, mullet, flathead, and sole. On these days, everyone fried fish or made fish soup. The sea at Odessa was everything . . . food, work, and pleasure!

In the new house, Klara made many friends, and Tanja Klyachkina became her best friend. She lived with her father and little sister, Zina. Their mother had died of cholera. Their father was disabled; he had been seriously injured during the war and had his leg amputated. While his wife had been living, he felt like the head of the family and earned money wherever he could. But since her death, he had lost all his spirit and had started to drink heavily. Because of this, his house was almost bare. If Zelda gave the girls dresses, Tanja's father would take them to sell. Klara tried to help Tanja, often letting her wear her clothes.

The girls went to the same school, where, for Klara, life was much more exciting than at home. Klara found that studying was not hard, and here she could forget about life's difficulties. She especially loved music lessons. A happy Ukrainian man came to class with his accordion, and the children learnt new songs, and Klara always tried her best. Her teacher noticed this and often stopped near her to stroke her head and say, 'Sing, little girl, sing!' Back at home, Klara had very little reason to sing. Her mother and stepfather both worked as hard as they could, but it was difficult enough to get food and clothes for the children. Zelda made dresses for the girls from her own old dresses; she made them so well that the other children were often filled with envy. Once she made a beautiful red dress trimmed with lace. Klara was so delighted with it that she went out into the yard to show it off. The boys were playing hide-and-seek, and Klara joined in their game. She decided to hide behind the shed, but as she tried to get out, her dress caught on a nail and ripped in two. Klara's grief was overwhelming. It seemed to be the worst thing that could have happened to her. But life shows that there is no limit for good or for bad!

·+·+·+·+·+·+·

In 1932, the big famine began. The whole family was starving, and Klara became so thin that she constantly felt dizzy. To help the family, Zelda sold her gold teeth and bought a bag of cornflour. She hid it on the top shelf in the kitchen behind some empty jars. Sometimes, when everyone was really hungry, she would cook them some porridge. One day, Klara came into the kitchen to find her mother sobbing bitterly. Klara rushed to her mother.

'Mother, what happened to you?'

Her mother wailed, 'My God, why do you do this to us?'

'What happened?' Klara asked again. 'Why are you screaming as though someone has tried to kill you?'

'How can I not scream when we have been robbed?' her mother answered.

'What could anyone steal from us?' Klara asked in surprise.

'Someone has stolen almost all of our cornflour, which I paid for with my teeth,' her mother answered, 'and now I have lost both!' She began to sob again.

The culprit was soon caught. Tanja's younger sister, Zina, was caught with a mug of the flour behind her back. Zelda took her by the hand and asked, 'How can you steal from friends?' Zina was silent but turned red with shame. Finally, she began to cry, pulled away her hand, and ran from the kitchen. 'Are you simply going to let her go?' Klara asked her mother.

'What else can I do?' she asked. 'She is just a hungry little girl.' Zelda made a gesture of hopelessness and left the room.

Soon, it was all the neighbours spoke about, and they all condemned Zina's rascally act. Zina's father flogged her in a fit of anger, and together they came to apologise. He promised that he would make some money and pay the family back. But Zelda knew that he couldn't earn enough money even to feed his own girls, and to hope that he would pay for the flour was futile. So it was necessary for everyone to tighten their belts even more. Klara's brother, Simeon, left school and started to earn money as the apprentice to a hairdresser.

All morning it had been drizzling. Jukan had taken a seat on a tree stump, and from there he could watch the sheep grazing in the meadow. They didn't seem to move; it seemed that they didn't like the rain either. Jukan felt weary as well. Why did he have to watch the sheep graze on such a horrible morning, like a stray dog, even though he hadn't yet had his breakfast? Why was he living in the house of the richest peasant in the area but still had to work so hard? The house he was living in had been built by his grandfather, who was born in 1875, in Mazine. From home conversations, Jukan knew that his ancestors had lived in Montenegro before the Turks occupied it. The Vignevich family was one of the first Serbian families to convert to Christianity and took part in the construction of the famous church, the Sacred Vasily.

The Turks had seized Montenegro and ruled by fire and sword. They plundered and killed, and the most beautiful girls were taken away to harems. They had wanted to take the most beautiful girl from Jukan's ancestor's family as well, but at night when the Turks were sleeping, the Vignevich men attacked and killed them all. Such rebellion the Turks would never forgive; they would find everyone who was responsible and publicly execute them. The family did not wait for the Turks' retribution; they collected all their belongings and ran towards the sea. But to hide from the Turks on land was almost impossible. They had to get to one of the Adriatic islands. Here, they had to learn a new art . . . they had to be pirates, Hussars, and attack passing ships and plunder them. Quite often the ships they attacked were Venetian. They lived this way for many years before they found themselves up against the mighty Venetian Republic. After a long search, the Venetians located the family. The Hussars were taken by surprise and hid on the island. The Venetians imposed a blockade. The only way out from the bay was by ship, but because it was getting dark, they decided to wait until morning to finish the Hussars off. Mountains surrounded the bay from all sides. To get through them was practically impossible, and how could they get the boats away? Without boats, they would stay on the island. Therefore, the Venetians simply waited until morning.

The Hussars couldn't wait until morning, however. They used the darkness, the clouds covering the sky. Under cover of the night, they killed their cattle and used the skins to cover the slope of the mountain. By watering the skins, they were able to drag two of the bigger boats to the other side of the island. They loaded the boats with the most important things and reached the mainland, disappearing into the mountains. The next morning, the Venetians began their attack, soon to discover that everyone had left the island. Furious, they burnt all the houses, taking with them the most valuable things. They returned to their ships and sailed back home.

It was unsafe for the Hussars to return to the island, so they moved on and started a new life in the town of Mazine, in Bosnia, where, later, Jukan's grandfather would be born. At that time, all the land in Bosnia belonged to the Turkish Begs, the higher ranks of officers, and the Serbs worked for them for practically nothing. Grandfather couldn't agree to this situation, so he decided to go to America to make some money. At that time, 'gold fever' was raging through Alaska, and Grandfather joined the other miners. In his first attempt, he found very little; but in his second attempt, good luck smiled at him and he found a lot of gold. He came back to Bosnia a wealthy man. With this money, he bought land from Mustafa-Beg. It was a lot of land, but not good land. The Turks kept the best land for themselves. So it was necessary for all the family to work hard. Grandfather's family was not a small one, with five sons and five daughters! He sent one of his sons to America, and he regularly sent home money. With this money, Grandfather bought more and more land and became one of the richest peasants in the area.

Grandfather's eldest son was killed during World War I; he left behind his wife, Nana, and two children, Rade and Mirko. They were fortunate to be surrounded by a loving family, so they never felt themselves to be orphans. Another of Grandfather's sons was Mile, and Jukan was the oldest of his three children. Now all of Grandfather's children had children of their own, and while they didn't all live in Grandfather's house, there were still plenty of people around. But Jukan's grandfather wasn't just rich; he had a beautiful soul. Although no longer young, he was still very handsome. His face was always tanned, dominated by his huge black eyes. He had a magnificent black moustache, the ends of which turned upwards. For Jukan, only one face was dearer, and that was the face of his mother.

Despite the fact that Grandfather had many grandsons, some older that Jukan, Jukan was Grandfather's favourite. They were real friends. Even on the big holy days, when 'God's Glory' was celebrated, Jukan was allowed to sit on Grandfather's knee, next to the high priest, and listened to his blessings. The first blessing was for the homeowner and his wife and then for each son and each guest . . . so it went for three days from morning to midnight! Together they went to the church, where Jukan saw the fat bearded priest singing the prayers. 'He is praying to the Lord for us so that God will love us more,' explained Grandfather. Jukan was overcome with fear and after that didn't like to go to church very often!

Grandfather's wife, Marija, was a small and very serious woman. She seldom smiled. She was, however, the perfect mistress of the house. Most of all, she hated when someone was simply lounging around, not doing anything. If Grandfather was the head of the family, Marija was most certainly the neck! She told everyone what they were supposed to be doing around the house. Grandfather could give everyone a hard time; it didn't matter whether it was a son, daughter, daughter-in-law, or grandson.

Once, when Jukan was naughty she told him:

"Jukitsa not even the Black sea will stop you!" Though she probably didn't knew were it was.

But nobody in the house dared to raise their voice to Baba Marija! Everyone was afraid of her, though they all loved her. Usually, Marija was kind, but too often her mood changed, and that would ruin Grandfather's mood. At that time, it was better to get out of sight until they calmed down.

Daughters-in-law (Snahas) had to work in turns with Grandmother around the house. The job wasn't hard, but it lasted all day long. They had to wake up early in the morning to give food and water to the animals, to milk the cows and sheep, to feed all the other living creatures, to carry water, and to clean and cook for the men. The Snahas didn't like this job very much and often complained to each other. The fieldwork was much harder, but they liked it better because they could talk, laugh, swear, and make amends to one another.

Sometimes it was necessary to go to market. On Mondays, the market was in Bihach; on Wednesdays, in Bosansky Petrovats; and on Thursdays, in Kulen Vakufu. Each market was well known in its own way. At one, cows and pigs were sold; at another, potatoes and beans. Usually, Grandfather and Jukan's father went to the markets, but sometimes they took one of the grandsons with them, and it was a big holiday for the children. They always bought the children ice cream, sweets, and even toys. But most interesting for Jukan was the railway station. He saw the steam locomotives as huge monsters letting out puffs of steam, their whistles screaming, while they dragged their heavy freight cars and passenger carriages.

But that was not the most amazing thing. In Lipa at night, the rooms were lit up with oil lamps. Here, the platforms and streets shone with bright lights, and they could see everything as if it was daylight. But the radio caught his imagination even more. Loudspeakers hung over the platforms, and the stationmasters made announcements about the arrival and departure of the trains. Jukan was delighted to hear all this. What was even more unbelievable to Jukan was that, many years before in the Mandich house where his mother had been born, a boy called Nikola had been born. He had been born on the same day as Jukan's grandfather; they had gone to the same rural school and had behaved outrageously in class together. And now this Nikola had become a scientist, working in electrical science, and had gone to America.

But now, Jukan was growing up in a hard-working family, and his path often crossed with that of his grandmother, the one that gave jobs to everyone! Sometimes she would say to him, 'Go and see where the chickens are,' or 'Go and see that the pigs don't get into the wheat.' But most of all, he hated to be forced to pray! Usually, after work, the family gathered for a prayer in the big room, or sometimes in the kitchen, closer to the fire. Grandfather and Grandmother stood in the first row, behind them their sons and daughters-in-law and then the older grandsons, and behind them all, the younger ones, who just stood and waited for it to be finished. When it was all over, they could eat. The discipline was as strict as if they were in church. When the prayers had been said, everyone sat down to eat; the adults at a big round table, about three meters in diameter, and the children sat at a smaller similar table. The food was eaten very quickly, and straight after that, they all went off to bed, knowing that the next day it would all start over again. Every Friday, they had to fast. It was forbidden to eat any meat, only baked fish. But where could they get fish in Bosnia, especially in Lipa, where there was hardly enough water to drink? They brought water to the house from a source located several kilometres away, and this water was so sweet, it was impossible to stop drinking it.

To stand in prayer behind everyone else was very convenient . . . nobody notices you, but everything is visible to you. Here, Stric (Uncle) Toma stood silently; he didn't like to pray and said that he couldn't see much sense in it. Others, too, didn't expect much from God but kept quiet out of respect for Grandfather and Grandmother. But all that Jukan wanted to know was, why did they need to fast? Why did they need to pray? These questions he addressed to Nana, the wife of the eldest son who had died during the war. She always loved the children and tried to keep them from being punished, particularly as she was often punished herself. She answered their questions and was their first teacher. The children asked: Who prays? What do they pray for? Which God do they believe in? Which church or mosque do they go to? But Jukan was more interested in just one question: do all regions have fast days? 'Yes,' Nana answered, 'all religions have fast days.'

'That's a pity.' Jukan was disappointed. 'I would prefer a religion where there was no fasting!'

On the fast days, Jukan found things for himself to do. He would go out into the courtyard and listen for when a hen laid an egg. Then he would run to grab it quickly, put it in his pocket, and hide it. Then he would gather the other eggs for Grandmother. Thank goodness the hens were laying well and there were enough eggs for everyone. Besides that, there was always smoked meat and lard in the house. To get them, Jukan worked with Mirko, who was usually on guard, and Jukan was the main 'getter'. Now they had enough to eat and even more! The boys' paths often crossed with Grandmother's. She had keys for all the storerooms and knew all the passageways to get to them. She usually sat in the kitchen, preparing dinner for all the family, and the boys helped her by watching the fire and throwing in some wood or dry cane. If they threw in a damp cane, it would burn longer but make more smoke. This was the moment the boys waited for. Grandmother would turn away, sometimes turning her back on them. Then one of the boys would rush into the storeroom holding a hard wheat or rye straw. He would punch a hole into the skinthat on a top of the milk and drink from it. They had to do it carefully so Grandmother wouldn't notice anything.

For a long time, they were successful. But one day, Grandmother came out of the storeroom, crossed herself, and called Jukan's mother. 'Milka, come and look. See how the milk in the skin has fallen? What could have happened to it?'

Milka just looked surprised but couldn't explain it. Then Grandmother decided, 'I think someone has put a spell on our cows. As God is my witness, this was all done by a witch from Chukovo. I gave her some milk yesterday, and she liked it and praised our cows so much that she has hexed them!' Grandmother consulted with others in the house, and they decided to call somebody to take away the hex. After a few days, Jukan noticed that all the cows had red wattle tapes made from red wool on their tails, which should have rescued the cows from the hex. But Jukan and Mirko continued their attacks on the storeroom, and the level of milk in the skins was falling even more. Grandmother came to recheck the storeroom and noticed that the level of milk had fallen even more, but the skin seemed untouched. She left the room and crossed herself. This meant that sorcery didn't help.

Again, the family got together and decided to call a deacon from the next village. They thought that he was closer to God and that God would listen to him. One day soon after, a man arrived, dressed all in black, very similar to the priest, only a bit leaner and with a beard not quite so dense. He brought with him a knife and a piece of hardwood, and with two other people, he went out to the cowshed. What happened in the cowshed, nobody knew, but they came out covered in sweat! The deacon went into the kitchen, crossed himself three times, and sat down to rest. Grandmother offered him rakija and coffee. He tried to leave, but Grandmother gave him another glass. Finally, when the deacon was leaving, Grandmother gave him a head of cheese and prshut, a leg of ham, not as big, though, as the ones she gave to the priest or judge!

When Jukan and Mirko saw this, they almost cried. Such special gift given to the deacon, and for nothing! If they had known this would happen, they wouldn't have drunk any milk from the skin for the past month. They were interested, though, to find out what the deacon had done to the cows. They started to examine the most beautiful of the cows, Sharulja. She had an udder much bigger than the others, and, for this reason, she was often compared to Mileva from Kulina; her breasts were the subject of much admiration from the men in the area! The boys noticed that Sharulja's horn was changed. In it was a piece of mahogany wood, firm as steel. The boys knew that it was all fake and felt very sorry for Grandmother. They were so upset that they stopped stealing the milk, and their house became peaceful again. Because of this, Grandmother always thanked the deacon in her prayers. And she became more kind and cheerful.

Jukan had changed too. Now the fasting was over, but they all had to go to church for communion. But, Jukan thought, how could he participate if he had not fasted even for one day? He tried to find out from other people, could anyone participate if they had not fasted? Everyone he asked said it was a big sin, and such people could not take part in the service. Jukan and Mirko couldn't sleep at night, whispering and wondering about their futures. In the morning, a bright idea came to them. Stric Toma had also not fasted. The boys would let him go first, and if nothing happened to him, then they would stop worrying! Still, they were frightened. The day arrived. In the morning, everyone got washed and dressed nicely. Mother dressed Jukan in a snow-white suit; she had spun the wool all winter and then wove and bleached the yarn and sewed the suit on her sewing machine, which had been part of her dowry. Grandfather had made opanki, traditional shoes in Serbia, from the skin of a dead cow. The cow had died the previous year from an unknown cause, so the skin had been removed and the body buried. On Jukan's head was a Lichka Kappa, a hat given to him by Grandfather, to show that Jukan was Grandfather's heir.

All the Manville men brushed the horses, putting on golden bridles. Their manes looked like pure silk, their hooves in steel shoes like girls. The cart was upholstered, the wheels made of ash wood and steel. The family took their seats in the cart; the aunts in their gold jewellery, looking beautiful and proud. The horses went slowly down the road but then broke into a run. Soon, they reached the church; everyone got down from the cart, and the horses were tied to a tree and wiped and given hay. On these days, people came from all the surrounding villages to the church; they sang and danced the kolo. Here, brides were selected for sons, and while beauty was appreciated, it was not the most important thing to look for. Certainly, no one was against a beautiful bride, but more important was that she was strong, tall, and hard-working so that she could give birth to big, healthy children.

The service in the church had not yet started. Finally, a carriage arrived, and the two priests and the deacon came out. They opened the church doors, and people began to enter and take their seats. Those without seats stood near the door. Someone rang the bells, and the noise seemed to crack open the skies! People began to cross themselves. The priests began to sing the prayers, the deacon joining in. Jukan and Mirko stood nearby, with small Easter cakes in their hands. Their stomachs were empty and growling with hunger. The boys looked at each other and began to make their way closer to the door. Here, the church walls were much thicker, and, more importantly, they could hide under the bell tower. They decided that even God could not see them there, and they quickly ate their Easter cakes! At once, they felt better and began to make their way back to Grandfather. He saw them and said, 'Hey, you children are probably hungry. Go to communion quickly, and after that, you can eat.'

Jukan heard this and began to sweat. Mirko asked, 'Where is Stric Toma?'

'He had a terrible toothache and had to leave,' Grandfather replied.+

Jukan heard this and stiffened, stunned. They didn't know what to do! Grandfather pushed them closer to the bearded priest, with a silver tray in his hands, holding two plates. On one plate, he held 'Christ's blood', like wine. The priest asked everyone if they had sinned or not, and everyone whispered their answer. Then he allowed them to drink a spoonful of 'Christ's blood', and under the spoon, he held a towel so that not a drop would fall on the floor. After that, everyone threw money onto the tray as much as they could. If someone threw too little, the priest stood in their way until the person threw some more money. After that, the priest moved aside, put a drop of holy water on them, and allowed them to kiss a cross. Then it was the boys' turn, and Jukan's legs began to tremble so badly, he could hardly stand. He didn't know what to say to the holy father, so he didn't say anything. If Jukan didn't want to speak, the priest had no time to listen! After all, children didn't have money yet, and they had not lived long enough to really sin, so the priest put a spoonful of the wine in his mouth, followed by a spoon of kovilja, a sweet boiled wheat drink, made the sign of the cross over him, and moved on into the church.

The boys ran joyfully out into the street, where Grandmother was waiting for them. 'Now you can eat your cakes,' she said, but the boys ran off before she could notice that they had already eaten their cakes. For a long time after that, the boys remembered their sin, especially during a thunderstorm, because, once, Jukan had asked Nana why thunder was so loud, and she had explained that it was God hitting a sinner. Jukan's eyes nearly fell out of his head when he heard that. For a long time, all that was on Jukan's mind was when God would get him. Nana saw this and said that God only hit big sinners; he forgave small ones. After that, Jukan calmed down a bit, but his problem with fasts continued. There were just too many of them in a year, not just fasts but holidays as well. Most of them fell in winter, not because the sacred suffered more in winter but because, at this time, there was a lot less work and people could relax more. During winter, everyone prepared their tools for the spring and took compost out onto the fields. Grandfather always used to say, 'The crop that you get in autumn depends on how well you prepare in winter.'

In February, the sheep are the first to give birth and then the cows and, lastly, the horses and pigs. They all need a warm and dry place, but more for the pigs. Someone always needed to be on duty to see that the mother pig didn't accidently roll onto her piglets and crush them or forget to feed them. Jukan loved the little piglets, seeing how clean they were and how quickly after birth they stood on their little legs. Each of them knew their own nipple; the firstborn always got the first nipple, so it had more milk, and it grew larger than its brothers and sisters. Lambs, too, stood on their feet almost at once, but they were usually unsteady as if they were being blown by the wind. The calves and foals took a bit longer, and sometimes days passed before they could stand confidently. All the young animals were beautiful and happy, especially the kids and lambs. They liked to play in groups, to skip and butt their heads. Sometimes they stood with their legs straight and began to jump. Then one would run through the valley, and if it saw another herd, it would join in there. Jukan thought that if he looked really hard at the animals, he could see human features, only they didn't smoke or drink! By March and April, though, it was time to plough the land, and everyone was very busy. There was no time for sleep for anyone, not even for the horses and oxen.

When Jukan grew up, he would harness the oxen, and his father or uncle went in turns behind the plough. The plough had only one ploughshare, so the work went slowly. If the horses and oxen were healthy, the work went quickly, and people didn't notice their tiredness; but as evening came, everyone was so tired that they could not feel their feet! The hardest work of all was the harrowing. People walked behind the plough, sinking into the friable soil, and so they chose light people for this job, usually the children. In spring, everyone was happy to see the rain, because that would mean good crops. Even Jukan was happy to see the rain, even though as a sinner he was scared of the thunderstorms!

Then came the time for haymaking. Everyone got ready for this by polishing their blades, and the mowers were as proud of their blades as the girls were proud of their dresses or jewellery. Mowers went to each farm in turns, usually for money. The farm owners were responsible for providing food; usually it was baked mutton, pita bread, and a lot of rakija. The mowers worked one behind the other, the strongest at the head and the others following his orders. The owner never went first, even if he was the best mower. His place was behind, where he could see how the mowing was progressing. The work was hard, but everyone was cheerful. A lot of jokes and stories were told during the breaks; people laughed and then went back to work. It needed three, maybe four days for the hay to dry, and then it was collected using rakes and pitchforks and put into sacks and brought home. All that had to be done before the grain ripened. That was a hectic time.

15

First, they harvested the barley and then oats, and only then could they harvest the wheat and rye. It was necessary to collect everything while the weather was still good. The last laborious job was to gather the corn and potatoes, and after that came the weddings! Weddings were autumn fun! At this time of the year, there was plenty to eat and drink. The most important thing, though, was it was much easier to propose, because all hands were not needed as much in the house. For the girls, it was easier to get used to a new home in autumn. The girls were worried at this time, like young actresses making their stage debut.

At home, the best time for Jukan was the time after supper, when all the family sat around the table. In the middle of the table stood a big bottle of rakija and small glasses. People drank and got more cheerful; sometimes they sang, and often they talked about the past. Then everyone felt that their ancestors left the walls of the house and joined them at the table. The elders often remembered the remote past, when they lived happily in Montenegro and built the first temple of 'Sacred Vasily', and the Turkish invasion and the battle on Kosovo fields, after which the Turkish yoke had begun. A lot was told about the free spirit that belonged to their ancestors. Sometimes Grandfather told about his American adventures, about life on the gold fields, and about the courageous, tough people who searched there for happiness. Jukan and the other children listened closely to these stories and drew bright pictures in their minds.

But if Jukan knew a lot about his Grandfather Jurech, he knew almost nothing about his grandfather on his mother's side, who had died before Jukan was born. He knew only that his name was Petar and that he was a well-known Chetnik who fought against the Turks. But after the Turks left, defeated, the Austrians replaced them with new rules. One day, Petar had gone to the Banja Luka markets; here, he saw the police dispersing a crowd of student protestors. He was angry at the police's behaviour and told them that the Austrian pigs were no better than the Turkish dogs. They arrested him for insulting the Austrian Crown and demanded that he apologise publicly. Petar categorically refused to do this and so was shot in the town square. Very few people understood why he acted this way and said it was silly. But Jukan was too young to judge.

So the years passed in the country house where everyone worked from sunrise to sunset. Jukan was growing up, and more responsibilities were placed on his shoulders. Now he had to wake early and graze the sheep, no matter what the weather. One cool spring morning, Jukan caught a cold and began to cough. The illness didn't go away, so Jukan was taken to hospital. Here, he gradually recovered and soon became everyone's favourite. To be ill was not funny, but one man decided to play a joke. They taught Jukan some dirty words and encouraged him to say them to the young nurse. Jukan, not knowing better, said these vulgar things to the girl's face. The nurse was so angry that she took a wet towel and whipped Jukan. Despite the pain and insult, Jukan didn't cry a tear or say a word. The older man thought it very funny, and the next day, he told a doctor what had happened. The doctor condemned the older man and spoke to Jukan. 'You are a true Bosnian. You suffered but didn't drop a tear or utter a word.'

The next day, the doctor took Jukan back to his own home for dinner, and Jukan met the doctor's wife. She like Jukan very much, and as they didn't have children, she suggested that Jukan stay with them and go to school. Jukan didn't know how to answer. But when Jukan's father came to pick him up, he absolutely refused to even think about it and took Jukan back to Lipa. That same autumn, Jukan started to attend the rural school. There were not many students and even fewer teachers. In Jukan's class, there were students from three different age groups, and one teacher had to teach three classes at the same time. Nevertheless, Jukan preferred going to school than grazing the sheep. So he always did his best, and his teachers often praised him and used him as an example to the others.

Part 2

My god, how good is that? Klara thought. She and her school girlfriends had just acted on the stage of the Tram Drivers' Club, under bright projector lights, and accompanied on a grand piano. The girls had sung enthusiastically,

> We are the blue-shirt girls,
> We are trade union girls,
> Let our country sing about us.

They were dressed in new dark-blue blouses and frilled skirts. They had marched onto the stage. Klara thought it was the happiest day of her life. Next to her, equally happy, marched her childhood friend and schoolmate Tanja Klyachkina. Neither of them had any doubt that their life would be long and happy and that every door in this world would be opened for them. And all of this was thanks to Stalin, their great leader with the magnificent moustache, smiling down at them from the big portrait hanging over the stage. The girls finished their act, bowed to the audience, and ran off the stage. After they heard the loud applause, they ran back for a second bow. 'Excellent performance, girls,' praised the musical director. He stroked Klara's hair and added, 'You sang wonderfully today.'

Klara was incredibly pleased that he had mentioned her voice only. She blushed and burst out laughing and ran to the exit.

As she ran down the steps, she almost collided with the tall, lanky Mitja Tabachnikov. He grabbed her by the hand and asked, 'Where are you running to like mad?'

'I'm running home, and I'm in a rush,' she answered, pulling her hand away.

'If you want, I'll see you home,' Mitja said.

'Thanks, but I'll find my way,' Klara said and then felt sorry for Mitja. She had sympathy for him, but right now she had no time for him. She ran out onto the street to a bright clear sky where the sun shone brightly, filling the crowded street with light. Noisy lorries passed by, brightly coloured trams roared by on their rails, and frightened horses and pedestrians jumped out of their way.

Tanja was waiting for her. They always walked back home together, frequently stopping to look into the shop windows. It didn't matter that they didn't even have enough money for a glass of sunflower seeds; nobody could stop them from dreaming. Tanja was already an attractive girl, and through her cheap dress, it was possible to make out her beautiful breasts. She had many admirers, and when she went to meet them, she borrowed Klara's dresses. Klara still felt like a child, small and thin, with no breasts, just like a boy. She didn't think about boys at all; inside her head were other thoughts. Above all, she liked to sing and dance. Here, she felt like a real actress, right at home on the stage where it was bright; that's why she didn't hurry home to the small, dirty apartment that was waiting for her. On stage, she could sing and dance. In the club, she had many friends, even boyfriends. Mitja was one of them. He was very tall and round-shouldered, with long hands, and he was very clumsy. But when he was sitting in front of the piano, he became graceful and confident. He was an excellent pianist, and Klara could listen to him for hours. Lately, Mitja had begun to pursue her persistently. And now he was again trying to catch up with the girls, taking large steps and waving his hands.

Klara turned to him. 'You again?' she said irritably.

'Please let me walk you home,' he begged.

'We are going to see my brother, and you know how much he hates it when boys hang around me,' she answered. It was true that Simeon didn't like boys following Klara. Simeon was only two years older than Klara, but he looked like an adult. He was tall and broad-shouldered with thick curly black hair, and over his upper lip, a small moustache was beginning to grow. He loved Klara and was always ready to come to her rescue. The local boys knew this and avoided Klara. So now, when she mentioned her brother's name, Mitja's desire to walk Klara home disappeared. He said goodbye to the girls, and the girls walked towards Simeon's hairdressing salon. It was located on a corner next to a tram stop. Like all salons, this place was usually crowded. Only a year and a half ago, Simeon had started there as an apprentice, and now he worked for himself and made decent money.

Thanks to him, life for the family was much easier, and Simeon felt like a real man. Klara came to the salon window and looked inside. Simeon noticed her and waved his hand. The girls opened the door, the bell ringing, and at once they could smell perfume and cologne. The girls loved the smell of the salon. Workers smelled of oil and sweat from the carriers, or horses and manure, but the hairdressers always smelled fresh and perfumed. 'Well, my beauties, sit down and wait until I finish this haircut.' The girls sat down obediently while Simeon straightened the sides of the client's hair with a razor, brushed the hair from his face, and moved the chair. The client stood up, paid, and left. Simeon turned to the girls and said, 'Come, let's go and I will buy you an ice cream.'

'Why?' Klara asked. In their house, it was very unusual to spend money on sweets.

'There is a reason. Let's get out and I will explain it to you.' Simeon took off his apron, shook off the hair, and said something to the owner, and they left the salon.

'And what is the reason?' Klara asked again.

Simeon looked at her sadly. 'The reason is that I am going away.'

'Where are you going to?' she wanted to know.

'Far away, to the very north. You know Arkhangelsk City?'

'We all know Arkhangelsk. What will you do there?'

'I will work in a hairdressing salon, of course. Do you know how much money they pay there?'

'You think they are waiting for you? Who will give you a job?'

'Three of us are going together, David, Rose, and myself. David will open a hairdressing salon, and we will work there.' Rose was the eldest daughter of their stepfather. Only a couple of months ago, she had married David, another hairdresser. He was a small man but a good businessman.

'How will you live there? You know it's a ten-month winter there.' Klara continued to be doubtful.

'Don't you worry, Klarochka, we will survive somehow and come back with so much money that we will be able to sunbathe on the beach for the rest of our lives. I will buy you so many dresses and shoes that you will be the most beautiful girl in Odessa.' Klara didn't really believe this fairy tale, but it was so pleasant to listen to that she blushed in excitement. They reached the ice cream stand, and Simeon bought an ice cream for them. 'Here you are, my beauties. A new life begins soon. Eat your ice creams and go and do your homework.' He patted their head and returned to the salon.

At this moment, a car stopped next to them, and two young men and a woman all dressed in black leather jackets got out. They all looked very serious, important, and frightening. NKVD officers had become more and more common on the streets lately. They usually appeared in groups, and people tried to disappear as soon as they saw them. But if in the daytime people wanted to avoid them, at night everyone panicked when they saw them. They appeared like black ravens when no one was expecting them. If they visited someone, then everyone else knew that this person was in big trouble, and often these people simply disappeared. Neighbours pretended that they saw nothing at all and refused to speak about it. Klara tried not to think about it, but in school, they learnt that there was a big fight going on against the enemies of communism, who had sold their souls to the imperialists. But Klara thought she had nothing to worry about. She lived in a country of free labour, and she really believed that one day they would build a future where everyone would be happy.

There were times when Klara's beliefs almost vanished. One morning, the wife of Zelda's brother, Grisha, ran into their room. Eva looked terrified, her hair was dishevelled, and her tear-stained eyes were bright with shock. She clutched her head and shouted, 'My God, why do you punish us so badly?' she cried out repeatedly and howled.

Zelda couldn't understand her. She grabbed her by the hand and asked, 'Can you calm yourself and tell us exactly what has happened?' Eva stopped shouting and began her story. It seemed that someone had informed the NKVD that Uncle Grisha had hidden gold and diamonds. Late the previous night, people in black leather jackets had come to their place with a search warrant. They searched the apartment all night long and turned everything upside down. Despite their diligence, they found nothing in the house. This was no surprise; where would Grisha get gold? Uncle Grisha was an ordinary blacksmith and had nothing but iron. His family hardly made ends meet.

Uncle Grisha had tried to explain this to these employees of the People's Commissariat of Internal Affairs, but he could not convince them. Despite having found nothing at all, at daybreak they took Grisha with them. Eva finished the story and again became hysterical. 'My God, why am I so unfortunate? Why do you torture me this way?' she shouted.

Klara watched this from her corner of the room and saw her mother try to calm Eva. 'Don't kill yourself by shouting so,' she said. 'Believe me, this is a misunderstanding. You'll see, they will realise that they've made a mistake and let Grisha come home.'

These words calmed Eva a little. She wiped her eyes and tidied her hair, saying, 'Maybe you are right. Maybe everything will be settled.'

'Yes, certainly it will be resolved,' Zelda said. 'You know that Grisha has never had any gold,' she added confidently.

'Should I go to the jail?' Eva asked.

'Wait at least one day and then go,' Zelda suggested, and Eva agreed.

The next day, Klara went with Zelda to visit Eva to see if there was any more news. Eva and Grisha lived on Moldovanka, and to get there, they had to catch a tram. Eva lived in a building with a courtyard surrounded by metal balconies connected between floors by metal stairs. Large families lived in every unit, and the balconies were always full of people; neighbours loudly shared their news, and children ran around through the drying linen. Usually, it was very noisy, but this day, intense silence reigned; only from Uncle Grisha's apartment, Eva could be heard sobbing.

Klara and Zelda walked up to the second floor and knocked on the door. The door was opened by Klara's cousin Petja. Grisha and Eva lived in a small two-room apartment, and they had five children: the oldest was Petja and then Rose, twins Syoma and Rahil, and, lastly, Sonja. They hardly made ends meet and never had any spare money. Now all the children were sitting around crying, and Eva was dressed all in black. When she saw Zelda, she stopped crying and asked, 'Zelda, what am I supposed to do now? I took your advice and waited all day long, but as you can see, he hasn't been released. I won't be able to last through this. I will take my own life!'

'Don't talk nonsense!' Zelda said, trying to calm Eva down. 'You have to look after your children!'

'How can I do that? We don't have any money,' Eva answered.

'Tomorrow, you will go to the prison, but before that, we will ask for advice from some other people. Maybe they can help us,' Zelda suggested. So they went around the neighbours, seeking advice, which ranged from really stupid suggestions to some that were quite reasonable.

The next morning, Eva packed a parcel for her husband and made her way to the prison. The correctional officer confirmed that Grisha was locked inside and took the parcel. Then Eva went to the reception area for the chief prison officer. The officer was a tall, thin man with a very unpleasant face. When Eva asked why her husband was being held there, the officer answered, 'We received substantial evidence that your husband was hiding gold.'

'What are you talking about?' Eva screamed. 'He has never had gold in his life.'

'Woman, listen! Do not shout at me. I told you that we had information. And it's not in your interest to spoil your relationship with me! Go home and think carefully about what I have just said and where your husband could have hidden gold. And after that, come back to me!' So, having achieved nothing, Eva went back home. She was very close to panic. She couldn't understand where the information could have come from. Who would tell such nonsense? After that, she visited the prison every day, taking parcels that were received happily, though Eva was not sure that they even reached Grisha. Here, she became acquainted with other women. At first, she tried to avoid them, but then she understood that they were just like her and that they had no idea why their husbands had been arrested. There were also the wives and girlfriends of real thieves and murderers; they looked and acted like ducks in water!

On the fourth day, she was allowed to see Grisha. She was taken down a long, narrow corridor to a small gloomy room with no windows and only two dim lamps. Along opposite walls were wooden chairs that had been nailed together. The guard told her to sit down on one of the chairs, while he stood near the door. In the room, there was another woman. She was grey-haired and thin, and she reminded Eva of a small tired animal. Only in her sad eyes was there any sign of human intelligence. After a few minutes, another security guard came into the room and called the small woman. 'Citizen Savelyeva, follow me!' She silently stood up, and without saying anything, she obediently followed the guard out of the room.

Eva was left in the room alone with the guard. At last, the security guard came back into the room and called to Eva. They went into the next room, which was divided in two by lines of screens, and between these walked another guard. 'Citizen Podvysotskaja, your meeting will last only ten minutes. Therefore, hurry and say what you want to say!' He showed Eva a chair where she sat and peered through the screen, but she couldn't see anyone.

At last, another door opened, and the security guard pushed Grisha into the room. Grisha, a blacksmith by trade, had been a healthy, strong, good-looking man, but the man on the other side of the screen was a thin, round-shouldered, bald man with a twitch in one eye. When he came closer, Eva was horrified when she recognised her husband! He looked so miserable that she cried out in horror, 'Oh, Grisha, what have they done to you?'

But she was forcefully pulled back by the security guard. 'Silence! Don't shout or this meeting will be over!'

'Why did they do this to you?' Eva whispered, but Grisha gave her such a fierce look that she stopped her crying.

'Listen to me attentively and do not interrupt. We don't have enough time. They said that I hid gold, and that means that you have to bring it,' he quickly explained.

'But where did you hide it?' Eva asked in surprise.

'I never did have any gold,' he whispered, and Eva could see that his two front teeth were missing. 'If you want to see me alive, you must bring this gold.'

'Where will I get it from?' Eva didn't understand.

'I don't know, but if you do not bring them some gold, I will never get out of here alive. That's what they told me.'

Eva was shocked by his words. Her head was spinning. Later she didn't even remember leaving the room or how the meeting ended. She regained consciousness in a chair out in the corridor. The same security guard was looking at her closely and said, 'Well, I hope you understood everything that your husband said?' Eva nodded her head, and the guard went on. 'Then go home and do what he told you to do!'

Eva arrived home in such a dreadful state that her neighbours thought she had gone mad. She moved as though not aware of her surroundings. Her hair was dishevelled, and every now and then, she threw up her hands to cover her face. Her children made her sit down on the bed and drink some water, and gradually she was able to tell them what happened. Grisha had been a very kind man who didn't quarrel with anybody. All the neighbours loved him, so when they found out what had happened to him, they all got together and agreed that they would help him. They decided to raise the money to buy the gold. Eva and her children went to their relatives with the same request to help with money, and surprisingly, even though they were all poor, people gave them money, and Eva managed to collect a decent sum. Zelda gave her some money as well, even though they had hardly anything to eat. With the money, they went to the pawnshop, where Eva bought some gold and took it to the prison chief. Although he was very dissatisfied at the amount of gold that she brought, he took the gold and promised that they would release Grisha. And he did keep his word. Two days later, Grisha was allowed to leave the prison, but he returned home a different man. Nobody saw him smile anymore, and he had a nervous tic for the rest of his life. He was always depressed!

Nobody wanted to talk about this anymore, or they were afraid to speak of it. And so Klara quickly forgot about it and continued to sing and dance at the Tram Drivers' Club. But there was a saying, 'When trouble comes, open the gates!' Simeon and his stepsister and her husband had gone to Arkhangelsk. As soon as they arrived, they had opened their hairdressing salon and soon had a lot of clients. In the letters home, Simeon mentioned that while he hated the climate and the lack of sunshine, he loved his earnings. People in the north earned big money and spent it much faster than in other cities. Simeon wrote that in a year or two, he would come back to Odessa a rich man.

But then news came from Rose. In her letter, she wrote that Simeon had gotten himself into a lot of trouble. One evening after work, he had gone to a restaurant to eat and drink. There, he unintentionally met up with three foreign seamen. They had all had a drink together, and one of the seamen showed Simeon some Swiss watches. One of them, a beautiful small watch, really appealed to Simeon. He thought how lovely it would look on the wrist of his little sister. He bought the watch and put it in his pocket. As he left the restaurant, he was stopped by two men in civilian dress, and they took him away to the militia office. Here, they searched him and, of course, found the watch. They accused him of an illegal transaction with foreigners and sentenced him to serve ten years of corrective service in a camp near to Arkhangelsk. For Klara and Zelda, this news came as a thunderbolt! For Klara, it was worse, thinking that this had happened partly because of her. And Zelda was in shock. She cried for hours, loudly damning her destiny and periodically appealing to God, 'My God, why are torturing me? Why am I so guilty in your eyes? First, you took away my husband and now my son. Why?' And suddenly she seemed to understand. She covered her mouth with her hands and whispered, 'Probably because I refused to go to America with my family? They live now in God's bosom, and here we suffer like the most dreadful sinners. Damn the day I stayed in this godforsaken country!'

Gradually, though, she came to her senses, put her hair in order again, and went to ask her neighbours to help raise the money for her trip to see Simeon. People felt so sorry for her and helped with everything they could. She travelled by train to Arkhangelsk and from there to the camp where Simeon was logging trees. She organised to meet with him. At first, she didn't recognise him. In front of her was a young man in prison uniform. His face was covered by a think, untrimmed beard. He rushed to her, and only then did she recognise him. It was terrible to see how these animals had changed her son. But Simeon was in good spirits; he didn't cry or complain. On the contrary, he tried to support Zelda. 'You will see, Mother, I'll stay here for a couple of years, and when amnesty comes, I'll come back home. And we'll start a new, happy life.'

Zelda did not believe in this bright happy future and returned home very depressed. At home, life was getting harder. After Simeon's arrest, the family had lost their primary source of income, and without it, they were practically starving. So when the school holidays arrived, Klara was sent once more to stay with Uncle Naum. This time, no one came to collect her; she was to travel by train alone, and she was very excited. She had never travelled alone before, and this seemed like a real adventure. She woke early in the morning, washed her face, and checked the bag that she had packed the previous night. Her mother went with her to the station. Mother gave her some last-minute advice. 'Don't you dare leave the train! Don't talk to strangers, and don't go anywhere with anyone, no matter what they promise. Only get out of the train at the station at Vesely Kut, where Uncle Naum will be waiting for you. Behave modestly, and I will come to pick you up in a month.'

They arrived at the station and went onto the platform to wait for the train. There were people everywhere. There were peasants coming home from the city, carrying gifts for their families. The train had not yet arrived, but it was clear that there wouldn't be enough seats for everybody and some people would have to stand the whole way. At last, they saw the train and carriages. The crowd began to move, trying to choose a vantage point. Klara was surprised at her mother's aggressiveness. Though she was small and fragile, she managed to force her way so that she was one of the first to get into the carriage, dragging Klara behind her. Klara felt awful that they had to push other people for vacant seats. They managed to get a place next to a window. Next to them sat a well-built muzhik . . . he put his large suitcase on the seat opposite. Some people tried to push his bags off the seat, but the muzhik refused to budge. At last, his wife and child came. Then the muzhik took his bag off the seat, and his family sat down. His wife greeted Klara and Zelda politely and asked where they were going to.

'I'm not going anywhere,' Zelda explained. 'I'm here to see my daughter off. I'm worried for her, and I would like to ask you to look after her and see that she doesn't miss her station, Vesely Kut.'

'Don't you worry,' assured her neighbour. 'We will look after her. Is that right Senja?' she asked her husband. He nodded vigorously, and this dispelled Zelda's last doubt.

'Well, then, I must go. Who knows when the train will get under way!' She kissed Klara on the cheek and ran to the exit. Just as she stepped down onto the platform, the whistle blew and the train started. Klara waved goodbye to her mother, and now that she was left alone, she began to feel uneasy.

'Sit down, girl, and tell us where you are going,' her neighbour said.

'I'm going to visit my uncle for my school vacation,' she replied.

'And where do you live?' Klara was asked again.

'I live in Odessa with my mother,' she replied again.

'And where is your father?'

'He died of cholera when I was still little,' she told them.

'Oh, you poor little orphan,' her neighbour said pityingly.

Klara pressed her forehead against the glass and watched the landscape running by. During the stops and the stations, local peasants gathered near the carriages and tried to sell their produce. The train stopped at almost every station. Passengers got out to smoke or buy something, but Klara followed her mother's advice and didn't leave the carriage. However, when her neighbours took out a loaf of black bread and began to eat it quickly, Klara thought she might be sick from hunger herself. She stood up next to the window, but even here the smell of the food didn't go away. Klara got up on a small step and hung her head out of the window. The fresh wind from the steppe blew in her face and ruffled her hair. Klara instantly forgot about being hungry and took in the wonderful smell of the fresh air.

By the time that the train arrived at Vesely Kut, it was already midday and the air was hot. It had become very hot in the carriage, and the smell of human sweat filled the carriage, even though the windows were open. The train stopped at Vesely Kut for just a few minutes, and Klara quickly jumped out onto the crowded platform, where there were local dealers and people from the train smoking cigarettes. Klara walked along the platform, looking carefully at each face, not wanting to miss Uncle Naum. Finally, she saw him standing near a small station building. Klara came closer to him, but he continued to peer into the crowd. When she was only a few steps away from him, she waved and greeted him. 'Hello, Uncle Naum!'

He looked at her carefully and then said, 'Klarochka, is that you? I didn't recognise you! You look so mature and have become a real beauty.' His compliments embarrassed Klara, and she blushed.

'So, should we go?' he asked as he took Klara's bag, and they went towards the exit from the station. Klara followed, and they made their way to a cart harnessed to a skewbald horse that stood nearby. 'Let's have something to eat before we get going. The trip will take some time, and I'm sure you must be hungry by now.' Trying to hide her delight, Klara nodded. Uncle Naum took a bag from his pocket and pulled out a sausage, just like the one they had eaten on their first trip. He cut off some bread and found some tomatoes from the bottom of the bag. He gave Klara some food, and then they began to eat. The sausage was just as tasty as the first time, and the tomato was fresh and juicy. They ate slowly, and Uncle Naum asked about her mother's health and if there was any news about Simeon. Klara answered his questions, but her mind was really concentrated on the food. After the last piece of sausage had been eaten and Uncle Naum had shaken the crumbs from his beard, he took the whip and shouted, 'Noo!' and pulled on the reins. The horses were exhausted by the heat, but reluctantly they got on their way. The wheels creaked, and a cloud of dust rose around them. The road was rough, covered in stones, and the cart was noisy as it travelled along. Klara couldn't tell how long it took to get to Tsebrikovo, where they bought salt.

All morning long, Mishka had been excited, waiting for Klara's arrival. He hadn't seen her now for almost four years, and then he had just been a child. Klara had stayed in his memory as a bright light. Now he waited with such impatience, as if it was the most important thing in his life. Over the years, he had grown and was going into year three. His best friend and schoolmate Petka was also excited. Here in this farmstead of Freiberg, there were mainly Germans living, and all of Mishka's friends were German. He spoke German as well as Russian. Mishka had told Petka about his beautiful city cousin, and Petka waited for her arrival with the same enthusiasm. Petka's family house was not far from Naum's house, and Petka's father, Markus, had been friends with Naum for many years. They did not bother with religious differences. Markus grew pigs and had some cows too. His cheeses and oils were the best in the district, and Markus was very proud of his produce.

Mishka had woken early that morning, washed his face thoroughly, and started to help his mother around the house. It was important to him that Klara like the house so that she would stay as long as possible. He had wanted to go with his father to meet Klara, but he had not been allowed. Father had explained that the cart could only comfortably sit two people and that Mishka should stay and help his mother get the house ready. All day long he waited impatiently and kept looking down the road from where the cart should arrive. Petka came over in the afternoon. Together they began to plan how they would entertain their guest. They had waited a long time, and they were exhausted. Then as evening began to fall, they noticed a cloud of dust along the road, and finally they saw the outline of the cart. The boys ran into the house to warn Mishka's mother and sisters, and all of them came out into the courtyard just as the cart rolled in.

Mishka stared at Klara. She sat next to Uncle Naum, and her hair was covered in dust. After the long journey, her bottom was sore, and she thought that if she stood up, her legs would fall off. So when she got down from the cart, she almost fell, causing Petka to snicker mischievously. Mishka gave him a punch in the stomach, and Petka almost choked. Aunt Sima came closer to Klara, kissed her, and turned her around. 'What a beauty you have become, just like a real lady.'

'Aunt Sima, what are you saying? What kind of beauty am I?' Klara asked, confused. Just then, her cousins ran up to hug her. Mishka shyly stood at a distance, waiting for his turn. At last, Klara turned to look at him, and he just froze, astonished by her beauty. He had never before met such a well-dressed city girl. 'Is this Mishka?' Klara asked her uncle.

'Indeed it is, but I've never seen him so quiet!' her uncle answered. Klara came closer, and the two cousins shook hands. Then Klara gave him a resounding kiss on the cheek, and Mishka was stunned!

At this moment, Aunt Sima called everyone in to the table. She put her hand on Klara's shoulder and led her inside. They all followed, except for Mishka, who remained in the yard with Petka. 'Well, what are you laughing about? Do you like Klara or not?' Mishka asked.

'She's nothing special, and she walks like a cow!' said Petka.

'You are lying! Didn't you see how nicely she is dressed?' Mishka had never seen anyone as beautiful as Klara.

'She dresses like a prostitute!' Petka said, clearly not knowing what this word meant. Blood rushed to Mishka's head. He would never forgive this. He rushed at Petka, fists raised. He hit him a few times, and one of his blows got Petka on the nose. After that, it was Petka's turn, and because he was bigger and stronger, he managed to get two punches to Mishka's head. But that didn't stop Mishka; he could not forgive Petka's insult, and he struck again, kicking at Petka's legs, and they tumbled down onto the ground. Hearing all this noise, the family came out again. Uncle Naum stepped between them, grabbed them both by their collars, and lifted them into the air. Even here they tried to hit one another. Uncle Naum, in a thunderous voice, ordered them to stop, or they would both be punished. He put them back on the ground.

'He insulted Klara!' Mishka sobbed.

'Is this the truth?' Naum asked Petka, and Petka nodded. 'Then leave this house and do not come back here again!' Petka wiped the blood from his nose, turned, and left the courtyard.

⁘ ⟡⟡⟡⟡ ⁘

That year, the drought in the region was so dreadful that the peasants had no money to feed their families, let alone pay taxes. Grandfather had borrowed money from the bank at such high interest that this debt destroyed the family. Their uncle in America could not help them either. So Jukan could not resume his studies and was forced to join in the hard labour that went with the country life. He became a full-time shepherd. This work was not hard, but it was very dull because the sheep could not be left unguarded. There were plenty of sheep on the farm but not enough meadows. Jukan secretly drove them onto Beg's meadow. By doing this, it was possible for Jukan to get into a lot of trouble, but he tried to be very careful. Sheep are gregarious animals, and it is hard for them to get used to a different flock. If a strange sheep joins a flock, the other sheep will sniff at her because each flock has its own smell.

Sheep are also very mobile; if you lose sight of them, especially in the rain, they can travel quite a few kilometres before coming across anything to stop them. A herd always moves behind its leader, which usually wears a bell. Sheep have excellent hearing and will follow this sound, seldom getting lost, even in dense fog. In the heat, the sheep stand close together so the wind can't pass between them. This way, it's easier for them to survive, though in the heat, people will stand as far apart as possible.

Just as the heat starts, so does the shearing. This demands great skill of the shearer. Any man can understand this, as when they shave, it doesn't matter how hard they try; they will cut themselves at least once! But with sheep, the shearer has to tumble them down, hold their front feet with one hand, press slightly on the sheep's feet with his foot, and only after that can he begin to shear. It isn't known how the sheep feel about all this, with no chance of resisting, or why they wait patiently until the end! When finally released, they probably feel light and indecently naked! They will be in shock for some time, considering what had happened to them. Then they will suddenly come around, jump, run, and fall. Then to show the others that they are still alive, they will run more and finally calm down.

Now, Jukan had also begun to shear the sheep. As he did so, he began to notice what he saw as an injustice. Grandfather and his wife had ten children, and so the herd was divided into many parts. Only a small group of sheep was held by the whole family; these were used to pay for food and debts. The daughters' sheep were even free from taxes. Jukan began to think, where were the sheep that belonged to him and his father and mother? And then he understood that actually nothing belonged to them and that they were just servants. Never before had he felt so sad in his grandfather's house. He was standing in front of six heaps of wool, a bigger one for the home and five smaller ones for his aunts. He went up to the heaps and pushed them all into one big heap. Angrily he went into the house where his father sat with his head in his hands. His face was gloomy.

'Well, how many sheep have you shorn?' he asked Jukan.

'All of them,' Jukan answered.

'So now you go and watch them grazing,' his father said.

'Why don't the owners graze their own sheep!' snapped Jukan. 'I will never do it again!'

Father said nothing, simply took his sweater, and went to check on Jukan's work. When he saw what Jukan had done to the wool, he almost hit him. But then another thought ran through his head, and he simply smiled and said, 'God has witnessed that you did your job well. Now, not even God can tell who owns the wool! I have wanted to do this myself for a long time, but I never dared. Trust me, there will be no more of other people's sheep in this house. That is the end!'

The next day was Saturday; nobody went to work, and everyone was talking about something. His father came to Jukan and said, 'Listen, son, take the sheep to graze just one last time.' Jukan thought, not quite knowing what to do. Only yesterday his father had told him that he would never again graze someone else's sheep, and today he told him again to graze them? 'What are you waiting for? I told you, it's the last time.'

'The last time, so let it be the last time,' agreed Jukan, and he went out to drive the sheep from the sheepfold. He sent the herd through the courtyard and then up the hill to the meadow, where he spent all day. When he brought the sheep back, it was already getting dark. The house was full of people, even though it wasn't a holiday, and nobody had died. All the aunts arrived with their husbands, but they were not very cheerful, and nobody spoke very much.

Grandfather was in his room, and everyone could hear him coughing. That meant that he had been drinking rakija and smoking; after that, he always coughed. At last, he came into the room holding his pipe between his teeth, puffing big clouds of smoke, and sat down at the table. Everyone waited impatiently for him to speak, but he remained silent for quite a while. Finally, he spoke. 'So let's do this the way we said!' He didn't say another word. The aunts who lived close by sent for help to get their sheep home. Jukan helped to separate them and marked them if he was asked to. When Jukan woke in the morning, the remaining sheep were standing in their stall, bleating. They felt deserted by the rest of the herd. Jukan felt sorry for himself because it was embarrassing for him to graze such a small herd. He thought all the girls in the district would laugh at him.

Father saw him standing here and asked, 'Why are you still here? Graze them. There are no more other people's sheep in this herd!'

There was nothing to answer back. Jukan opened the gate and let the sheep out. They ran out very quickly, trying to catch up with the rest of the herd, but soon they stopped and bleated sadly, trying to call them back. Now, he had only seventeen sheep in his herd. But what could he do? As people said, he got what he asked for! He tried to graze the sheep where no one would see them. Father noticed this and said, 'Why aren't you happy now that you got everything that you wanted?'

'Now I'm a bit ashamed to graze such a small herd,' Jukan confessed.

'It doesn't matter how many you have. Now you know that they are all yours. But don't worry, we'll buy more sheep so that my son doesn't die of shame,' his father assured him. On Wednesday morning, they got the cart ready and drove to the Petrovaf market. Here, they bought forty-five sheep and started them on slow walk back home. The next day, Jukan happily sent his herd into the meadow. Not only was he pleased, but the adults in the family were pleased too, even Grandfather and Grandmother. Now they all treated Jukan as an adult, because he had started this, and now he was a winner.

He continued to graze his sheep, but there were many new adventures. One day, he fell asleep because he was so tired, and when he woke up, he found that the sheep had vanished without a trace. He ran around and searched. Luckily, after running many kilometres one way and then another, he found them in a secluded place. He didn't want the sheep to get into other people's grain crop and get caught by the owner, or even worse would be if they took the sheep into a community shelter. There the punishment for the owner of the sheep would be very hard. One time, he grazed his sheep just above the Ripach cemeteries. There was no fog, but Jukan was freezing. He decided to sit down and cover himself with a cloak to keep warm. Here, he fell asleep, and when he woke, the sheep were gone. First of all, he ran to Milka's field, but they were not there. Then he rushed into a long ravine but again found nothing. Suddenly, he heard the bell that his leader sheep had around its neck. Jukan rushed to the Bujader house. Jukan was more afraid of Bujader than he was of thunder! He wasn't a very tall man but was solidly built and had a magnificent moustache as black as the priest's. Nana often told the children stories about Bujader's father, who was a great Chetnik, one of the men who created Yugoslavia and a hero of the First World War.

As he got closer, Jukan saw that the sheep were not on Bujader's land but on the land of a Polish neighbour, Pevich. Jukan was not afraid of Pevich at all; Pevich often visited their house, and Grandmother treated him so well that Pevich usually turned a blind eye to these happenings. But this time, he caught the sheep and tried to send them away. Jukan caught up with him and began to send the sheep back the other way. Jukan could stand up for himself now, and some of the local boys the same age were afraid to argue with him. Pevich was a small man and started to call for help.

'Hey, people, look! For how long do I have to put up with this?' But nobody heard except the sheep!

'Why are you shouting? My sheep ran unintentionally onto your land. It will not happen again, I give you my word!' Jukan tried to calm him down.

'No, this isn't the first time this has happened,' Pevich answered. 'I will take them to the police and let them decide.'

Jukan was enraged. He lifted his shirt to show a holster that was hanging from his belt. It was empty, but nobody knew that. He grabbed the holster with his right hand and Pevich with his left. 'Listen to me, if you do, I will kill you. I don't care what happens to me!'

Pevich turned white with fear and squealed, 'What's wrong with you, you know I'm only joking! You know I am friends with your grandfather.'

'Then remember, if you tell anyone about this pistol, you will regret it,' Jukan added.

'Word of honour, I won't say a word.' Pevich crossed himself, and the two walked off in different directions. But Pevich didn't keep his word, and soon other people began to think badly of Jukan. In some ways, though, this made Jukan even stronger. Soon, his herd had grown to 150 sheep. They grazed mostly by themselves in the forest. It was amazing that they were never attacked by wolves. Every summer, the wolves took at least one of their neighbour's sheep, but it seemed that the wolves passed by his herd, maybe even looking after them. The changes to the house, however, didn't bring them prosperity. All the family members were working like slaves from morning to night but had barely enough food or wool to make clothes.

That year, it was hard everywhere. Taxes were high, and the price for agricultural produce was very low. It became difficult to sell, and what they were able to sell sold for almost nothing. Grandfather also had legal proceedings with his neighbour Zorich over a small piece of land. The argument had been going on for about twenty years, and the costs of the court case were greater than the land was worth. One year, the land was awarded to Grandfather; the next year to Zorich. Grandfather couldn't see a way out and began to drink; almost all business came to a halt, and the family decided that Mile, Jukan's father, should become the head of the family. Now Grandfather stopped going to the markets and lost touch with his friends. He was entirely dependent on Grandmother. The house affairs began to go better, but for Jukan, there was little change. For adult men, it was easy to go to the city, but not having a passport, Jukan could not go anywhere. Meanwhile, poor men from all over the country were going out looking for work. Local men gathered together to get on carts that took them to Bihach. Men played music and sang, and from the outside of the cart, it all looked very cheerful.

Late in the autumn, these same men were coming back home with money, dressed like gentlemen. Jukan looked at them with envy, and tears came to his eyes. He was wearing shabby trousers, the shirt had been sewn by his mother, and on his feet, he wore the opanki that his grandfather had made, while on his head he had Lika's cap. Jukan decided then and there that next spring he would go and look for a job. He kept it a secret and hid some clothes, socks, and a towel at the house of a distant relative, Rade, who also wanted to go.

The day came when instead of going to graze his sheep, Jukan ran away from home. He ran as fast as he could down the road so that no one would see him, and only after that could he walk slowly to show that he was not afraid of anything! Many men were already gathering; Rade was there too, holding Jukan's things. They were to travel in the cart of one of Jukan's father's friends, Micho. Micho noticed Jukan and was surprised. 'Where are you going?' he asked.

The blood pounded in Jukan's head, and his throat closed up. But Rade came to the rescue. 'He's going to visit his aunt in Bihach,' he said.

Micho was satisfied with the answer, and the carts got under way. The men started to sing, but Jukan had no rest, because for the whole trip, Micho asked questions about Aunt Danka, whom Micho had adored his whole life. In Ripach, they decided to give the horses a rest, and the men decided to have some rakija in Michael Pilipovich's tavern. Michael was a well-known friend of Jukan's grandfather, so Jukan didn't want to go inside but instead stayed out next to the cart. Even here, though, he was noticed by one of the waiters. 'Come here and I'll serve you.'

'I'm not drinking, thanks,' Jukan said.

'How is it possible not to drink? Then you are not like your grandfather,' the waiter said. Jukan didn't want to be too obvious, so he ordered a spritzer and a coffee. He wanted to drink and leave quickly.

Luckily, the owner didn't notice Jukan, and soon the others came out and took their places on the carts. They started singing again, and they got to Bihach very quickly. Here, they went to the station to get their tickets to Belgrade. They had plenty of time before the train was due to leave, so the men crossed the road and sat under apple trees to play cards. Jukan didn't play but watched on from the edge. He felt as though there was a massive stone lying on his soul, for, by now, his family at home would have learnt that he had run away. Soon, it began to rain, and the men moved back to take shelter in the station. As soon as the boarding announcement was made, the men all found their seats, and even before the train started off, the conductor began to check their tickets. At last, the train began to move. Jukan took a big breath and began to feel a bit better. Soon, the conductor reached them, and Jukan gave him his ticket. But the conductor did not look at the ticket but looked closely at Juan's face.

'Where are you going, and where is your grandfather?' he asked.

'Grandfather stayed at home, and I am going to Belgrade,' Jukan answered.

'And what will you do there?'

'I'll get work, like everyone else,' Jukan answered again.

'And do you know that you will be eaten alive by lice? Even now it is hard for people with a trade to find work in Belgrade. Why are you leaving a house as rich as yours?' the conductor asked him.

'That's my business, and I will find a job!'

'Good, so now, where is your passport?'

Jukan didn't know how to answer, but Rade tried to stand up for him. 'What do you want from this man?' he asked. 'Leave him alone!'

'Best you keep quiet if you don't want to get into trouble yourself,' the conductor told him. 'Jukan will get out of the train at the next station, and I will return him to his grandfather,' said the conductor and went on his way, checking tickets. All the other travellers advised Jukan to agree and go back. Even Rade was scared and remained silent.

When they arrived at Krupa, the conductor came back, and this time he had a policeman with him. He said, 'Well, now you and I have arrived, let's get out here and go in the opposite direction.' Jukan took his things, said goodbye to the others, and got off the train. As soon as they stepped onto the platform, the train left. Now they had to wait for a train going the other way. 'I'm sure you must be hungry?' asked the conductor.

'Not yet,' Jukan answered.

'Then let me buy you an ice cream.'

'I can buy one for myself!' Jukan insisted.

'Looks like you have a lot of money,' said the conductor.

'Enough for an ice cream,' said Jukan.

'Probably your grandmother gave you the money,' the conductor said, knowing perfectly well that Jukan's grandmother never threw any money to the wind.

'No, Ujak (the name given to an uncle on the mother's side of the family) gave it to me so that I could buy a gift,' answered Jukan, and that was the truth. Ujak loved him very much and was always buying gifts for him. When Jukan had been born, Ujak had presented him with a pistol. It was a custom in Bosnia to buy a gun for a baby boy, as a man in the future. Every man in Jukan's house was armed.

All the way back to Bihach, the conductor was preaching to Jukan. 'You have to understand that work in the city is hard. And there is not enough of it. Take me, for example. I don't always go to sleep on a full stomach, but, thank God, my children don't starve! It's good that my job comes with a uniform and I look like a respectable person. But many people have so little food that they could leave their teeth on a shelf! In your house, you never starve, but in the city, two families live on what your horses eat! And what horses you have, I saw them once at the market. They were not just ordinary horses. It's difficult to find anyone in Bihach who does not know your grandfather, and you ran away from him! Return to your home, grow up, get married, enjoy your life, and never again make such a stupid mistake. Now you will sleep in your aunt's house. When you wake up in the morning, you will go back home and tell them that you went to Bihach to buy something for yourself or some girl!'

The conductor walked almost to the front door and then left. Jukan went to the door and turned to see if the conductor was still there. As he turned, he saw that his father was right behind him. He almost fainted with shock. But his father saw this and put his hand on Jukan's shoulder. 'Come, let's go inside the house,' he said. They went in.

In the middle of the room at the table sat his tear-stained aunt Danka. As a good actress, it was never difficult for her to shed a tear! 'Are you not ashamed to make your father and family worry so much?' she asked Jukan reproachfully. She didn't wait for an answer but went into the kitchen to prepare a meal. They ate silently, as if trying not to think about what had happened. Soon, they were ready for their homeward trip. The horses had rested well, and as the rain had just stopped, Father tied up the horses' tails so that they would not get dirty in the mud. The horses were not used to running with their tails tied up, so they ran very quickly, snorting through their nostrils. Very soon, they reached Ripach and then, without stopping, continued on their way. Until that point, they had been sitting silently, but now Father began to speak.

'Tell me, my treasured son, how does it look when a son runs away from his father? And why did you decide just now, when everything had been changed to the way you wanted?'

'I can't see any difference between now and the way we used to live,' Jukan answered. 'We are still working just for a piece of bread, which doesn't even make you feel full. We still have no water in the house, not even enough to wash in. We don't have toilets like other people do, and we have to run into the bushes, like dogs. Why should I live like that?'

Now it was father's turn to speak again. 'Believe me, my son, as soon as we pay off our debts and the lawyers, we will find water in the lowlands and we will build a big dam, and then you will not only be able to wash but also be able to have a bath. We will build a toilet so fine that even gentlemen from Bihach will be envious. And for you and the other children, this year, we will buy suits so that you look like real men.' He looked at Jukan and immediately understood that this had been the problem all along. They smiled at one another, and both burst out laughing.

But this didn't last long. Jukan stopped laughing and said, 'No, Father, I don't think that will happen. The interest on our debts grows so quickly that we will never be able to pay them off, even if we sold all our cows and sheep.'

'No, you are wrong,' his father objected. 'If we sold even half of them, we could pay them off!'

'Then let's sell them and pay off the debts!' Jukan was quick to reply.

'We have to wait,' Father explained. 'Soon, the prices will rise again, and my brother Stefan writes from America that as soon as their crisis is over, they will be able to help us.'

'Well, I am prepared to wait another year, but no longer,' Jukan said.

'It seems that you have completely lost faith in our house,' Father said sadly.

'Is it only me?' Jukan asked. 'Your brothers ran away and came back only in the winter. And when they do settle in the city, you will not see any trace of them, because they lost their faith in the house a long time ago!'

Father dropped his head and thought about Jukan's words. 'Well, then, we will wait one more year, and after that, we'll decide.'

As they finished this sad conversation, they reached home. All the family was waiting in the courtyard, and when they saw Jukan with his father, they were all overjoyed. Grandfather was the only one not to come out. After a quick supper, everyone left the room, leaving only Jukan with his father and mother at the table. Father got up, and as he left the room, he said to Jukan, 'Tomorrow morning, you do what you are supposed to do!' That meant that in the morning, Jukan would be grazing the sheep again. Now he stayed alone with his mother. She raised her eyes, and Jukan could see that they were filled with tears. Jukan felt these tears tearing at his soul. Why do we torture the people we love the most? Jukan and his mother embraced and silently held on to one another for a long time. It is comforting to feel close to the person who had given birth to you. We always think we have plenty of time to give our love back. We think that this person will always be close by and we still have plenty of time to say everything that we want to say. But we often forget, and when we do decide to do it, it's usually too late.

Part 3

Klara got out of bed just as the first rays of sunshine were touching the bedroom wall. Because she was so excited, she had not slept well, but today wasn't the day for self-indulgence. This past year, she had graduated after eight years at school and was now enrolled at Rubfak. But now she had to find a job. Just next door to Klara's house was the Seventh Tanning Factory, and Klara had decided to begin her search there. She washed her face and hands and dressed in her grey dress and put on her only shoes. She brushed her hair, and when she was satisfied with her appearance, she went out onto the street. The streets were filled with the usual noises; trams overcrowded with passengers hanging on the footboards, cars hooting their horns, horses neighing, and people going about their business all rushed past her, going in different directions.

Klara crossed the road and went up to the factory gates. Here, she was stopped at the checkpoint by a security guard. 'What are you looking for, girl?' the guard asked her.

'I'm looking for work,' she answered.

'Then you need to go to the Staff Department,' he told her.

'Could you please show me where I have to go?' she asked.

'You see that door?' He pointed to a big wooden and metal door. 'You go through that door and go upstairs to the second floor. Ask for Anju Jamshchikinu. She is the chief of the Staff Department.'

Klara thanked the guard and followed his directions. She walked up the dimly lit steps and followed a long corridor where she found the Staff Department behind the second door. She knocked quietly and went inside. The room was large with shelves along the walls stuffed with papers and books. A young woman was sitting at a big table that was covered with documents. She looked at Klara and asked, 'What do you want, girl?'

'I'm looking for work,' Klara answered.

'How old are you?' the woman asked her.

'I'm fifteen,' Klara answered again.

'You are too young for a job,' said the woman. 'What can you do?'

'I can't do anything,' Klara confessed, and the chief of staffing burst out laughing.

Just at that moment, a bald man in a black suit came into the office. The woman asked him, 'Michael Izrailevich, does the Accounts Department need a new employee?'

'We do actually need someone, but what can this girl do?' he asked.

'That's just the point, she says she can't do anything!' Anju continued to laugh.

But Michael Izrailevich came closer to Klara and looked at her carefully. He asked, 'What is your name?'

'Klara,' she answered.

'Well, Klara, are you a clever girl?'

'I think so,' she answered again.

'Will you try hard?'

'Certainly I will. You give me a try and you will never regret it,' she said confidently.

'Well, Anechka, I like your protégé. I'll take her as an assistant bookkeeper and check out how clever she is.'

'All right, then, Michael Izrailevich, you go now, and when she has completed the application form, I will bring her to you.'

Klara could not believe how quickly she had been given a job. After she had filled in the form, Anja Vasilevna took her to the Accounting Department, which was on the same floor, further down the long corridor. Her new boss, Bubnov Michael Izrailevich seemed to be a very likeable man. He introduced her to the other nine workers in the Accounting Department and then took her around the factory, showing her every department and introducing her as a new employee. The workers all greeted her; some smiled and winked playfully. It looked as though Bubnov was greatly respected in the factory, and Klara felt that this respect extended to her as well. They then returned to their own department, and Bubnov explained to Klara what she was to do. 'So, Klarochka, your job is very straightforward but very important. You will be responsible for putting all the data into the books, and many things depend on that data. At the end of each quarter, you will make sure that debits and credits balance. That is the main task of our department. Do you understand?' Klara nodded her head, though her brain was spinning with all this information. Bubnov noticed this and said, 'You know what? You should go home now and have a rest. Think about everything, and tomorrow come back and we will talk some more.'

Klara was very excited, and she knew she needed to calm down. She said goodbye and went home. Her mother was already there, and Klara was excited to share her news. But her mother was not listening carefully . . . it was clear that she had something else on her mind. 'Mother, aren't you interested in what I'm telling you?' Klara said, feeling hurt.

Her mother hugged her gently and said, 'Of course, I'm interested. It's just that I had a letter from Simeon today.'

'Has something happened to him?' Klara asked.

'No, he said everything was all right, but it seems to me that he can't write the truth. In my opinion, he's very depressed,' Mother said.

'How can we help him?' Klara wanted to know.

'I don't know,' answered her mother. 'I think I will go and visit him before the winter starts.' And as she had said, Klara's mother left to visit Simeon in Siberia, and Klara started her new job.

At the factory, they prepared a workplace for Klara, a small table in a corner of the Accounting Department. To get to it, she had to pass all the other employees. That should not have been a big problem, as everyone was very friendly towards her, except for one man, Tsukerman Alexander Azarovich. For some reason, he hadn't liked Klara from the start and continually criticised her. He criticised everything that she did, often complaining to Bubnov. But all the others were very kind to her, and she became great friends with a blonde girl called Olga. She was the most beautiful girl in the whole factory; she was tall and elegant, with a thick plait and long legs. But Olga wasn't arrogant at all; on the contrary, she was easy and straightforward. They would go to eat together, and in the evenings, they studied at Rubfak. Studying after a long day's work wasn't easy, but Klara found it fascinating. The people she met there were of different ages and ambitions, but all of them looked optimistically to a bright future for their country and to the fulfilled dream of the proletariat. Klara hoped that after graduating from the Rubfak, she could enrol in the medical institute, wanting to cure the sick.

Lyonka Rjaboy shared a desk with Klara. He was not tall but was very energetic, and he dreamed of going to a military college to become an officer. He fell in love with Klara almost immediately and wanted her to be his girlfriend. Klara didn't want to even consider this and always turned it into a joke. However, Lyonka was very persistent and often joked back, 'Eh, Klara, you don't understand how lucky you are. When you grow up and marry me, you will never regret it. I will always love you, and one day you will be a general's wife!'

'What are you talking about?' she asked, laughing. 'And what is your surname?'

'Rjaboy,' he answered, not realising that she was making a joke because the word meant 'speckled'.

'Well, if I marry you, everyone will call me Madame Speckled!'

'Then I will take your surname,' he answered back quickly, not wanting to give in.

'Listen, Lyonka, I'm still much too young to even think about marriage,' Klara cut him short.

'All right, I will wait!' he said.

It was difficult to work and study, but Klara also continued to sing in the amateur chorus. Without singing, she didn't think she could live. At work, after a short training period, Bubnov entrusted her to put all the data into the main accounts book. When Tsukerman learnt this, he was horrified! 'You trust it to her and you will see, she will mix it all up. Then you will regret it.'

'Perhaps,' Bubnov agreed, 'but it could be the opposite. We'll wait and see when the quarterly accounts are due.'

Klara tried very hard not to miss or mix any of the figures, and she was dreading the day the accounts were due. When the day arrived, the data of debits and credits balanced the first time, for the first time ever; no one expected this, not even Bubnov himself. Tsukerman became silent. Then Bubnov asked him, 'Well, what can you say, Tsukerman, the numbers have balanced!'

'So what,' he sniffed contemptuously.

'Well, this is something that you have never achieved,' said Bubnov in a low voice. He turned his back and left the office. After that, Tsukerman stopped his attacks on Klara, and life was quiet.

Klara's mother returned from her trip to see Simeon very upset. Klara had many questions, and her mother replied that now he looked and acted like an old man. He was chopping trees, and this job was terrible. His hands had been injured from working with an axe, he had a thick unshaved beard covering his face, and many of his teeth were missing. Mother felt the pain of seeing him, and she cried all the time. But Simeon's spirits remained high, and he kept assuring his mother that he would do his term, and then he would return to them. Zelda had gone to the chief prison officer, trying to make life easier for Simeon, but she achieved nothing. So she had returned to Odessa. By that time, her two older stepdaughters had married and were living separately away from the house, so things were a little easier.

Klara was paid a small salary, and she was able to buy a beautiful silk dress and some rubber shoes. Sometimes she had enough money to go the cinema with friends. Tanja Klyachkina was not able to go with her very often. Tanja had a boyfriend, Shurik. He was tall, with beautiful curly blond hair. His parents were Bulgarians but had lived a long time in Odessa, and they lived in the Lanzheron area. All the girls were crazy about Shurik, but he had eyes only for Tanja, and he didn't let any of the other boys get near her. Whenever she had a date with Shurik, Tanja borrowed Klara's dress. Klara didn't want to even think about boys just yet!

Time flew quickly! Klara didn't notice that two years had passed since she had begun in the factory. Now she felt very much at home there, and everyone knew and loved her. Greetings and jokes always came in her direction. Bubnov treated her as his own daughter, and Tsukerman was reconciled and didn't bother her anymore. Everything seemed to be going well, but Klara's mother could not get used to the fact that her son was a convict. She stopped looking after herself; her hair turned grey, and grief stiffened her face. She lived in constant fear for herself and her children, and she seemed to be always waiting for life's next blow. Zelda's brother, Grisha, and his family were not much better. He had never recovered after his arrest; he remained hunched and very scared for the rest of his life. He hardly talked to anybody and never laughed.

From America, they received very good news; all their relatives had started their own businesses and had their own homes. Their children studied in expensive schools and were going to become future doctors and lawyers. They didn't ask Zelda to come to America, understanding that this would never happen, but they were always interested to hear what was happening in Zelda's life. Zelda didn't want to tell them the sad truth and didn't reply very often.

After graduating from Rubfak, Lyonka Rjaboy decided to go to Leningrad and enrol in the military college there. Before leaving, he visited Klara. He looked very serious and solemn. He went to her and said, 'Listen, Klara, I am going to Leningrad.'

'I'm so glad for you,' Klara said, but Lyonka went on.

'Will you promise me that when I come back, we will be married?'

Klara felt uncomfortable about rejecting him, but at the same time, she did not want to make this promise, so she answered simply, 'You go to Leningrad, and when you come back, we will decide!' So Lyonka left, enrolled in the military college, and for some time, he disappeared from Klara's life.

That year was a very eventful year for Klara's best friend, Tanja. One evening in late autumn, there was an impatient knock at Klara's door, just as Klara was heading for bed. She opened the door, and there was Tanja, radiant with happiness. That evening, she had borrowed Klara's dress. 'What are you doing coming now?' Klara asked. 'You could have returned the dress tomorrow. Why?' Klara asked again.

'Because today, Shurik asked me to marry him.'

'And you agreed?'

'Of course, I agreed,' Tanja said, laughing and spinning around.

The next day, Klara went with Tanja and Shurik to the registry office to apply for a wedding license, and two weeks after that, Tanja and Shurik were married at a solemn ceremony. Shurik had bought Tanja a beautiful dress, and she looked wonderful, shining with happiness. The ceremony was a simple but formal affair. All Tanja's friends were envious of the handsome Shurik, but he had eyes only for Tanja. After the service, they all had a glass of champagne. Tanja moved into Shurik's family's house, though they were not very happy about having a Jewish daughter-in-law.

After Klara's graduation from Rubfak, she enrolled in evening study at the national economics faculty and continued to work at the tanning factory. She was so used to the work by now that each day was the same as the one before. But one day, news spread around the factory that a new deputy director, a young, handsome, brown-haired man had arrived. Everyone was talking about his wit and knowledge, and many of the girls were already mad about him. One day, Klara was going to the warehouse, a notebook in her hand. Just at that moment, the new deputy director came out. Klara kept walking, looking at her notebook, pretending that she hadn't noticed him. Suddenly, he stopped, blocking her way.

'Hello, Klara, what are you doing today?' he asked.

'I'm going to the warehouse,' Klara answered, confused.

'I'm not asking where you are going now,' he said. 'I meant to say, what are you doing tonight?'

'As usual, I'm going to the institute,' she explained.

'Which institute?' he asked again.

'Narhoz!' she said.

'Well, you are a good girl. After that, I will wait for you near the main entrance.'

'Why?' Klara asked again.

'Because I want to see you' was his reply.

'And if I don't want to see you?' Klara tried again.

'If you don't want to, it is all the same, I will wait for you!'

'Well, then, you will wait alone!' she replied quickly and ran off to the warehouse.

At the end of the day, after studying, Klara went out through the side entrance to avoid the central entrance and ran home. The next day, he again met her in the corridor. Klara had the impression that he was stalking her.

'Hello, Klara,' he greeted her.

'Hello, Lev Davidovich,' she answered.

'You can call me by my first name—after all, I am not your father!' He was quite indignant.

'I am not comfortable with that,' Klara said.

'It seems you are not comfortable with many things. You didn't even show up for our date! Why did you escape like that?'

'I didn't want to come,' Klara said stubbornly.

'Fair enough,' Lev said. 'But tonight I will wait for you in the same place.'

'And I will not come again,' she said.

'And I will wait for you anyway!' he said and left.

Klara stayed where she was, thinking about this situation. Why did he keep following her when there were so many beautiful girls around? Then the thought struck her . . . he was simply wanting to get acquainted with Olga! With this thought, she ran to find Olga. 'Listen, Olga, today after work, let's go for a walk with our new deputy director.'

'With whom?' Olga asked, surprised.

'With our deputy director,' Klara said. 'I think he really likes you but doesn't know how to approach you, which is why he came to me,' Klara explained.

'Well, then, we will go!' Olga agreed.

In the evening, they went together to the main entrance where Lev was waiting for them. 'Hello, Lev Davidovich,' they greeted him, but he stopped them at once.

'Sorry, girls, here, we are not at work, so please call me by my name, Ljova Miroshnik! I want to invite you to the café Falcone.' And off they went quickly towards Deribasovskaja Street. The café was ablaze with lights, and it was very crowded and noisy. It turned out to be a wonderful evening. Lev was gallant and confident; he joked, and the girls laughed cheerfully, enjoying ice cream and juice.

41

The time flew by so quickly that Klara was surprised to see, when she looked at the clock, that it was already ten o'clock. 'It's time for me to go,' she said, getting up from her chair.

'Where are you off to? We will go with you,' Ljova said.

'No, you can take me to the tram and then you can take Olga home,' Klara insisted. But Ljova didn't want to listen to this.

'No, we will take Olga home, and then I will take you home,' he said. Olga was very confused by this, but they did as he said, and when finally they reached Klara's house, he asked her, 'Why did you bring Olga along? Did you think I would eat you alive?' and with that, he left.

Next morning, Olga was very frustrated, but at once, Klara began to make up another story. 'Yes, he does like you, but he is reluctant to be alone with you,' she said. After a long conversation, Olga agreed to go with Klara and Lev the next night, so there they were, the two of them, waiting when Ljova arrived. When he saw them together again, Lev was a little on edge, and after about an hour, he spoke up.

'Listen, Olga. I think you are a lovely person, and I don't want to offend you, but please don't come again with Klara. I want to be by myself with her. If you are worried about her, I give you my word that I will not hurt her in any way.' Olga was so embarrassed by this unexpected information; she blushed deeply and ran away.

The next day, Klara tried to explain how guilty she felt, but Olga waved her away. 'Go away from me. I don't want to see you anymore!'

But Klara decided that she would not be put off. 'I apologise; I couldn't believe it myself. What fool would choose me when he could have you?' she asked.

'Don't pretend to be such a such a foolish, modest woman,' Olga replied. 'You know your value perfectly well! Because of you, I have made a fool of myself. Yes, I looked like a fool!' she finished.

'I apologise, I never for one moment thought such a thing would happen,' Klara tried again.

'You can say what you like. Because of you, I made a fool of myself, not just once but twice,' Olga said angrily. But then she stopped, thought for moment, and said, 'If Ljova Miroshnik has his eye on you, it means he sees something special in you. Such a man does not make mistakes.'

After that, they met almost every day. Ljova looked after her as though she were a princess, buying her flowers, writing poems for her, and taking her to the theatre and cinema. On her birthday, she received the most wonderful surprise. Early in the morning, a man all dressed in red with a cap on his head came into the courtyard. He was holding a huge bouquet of roses. The neighbours had never seen anything like it before! The man went to Klara's door and knocked. She opened the door and froze with surprise. The man began his solemn speech: 'Dear Klara, please accept these flowers for your birthday from the person who dreams of being with you for the rest of his life!' He handed her the bouquet of flowers, bowed, and left. In the bouquet, Klara found a note. She opened it and read:

> For Klara, on her birthday.
> You were born in the year 1920,
> On the eve of a great and promising epoch.
> And everyone has noticed
> Your eyes, your smile, the air about you.
> Growing in this amazing time,
> You have blossomed as have the years.
>
> It is impossible to tell of the scale
> Of my love and feelings for you.
> I wish, darling, that from now
> You will live happily for one hundred years.
> To love this world and be loved in return,
> As every person deserves.
> Odessa, 29/3/1938
> Ljova Miroshnik -----

After reading this note, Klara was almost crying with happiness. She had never felt like this in her entire life. Then one beautiful evening, only a few months after meeting, Ljova proposed to her. 'Klara, will you marry me?' he asked.

Klara had been expecting this question for a while now, but even so, it took her by surprise. Just at that moment, though, Klara remembered a prediction that her neighbour Aunt Sonja had made. 'I'm sorry, but I can't!' Klara answered, close to tears.

Ljova was not expecting this answer and was hardly able to contain his emotions. He asked, 'Why ever not, if it's not a secret?'

'Because I will never be able to give you children,' she explained.

'How do you know this?' he asked again.

'Aunt Sonja told me,' she answered.

'And who is this aunt Sonja? Is she a doctor or something?'

'No, she is just one of our neighbours, but she knows everything,' Klara explained.

At that moment, the frightened look left his face, and Ljova said, 'Well, we will check what this aunt Sonja knows. Do you have any other reasons to refuse me?'

'No,' Klara answered, smiling.

'Then you will marry me?' he asked.

'Of course,' Klara answered again.

After that, he slapped himself on the knee and almost danced. 'Then we can put in our application to the registry office?'

'No,' Klara laughed. 'First, we need to talk to my mother.'

But Ljova was flying on the wings of love. 'I will talk to your mother!'

⋄⋄⋄⋄⋄⋄

This was an important year for Mishka. He had graduated from school, and what had seemed to him to be an infinitely long childhood was at an end. All these years, he had spent on a remote farm, far away from the world's problems, and life passed slowly, hardly changing. The news from Odessa and Moscow reached them occasionally. Sometimes officials from the regional centre came for an inspection, and then the locals shivered in fright. But mainly they lived as if in a bubble. Their poor farm at Freiberg wasn't attractive to anyone. Here, among the boundless Ukrainian steppes, they mainly spoke German at home, Russian at school. The days when Klara had visited were the brightest in his life. For Mishka, she was like a princess in a fairy tale. She dressed differently from his sisters and was very outspoken, while the village people were not at all talkative. He could still recall her laughter, loud and unchecked. He thought he would hear her laughter for the rest of his life. It didn't matter that during her last visit, he had lost his good friend Petka. Mishka couldn't forgive him for those rough words he had used when talking about Klara. Petka also hadn't forgotten, and though they didn't fight anymore, they avoided each other. Mishka had other friends, but he spent little time with them.

Above all, Mishka loved to draw. He spent all of his free time with his pencils and paper, drawing people, animals, landscapes, and even sometimes his dreams. But nobody in the house took his hobby seriously. In a village, people were supposed to engage in serious work, not drawing pictures. His father dreamed that one day his son would live next to him and start his own family. But Mishka had other plans. He dreamed of leaving the farm as soon as possible and go far away to live in a big city, where life was in full swing. From Germany came dreadful news. After Hitler had come to power, Jews were exposed to mockery and violence. Mishka had decided that he would help fight against the evil of fascism and become a military officer. He hadn't shared these ideas with anyone, and only after graduation did he talk to his father about them. Father was stunned by the news.

'Don't you know that Jewish men cannot be officers?' he asked.

'Why is that?' Mishka asked.

'Because Jews cannot bear arms!' his father replied.

'But I am also a Soviet citizen. That is why I want to protect you and our homeland,' Mishka said, refusing to give up, and no one could make him change his mind. Eventually, his father gave in, and Mishka went off to join the military college.

xxxxAnother year passed but very little changed in life in the village. Nicola bought a piece of land in Vakup and began to build a kafana, a café. At that time, the government began to build the new Una railway, and life there was busy. All Nicola's family's money had gone into building this kafana, and it was finished very quickly. Three people worked there, and their income was better than it was in the homeland, where twelve people worked hard for eight to ten hours a day to earn the same amount. At that time, Jukan decided that he would go. He found an opportunity when no one else was at home except his father and mother. He went to them and said, 'That's it, Father. After today, I'm not taking the sheep to graze. I'm leaving to make some money.' With these words, he took a bag with spare clothes and a bit of cheese and bread and went out the door. His father ran after him and pulled him back. But Jukan pulled the other way.

'Where are going?' Father asked Jukan.

'To Vakup railway construction,' he answered.

'No, I wanted to go to work there,' Father said.

'Then leave my bag, get another bag from Mother, and we can go together,' said Jukan.

'And what will you do there?' Father asked again.

'What all the other people do!' Jukan said.

'But you don't have any trade, and you are still too young to live alone,' Father objected.

'It's all right, Father,' said Jukan. 'I'll learn from what other people do.' Jukan pulled his bag from his father's hands and walked away.

He walked all the way to the end of the road and then stopped and looked back. He saw his father standing motionless, looking after him, and Jukan felt very, very sad. Suddenly, he saw Mirko run out of his house, also carrying a bag, rushing in the same direction. That meant that he had left the cows and taken his belongings. So the family was left with no shepherds.

That evening, they reached Vakup and for a while could not decide whether to go to Stric's hotel or somewhere else. They decided to go to Stric's hotel. As it turned out, Stric was not at home; he had left for Dalmatia to buy wine for his kafana. His wife met them happily and gave them food and a bed. The boys got up early in the morning and went out to search for work. They found a job very quickly, despite the fact they neither of them had a trade. The work was very hard; they had to dig the dirt with shovels, load it onto wheelbarrows, and move it to where the future platforms would be. The supervisor watched them closely, so it was important to work quickly. 'You will get paid according to the amount of work you do!' he shouted. Everyone hated the supervisor and silently cursed him. Every day the work was getting harder and harder. Jukan's hands were filthy, and the blisters were dreadful.

A few days passed like this, but one morning, an inspector called them and asked, 'Could any of you build the barracks?'

Jukan quickly stepped forward and said, 'Yes, I could do that!'

'Then go to the warehouse and leave your shovel here.' Jukan walked to the warehouse, took a seat on a tree stump, and waited. Soon, the inspector with two more senior men arrived. They went into the warehouse and called to Jukan.

When he came closer, he saw that they were looking at some papers and talking. One of them showed him a drawing and asked, 'Do you know what this is?'

'It's a drawing of a building,' Jukan answered.

'Who taught you that?' the man asked him.

'My grandfather did.'

'Is he a tradesman?' the man asked again.

'My grandfather could do anything. He built all the schools in our area. I helped him and I learnt,' Jukan replied.

At that moment, another man entered the warehouse and heard what they were saying. 'Give him the plan and let him show what it will look like on the ground.' He took Jukan to the courtyard and showed him two pages of plans.

'You see, there has to be a facade. You should make other markings on the ground. I will give you the key to the warehouse, and there you will find everything you need.' He turned and walked away, leaving Jukan alone. Jukan thought for a while and went into the warehouse. Everything was stored neatly. He found a pole-axe, a saw, a ten-metre measuring tape, twine, and pegs. He came out again, examined the plan, and orientated it on the pegs. Then he marked the four corners and internal walls. Then he began to drive the pegs into the ground.

He didn't notice that the boss and some other men were watching him. The boss spoke. 'It seems you know what you are doing. But do you remember the primary sizes?' Jukan replied from memory. 'You have a clear mind, young man. That means you will be the main carpenter here, and you will give me the keys when the barracks are finished.' So, unexpectedly, Jukan had a well-paid job, and he and the boss became friends, and quite often they visited Stric's kafana after work.

A Muslim lived next to Stric's house; he was the brother of the man who had sold the land to Stric. In the city, there was very little land, and so the houses were built very closely together, especially in the Muslim area. They had a law that a father could not allow his son to marry unless he has built him a new house . . . that's why the houses grew like mushrooms, built closely to the house next to it. The houses were built primarily of thin timber. In the summer, they were cool; in winter, they were very cold. From Stric's house to the Muslim neighbour's house, there was practically no distance at all, and it was possible to shake hands from one window to the next. The room where Jukan slept faced four windows of the Muslim's house. Just in front of his room were the windows where the owner's daughter, Zlatina, lived. She was a beautiful young girl, tall and graceful, with a long neck and long legs. Her long chestnut hair was braided and fell to her knees. Her face was an oval with a small mouth and a lovely chin. Her beautiful blue eyes shone and were graced by beautiful half-moon brows. Never before had Jukan seen such a beautiful woman. He lost sleep thinking about her and couldn't concentrate during the day.

Soon, Zlatina and Jukan became acquainted, and so their love story began. They started sending love notes to one another. There was no electricity in Vakup; the housed were lit by oil lamps, and everyone usually went to bed early. But Zlatina and Jukan were in no rush to go to sleep. They opened their windows slightly and whispered quietly to one another. All day long, they waited for the moment when they could be near one another. It was their first real love, but between them, there were two religions, so they were without any help. Nobody wanted to understand. Jukan's friends did not condemn them, though they advised the couple to end their relationship. No one would allow a Muslim girl to become the wife of a Serb. When Zlatina's father found out, he was furious, and Zlatina's windows no longer opened, and Jukan had to leave Stric's house. It was hard for him to understand why religion should separate people who were in love and cause others to hate.

After that, Jukan did not want to stay in Vakup, preferring not to visit friends and not to disturb the wound of his love for Zlatina. He continued to work at the station for another two months. By then, he had many friends and acquaintances with whom he spent his free time. The owner of the local bar was the father of his uncle's wife. He had two sons and two daughters; the younger daughter was called Ljuba. She was the most beautiful girl in the area, and everyone loved her. She wasn't just beautiful; she was kind and friendly. Though she was more than three years older than Jukan, they were good friends. They had met several years ago, when she had visited Lipa and helped Jukan to graze the sheep. Now they were still friends, and Jukan liked to go shopping with her. When the job at the station ended and the workers had to move further down the line, Jukan decided not to go with them. He took his money and went shopping . . . he bought two suits, one for every day and one for weekends. He bought three shirts, some scarves, two pairs of socks, two elegant pairs of shoes, a tie, and a hat. He still had some money left, and he spent that on a few days in the city with Ljuba. Then on the Saturday, they travelled together to Lipa. Ljuba always dressed beautifully, and now Jukan looked like a gentleman too. He loved the feeling of his well-fitted suit, knowing that he had paid for it himself from his own money. He felt that Ljuba liked walking with this well-turned-out young man.

When they arrived home, everyone ran out into the courtyard to look at them. Jukan's relatives were glad to see him looking so handsome and well, particularly Mother and Father. Mother came to him and patted his hair. She said with tears in her eyes, 'I didn't recognise you. I was wondering who this young man was, and it's you!' They embraced one another; he had not been home now for several years.

Jukan wanted to see Grandfather, but he was not at home. Jukan didn't want to wait. He left to visit the Mandich house, where his mother had been born. He stayed there until evening, and by then, Grandfather was in bed. So, early the next morning, Jukan washed his face and dressed in his new suit and tie. He looked in the mirror and was happy with the way he looked. He went to the part of the house where Grandfather slept. He opened the door and saw his grandfather sitting on his favourite three-legged stool, drinking his coffee. His moustache was dashingly curled, and he had the look of someone who is pleased with life. Suddenly, he saw Jukan standing there in his suit and tie. Grandfather jumped from his stool and shouted, 'What is that dog collar you have around your neck? Get away from here, and make sure I don't see you ever again wearing this dog collar!' He stretched out his hand and grabbed his shtap (walking stick) and raised it. Jukan had just enough time to run out of the room before he heard the shtap hit the door. Jukan knew that Grandfather had not intended to hurt him, just to frighten him. He often threw the shtap, but no one had ever been hurt. Jukan understood what Grandfather had said and never again showed up before him wearing a tie!

Again, Jukan became a shepherd, but he tried as much as possible to help his mother. In the house, there were now only three women, but the amount of work stayed the same. Besides that, Mother had given birth to a third son, and she had to give him a lot of her attention. Jukan by that time had become a very passionate young man and was always seeking out girls. That year, all the older boys had left to join the army, and Jukan became the leader of the other boys and the defender of the local girls.

One fine August afternoon, all the young people gathered in the valley. They played cheerful music, and the girls danced 'kolo'. Jukan had come with his friends from Kulina. Everyone knew everyone else, and the young people were getting along very well. Suddenly, there appeared among them six unfamiliar boys, and the news spread that these were boys from Gorevats. They were a bit older than the local boys, stronger and ruder too. They began to dance, and everything was going well until one of them, a spindly legged youth, started to get rough with one of the girls, who did not want to dance with him. The youth continued to pull at her until Jukan stepped in to stop him. 'Leave her alone, don't force her if she doesn't want to dance with you!' he said. But the spindly legged youth continued to pull at the girl. Jukan again stepped in and in a firmer voice said again, 'Leave her alone!'

The spindly legged boy grabbed Jukan by the collar with one hand and, with the other, slapped Jukan across the face. Jukan fell to the ground. He stood up quickly and rushed at his attacker, but this time the youth's friends grabbed Jukan by the arms, and the youth made a move as if to pull out a pistol and began to shout, 'I will kill you!' and he struck Jukan again. The local girls began to drag Jukan away, begging him not to fight this hooligan. The situation was made worse by the local boys who did nothing to help Jukan. The spindly legged youth's friends did try to stop him, but he continued to shout, 'Let me go! I will kill him!'

Jukan realised that, unarmed, he could do nothing. He remembered that his pistol was at home. Blood rushed to his head, and he turned and ran, followed by the loud laughter of the gang. His home was about two kilometres away; he ran the whole way but didn't feel any tiredness. His face stung from the slaps and anger welled up in his throat. He didn't see anyone in the yard when he got there. He quickly drank some water and rushed to his room where his pistol was hidden. He pulled the gun, wrapped in a rag, from a big jar, and put it in his pocket. He took twelve cartridges, put them in his other pocket, and ran back to where they had been.

When he got there, he saw that everyone had left. He decided to catch up with them to pay the youth back. In the highlands of Bosnia, blood flows hot through human veins. People cannot live with an insult. Jukan's pulse was racing, and he was aware of the gun in his hand. Nothing could stop him. A neighbour asked him, 'Where are you running to?'

But Jukan answered, 'Don't ask me, tomorrow you will know!'

At last, Jukan saw the group. They were in a cart, and Jukan's attacker was there. Jukan immediately decided on a plan: he would run straight across the woods and get in front of the cart. Branches hit him as he ran, but he paid no attention to them. At last, he got ahead of the cart; he took a few seconds to recover his breath and moved forward. His offender saw him, jumped off the cart, and began to run. Jukan raised his pistol and shot, but he missed his target because the youth was running very fast. Jukan ran after him and shot again. Despite the distance between them, this time Jukan hit his target, and the youth stumbled and fell. But a second later, he was up and running again. Then Jukan shot a third time, and again the youth fell to the ground. A few of the others had gathered at the stream, and they rushed to help the wounded boy. One of them swore loudly at Jukan. But Jukan turned and began to move in his direction, and the boy fell to the ground, realising that he, too, could be shot.

Nobody ran to Jukan again. He dropped his hands, feeling chilled, knowing that he had killed a man. Now he felt sorry for what he had done. He walked home through the forest. His home was silent but alert, as everyone had already heard what had happened. When he entered the courtyard, all of his relatives were gathered, but no one spoke to him, no one approached him except for his mother, who asked quietly, 'Why did you do it?'

It was very late when his father arrived home. In the morning, he had gone to Bihach, and on the way back, he had to pass through the village where Jukan had killed the man. This could have developed into a blood feud, but his friends warned him, and Father had bypassed Gorevats on foot. Once past the village, he got back on the cart and arrived home. When Jukan heard the sound of the approaching cart, he rushed to open the gates. The horses entered quietly, as though they knew that something was wrong. Jukan sat down near the well. Everyone watched as his father went up to Jukan, as though about to speak, but when he saw Jukan's face, he changed his mind and instead hugged and kissed his son. Then he turned to his family and said, 'Why are you all here? Go to bed! And, Milka, can you make us some supper?' All the relatives went inside, leaving just Jukan and his father, who was stroking Jukan's head. His eyes showed how angry he was, but he loved his son and felt sorry for him. So they walked together into the house, where they had some supper, before Father said to his wife, 'Milka, please go to bed now, and Jukan and I will lie here together.' So Mother left the room, Jukan giving her a sorrowful glance.

Now that the anger had left Father, there was only sorrow. The two of them lay down on the bed, but it was a long time before Jukan could fall asleep. He tossed and turned, and in the few moments when he did start to doze, he had a nightmare that he was wrestling with someone. He woke again, to feel his father still stroking his head, and eventually fell asleep again. In the morning, when he woke up, Jukan decided to change the pistol for a very old and almost useless one of the same calibre. He went to the storeroom and swapped over the guns and left the house. He walked far away from the house, wrapped the pistol in a rag, and shot three times into the air. After that, he went home to wait for the police to arrive. The police appeared not to be in any hurry and only arrived at three in the afternoon. The family offered them dinner; this was refused, but they had a glass of rakija before the senior policeman called Jukan and said, 'Do you know what you have done?'

'Yes, I know that I killed the person who insulted me in front of my friends and the girls,' Jukan replied.

'No, you are wrong, you shot his friend,' the policeman said maliciously.

'It can't be, I remembered him well,' Jukan answered without hesitation.

'Perhaps they looked alike?' the policeman questioned.

'No, I shot the one who insulted me. I didn't lose my mind!'

'Then bring me the pistol that you used,' the policeman demanded. Jukan went and brought back the pistol he had just used. The policeman turned it in his hands and said, 'Is it possible to shoot from a faulty pistol?'

'I threw it against a rock after I had used it,' Jukan lied.

'Can you show us this rock?' the policeman asked.

'I can, but it's a long way from here.'

'That's OK, the main thing is that you remember where it is. How many times did you fire it?' he asked.

'Three times,' Jukan answered him. The policeman handed the gun to the second policeman, who examined the pistol and sniffed the barrel and nodded his agreement.

Jukan began to feel better; at least he had saved the pistol that Ujak had given him. 'Go and collect your things,' the first policemen said to Jukan. 'You will come with us to the police station.' This was not what Jukan had wanted to hear, but he went to the other room where his mother was waiting for him. Grandfather had gone in to talk to the policemen.

'You see what you have done, my son,' Mother said. 'What will happen now?'

'I don't know,' Jukan answered her. 'The police said to collect some things that I will need and go with them.' Mother was crying as she began to help him with his things, and then Grandmother came, wanting to help, but crying loudly.

'Never have the police taken anyone away from our house,' she cried. 'How unlucky am I to feel this shame in my old age!'

Jukan was tormented by the thought that maybe he had killed the wrong man; if so, it was terrible. But he thought again that this could not be true; Jukan remembered the youth well, and why would he have run if he was innocent? No, he hadn't confused spindly legs with anyone. So now he didn't hesitate when he said to his mother, 'Mother, you don't have to collect anything. If I need something else, I will let you know later.' He took just a few of the most important things and went out to the policemen. They stood up and walked with Jukan out of the door.

Outside, Jukan could still his grandmother crying, 'My God, what is happening? This never happened to our home, not even under the Turkish yoke!'

'It hadn't happened before because I hadn't been born yet!' Jukan replied, and everyone burst out laughing. Even the moustached policeman agreed! Jukan tried to behave naturally to help his family feel better. But as they left the courtyard, Jukan remembered what was happening and became silent. For the rest of the walk to the police station, no one spoke.

When they arrived, one of the policemen went to report to the chief, who was well acquainted with the Vignevich family. The chief ordered that Jukan be brought to him and that they be left alone. He then began to question Jukan loudly. 'What is your name? family name? date of birth?' Jukan answered quietly, but the chief suddenly shouted, 'You are still a minor, and already you have brought shame to your family! From where did you get this pistol, and why did you idiot do it?'

'Please don't insult me, you have no right to do that,' Jukan said quietly. 'I know that I am guilty, and I will answer according to the law.'

The chief was infuriated by these words; he got up and approached Jukan. 'You are teaching me how to speak? You will not forget me!' and he put his huge fist right in front of Jukan's nose but then cooled down a little and called in another officer and ordered, 'Lock this rude man away, let him sit by himself for a while, give him time to think!' There was no special cell at the police station, so Jukan was locked in an empty shed where the firewood for winter was stored. He was left there for about an hour and then taken back to the chief.

'Tell me, which of these pistols is yours?' he asked, placing five handguns on the table in front of Jukan, who pointed to his pistol without hesitating. The chief took the pistol and slowly turned it. Then he pointed it right at Jukan and shouted, 'No, this is not your pistol! You will go home and bring me back the real one! Do you understand me?'

'I shot from this pistol, and I don't have any other,' Jukan said calmly.

The chief burst out laughing and then got serious again as he resumed his questioning. 'Tell me, why didn't you calm down and change your mind after your eight-kilometre run?'

'Even now, I would do the same thing,' Jukan answered.

'Did you know that the penalty for murder is the death sentence?'

'I know, but it is better to die than live in humiliation,' Jukan answered seriously.

The chief looked at Jukan carefully. 'Who do you take after? Only decent people live in your house.'

'I tried to explain to the boy he had to behave decently with the girls, but he wouldn't listen to me. And he offended me in front of all my friends,' Jukan added. 'For that he had to answer!'

'So,' said the chief, taking a deep breath, 'you will have to go to court for what you have done, but because you are a minor, I will release you to your home. You can continue to graze your sheep, but you cannot leave home without permission. When you reach adulthood, you will go to court, and there your destiny will be decided.'

So Jukan was sent home, where everyone had been expecting his return. His father simply asked him, 'Well, son, do you want to eat?'

'Yes, please!' replied Jukan.

'Mother, would you bring this gangster something to eat?' Father shouted. And Mother appeared almost immediately, as if that was what she had been waiting for.

After a while, the court sentenced Jukan to seven years in a high-security prison, and his sentence was to start as soon as he reached adulthood. After an appeal, the sentence was cut to three years, and after another appeal, to one and a half years. This term was final, and there were to be no further appeals. But a lawyer told him that soon there would be the coronation of the new king, and a big amnesty was expected; Jukan could be completely pardoned. All his friends advised him to go away somewhere to wait for the coronation, and finally Jukan agreed to go to Belgrade to Stric Nicola using the passport of one of his friends, Pepo, from the Muslim village of Chukovo. He woke up early that morning, said goodbye to his family, took his bag, and left. When he got out on the road, he turned and looked back; there was his mother waving her hand and father standing next to her, his hand on her shoulder. Jukan didn't know then that he would never again live permanently in that house again, only as an occasional visitor.

The two boys arrived in Belgrade without any trouble and at once found jobs.

They were doing concrete work on a construction site, and it was very hard work. Jukan was not used to this sort of work and found it very tiring. Because he was the youngest, the men gave him the simplest and easiest job . . . he had to carry the water to the two Slovenes who made plaster ornaments. Though he wasn't tired anymore, morally it was much harder for him now. Neither of the Slovenes had any respect for him or any other Bosnian. They were continually correcting him and criticizing his work. Also, they often made remarks about his 'Bosnian mother!' At one point, Jukan couldn't take this anymore and in turn insulted their 'Slovenian mother!' It was about to become a fight when Jukan remembered all the trouble he had been in and that he was living in Belgrade on another man's passport. It would be unwise to get involved with the police again. The next day, the owner of the building site told them they had no more work. Jukan had no money and decided that the best thing to do would be to go and see his stric Nicola. He was a waiter in a hotel, and Jukan went straight to the hotel.

'At last you're here,' said Stric Nicola. 'We've been waiting for you; we knew you were in the city.'

'Please don't nag at me!' Jukan asked. 'I'm here now!'

'All right,' agreed Stric. 'Now I am busy, but when I finish work, we will go home together. But on the way home, we will stop off and disinfect your clothes. I don't want you bringing germs into my house. Who knows where you've been with your Muslim friends? And remember, from now on, you need to listen to me. If you don't, I will send you back home! Do you understand me?'

'It's hard not to understand you!' Jukan answered.

With that, Stric went back to work, leaving Jukan with his thoughts. He realised it would be hard to live with Stric, who still thought of him as a child and still felt that he had to teach him. Just then, one of his friends, Sayo, came into the hotel. Jukan called to him, 'Hey, Sayo, come and sit down.'

'I can't, I'm in a rush to meet someone about a job, and I still have to find some more people,' Sayo said.

'Well, then, take me!' said Jukan.

'OK,' agreed Sayo, 'though you don't know what work we have to do.'

'What's the difference?' Jukan said. 'A job is a job, and anything you can do, I can do!'

'That's good, then,' said Sayo. 'Meet me at six o'clock in the morning on the landing stage under the Savitsky Bridge,' and he ran out of the hotel. Jukan decided that he would be better off staying with friends than go to Stric's home, and he, too, ran out of the hotel. Just then, a tram was passing, and Jukan jumped onto the footboard. When he went into his friends' room, he found a card game in progress, and he was invited to join in. Jukan had never played cards for money before but had watched others playing. This time, he decided to take a risk and accepted their offer. Whether he was incredibly lucky or just playing well, he won almost every hand, and soon his friends had run out of money and went to sleep. Jukan went to bed very happy, convinced incorrectly that he was a good card player and could read other people's thoughts!

Early in the morning, the boys all washed their faces, ate some breakfast, and went to work. On the way, they told jokes and arrived at work very pleased with themselves. Then they were shown what they had to do . . . they had to load a coal barge in one day. That meant carrying heavy bags filled with coal. Sometimes Jukan thought that he was totally exhausted and could not keep going. The ground felt unsteady under his feet, and sometimes he wasn't sure where to go. But he kept going, and eventually the job was finished. The boys were paid and went down to the quay. They bathed in the river, washing the sweat, coal, and dirt from their bodies. Then they fell asleep on the pier. When they woke up, the sun was high overhead and too hot to sleep. They decided to bathe a second time; they did it very carefully because none of them could swim. It was almost impossible to learn to swim in Bosnia, where there is not enough water for a wash, let alone a swim! It seemed to some that God had made Bosnia either at the very beginning or the very end of Creation, because at the beginning he had no experience, and at the end, he had run out of materials! That's why Bosnians, who are not afraid of guns or knives or fire, are frightened by water. Yes, they will collect water in buckets from wells, but the ocean or rivers always frighten them.

After bathing, the boys walked to the kafana where they ordered food and drink. Some had wine or rakija, and the younger ones, beer. They were drinking slowly, but when they got out on the street, they felt how tired they were . . . maybe from the alcohol, maybe from the work. Jukan felt that his legs were made of lead. They boarded a tram, and when he leant his elbows on the side, his legs gave way and he almost fell on the floor. The boys finally arrived home, and all fell asleep. The next morning, Jukan felt a little better, but his hands and shoulders still pained him. He decided that he did not want to work like that anymore, and he began to think about how he might live in the future. He knew that he didn't want such a life not onlybecause he had to work like a horse but also in poverty and dirt. He decided that he would go again to see Stric Nicola and ask for his advice. But, first, he had to think of a reason for leaving the hotel last time. But this time, Stric was very friendly and did not lecture him.

'You don't have to tell me why you ran away before, but I hope you won't disappear again,' he said.

'I promise not to run away again if you promise not to lecture me,' Jukan answered.

'I promise,' agreed Stric, 'but now you have to tell me your plans, how you are going to live, and whether you want to study a trade.'

'That would be good, but I don't know which trade to learn,' Jukan said.

'Well, we'll think about it, but, first, we need to get you home and into a bath and then rest, and I will talk to some of my friends to see what they think,' Stric said.

The two of them walked home, discussing possible trades, and both agreed that it would be best to learn to be a mechanic. As soon as they got home, Stric showed Jukan how to use the hot and cold water in the bath and gave him two towels. 'Take your clothes off and have a bath, and I will make some dinner,' Stric said.

'Why do I need two towels?' Jukan asked.

'You use the big towel for your head and body, the small one for your feet,' Stric explained.

'Aren't my feet part of my body?' Jukan asked.

'Yes, but they have a special towel,' Stric laughed. Jukan closed the door and began to undress. No sooner was he undressed than there was a knock at the door. 'Open the door, it's me,' said Nicola.

'I can't, I'm naked,' Jukan said.

'You are not a woman, and it's only us here,' said Nicola. Jukan opened the door and jumped into the bath. 'Are you embarrassed by me?' Stric asked as he came in.

'No, I somehow feel uncomfortable to face you naked!' confessed Jukan.

Stric just turned around and left again, and Jukan wondered why he had come in. Then he looked around and saw that his clothes were missing. But the warm water in the bath interrupted his thoughts, and he relaxed and felt blissfully happy. If they had such a bath in Lipa, he would never want to leave, he thought sadly. He lay motionless with closed eyes, enjoying the hot water until he started to feel very hot. He opened his eyes and saw that the water was black! He understood that it was from the coal that they had unloaded on the dock. He let this water out and refilled the bath to wash again. This water soon became dirty again. He did it a third time, and the water still wasn't clean. He took a shower and was just getting out when there was another knock at the door.

'Who is it?' Jukan asked.

'It's me, who else?' answered Stric. 'I'm wondering how long you are going to stay in the bathroom; what is taking you so long?'

'I could spend my whole life here; I feel like I am in paradise!' Jukan answered.

'I'm glad that you like my bathroom so much, but get down to earth and get out quicker!' said Stric. Jukan took the big towel and wiped himself dry, forgetting that he had been given a small towel for his feet. After that, he went out into the room where Stric was waiting for him. 'My goodness, what a handsome man you are, looking so good in those pyjamas,' Stric said.

'Why do I need these pyjamas? Give me back my trousers and shirt,' Jukan objected.

'No, you'll dress what I give you,' said Stric. 'Pyjamas in the house are more convenient!'

'Where are my clothes?' Jukan asked.

'I took them to be cleaned, but everything that was in your pockets I have put on the table near your bed.' Jukan went to see, and there was the note with the address of his friends. He read the address to Stric and asked if Stric knew where it was. 'Somewhere around Karaburma,' Stric answered, 'but you can't go there today, you have no clothes to wear!' Stric laughed.

That night, Jukan slept in a clean bed, like a gentleman. He slept very well, and when he woke up, he found that he was alone. There was a note on the table telling him where to find something to eat. He washed his face and ate and then sat in the armchair and read the newspaper. *I wish Mother could see me now,* he thought. *She would be so happy to see how I am living.* He went to the window and looked out to see what was happening. Stric's house was at a crossroad, and from the window, it was possible to see three roads at once. On one road, people streamed past going in all directions, people of every size and shape dressed as gentlemen or peasants. Jukan watched the women, looking at the different way they dressed. He was so busy watching that he didn't see how quickly the time had passed, and he realised that he was hungry again. He ate some food that had been left for him and then washed the plates. He cleaned the room and then sat again at the window, watching for Stric and his wife, Sofia, to come home.

Strina Sofia noticed at once that Jukan had cleaned the house and praised Jukan. 'Look how good he is, he's cleaned the room,' she said in surprise. She then went off to the kitchen to prepare dinner, and Stric spoke to Jukan.

'Well, my friend would like you to study music, to become a musician,' he said.

Jukan didn't know how to answer. 'I don't know, maybe I don't have any talent, and who would take me?' he asked.

'We'll see tomorrow,' Stric said, 'but, first, I have to get your suit back.' Stric left, leaving Jukan to think about becoming a musician. He knew that his grandfather would not approve, but how could he tell Stric that? Jukan decided not to say anything more about it to Stric, not wanting to disappoint him.

Soon, Nicola came back with his suit, happy to see that it was still in one piece. 'I was afraid they would damage it and I would have to buy you a new one,' he confessed.

Jukan asked him, 'Then why did you have it cleaned?'

'I didn't want lice coming to my house. Who knows how your friends live!' he answered. Just then, Strina Sofia called them for dinner. As soon as they sat down, Stric told Sofia the news, 'Do you know, Sofia, that this young man is going to be a musician and will make more money than you can dream of?'

'I'm not too happy about this gypsy trade,' he blurted out.

'This gypsy trade!' exploded Stric. 'This is a wonderful trade, to play at weddings and funerals, in restaurants and at dances!' They talked about it for the rest of the evening, and when Jukan finally got to bed, he thought for a long time about what he would tell Grandfather. When he fell asleep, he dreamed that he was playing a violin and playing it so beautifully that he surprised himself. Suddenly, his hand got stuck, and he couldn't move. He woke up covered in sweat!

The next day, after breakfast, Stric and Jukan went into the city. On the way, Stric gave Jukan some advice: 'Try to look modest, don't move around too much, and only answer their questions,' he said. Soon, they came to a big hotel and went into the foyer, which was decorated with a crystal chandelier. They went to a small door, and Stric told Jukan to wait there before disappearing behind the door. Soon, he came out and called Jukan. When they went into the room, Jukan saw two men, one with a small beard, the other a very handsome man with neatly combed long hair. The man with the beard spoke to Jukan.

'What is your name, and how old are you?'

'I'm Jukan, and I'm twenty-one,' Jukan lied.

'It would be better if you were younger,' the man said. 'Now your mind will be full of girls and you'll find it harder to study. Music is easier to learn when you concentrate just on the music. So, will you study or chase girls?'

'If you think I am capable of learning, then I will. Only, how long will this last?' Jukan asked him.

'It all depends on you. If you work hard, it will go quickly, and if you don't, it will take forever!' Everyone laughed at that. 'I know you will work hard. Now, where will he live? He could stay here with me,' he offered.

'He doesn't have money for an apartment,' Stric said, 'so let him live with me for a while.'

'Let's do that,' agreed the bearded man. 'He must be here at half past eight on Monday.' After that agreement had been reached, Stric and Jukan said goodbye and left.

For the next two days, Jukan thought about his future as a musician and which instrument he would play. Finally, he just considered two, the first was the accordion. In Bosnia, very few people played it, but accordion players were often called to celebrations and earned excellent money. And he thought that his parents would like that. But, on the other hand, it was difficult to play and would take a long time to learn. So then he thought of the drum. He would only have to control the sticks, hit them against the drum, and shake his head in time. The worst part of that was that you couldn't play solo and you couldn't earn good money. And Jukan thought that his father and grandfather would not like this instrument. In Bosnia, the drum was always played to sound an official decree. From the time of the Turks and Austrians, the sound of the drum always sounded trouble. No, he shouldn't play the drum!

On Sunday morning, Stric decided to walk with Jukan to work, to show him how to get there. They walked for about twenty minutes and reached the hotel Slavija. Here, they met columns of students, singing and calling out slogans, all going to the royal palace. On one square, there was a meeting where young people were making speeches.

'Who are these people, and what do they want?' Jukan asked.

'They are workers and students demanding more money and better working conditions. They also want their professors released from prison,' Stric told him. Jukan wanted to listen to the speeches, but Stric grabbed his hand and pulled him away.

'Why did you do that?' Jukan asked.

'Let's get away from here while we still can!' Stric said. They went down another block and came out on the street where the hotel where Jukan was to work was located. 'Well, do you remember the way?' Stric asked him.

'Don't worry, I know this part of the city quite well,' Jukan reassured him.

'Then let's go and get something to drink at the Russian Tsar hotel.' They ordered coffee and water, but the noise out on the street started up again. Jukan wanted to go out on the street to see what was happening, but again Stric grabbed him by the hand. 'Sit down and don't go anywhere. You don't want to get into trouble again,' he said.

'I won't go anywhere,' Jukan agreed.

Just then, a young man ran into the restaurant and told everyone about the latest developments. It appeared that when the demonstrators got to the palace, they were attacked by police, and there was a skirmish. The students beat off the police by throwing stones, and the police retreated to the station. Jukan admired the students' bravery. 'They were real heroes; even the police couldn't stop them!' When it was quiet again outside, they left the restaurant and walked to Kalemagdan, where from a height they could see where the Danube River merged with the Sava, the two enormous rivers joining together and rushing down to the Black Sea in the distance. Jukan had never seen so much water in his life and was bewitched by the scene. Soon, though, he was ready to go home, but Stric thought they should go to lunch first. They went to a restaurant that was well known for its fish, and while the smell was wonderful, the fish were small and very hard to eat. Jukan had to wash his fish down with his beer! Stric thought that this was very funny, and when they got home, he told Strina Sofia about it. That night, Jukan slept badly, dreaming that he was one of the demonstrators and was being chased by the police!

In the morning after breakfast, Jukan went off to work, very afraid of what would happen. He was there at precisely eight thirty, and there in the doorway was the boss. 'Good morning, young man,' he greeted Jukan, and Jukan at once felt better. He was taken into a room where he was introduced to the other musicians. Then Jukan and the boss were left alone in the room, where the boss showed him all the instruments, how to play them and how to look after them. The instruments were always to be clean and in perfect working order. Looking after the instruments was Jukan's main job. 'Well, do you understand what you are to do?' the boss asked.

'Yes,' answered Jukan, 'but when do I start my job?'

'This is your job for now,' the boss said. 'You will do everything that I ask you to do, and after a while, you will study music!' He left the room, leaving Jukan alone with the instruments. Reluctantly, he began to clean, first the grand piano and then the other instruments, and finally he cleaned the room. But all the time he was thinking that he would not be able to clean for everyone for very long. But he continued to work, and when the boss came back, he was pleased with what Jukan had done and praised him, 'You did well, young man. If you keep on like this, we will not have any problems. Now you can go back to your house and have dinner, and be back here by two o'clock.'

Jukan went home quickly, and as soon as Stric saw him, he asked how Jukan liked his work. 'What I did today, I didn't like at all. If it stays like that, I will leave!'

'Dear boy, all work starts like this. Did you think they would let you play in the orchestra today? Do what your boss says, and everything will be OK!' After that, Stric gave Jukan some dinner, and Jukan went back to work.

When he got back, the musicians were rehearsing on stage. Jukan listened to how the different instruments sounded. The loudest were the accordion and the violin, and he liked their sound. The pipes were less pleasing and quieter. But the idea that this trade was not for him would not leave his head. He was so deep in thought that he didn't notice the boss approach him. 'What are you thinking about, young man?' the boss asked.

'I think that this work is not for me. Soon, I have to go into the army and I won't have time to learn anything,' Jukan replied.

'You don't have to worry; I know that you are waiting for the coronation for your pardon. Then you will see. Your stric and I are good friends, he told me everything.' At first, Jukan was upset that Stric had told anyone his secret, but then he was pleased that the boss and Stric were good friends. Despite that, he decided that he would leave this job.

At home that evening, Stric said, 'Well, Jukan, I have just spoken to your boss, and he praises you, even though he knows so little about you.'

'No, he knows a lot about me, even that I am hiding from the police!' Jukan answered.

'How does he know that?' Stric asked, surprised.

'I think you must have told him, because there were only two people in the city who knew that, you and me!' said Jukan.

'I don't remember that, maybe you're making this up!' said Stric again.

'Don't worry, since he is your friend, I don't think he will tell anyone else,' said Jukan.

'Still, I am angry with him,' said Stric.

'If you are such good friends, maybe you could find me a better job!' laughed Jukan.

The next morning, Jukan was back to his cleaning. When he went to lunch, he met a fellow countryman, Stevo. Jukan suggested that they sit down and catch up on all the news.

'I can't,' said Stevo. 'I have a train to catch.'

'Where are you going?' Jukan asked.

'To Kupinovo, to work in the forest.'

'How much will they pay you?' Jukan wanted to know.

'It all depends on how good your partner is. There's a lot of work there. You should come with me,' Stevo said.

'I'll think about it!' promised Jukan, and Stevo ran off to the station.

Jukan walked for a while and then went back to the hotel. His boss was there, just finishing a conversation with another man. 'Well, did you find yourself a girl to marry already?' he asked Jukan.

'I'm not even looking for one,' Jukan answered him. 'It's too early for me to think about marriage. I don't have a trade yet, and I think it is too late for me to study music. Can you find me other work?'

'I don't know, ask your stric to come and see me tomorrow morning,' said the boss, and he and the stranger left the room.

In the evening, when Stric came back from work, Jukan told him what the boss had said. 'I know, I saw your boss and his friend, and he has offered you another job,' said Stric.

'What kind of job?' asked Jukan.

'The boss's friend is the boss of a big warehouse, and he needs an assistant. It's an important position, because you would be dealing with expensive materials. The pay is decent, and if you do well, you could become a senior assistant,' said Stric.

'So, what would I have to do? Maybe I won't like this job either. I should look at it before I give an answer,' Jukan said.

'That sounds good,' said Stric. 'We should go to bed now, and in the morning, I will take you to the warehouse. Just remember that your new boss is a worker himself, and he treats his men well. The main thing is to work hard and everything else will be fine!' Jukan was really excited about this new job and for a long time could not go to sleep.

Stric woke him up early. 'Come on, working man,' he said, 'this job starts early.' So Jukan quickly washed, and the two caught the tram, getting off near Savsky Bridge, and walked down towards the river. Less than half a block further, they stopped next to a warehouse that handled parquet flooring and other wooden materials. They walked up the steps to the second floor and walked into the office where there were two men. Stric spoke to the older of the two and asked to see his boss.

'He's busy just now,' the man answered. 'Can I ask who you are?'

'I'm his friend,' Stric said.

'I will talk to him,' said the man, going to knock on a door leading to the next room. He came back almost at once, accompanied by the boss, who smiled at Jukan and his stric and shook their hands.

'It's a pity you didn't bring Jukan here at the beginning,' he said to Stric. 'He'll feel better here. A musician's job is not for him, am I right?'

'You are right,' said Jukan. 'What kind of work will I be doing here?'

'The most important thing here is to want to work. There is always plenty of work to do. So much in fact that it is impossible for me to do it all,' said the boss. He then called up a young assistant and told him to take Jukan on a tour of the warehouse, to show him what they were doing there.

The young man took Jukan to a big room on the second floor, where there were rows of parquet tiles sorted by colour, quality, and size. These rows almost reached the ceiling, and the space between them was just big enough for a small wheelbarrow to pass through. Jukan had the feeling that they were about to fall on him. The young man showed Jukan around the warehouse, but without any enthusiasm; he looked weak and sick and walked as if he carried the whole warehouse on his shoulders. He answered Jukan's questions reluctantly and sometimes ignored them altogether.

When they got back to the office, the senior assistant was furious with them. 'What took you so long?' he demanded to know, but the young assistant just shrugged his shoulders. Before he could answer, the boss, Mr Dushko, called Jukan into the office.

'Well, what do you think?' he asked.

Jukan didn't know how to answer. 'Honestly, I saw only that the warehouse is big, and it's difficult to see everything,' he answered.

'That's good. You can start to work and get everything in order,' the boss said.

'So all the problems have been solved,' Stric interrupted. 'Let's go and have dinner!' Stric left the room with Jukan, but Dushko stayed behind to give the assistants some orders.

When he joined Jukan and Stric again, he was angry. 'God alone knows how much this senior assistant annoys me,' he said.

'Why do you keep him, then?' Stric asked.

'I would be happy to see him go,' said Dushko. 'He is always in the way, poking around and making things more difficult. He is not a nice person and doesn't get along with the others. I think he is a police informer and would sell his own mother! But, on the other hand, he has worked at the warehouse for twenty years and knows everything. It would be hard to replace him. So, Jukan, you have to learn fast and take his place. I have been watching him for a long time. It would be easy enough to sack him, but in the meantime, I have to put up with him. My young assistant is a very fine man, but he can't get over his father's death. He was arrested at a demonstration and put in jail. But he caught pneumonia and died in the prison hospital. He was a wonderful man, worked in Germany, France, and America. He was my good friend.'

After dinner, Stric Nicola and Dushko shook hands and walked off in different directions. Jukan was uncertain whom he should follow, but Dushko called him. 'What are you waiting for? Now we go to work!' Jukan was pleased to hear this and went back to the warehouse, where they began to inspect the stockroom. 'It looks as though everything is in place,' Dushko said, 'but there is no order. The passage ways are blocked. We need to make a better order.' The senior assistant tried to keep calm, but it was clear to Jukan that he was very angry. 'So, tomorrow, everyone will start cleaning, otherwise I will send for the fire inspectors, and they will fine you! And now,' he said to them all, 'I will give you your instructions. You will read them and then repeat them to me!'

Jukan and the two assistants went into the office, where they were given some information sheets, and they started to read. After half an hour, Dushko began to ask them questions, but because the senior assistant had not read any of the information, he could not answer much. The younger assistant was better but answered without any enthusiasm, and when it was Jukan's turn, he answered everything almost by heart. 'Well done!' Dushko said to Jukan and then embarrassed the senior assistant. 'You have been here twenty years and still don't know the rules. This young man reads the rules just once, and already he knows them almost by heart.'

'I'm younger, that's why I remember so well!' Jukan tried to be modest.

'Nonsense,' said Dushko. 'So, tomorrow, we start cleaning up, and you have two days to get it finished,' he said. So the next day they began to clean the stockroom. At one time, the senior assistant walked up to Jukan. 'Have you known Dushko for long?' he asked.

'Not at all,' replied Jukan, 'only for two days.'

'I thought you must have known him for a long time. I have worked here for a long time, but I have never been called into the office. You have known him just two days, and he talked to you for about an hour.'

'Has Dushko been here a long time?' Jukan asked.

'Not really, just three years,' replied the senior man. Jukan then understood why he was so dissatisfied; he was a bundle of envy!

The men sorted the parquet for some time, but during the whole time, the young assistant didn't utter a word. When Dushko called to the senior assistant, Jukan tried to speak to him. 'What is your name, Mister?' he asked.

'I was never a mister, and neither was my father. You can all me comrade, and my name is Milenko,' he answered. His voice was serious, and he looked straight into Jukan's eyes and held out his hand. 'Here is my hand. If you decide that you, too, belong to the working class, you may shake it,' Milenko said.

Jukan knew very little about the working class, but he willingly shook hands with Milenko. Then he asked, 'What kind of man is our senior assistant?'

Milenko got serious again. 'He is not a working-class man, though he should be. He will willingly betray anyone if it is to his benefit. I advise you to stay away from him, and talk less.'

'Then why does our boss keep him here?' Jukan asked.

'This warehouse doesn't belong to Dushko. It is owned by a big company, and Dushko is merely our boss. If I was stronger, I doubt that the boss would keep the man here, but I must admit that the senior assistant knows his job, and that's why we need to work together,' Milenko conceded.

For three days, they worked on the cleaning and tidying, and when a new load of parquet arrived, the four men worked together. The work was not hard, and Jukan was able to talk with Milenko, who took pleasure in answering Jukan's questions. He talked about the working class and how it was different from the peasants. He spoke about Marx and Lenin, about revolutions, and about Russia, where the revolution had already been won. 'Power has to be in the hands of the workers,' Milenko said. 'We should all be living under the slogan, "Who does not work does not eat!"' he said.

'There is nothing unique in that,' said Jukan. 'In our village, who does not work does not eat because he will have nothing to eat! And where is Russia?'

'This is the result of our education.' Milenko was furious. 'People do not know where Russia is, even though it occupies one-sixth of all the land in the world. This is the native land to all Slavs. People knew about it even at the time of the Austro-Hungarian Empire and of our kingdom, and you don't know about it. Shame!' Just then, the senior assistant came back, and the two younger men stopped talking.

'Why have you stopped talking?' he asked, 'though it's probably a good thing because you work more. Just now the police were here looking for a communist who disappeared in this area. Recently, at a nearby factory, he called on the workers to strike. They only like life in Russia and conversations about revolutions. They want our kingdom to collapse and to seize power, though half of them are illiterate!'

Jukan could not listen to this and said, 'They are not the enemies of the kingdom. They strike because their wages are so small, and it is not their fault if they are illiterate.' Just then, Milenko stepped on Jukan's foot, and Jukan screamed, 'Why did you do that?'

'You have to talk less and work more,' he answered. 'That's what you get paid for!'

'Right!' said the senior assistant, his eyes boring into Jukan. 'It seems that you are even worse than these city rebels, the police will beat that from you. It looks as though the Turks haven't taught you anything!'

'You think I'm an enemy of the country just because it is hard for me to watch poor people breaking their backs and being so badly paid? They have nothing except tattered clothes and shoes with holes!' The senior assistant gave Jukan an angry glance and left the room.

Milenko came closer to Jukan and whispered, 'Never speak to this bastard about politics. You were speaking the truth, but there's no point in talking to him. Now he thinks that you're a communist sympathiser, and he can inform on you to the police. If you want, we can go after work to the park and talk about things, even read books. Do you like books?'

'Of course, I like books, but at home, we didn't have time to read and books were hard to find. Even if you did find one, Grandmother would immediately find work for you to do!'

'So, she was strict with you?' Milenko asked.

'Strict but fair,' Jukan said. 'She works hard herself, that's why she doesn't let others rest.'

'I believe you that she is a good woman,' Milenko laughed, 'but it's impossible to be honest with everyone. When you are with wolves, you must be a wolf. You and I are workers, and everything in this world is made by hand, yet we have nothing. This injustice should be eliminated, don't you think?' Jukan agreed, and they got back to work.

They worked together for about three months, and in this time, they became good friends. Then, suddenly, Milenko disappeared. Dushko said he was in hospital, though he wouldn't say which one. Jukan and the senior assistant were still not friendly with each other, and once he threatened Jukan with his fist. Jukan warned him. 'You had better take your fist away from my face, otherwise I may not be able to control myself!' This cooled the situation, because it was rumoured in Belgrade that it was nothing for a Bosnian to kill someone.

One morning soon after that, Dushko called Jukan into the office and gave him the news that the senior assistant had handed in his resignation. 'Now it will be just the two of us, and we will do all the work. Soon, I'll find another assistant for you, but for now we continue as though nothing has happened. But please watch carefully what this man is doing behind my back. He could be trying to pull some dirty trick at the end. If you notice anything, tell me at once,' Dushko said.

Now that the senior assistant said that he was looking for a new job, Jukan was running around like a mouse on a wheel, hardly having time to do everything. Once, he lost his temper and said, 'I can't stand this anymore, I can't get everything done on time!'

The senior assistant just said, 'Do whatever you want, I don't care at all. You need to talk to Dushko, not to me!'

Jukan spent more than three months on this job, and despite all the problems, he loved it. The salary was good, and he felt more at home here than at his grandfather's house. Besides that, Milenko came back, and Dushko was happy too. 'Now everything is going well and no one can spoil it!'

But their joy was premature. The senior assistant would not leave them alone, coming back to the warehouse on the pretext of borrowing tools, but he never returned them to their right place. Jukan decided to hide the tools, and the next morning when the man came in searching for tools and swearing angrily, Jukan said, 'Excuse me, what are you looking for?'

The senior assistant turned, and Jukan saw that he was grinning maliciously. 'None of your business,' he replied and began to insult Jukan and his mother.

'You'd better leave my mother out of this,' Jukan warned. But it was too late. The senior assistant grabbed a big piece of wood and threw it. Jukan just managed to avoid being hit, and the board flew by him, just centimetres from his head, breaking the plaster behind Jukan. If it had hit him, it would have made Jukan a cripple. His pulse racing, Jukan grabbed a stick and moved towards the other man, who turned pale and ran down the steps. Jukan caught up with him and hit him on the back. The former senior assistant lost his balance and slid down the steps. Jukan saw that the man was no longer moving, and then he saw blood on the steps. Jukan threw away the stick and bent down to pick the man up, but he could see no signs of life. He leant the body against the wall and then ran back to the office.

It was still early, and no one else was there. Jukan switched off the lights, closed the office door, and ran back downstairs. The man was still in the same position, and he seemed dead. Jukan threw the key through the open window of the office and ran down the steps. Whether the man was dead or not, Jukan knew that he had to get away before the police arrived. He ran to the tram stop, and here a police car passed him. Jukan knew he had to leave Belgrade, not even returning to Stric Nicola. He walked to the Savsky Bridge and there caught a tram to Zemun. He decided to join his Bosnian friends who were chopping wood in Kupinovo. In Zemun, he had some breakfast and caught the bus to Kupinovo. On the bus, he mentally berated himself for his temper that was so quick to flare up and that he could no longer control. It had gotten him into trouble before, and now here he was in trouble again.

The bus finally reached Kupinovo. The village was quite big, like a small city. Jukan asked people where he could find the woodcutters. Finally, he found an old man who was able to explain with hand gestures how to find the camp, and following these instructions, Jukan located the camp about half an hour away. There his countrymen were delighted to see Jukan, but Rade asked, astonished, 'What are you doing here? Why have you left Belgrade and your fantastic job? Why do you want to be here in the forest?'

'I've missed you,' Jukan said. 'Can you find me a job here?'

'It's not so easy. You need a partner, without one you can't cut trees,' answered one of the boys.

Jukan was disappointed, but chiko Pero encouraged him. 'Don't worry, just write a letter to someone in Bosnia and ask him to come and be your partner. Everyone these days in Bosnia is looking for work. Until then, you can do the cooking for us. You can be the cook and you won't be hungry.' So Jukan wrote to his friend Micho. Though his father was a policeman, Micho was a good friend and very strong. In ten days, he had arrived in Kupinovo, ready to work.

By that time, Jukan had bought tools: two poleaxes and one cross-section French saw. They began work the day after Micho arrived, and they were doing very well to start with. But this did not last for long. At first, they were working far away from the village, and here it was easy to cut a lot of timber. But later they were sent to chop trees close to a village. Here, the forest was not as thick and it was much harder to cut it. Besides, here, local children visited them, and the boys were flirting with the local girls. They had fun swimming in the river and called for Jukan and Micho to join them. They couldn't understand why the boys could not swim. They didn't know that the rivers in Bosnia were usually small, fast, and cold. To get into the water was almost impossible, let alone to swim. Then things got even worse because the trees were growing close to the river, so that when the boys chopped down the trees, they often landed in the water. Luckily the trees were small and the boys could pull them out, but their work was getting slower. The work was harder, and their hands were badly callused. But still they didn't get gloomy, and they often had competitions, seeing who could lift the most logs. In the end, Micho developed a terrible stomach ache, and when he was examined back at the barracks, they discovered that he had developed a hernia. He was sent to hospital that night and then home, so again Jukan had no partner.

Autumn arrived, and it began to get colder. Now the men had to build barracks where they would be out of the rain and cold. Jukan was busy supplying milk, bread, and other foods from the nearby village, where he had made a lot of friends. They thought he was a young student who had run away from Belgrade, because he was well dressed and loved to talk . . . rural men usually were silent! The local girls often turned around to look at him, and this gave him even more confidence. The girls here were well-groomed and wore beautiful coloured dresses, and it was obvious that they had never milked a cow! Life here was lordly compared to Bosnia. In their houses, they had kitchens, bedrooms, and bathrooms, just like houses in the city. Here in Kupinovo, they had a few kafanas where musicians played; they had a church, police station, post office, and even a firefighting crew. For the children, they had a grammar school, and Jukan became friends with one of the grammar school girls, Militca. She was very beautiful and graceful.

Once, she invited Jukan to her home and introduced him to her brother, who was the local forest warden and needed an assistant. 'Meet this man, Jukan,' Militca introduced him.

'Would you like to be my assistant?' her brother asked.

'I don't know whether I would suit you or what the work would be,' Jukan answered.

'Did you serve in the army, and can you use a weapon?' the brother asked.

'I was never in the army, but I can use a gun,' Jukan said.

'What sort of gun?' Jukan was asked again.

'Any light gun,' he answered.

'Of course,' the forest warden laughed. 'I forgot that you Bosnians couldn't live without a weapon, or at least a knife!'

'That's true, a knife for us is more important than teeth, and everyone has at least one pistol.'

'Then this job is exactly for you!'

'What would I have to do?' Jukan asked.

'Don't you know what a forest warden's job is? He protects the forest and gets paid to do so,' the warden answered. 'I will protect the forest by day, and you can do it by night.'

'And what do we guard?' Jukan wanted to know.

'You guard the cut wood, to stop it being stolen and taken down the river.'

'What can I do by myself?' Jukan asked.

'Nothing special. As soon as you see anything suspicious, you just shoot into the air, and the thieves will run off,' the warden assured him.

'And if they don't run away?' Jukan wanted to know.

'Then shoot in the air again!'

'And if they still don't run away?' Jukan went on.

'Then you must run away from them!' the warden said, and Jukan became worried.

'And how much will I be paid for this work?' Jukan asked again.

'More than you get waving an axe around,' the forest warden said, winking, and then continued. 'It all depends on how well you do your job. If there are no thefts, then you will be well paid. But if you allow thefts to happen, then you can lose from 15 to 75 per cent of your salary,' he finished.

'In that case, I'm not sure how to answer,' Jukan hesitated. 'I will think and give you an answer tomorrow.'

'I'm not in a rush. Go and think,' agreed the warden.

On the way back to the barracks, Jukan decided that any job was better than no job at all, but he decided not to say anything because finding work was very hard at this time of year. He woke early, washed, and left. By seven, he was already at the warden's house. Here, everyone was up already and working around the house, and there was a lot more to do than in a normal country house. They had two cows and a calf, geese and ducks, and in the kitchen garden, they had beehives. But most importantly, they had horses. Especially fine was a young stallion, standing on long thin legs, with a small head and a white arrow pointing to his eyes. Next to it, the warden was combing the horse with a brush, and it trembled when its owner brushed its belly. Jukan remembered how his grandfather combed the horses, but this one was entirely different, used just for riding. It was clear that the warden was a good owner. He was so involved in his work that he didn't notice Jukan and was surprised when Jukan spoke to him. He smiled when he saw how Jukan looked at the stallion, and asked, 'Well, my assistant, did you come for me or the horse?'

'For you, of course, but it's hard to take your eyes off such a beautiful horse,' Jukan answered.

The warden smiled. 'Where did you get your love of horses?' he asked.

'My grandfather taught me. We always had beautiful horses,' Jukan explained.

'Then what are you doing here?' the warden asked again.

'Looking for a better life. In Bosnia, we were very poor,' Jukan answered.

Just then, the warden's wife called to them to come and eat. She was a real townswoman, beautiful and with golden hair. 'Well, come and eat,' said the warden.

'I'm not really hungry,' lied Jukan, but the warden stopped him.

'Don't try to tell me that you're not hungry, and it would be terrible to offend my wife. And you should eat now, because we won't be back until evening,' and with that, the two went in to eat. After breakfast, the warden went to change into his uniform and came back with a gun and a box of cartridges. 'Ready to go?' he asked.

'Certainly,' said Jukan.

'We will walk, because we both can't ride the horse.'

'You take the horse, I can walk,' said Jukan.

'No, that's not very friendly, and I would look like a high-ranking Turkish officer, and you don't have any love for them. Besides, we can talk as we walk and the time will pass more quickly.' The warden took with them a thin dog with long ears, and they set out. They were both good walkers, and as they walked, they talked about the job. The dog sometimes walked with them and sometimes ran ahead. It was clear he knew where they were going. The road left the village, and the two men turned onto a smaller road, which soon became a goat track. The warden showed Jukan places where he needed to be alert, and soon they came to a clearing where they stopped for a rest, sitting on tree stumps.

'Who cleared this area?' Jukan wanted to know.

'Hunters cleared it. They also had a table where they ate dinner, but it seems your Bosnian brothers took it to their barracks,' the warden answered him.

'What animals are here?' Jukan asked.

'Mostly wild pigs, but there are pheasants, ducks, hares, sometimes foxes, and occasionally wolves, and also deer,' the warden said. They rested a while longer, and then the warden said, 'Now we go down to the River Sava.'

'How can you say you go up and down when there are no mountains?' Jukan asked. 'It's different in Bosnia, up means up a hill and down means go away from it.'

'Only in Bosnia is it so easy,' the warden explained. 'Here, we need to be guided by parts of the world, north, south, east, and west. "With the current" means down, and "against the current" means up.'

He burst out laughing as Jukan said, 'But you can't see the river from here.'

'We can't see the river, but I know where it is and where it flows. But I forgot whom I'm talking to. You Bosnians believe only in what you can touch with your own hands!'

'That's true,' said Jukan, 'we only believe in what we can touch.'

'Then how can you trust God—you never see him?' asked the warden.

Jukan shrugged his shoulders. 'You know, my grandmother always frightened us with God. When she got angry with me, she shouted, "God should kill you!" and I got scared and stopped being naughty. But as I grew older, I saw that some people believe in God, some in his Son, some in the Divine Mother, and others in Allah. Everyone believes in their own God and defends him. But when you look closer, you see that they are not true believers; when they swear in the name of God, they are not afraid, but if they begin to damn the king, they are afraid that they will go to prison.'

'Does that mean that you don't believe in God?' asked the warden.

'I'm not saying that, but as my father taught me, I question everything. It seems that God forgot about our Bosnia and we have forgotten him. And the rich only pretend to believe because the church supports power.'

'It seems that you are a very dangerous person here in our state,' observed the warden.

'I have nothing against the state; I'm just telling you what I have learnt and understood in my short life,' said Jukan.

'I believe that you are speaking from your heart,' said the warden, 'but now is not the time to speak like this. It's good that you left the city; over there, with such ideas, you could lose your head. People are saying that war is close and the times are dangerous. Learn to be silent. The big question is, what will happen to our Yugoslavia? The Germans are arming themselves and want to take all Europe, but no one is ready for war. As you can see, the situation is dire; they lock people in prison: communists, socialists, democrats, and even simple workers and peasants. The kingdom is trembling, and each party is dragging it in a different direction.'

'I don't trust these parties,' Jukan said. 'They promise us a lot before an election and then forget about them. They don't care about the poor; they look after the rich. Working people just want to be paid for their work and to be able to live decently. Everything in this world is made by hand, from needles to steamships, but the working people have nothing for themselves. But in Russia, the workers have seized power and rule the country.'

The forest warden looked at Jukan seriously. 'You are not the son of a peasant. Who taught you all that?' he asked.

'In Belgrade, I met some interesting people,' Jukan answered.

'Maybe you've read Karl Marx?'

'I haven't read Marx, but I've heard about him. But can you tell me what you believe?' Jukan said.

'Listen, my friend, I don't want to hear these speeches. I work for the state!' the warden answered.

'You started this discussion.' Jukan tried to defend himself.

'You must learn to speak less, even when someone asks your opinion. Let's finish up now and get on to work.'

Now they walked in silence. The forest in front of them was getting thicker, but it unexpectedly cleared, and there in front of them was the River Sava, broad and smooth, slowly carrying its water to meet the Danube and then together to the Black Sea. Jukan was captivated by this view and thought that life for a river was easy . . . it carries its waters on a set channel, unlike people who never know where life will take them and how to avoid those places where it's possible to be killed. His thinking was interrupted by the warden's question, 'Well, now that you've seen the Sava, do you understand where down and up are?'

'Yes, now I know,' Jukan said, and they both laughed. It was clear that the warden was not angry with him, but Jukan had decided that he would not talk about delicate subjects anymore.

They walked on a footpath for about a kilometre past a settlement and back into the forest. 'What settlement was that?' Jukan asked.

'That was a timber warehouse, where the logs are stored before floating them down the Sava and Danube before reaching their destination. The warehouse watchmen live there, and they can always help us if any timber is stolen,' the warden said.

'With so many guards, it should be impossible to steal the timber,' Jukan remarked.

'It's difficult only for people who don't know how,' the warden said. 'For real thieves, it's much easier, even with guards. Now I'll show you where our logs are lying. This timber hasn't been brought to the landing-stage yet, and it is less guarded. To steal it is harder, but it is spread over a wide area, so it's harder to look after it. You and I are responsible for this timber.' They walked all around the area where the trees were lying, looking carefully at the area closer to the Sava, where it was easier to steal the timber. Then they found a couple of tree stumps to sit on, and the warden opened his satchel and said, 'Now we can have lunch. I am hungry!' Jukan tried to refuse, but his boss insisted, and they ate tasty sandwiches and even drank a glass of wine. It was good quality wine, and Jukan enjoyed it.

'What do you Bosnians know about wine?' the warden asked Jukan. 'You don't have wine in Bosnia, only rakija.'

'Yes, we don't grow grapes in Bosnia, but we do know about wine. Your wine is good, but the wine from Dalmatia is better. You should try the wine that is delivered to Lazo Shagret. You would be surprised,' Jukan said.

'Who delivers to your mountain?' the warden asked.

'I don't know, but we always had Dalmatian wine in our house.'

'Enough, let's stop talking and get back to work,' the warden said.

They finished just as the sun was on the horizon and very close to the barracks where Jukan lived. 'Here are your barracks,' the warden said, slapping him on the back. 'Go, and I will see you in the morning.'

'I'll definitely see you in the morning,' Jukan said as he ran down the hill. When he entered the barracks, there was no one about, just two older men outside preparing supper. It was almost dark when the others returned, tired and disgruntled. All day they had been using their axes, and now they had no energy left. They sat down at the table and called for Jukan to join them.

'Thanks, but I've only just eaten with the forest warden,' said Jukan.

'Oh, so he has dined with Mr Forest Warden and now we mean nothing to him,' one of the boys said sarcastically. 'Did you get the job?'

'Yes, I did,' answered Jukan.

'What will you do?' the boy asked again.

'I will work in the forest!' Jukan said.

'I don't know of any jobs in the forest right now,' someone said.

'The forest warden has asked me to be his assistant,' Jukan said. 'I'll help him protect the forest . . . he will do it in the daytime, and I will work at night.'

'But there is no one in the forest at night except wild animals. Who will you protect it from?' and everyone burst out laughing.

Finally, they all went off to sleep, leaving Jukan alone considering his future. At last, he fell asleep but had a nightmare. He dreamed that someone was stealing his grandfather's horses, and while he wanted to run for help, his limbs were frozen. He tried to shout, but no one heard him. Then someone hit him on the back, and he woke to see Pero was trying to wake him.

'Why are you screaming?' he asked.

'I was dreaming that someone was stealing our horses,' Jukan said.

'So, will you scream like that if someone comes to steal your timber?' he was asked.

'No, I will run away and call for help,' he said.

Early in the morning, before dawn, he set off. It was cold, so he walked fast to keep warm. He got to the warden's house quickly and went straight to the stable. The warden was there, grooming the horse, combing his mane. 'Good morning,' Jukan called.

The warden was surprised. 'What kind of morning is this with the sun not yet up?' he asked.

'In Bosnia, we call this morning.'

'Yes, you Bosnians are extraordinary people,' the warden said.

'Will you let me groom your horse?' Jukan asked.

'He will never let you near him, let alone groom him,' the warden said.

'Just let me try, and we will see,' Jukan asked again.

'He will kill you!' warned the warden.

'Let's see what happens,' Jukan persisted.

'Well, you can try,' agreed the warden and stepped aside.

Jukan carefully raised his hand and extended it towards the horse as if to give it something. The horse looked at Jukan, but as soon as he tried to get closer, the horse lifted his head and snorted, pawing the ground. Jukan did not pull his hand back, showing he was not afraid. Then he started to talk to the horse in a soft voice and again began to move closer. At last, he touched the horse with his fingers; the horse shuddered but didn't move its head away. Jukan began to scratch the horse's head, and the horse stretched his neck and took a step towards Jukan. Now they were acquainted, and Jukan knew that he would have no more trouble with the horse.

The forest warden had been watching carefully. 'Well,' he said, 'I see that you know how to communicate with horses. This horse has never allowed any of my friends to touch him.'

'Why should he let them? They are your friends, not his,' Jukan said with a smile, and the two men laughed.

The forest warden's wife came into the shed and interrupted their conversation. 'How much time do you need to spend with this horse? I'm sure you love it more than you love me! Come now and have breakfast,' she said to them.

This day, they decided that the warden would go on the horse and Jukan would ride a bike. They got ready and soon left the house. To start with, the road was good, and Jukan was able to get ahead. But soon the road narrowed and then became a footpath, which often disappeared altogether, and here Jukan could hardly keep up. Often they stopped so that the warden could explain where Jukan would need to be careful.

'Why are you so quiet today?' the warden asked Jukan.

'I see that this job will not be easy and maybe I won't be able to do it,' Jukan answered.

'The forest is not a herd of sheep and will not run away,' the warden said. 'That's why you need to protect it from the riverside. If something happens, just shoot in the air, and they will run away because they know that the other guards will come.'

'And if they have weapons?' Jukan tried again.

'So what? You are a Bosnian, not some coward.'

'Yes, but we love our lives no less than other men,' Jukan said.

'Who told you not to protect your life? You have to make decisions based on the circumstances. Now, let's get back.' They went by a different road, and Jukan found it hard to keep oriented; he had to keep looking at the ground so as not to hit any snags. A few times he seemed to be lost and had to call to the warden, who was happy to come back for him. 'Now, Bosna, do you know where you are?'

'I was never really lost, and I learnt as a child to find directions by the rings on tree stumps and moss on trees,' Jukan explained.

By the time they came out of the forest, it was already getting dark. 'Now you go to your barracks,' said the warden. 'Take the bicycle with you and bring it back when you come tomorrow. Tomorrow, we will go to the central office, and I'll introduce you to my boss. After that, you will receive a gun, and you'll need to sign for that. But that is all for tomorrow. Now, go back to your Bosnian brothers,' and he urged the horse on.

When Jukan got near the barracks, everyone came out to look at him and his bike. They all wanted to have a try to ride it, though he was sure that none of them could do it. 'Do it carefully, it's a bicycle, not a horse,' Jukan warned them.

'Yes, we know, but now you will see that we can ride it,' said Rade. Everyone came out to have a look, but only a few younger ones tried to ride it. There was a lot of laughter as they tried and fell off, asking Jukan again to show them how to do it. Then chiko Pero asked to have a try, and he surprised everyone by riding it down the path, turn, and ride back again.

'Where did you learn to ride?' Jukan asked him.

'I learnt a long time ago, in France,' Pero answered. 'It's not just the young who can ride,' Pero said. After that, nobody else wanted to ride, and they all went in to eat and sleep.

The next morning, two people complained about the pain in their hands after falling from the bicycle, saying they could not go to work. Pero asked for another chance to ride the bike, maybe the last chance of his life, and this time he climbed on the bike alone and rode off happily. When he came back, he said to the two victims, 'Let me give you a massage.'

'How will that help when I cannot bend my arm?'

Pero made the man sit on a bench and slowly began to massage his hand. He took his fingers and asked, 'Now tell me where the pain is.'

'I already feel less pain,' said the patient, but at this moment, Pero pulled his fingers, and the man jumped to his feet. 'Are you crazy? That hurt!'

'It's OK, now you can go to work.' In the same way, Pero quickly fixed the second patient, and within the hour, everyone had gone to work.

Jukan arrived in Kupinovo very early again that morning. The warden was again in the stable. This time, Jukan decided not to eat breakfast with the warden and his wife but to go to the kafana. As he came out of the stable, he heard a familiar voice calling him. 'HI, Jukan, why are you rushing off?' It was Militca. Jukan was a little embarrassed because he was so fond of her.

'I'm going to the kafana to eat before work,' he explained.

'Well, I hope we see you more often at our place,' she answered him.

'I hope so too,' he answered back. Jukan started to walk away but then stopped to look back and saw that she was looking at him. It was clear that she had feelings for Jukan too, and that excited him so much that he walked right past the kafana and had to turn and go back when he realised how hungry he was. After breakfast, he made his way back to the warden's house, and the two men, along with the warden's wife, walked to catch the bus. The driver had run out of tickets, so the warden told Jukan that the Forestry Department would pay.

They couldn't talk on the journey because they were seated in different parts of the bus. Next to Jukan was a fat elderly woman; she could hardly fit on the seat and continually complained about the overcrowding on the bus and insisted on opening the window. But behind her was another woman who was afraid of draughts and wouldn't let her open the window. All the passengers got involved in the dispute; some were on the side of the fat woman, and others on the side of the woman who was afraid of the cold. The noise on the bus was intolerable, and the driver had to get involved. He stopped the bus and warned them, 'If you do not stop this now, I will kick you all off the bus!' Everyone got quiet then and agreed that it was much better to travel this way. But small cheerful squabbles continued all the way until the bus stopped next to the Forestry Department building.

Here, they got off the bus, the warden's wife said, 'Don't wait for me on the way back. I have a lot to do here today, and if it gets too late, I will spend the night with my parents.' She turned and walked off towards the markets, and Jukan and the warden walked into the building.

The warden walked into an office, leaving Jukan in a small corridor where there were doors leading off to different rooms. There were rows of chairs against the wall, but having been so long on the bus, Jukan decided to stand and walked up and down the empty corridor. Occasionally some people came out of one office and went into another. Finally, the warden came out and said, 'We have to fill out this application form.' They sat at a table, and the warden told Jukan what to write. Then Jukan signed the form, and the warden took it back into the office. After a short time, he came and called Jukan into the office, where there was a fat man with greying hair who immediately began to question Jukan.

'Did you serve in the army, young man?'

'Not yet,' he answered.

'Then this job is not for you. Here, you must be able to use a weapon.'

'But I can use a gun anyway,' Jukan replied.

'How come?'

'As long as I can remember, we always had a gun in the house. In Bosnia, as soon as a boy is born, they buy a pistol for him. So back home, everyone is able to use a weapon,' Jukan explained.

'What about those who are poor?' the man asked again.

'They buy a cheaper gun, or as a last resort, they buy a holster, and then who knows what is in it? So, without a pistol or knife, nobody even goes to church!'

They all burst out laughing at this, but then the fat man asked, 'What kind of weapon do you have now?'

'A knife,' and after a moment's thought, Jukan took it from his pocket and put it on the table.

'And where is your pistol?' the man asked again more seriously.

'For a gun, you need a license here,' Jukan said.

'And in Bosnia you don't need a license?'

'At home, everyone knows who has what kind of weapon, but nobody talks about it. Another thing, with a knife or shtap, everyone can see it, otherwise, how would you beat off dogs? A good shtap passes by right of succession. It's usually made of hardwood, and you can take it to church or weddings,' Jukan explained again.

'This shtap sounds sacred?'

'Well, to tell the truth, I've often heard people curse something holy, but I've never heard anyone curse a shtap. Even my grandfather, if he loses his shtap, will not curse it but will call on someone holy to find it!'

'Does that mean your grandfather doesn't believe in God?' the man said, shaking with laughter.

'I can't say, I only know that he uses his shtap more often, and it helps him more.' With this, Jukan decided to stop talking because it might get him into trouble.

The fat official picked up a pipe, filled it with tobacco, and lit it. It seemed he smoked more from habit than pleasure, letting out almost all the smoke and only drawing a little in. Then he leant back in his chair and asked, 'Do you have big guns in Bosnia?'

'To tell the truth, I have never shot a big gun, but I know they have them,' Jukan said.

'Where do you get big guns?' the man was surprised and cursed the 'Bosnian God', though as Jukan believed, there was only one God.

'I don't know for sure, but our Muslim brothers from Chukovo and Orashtsa, when their fast comes to an end and the sun goes down, they start to shoot with their guns, declaring the end of the fast,' Jukan said. This amused the two men, but Jukan was feeling angry with their laughter because he knew he was telling the truth.

'Why hasn't your grandfather bought a gun?' the man asked finally.

'Once, he came very close to getting one,' Jukan remembered. 'A Muslim came to us from Chukovo and began to beg my grandfather for credit for some potatoes and sauerkraut, promising to pay it back in summer, during the haymaking. Grandfather said, "But you are not a good haymaker," and the man replied, "Then I will pay it back on at the harvest." "You will have to collect all the wheat in front of our house," Grandfather said. "I am prepared to do that!" the man said. "No," Grandfather said. "You are agreeing with everything now, but when the time comes, you will not show up!" "I swear by Allah!" the man said. "What do you think your Allah means to me? You had better give me your gun," Grandfather said. "How can I give you my gun when it is for protection?" the man spoke again. "That is not my business!" Grandfather laughed, but he never got hold of the gun!'

At that, the warden and the official were laughing so loudly that they were holding their stomachs and may have broken their chairs when the boss took himself in hand and said, 'Enough! Otherwise, we'll listen to these stories all day long.'

'I'm telling you what I saw with my own eyes!' Jukan was offended.

'Yes, we believe you,' the official calmed down and looked at the warden. 'What will we do with him?'

'I think we must take him,' answered the warden.

'It's easy to say, but I will be the one that's responsible for him,' the man said.

'We will take responsibility together,' the warden assured him.

'All right,' they agreed. 'The young man will have to wait outside while we discuss the details.'

Jukan went out into the corridor, and soon after, the warden joined him. 'Well, let's go and have some dinner,' he said.

'OK, let's go!' Jukan agreed.

On the way, the warden spoke to Jukan. 'You know, you made a very good impression on our boss. He felt a little sorry, though, that you are so young and have not served in the army. But I took the reasonability on myself. We just have to change your statement.'

'Good!' Jukan was delighted.

'It's not so good because now we have to lie to get this job!' the warden said.

They came to a small restaurant, sat down at a table, and wrote a new application, not being specific about Jukan's date of birth. In the meantime, the waiter came to them and took their order. This time, Jukan was determined to pay for the dinner himself. They didn't have to wait long before the waiter arrived with two plates of juvetch and a decanter of red wine. The food was tasty, and they ate quickly.

The forest warden leant back in his chair and stretched. 'Perfect, now for some coffee!'

'I'll go and get it,' Jukan offered.

'No need, the waiter will come!' the warden assured him.

'No, I'll do it faster,' Jukan said and went to the kitchen. There, he ordered the coffee and paid the bill before returning to his seat. They enjoyed the coffee, but the warden began to impatiently spin on his seat.

'Where is the waiter? When will he bring the bill?'

'The bill has been paid,' Jukan confessed.

'Look, Bosna, I could quarrel with you because you should not go behind the back of an adult.' Jukan was not sure why the warden was angry with him. After that, the warden took the application form back to the office, and they went straight from there back to the bus station. On the way home, they sat together, and the warden said, 'Congratulations, you got the job, but the truth is it is only temporary.'

'Temporary means how long?' Jukan wanted to know.

'About a month.'

'And after that?' Jukan asked again.

'That will depend on how well you do your work!' the warden said. Jukan didn't ask any more questions because sitting behind them was a friend of the warden, and they began to discuss local problems. He sat silently, considering the situation and asking himself whether he had made the right decision. But he didn't want to disappoint the warden, and the job was only temporary at any rate.

When they got back to Kupinovo, the warden suggested that Jukan go back to his house to finish up some of the details of the job. There was still no one at home. The two entered, and the warden went off, coming back with a long gun in his hands. He showed it to Jukan and asked, 'Did your grandfather have such a rifle?'

'No,' said Jukan, 'and I don't think he would have liked one.'

'Why not?' the warden wanted to know.

'Because it is similar to a shucker gun,' Jukan answered.

'What does that mean?'

'Guns like that, my grandmother told me, were carried at the time of the Turkish yoke. The Turks would often come to our house to drink rakija or to eat.'

'Again, you are telling me your grandmother's stories. You had better show me whether you can take this gun to pieces and put it back again.'

Jukan examined the gun carefully and asked, 'Is it loaded?'

'Certainly not,' the warden said. Jukan clicked the shutter a few times and gave it back to the warden, who praised him, 'Good man. Now, what can you tell me about the gun?'

'A rifle has no bayonet, has three cartridges, and has a long trunk. That means it's long-range. If it had a larger magazine, even my grandfather would mind it!' Jukan said.

'From tomorrow, this will be your gun. Remember, you can't give the gun to anyone, it doesn't matter whether you like the person or not. Look after it as if it is the apple of your eye. It would be better for you to rent an apartment nearby; now it's almost autumn outside, and winters are cold here. Living in the barracks would be difficult. So I have explained your job, be here at five o'clock.'

Jukan said nothing, just shrugged his shoulders.

'Why are you silent?' the warden asked him.

'I would like you to show me one more time the area I have to guard.'

'I have nothing against that, but you should get enough sleep, you will have a long night without sleeping.'

'That's all right, I will have a rest after dinner, that will be enough for me,' Jukan assured him.

'Then come in the morning,' the warden agreed.

In the morning, Jukan had to mend the bicycle tyre that had been pierced the previous night by the boss's sister. He did it successfully and was again praised by his new boss. 'You have good hands, young fellow. Now, where is your gun?'

'At home, in Bosnia,' Jukan answered.

'Forget for now about Bosnia,' he said and went into the house, coming back carrying the long gun. 'Hold it. Now it will be yours.' Jukan hung the gun over his shoulders, and they got under way. The forest warden went ahead on his favourite horse, and Jukan found it hard to keep up because the butt of the gun was hitting his bicycle. He had to rearrange the shoulder strap, and then it was much easier to ride, and he soon caught up with the warden.

'Why are you lagging behind?' he asked.

'The gun made riding harder,' Jukan answered.

'That's OK,' said the warden. 'In the forest, you will be more confident with the gun. You must realise that at work, anything can happen. On this job, we are responsible for the same things, but I am responsible for you too. I hope you understand that!'

'Of course,' answered Jukan.

'Remember that in the forest, there are a lot of wild pigs. You don't have to be afraid of them, but you also shouldn't be in contact with them. They can get aggressive, protecting their young, so it's better to avoid them. I will give you a lantern, and you can use it in the dark to scare them off. There's only one thing— we provide just one battery a month, so if you use the battery often, it will be at your own expense.'

'Certainly, where can you buy them?' Jukan asked.

'You can get them in Zemun or Belgrade, the thing is to have the money.'

They quickly went around the area and returned to the warden's house. Here, Jukan washed the bicycle and put it in the shed. The warden brought some papers from the house and gave Jukan a questionnaire, three cartridges, and instructions on how to carry a firearm. Then he left Jukan alone to read the instructions. They were written clearly, and after reading them, Jukan realised that it was better not to use the weapon at all, because it would be complicated to prove that the use was necessary. It didn't matter if you were a forest warden or a policeman; to use the weapon was not justified unless your life was threatened. How, then, to protect the forest? Jukan was thinking about this when his boss found him.

'What are you thinking about now?' he asked.

'I believe that it would be better for me to guard the forest without a gun, because I am not really allowed to use it,' Jukan said.

'Listen, the gun is not given to you to kill people with but only for your own protection.'

'Yes, I understand that, and I'm even glad. Now I will be less afraid of police officers.'

'No, they have different instructions. They guard the law, and the laws protect them. We only frighten people with our weapons, but we don't shoot at them. And now, when you've understood everything, you have to sign the paper.' Jukan obediently took the pen, signed the papers, and took his three cartridges and his lantern, which he liked most of all because he could use that when he wanted to, not like the gun. The sun was already low, and the warden said, 'Now we will have supper, and then everyone will do what they need to do.'

'Excellent,' said Jukan and took his things and made for the door.

'Are you going to work hungry?' the warden asked.

'No, I'm going to the kafana,' Jukan said.

'It's not the way we do business here,' the warden said. 'My wife made supper, and you can't refuse it. That's the rule for as long as you work for us . . . we have supper together.' Jukan wanted to have a rest, but the boss's wife came out, and it became harder to get away.

After supper, the boss's wife brought a satchel meal for him, and Jukan felt uncomfortable. 'How long will I be eating at your expense?' Jukan wanted to know.

'Quiet, don't offend me,' she said and gave him the satchel.

Jukan put the satchel on his back, thanked the warden's wife for her care, and went out. From here to the Sava River where his work was located would take him thirty to forty minutes of walking, and he hurried to get there before it got dark. When he was almost there, he slowed down and began to listen to the noises around him. The sun had set, and the moon had not yet risen, so it was difficult to see in the woods. The darker it got, the more miserable Jukan felt. Any person in a dark forest feels uncomfortable, especially if the woods are unfamiliar. At home, he wasn't afraid of anything, and even wolves were his brothers. But here he felt fear! The time was slow to pass. Occasionally he heard awful bird shrieks, which made his hair stand on end. He didn't know what sort of animals lived in the forest. However, he remembered that the warden had told him about harmless wild pigs, but Jukan knew totally different stories about the animals in forests. He decided to go to the watchtower that the warden had shown him; it was high above the ground, and pigs couldn't get him there. It wasn't easy to find the way, and he needed to use the lantern from time to time. The deeper he got into the woods, the darker it got, and now he needed to use the lantern almost all the time. However, at night, all forest animals are afraid of light, and as soon as the light reached them, they disappeared into the bushes, and Jukan didn't have enough time to recognise them.

These sounds made him feel miserable and cold to his bones; he felt that his skin was covered with goosebumps, and he looked more like a hedgehog than a man. He took the gun from his shoulder and loaded one of the cartridges and listened to the sounds around him. Soon, everything was still again, and Jukan decided not to use the lantern anymore so as not to disturb the animals. He had no idea how much time had passed, but now his eyes were getting used to the dark, and he began to recognise shapes around him. He was sure that he was on the right track and calmed down a little. At last, he found the tower. He walked around it, making sure that everything was all right, and then climbed up. It was very much like a military tower; it was impossible to sit down and he had to stand.

Now he felt safe and he started to take an interest in the forest around him. Soon, a bright moon appeared and cast a silver light over the forest, making it calm and bright. A sudden noise jolted him from sleepiness, and he understood that there were pigs grazing. The noise went on for some time but then went away. Jukan looked at his watch and saw that it was almost four o'clock and soon it would be dawn. Suddenly, he heard another pig scream. This time, it was further away, but the scream was so loud that it made him cold to his heart. Jukan was not sure what had happened, but suddenly the scream was cut off, and the forest became quiet again. By that time, the sky had already lightened and the stars were disappearing. Jukan carefully climbed down from the tower and walked in the direction from where he had heard the screams. Soon, he came to a small freshly dug area where the pigs had been grazing. Now everything was quiet, and he tried to understand why the pigs had screamed and who had frightened them.

The sun hadn't fully risen yet, but everything was visible, and now Jukan could walk quickly. He had walked about a kilometre when he saw in the distance the silhouettes of several people. He decided to get closer and see how many of them there were and came off the path and walked across the wood. When he came to the glade, there was no one there; they had disappeared without a trace. He began to doubt that he had seen anyone at all, and anyway, what would people be doing here so early? He walked a little longer and decided to go back to the forest warden's house. He walked slowly because it was still so early. The sun was rising, waking the forest animals with its light. Birds and animals began to fill the forest with their sounds, telling everyone that they were alive. There is no better time to be in a forest than the morning. He walked past the stumps made by the hunters and remembered the satchel meal. He sat down and ate with real pleasure surrounded by a chorus of birds. All his nightmares were dispelled by the morning light, for without light, people are like the blind and afraid of their surroundings.

When he got back to Kupinovo, the forest warden was already in the yard, saddling his horse. 'So, how was your first watch?' he asked.

'I don't know what to tell you. Have you ever been alone in the forest at night?' Jukan said.

'Not often. I usually have someone with me,' the warden confessed.

'With someone, it could be cheery,' Jukan said, 'but to be alone was a bit scary. In Bosnia, I was never afraid to be in the forest, but here I feel like a stranger.'

'What is the difference between your forest and this one?' the warden wanted to know.

'I don't know exactly, but here I feel different,' Jukan said.

'You will get used to it!'

'Perhaps. Last night I didn't see anything but wild pigs.'

'Don't worry, you will see more. Everybody around here knows that wood is chopped here, and many people are keen to steal it,' the warden said.

'I understand, and where will I put this gun now?' Jukan asked.

'In the special case in the hallway. It is not really convenient for you to come here every morning, walking such a long way from the barracks. It would be better to find a suitable place to live in the village.'

'It's easy to say, but I don't even know how much I will be paid, and if it is enough for an apartment,' said Jukan.

'You'll get enough for everything, and if you don't have money, I will lend you some,' said the warden.

'No, I don't need it. For a while, I'll live and eat with them.'

'Do what you want, but your gun has to be stored here, and you will need to bring it here every morning.'

'If that's what is necessary, then that's what I will do,' Jukan agreed reluctantly.

The warden noticed this and added, 'Well, if you change your mind, I will help you find a cheap apartment nearby.'

'If you think that's the right thing to do, let's do it. But we'll do it after the trial period. After all, we don't know yet whether I suit you,' he said.

'I'm sure everything will be fine. The main thing is that you like the job, and the rest we will fix later!' the warden replied.

'Thank you for your concern,' said Jukan and said goodbye quickly before he could be called again to breakfast.

When he got back to the barracks, there was no one there except for chiko Pero, who was tidying the place and cooking food. He was delighted to see Jukan.

'Where have you been all night?' he asked.

'At my new job,' answered Jukan.

'Did you work hard? Be careful you don't pick up any nasty disease at this work!' said Pero.

'Seriously, I was at my new job,' Jukan insisted. 'I told you that I work now as a forest warden assistant, guarding the forest from thieves who want to steal the wood.'

'Who would take wood?' Pero burst out laughing.

'It is possible. Do you have anything to eat?' Jukan asked.

'Today we have pork,' said Pero.

'Where did you get it?' asked Jukan.

'A man from Vrtoch brought us about ten kilos,' Pero said.

'And where did he get it from?' Jukan asked again.

'Who knows, he told us God sent it to them, and sold it to us for a low price.' He gave Jukan a plate of goulash, hot with a strong smell. When he tried it, he realised it was wild pig meat. With a smile, he remembered the screams of the wild pigs and realised that it was his countrymen in the forest. They had a business over there, and it apparently was very profitable.

'Good purchase!' said Jukan, 'and now I am going to sleep!'

'Go, sleep well, it's tough working at night,' said Pero.

He lay in bed, thinking that he'd had no reason to be afraid last night. After all, it was his fellow countrymen. But, on the other hand, it meant that quite often they were wandering over there, and maybe not always for pigs. He knew he had to protect the woods, and maybe from them too. It meant that it was possible he would need to shoot at them. No, he would never be able to pull his gun on them. He hadn't felt comfortable with this work before, and now he felt especially bad about it. But what would he say to the warden? He didn't know, and he didn't want to offend such a good man with such high hopes for him. He knew he couldn't tell him to his face; it would be better to wait until the end of the trial period, and then he would decide what to do. With this thought in his head, he fell into a deep sleep. But from that day, as he was doing his duty of forest protection, it would have been possible for anyone to steal everything all at once, not just by parts.

Part 4

Klara's wedding was very modest. That day, she wore her most beautiful dress and high-heeled shoes. Ljova arrived by car, and when she saw him, Klara again thought how incredibly lucky she was. He was dressed in a magnificent black suit and a white shirt. His dark curly hair was brushed neatly. And today, this man was to become her husband. The ceremony in the registry office was short but very solemn. The witness on Klara's side was Olga, and Ljova had a school friend as his witness. After the exchange of rings, the director of the registry office pronounced them husband and wife. Back on the street, they uncorked a bottle of sparkling wine, and everyone drank a glass. So the ceremony was over, and Klara's new life had begun. Now she lived close to Hospital Lane, near Atrada Beach, where the Miroshnik family lived in a small private house. At first, Klara felt very uncomfortable there because Ljova's mother did not appear to think of her as a suitable wife for her son, but when she became pregnant, everyone showered her with care. Klara seldom went now to the Sirota house where her mother lived, and her mother only occasionally visited her. At the Miroshnik house, they ignored Klara's mother, so she didn't like to go there.

Meanwhile, from Klara's brother, Simeon, there was no news. They only knew that he was chopping wood somewhere around Murmansk. Zelda decided to go and visit him again. She found Simeon in a remote gulag. When he went into the meeting room, Zelda didn't recognise her own son. The cheerful curly brunette had turned into an exhausted grey muzhik, and there was no trace now of his former happiness. When he saw his mother, he ran to embrace her; she held him, and they both began to cry. But they couldn't cry for long; they only had half an hour for their meeting. Simeon answered questions about his life, saying that everything was all right, while hiding his hands behind his back; they had been ruined by the hard work. Zelda looked at him and cried; she knew that life for her son was very hard. He saw her tears and said, 'Don't cry, Mother, only two more years and we will be together again.' Zelda left with a broken heart, but there was nothing she could do to help him.

Time passed quickly, and in the middle of February, Klara gave birth to a son, and they named him Dmitry. Like his father, Dima had clever brown eyes, and he brought a lot of joy and a lot of cares into Klara's life. Ljova was on top of the world, his face aglow with love for his son and his wife. Klara was happy with her life, trying not to jeopardise her luck.

By winter, Jukan came back home, like all other seasonal working men. Over the time, there had been very little change in the house, only more disturbing news coming from different parts of the world. In Europe, there was already the sounds of war, but in Bosnia, very few people were political. Both Grandfather and Father told Jukan that he should be quiet, not to go far from the house, not to church or the kafana, and not to catch the policemen's eyes. It was like being under house arrest. But, on the other hand, he had always been the favourite grandson, and because of that, he knew that he could get away with anything. It was hard to stay inside the house, but the weather helped a bit. So much snow had piled up that they had to force their way through deep drifts to get out and back again. The frost was so hard that sparrows sometimes froze in the air and fell to the ground. It was very dangerous to visit relatives because, also, there were many hungry wolves, ready even to attack people. So Jukan stayed at home, cleaning the cowshed and feeding the sheep, and he quickly became bored, thinking that life like this was no better than in the well-known Zenica prison.

But, on the other hand, autumn and winter were the best time for weddings! The truth was that it was very hard for a peasant to find a bride. Every parent wanted their daughter to find a rich groom, wishing them luck for their future. Policemen and security guards were popular choices, though Jukan despised them. His cousin Mileva, with whom he had always had a good relationship, had fallen in love with a young man from the next village. He was young and handsome but from a very poor family, and Mileva's father was categorically against the wedding. When Jukan came to visit her family, she found a moment when they were alone, and with tears in her eyes, she began to beg him, 'Jukan, I can't take it anymore. My parents won't even listen to me, but I can't live without him. God knows, if you don't help me, I will commit suicide!'

'Don't even think about that. We need to make a plan and make sure we carry it out. But the most important thing is that it must remain a secret.' This calmed Mileva a little. Jukan knew that no one would be patting him on the head for what he was doing, but he felt he had to help his cousin run away with her sweetheart. He considered himself morally right doing this because he wasn't doing it for himself . . . for himself, he wouldn't choose a girl so tall!

On the day they agreed on, Jukan went to his godfather's house in the evening. They all sat down around the table to have dinner. The table here was just like the one at home, where everyone could sit down together. While everyone was eating, Mileva collected all her things, and when it got dark, Jukan and Mileva met behind the house. Jukan took the bag from Mileva, and they began to run. It really looked as if Mileva was stealing Jukan . . . with her long thin legs, each of her steps was equal to two of Jukan's! She ran on the wings of love, dragging the loaded Jukan behind her. When they arrived at the place where the matchmakers were to meet them, they were both so tired that they couldn't stand. People picked them up and then began shooting guns and pistols as though a war had started.

Deep down, Jukan understood that he was not going to get away lightly from what he had done. He asked to be allowed to leave, but no one would listen to him, and he got dragged back to the party. Then he got really angry and started to pull away until finally he was left alone, and he hurried home.

In front of his home was Father. 'Where were you, my son?' he asked.

'I was visiting Godfather,' Jukan answered.

'What were you doing there?' Father asked again.

'We just talked for a while,' Jukan said.

'And where is Mileva?' Father asked again.

'Where she is supposed to be, at home,' Jukan said, pretending to play the fool.

'You do not have to lie to me,' Father was angry.

'If you don't believe me, go and check for yourself,' Jukan replied.

'I don't need to go and check it, your godfather was already here, looking for you both. And do you know what he is saying? That you helped to steal her!' Father said.

'Why would I steal her? After all, she is my relative,' Jukan asked.

'Yes, you stole her not for yourself but for those gangsters from Vrtocha.' Jukan wanted to say something more, but his father looked at him with his huge eyes and said, 'We agreed not to lie to one another.'

Jukan started to feel uncomfortable and confessed, 'Tell Godfather that I didn't steal her. I only helped her carry her things.'

Father shook his head and moaned, 'My god, how much longer will we suffer for your silly mistakes, my son?'

'What terrible mistake did I make? I didn't kill anyone. She loves this man so badly that she ran away herself. It wasn't necessary to steal her. Tell me how you married Mother. You stole her!' Jukan said.

Father was quiet and even smiled a little but then controlled himself and said, 'Why do you only remember the bad things?'

'Listen, Father,' Jukan explained, 'you don't have to speak to me as though I am still a child. I did nothing terrible.'

'And how will I be able to look at Godfather tomorrow?' Father asked.

'They will understand that they are the guilty ones; they are not supposed to go against love.' At this point, they stopped talking and went to bed.

In the morning, Jukan woke up early and went straight to the stables, where he met his grandmother. She was whispering to herself and shaking her head, but Jukan knew that she loved him and wanted the best for him. Meeting with Grandfather would be more difficult, because he was already losing faith in his successor. Jukan stayed in the stable for some time, not daring to go out. But at last, he heard Grandfather's cough, which let everyone know that he was up. Everyone tried to look as though they were busy, because Grandfather hated to see people doing nothing. If you had nothing else to do, you grab a poleaxe and begin to chop wood, which was always needed in the house. Grandfather always loved a good fire in the furnace and good smoke from the chimney so that he could forecast the weather. Standing in the stable, Jukan tried to work out his grandfather's mood. If he didn't cough a lot, it meant he was in a good mood. Jukan took a bucket and left the stable with it, giving the impression that he was bringing in water. There he came face to face with Grandfather, who asked him, 'Don't you feel embarrassed to look me in the eye, misfortune of ours?'

'Why, what did I do that was wrong?' Jukan asked.

'You did something that no one in our house has ever done before. You found a new way to break the law; you stole your godfather's daughter for the Vukshums.'

'Think, Grandfather, why did they need me to help them? They could steal anything themselves, even from God in heaven!'

After these words, Grandfather started to smile. 'So, you are saying that you didn't steal her?'

'Of course not,' Jukan answered, 'she simply asked me to carry her things, and how could I refuse that?'

'That means that you knew about this for a long time, but you didn't say anything to us,' Grandfather observed.

'She asked me not to! Listen, Grandfather, it's her destiny in the end, and you don't have to worry about it. And our godfather Puvach's house is full of brides!' Grandfather smiled and stepped aside and let Jukan go. Happy with the way the conversation had ended, Jukan picked up the bucket again and went to the well.

On the way, Grandfather said, 'Really strange people at your godfather's house. Everything that happens to them, they always accuse other people.'

'It doesn't worry me, let them say what they want. The main thing is that you understand me,' Jukan answered, and being afraid that he would cry, he ran back to the stables.

So this episode had ended, but Jukan's relationship with his grandfather had deteriorated so much that Jukan never again visited his house, though with the young men at the Puvach house, he remained good friends. Life went on as usual. But just before the New Year, Jukan again was involved in the stealing of a bride. This time, it was a girl from the same village; her name was Kovilka, and she was in love with a distant relative of Jukan's, a shoemaker from Rajnovats. Her father wanted her to marry a policeman who was much older. To prevent this wedding was much easier, because Kovilka was not a relation, and Jukan had a good relationship with Nikola and his brothers for many years. Almost all the young boys had a part in this theft. They helped Kovilka run away from home and across Milkin Mountain to where the matchmakers were waiting. The terrible shooting began again. Jukan was again blamed for all the trouble. And the next day, Kovilka's family went to the police station to accuse Jukan. They lied and said that Jukan had started the shooting and that he disturbed the peace. And they added that the shooting was so loud that they thought that the war had started and they had to hide under their beds!

For the police, that was enough, and they went to Grandfather's house that night, even though it was the night of the Sacred Vasily. Usually two policemen came, but this time, they arrived in force, and three of them came together. They went into the courtyard and waited. All the dogs were barking terribly, but the policemen didn't move. Eventually, Grandfather went out and invited them into the house, but they refused and said that they wanted to see Jukan. Now everyone knew for sure why they were here and told Jukan to hide in the house because it was too late to try and escape. But Jukan didn't want to hide like a mouse, and he told his family this. The main thing, though, was that Jukan was simply tired of these complaints from his relatives, and he decided that it would be better for everyone if he simply went to jail. He opened a window and told the police that he would come out. Everyone was surprised by this turn of events, and Grandfather began to ask the police if they would leave him at home, at least for the holidays. But the police were unshakeable, and soon Jukan came out to the courtyard and said, 'Here I am, I'm ready!' They didn't try to tie him up, and they all left together through the gate. They walked quickly and soon reached the barracks. Here, Jukan had to spend the night, and even though the bed was soft and clean, Jukan did not sleep well.

In the morning, he was taken forcefully by one of the policemen, who asked him, 'Well, are you ready?'

'Ready for what?' Jukan asked him.

'For a trip to Bihach,' the policeman answered.

'I'm ready,' Jukan said at once. No one knew who had ordered the cart, but it arrived, being driven by their good family friend Koyo from Dolova. Jukan was pleasantly surprised to see him and asked, 'Why did they send for you?'

'You're not pleased? Don't worry, everything will be all right.' Jukan didn't understand what Koyo meant, but soon everyone was seated and they got under way. As soon as they got out on the road, Koyo started singing and pulled out from under his seat a big bottle of rakija. He pulled out the cork, gulped a mouthful, and passed the bottle around. Everyone drank as much as they wanted, and soon everyone was singing, giving the impression that they were matchmakers going to collect the bride. By the time they passed Dubovsky, both policemen were already tipsy, and their heads were drooping so much that it looked as though they would fall off their necks! When they approached Ripach Klanats, both policemen were sleeping, leaning against one another. Then Koyo stopped the cart and said to Jukan, 'Well, now that they are drunk, you can run away!'

'Run to where?' Jukan asked.

'Wherever you want, to Italy if you want,' Koyo said.

'Then what will happen to these policemen? They will be expelled, and they both have families and small children,' Jukan said again.

'Why do you feel sorry for them?' Koyo wanted to know. 'They are policemen!'

'So what?' Jukan said. 'They are good people. Besides, I'm fed up with my home, "Don't go there, don't do that!" I feel as though I'm in prison.'

'No, prison is different. In prison, the lice will eat you alive!' Koyo warned.

'Let it be, I've already decided that I'm not going back,' Jukan said again.

'You will regret this, but it will be too late. Your stubbornness will cost you a lot!' Koyo warned again.

Koyo pulled on the reins, and the cart went on its way. 'You are not smart, Jukan. Your grandfather has a smart head, and your parents are clever too, but it seems that you are a fool!' muttered Koyo.

'Well, everyone is a fool before he grows wiser,' Jukan snapped back. Without noticing, they had arrived in Ripach. The policemen snored peacefully on the floor of the cart, and Jukan covered them so as not to draw attention to them. They didn't stop here, just passed through the village without letting the horses take a rest.

Now the policemen woke up and looked around in fright, not knowing where they were. They breathed a little easier when they saw that Jukan had not run away. 'We've already passed Ripach? Why didn't you wake us up?' one of them wanted to know.

'You were sleeping so nicely; I didn't want to wake you,' Koyo said.

'Do you still have something to drink?' the second policeman asked.

'No, you drank the whole bottle,' Koyo said.

'What, there is nothing more to drink? That can't be true,' the policeman said.

Koyo pulled out from the hay a second bottle, much smaller than the first. He gave it to the policemen, warning them, 'Only drink a little bit now.' They agreed with him, and this time, they took just a few gulps and returned the bottle. Then Koyo offered the bottle to Jukan. 'Have a drink,' he said.

'No, I don't want one,' Jukan said.

'As you wish, but you won't get the chance again soon,' Koyo reminded Jukan. The policemen liked this joke and laughed. Jukan laughed as well, though in his situation, it looked as little silly.

Soon, they arrived in Bihach and stopped at the Pavel Suchevicha kafana. Jukan had visited here often with his grandfather; he felt quite at home here. The owner, Pavel, recognised him at once and called him aside. 'Hi, Jukan, what are you doing in such strange company?'

'They have brought me to the local prison.'

'How come? You have avoided jail for more than a year, and now, just before the amnesty, you decide to go?' he asked.

'Please don't try to dissuade me. I decided it was better to go now,' Jukan tried to explain.

'Think again,' Pavel said. 'If you want, I'll talk to the policemen,' he offered.

'No, you don't need to. But if you can, tell them not to take me to prison under escort. I will go myself,' Jukan said.

Pavel straightaway went to the policemen, and within a few minutes, everything was settled. The senior policeman winked at Jukan and said, 'All right, you will go to prison by yourself, only don't dare run away!'

'Excellent!' Jukan was delighted, drank a glass of water, said goodbye to everyone, and went out on to the street.

Jukan crossed the bridge and walked to the prison. On the opposite side from the jail was the Low Court, and he had to go there first. He pushed open a heavy door and came into a big room where two peasants were sitting. Jukan didn't know what to do next, so he sat down on a chair and waited for an employee to come out. He was sweating with nerves. At last, a door opened, and a beautiful woman came into the room.

'What are you waiting for?' she asked Jukan.

'I just want to find out where I should register to serve my sentence,' Jukan answered her.

'Are you alone or with company?' she asked him and burst out laughing.

'I'm not joking,' Jukan said.

'That's great.' She smiled again and disappeared behind the door. Jukan sat back down and waited.

After a while, she returned, and Jukan said, 'I swear I'm not joking. I've come to go to prison.'

This time, she looked at him more seriously and said, 'Then, young man, follow me.'

Together they entered an office where a young-looking man, though with almost grey hair, was sitting behind a table. 'Talk to this man,' she said and left, closing the door behind her.

Jukan again asked his question, 'Tell me, where should I go to register to serve my sentence?'

'For which crimes are you to go to prison?' the man asked.

'For fighting and for murder,' Jukan said.

'When did this happen?' the man asked again.

'Almost three years ago,' Jukan answered.

'And why were you free for so long?' the man wanted to know.

'I was still too young, that is why no one touched me,' Jukan explained.

'Who brought you here now?' the man asked.

'Nobody, I came by myself,' Jukan said.

'Are you normal? I've never seen a person who wanted to go to prison.'

'Yes, I decided for myself. A man can't be free if he has a sentence to serve,' Jukan explained.

'Have you been to prison before?' the man asked.

'Certainly not,' said Jukan.

'If you have decided, then so it will be!' the man said and went to a shelf and finally found the folder he was looking for. He opened it and began to look through it. At last, he found what he was looking for. 'So, you are Vignevich, Jukan?' he asked.

'Yes,' Jukan said.

'Then don't try to look innocent. You have been hiding from the law for about three years,' the official said.

'It seems that they didn't try hard to find me,' Jukan answered.

'All right, now go out to the corridor and wait there,' he said in a voice that did not allow for objections. So Jukan went out and sat on chair.

Jukan had to wait for about an hour and was almost asleep when he heard his surname being called. He stood up and saw in front of him a man in a blue uniform looking at Jukan as though Jukan had killed his father. 'In the name of the King, hold out your hands!' he screamed, and it shocked Jukan so much that for a minute he couldn't understand what to do.

'Why are you putting handcuffs on me? I came here by myself,' Jukan asked.

'That means nothing to me. Put out your hands!' the officer roared. Jukan realised that he couldn't change anything and held out his hands. The man quickly put the handcuffs on his wrists and then ordered Jukan to sit back down. He went into an office where he stayed no longer than ten minutes. By this time, Jukan's hands were numb because the cuffs had been tightened too much. Jukan decided he needed to talk to the officer when he came out.

'Sir, could you please loosen the handcuffs just a little? My hands are numb,' he said.

'Nothing will happen to your hands, you will get used to them' was the reply.

'I'm not asking you to take them off, just to loosen them a little bit,' Jukan tried again. The officer looked around at the people sitting around and changed his mind and loosened the handcuffs. Then both of them went outside and walked in the direction of the prison.

Snow had begun to fall, and the street was slippery. Jukan was wearing his new shoes, and he was constantly sliding. Unexpectedly he received a blow on his back. Just then they were right in the middle of the bridge leading to the electric power plant. Jukan turned and looked angrily at the officer. 'You, sir, do not know me. You could lose your job for that!' he said and then turned his back and continued to walk.

They came to the iron doors of the prison, very similar to church doors, where the jailer knocked at the door and called out. The door opened with a dreadful screech. They walked through a small courtyard and went down stairs into a gloomy basement. Here, they were met by a man with the most enormous stomach. He gave Jukan the most evil glance as though he were a mad dog smelling his prey. 'Quickly take off all your clothes and stand there naked!' he screamed, and with trembling hands, Jukan began to undress. He dumped all of his clothes onto the floor and waited for the next order. It was freezing in the cellar, and he was covered in goosebumps. The jailer disappeared, and Jukan decided to put on a shirt to feel warmer. No sooner had he put the shirt around his shoulders than he heard the horrible voice again, 'Didn't I tell you to undress? Put that shirt on the floor!' Jukan was frightened and threw the shirt on the floor. Whether from fear or something else, he began to feel warmer, though maybe he was just getting used to the cold, but now he didn't shake anymore. After that, they took his fingerprints, photographed him, full face and in profile, and then he was ordered to pick up his clothes and follow the enormous jailer. They went up to the second floor, where the jailer opened one of the doors, pushed Jukan inside, and quickly closed the door again.

Here, there was not enough light and a lot of people, and all of them asked him for cigarettes. 'I don't smoke,' Jukan said.

'Maybe you don't drink either?' someone asked him.

'And I don't drink either,' he confirmed.

'And you don't like women either?' the same person asked him.

'No, I love beautiful girls!' Jukan said.

'What we don't have here are beautiful women!' the voice said again, and everyone burst out laughing. They snatched his clothes out of his hands and began to ransack the pockets. Someone found his holster with some cartridges in it and began to throw them on the concrete floor.

Jukan was frightened that the noise would bring back the jailer and he would be in trouble again. He explained this to the others, and they gave him back his clothes. He gladly put them on and was then bombarded with more questions. Jukan answered their questions and then asked one question himself: 'Why is the air so heavy in this room?'

'Because here we are in the most well-known health resort in our kingdom!' someone answered, and everyone burst out laughing again.

At this moment, the room leader ordered everyone to line up and, taking Jukan by the shoulder, introduced him to everyone, explaining why they were there and how long their prison sentences were. Jukan's fears began to disappear, and he even became cheerful following all their jokes. Then he was shown the place where he would sleep and introduced those who slept on the left and right. It was cheerful, not just in that room but in the neighbouring room too, because they could talk through the holes in the walls and ceiling. The last question was whether he played cards.

'I like to play cards, but I have no money and nothing to play with,' Jukan said.

'You don't need them. Here, you can play for a breakfast or a supper,' the room leader explained.

'Who will eat two breakfasts or two suppers?' Jukan asked, surprised. Again, the men burst out laughing.

The leader said, 'Brother, even four of them will not be enough for you!'

'Then what will happen to the one who does not eat?' Jukan wanted to know.

'Then he should try to convince himself that he isn't hungry,' he was told.

'How can a person live without food?' Jukan asked again.

'No one can live without food . . . that's why we are not allowed to play for dinner. Well, who wants to play cards now?' he asked, but no one was keen to play. 'Well, if no one wants to play, I suggest, in honour of our newcomer, that we play without money, simply for training.' Everyone then joined in the game, but Jukan decided to watch from the side. They sat around a plank bed as if around a table. It was easy for the Muslims to squat . . . the Croats and Serbs were uncomfortable, often changing position, but the game didn't stop for a minute. When it got too dark to see, they decided to go to sleep.

For a long time, Jukan tossed and turned on the hard plank bed, trying to fall asleep, but something was biting him, and he realised it was lice. His neighbours demanded that he calm down. Now, lying in a room on a plank bed, he began to regret that he hadn't run away when he had the chance. But there was no one to blame; he was guilty, and that was why he was suffering now. With these thoughts, he fell asleep.

He woke up to unfamiliar and loud sounds. He opened his eyes and saw that everyone was up and had their shoes on. He saw that everyone was doing something, brushing the plank beds, sweeping the floors, or airing the room. Everyone was busy. Only Jukan didn't know what to do. Finally, the room leader ordered everyone to line up and be counted. Jukan found out that there were twenty-one people in the room, and mostly they were young men. Just then, the door to the room opened, and the chief prison officer came in. The room leader made his report. The officer listened to the end and then said, 'Anyone with a complaint, step forward!' Nobody moved except Jukan, who stepped forward.

The room leader ordered, 'Quickly return to the line!' but the officer stopped him.

'Leave him, let the young man tell us his complaint.' Jukan took off his shirt and showed that his body was as red as if he had been stung by nettles. But the officer appeared not to notice anything, just pointed his finger at Jukan, and said, 'Lice bite you because you are lazy and sleep too much!' Then he turned his head and said to the room leader, 'Find him an all-night job, and then the lice will not bite him! And if you can't find one, I will find one for him myself. And if I take care of someone, lice will never bite him again.' The jailer darted a final glance at Jukan and left the room.

As soon as the jailer had gone, everyone crowded around Jukan. 'What right do you have to complain without telling us first? Remember, here no one complains, because it only makes things worse for you and for all of us.'

Jukan pretended that he was listening attentively but then said, 'I don't understand why you should be responsible for what I do and why I can't complain when we live here like animals.'

'They do treat us like animals here, but it's better to be quiet, otherwise they will lock you in the punishment room with just bread, ice water, and rotten soup. After that, you will not be able to drag your own feet around. And if that is not enough, they will force us to beat you until you are silent!'

'And would you do that?' Jukan asked, terrified.

'What else could we do? If we don't do it, they will find someone to punish us!'

'Where do they find such people?' Jukan asked.

'Easy, here there are a lot of people who would punish their own father if it made things easier for them. Therefore, suffer and be quiet!' Jukan listened to what they were saying and understood that they were telling the truth.

The next day, Jukan discovered that he didn't need to eat the prison food anymore. Twice a day, his favourite aunt managed to bring him food from home. The prison food he gave to his neighbours who needed it more. Now some people in the room started to treat him with respect, and even suspicion. One of them suggested, 'Maybe you are a policeman, otherwise, why would they do you such favours?'

Jukan decided to tell them the truth. 'It's simply because my grandfather is well known in this district, and he would do anything for his favourite grandson.'

'Why, then, are you in prison?' they wanted to know.

'It seems my silly tricks have annoyed not only my grandfather but also even my dear mother,' Jukan answered.

The next morning, they lined up again before the arrival of the chief officer. He came into the room, walked slowly along the line, and stopped next to Jukan. 'Well, did you sleep well last night?' he asked.

'I didn't,' Jukan lied. 'I had to clean the room.'

This answer pleased the officer very much, and he continued with a smile. 'So you have nothing to complain about?'

Jukan took a step forward and said, 'I don't care what you do to me, but the lice in this room make life impossible!'

'OK, we will try to help you, only I hope you don't come to regret it!' he said, and looking around the room, he left.

After dinner, two jailers came into the room and ordered Jukan to collect his things. 'We're moving you to another place,' they said.

Jukan felt that something unpleasant was about to happen, but not wanting to show his fear, he simply said, 'I'm ready!' He said goodbye to his new friends with whom he had spent these last days.

The officers took Jukan out into the corridor and downstairs into a cellar. Only one dim lamp burnt here, and it was not possible to see anything. The jailer opened a door to a room that smelled of rotten hay or potato. Jukan was pushed into the darkness. He touched a wall, and it felt damp and dirty. Jukan did not know what to expect. Gradually, his eyes became used to the gloom, and he saw that here there were people, but they were sitting in big metal cages. The jailer opened the door to one of them, pushed Jukan in, closed the door behind him, and said, 'Well, now the lice will not bite you. In this darkness, they will not see you! So you can rest here as if you are on a resort.' As soon as the jailer had gone, the two men in the next cage began to ask Jukan questions, who he was and where he had come from. But Jukan didn't answer; he decided to wait for a while.

After some time, the door opened again, and into the room came another man dressed in strange black-and-white striped clothes. He was locked in the cage opposite Jukan. Jukan thought he looked about thirty-five years of age; his face was dark although he was smiling, and he was built like an athlete, though he limped on his left leg. 'Where are you from?' Jukan couldn't resist asking.

'From Bosansky Petrovats, but they have brought me here a witness from Zenica,' answered the man.

'So we are almost neighbours! And after the trial, will they send you back to Zenica?' Jukan asked him.

'Of course,' he replied.

'How long are you in prison for?' Jukan asked him again.

'For life!' he answered.

'What does that mean?' Jukan wanted to know.

'It means that I will never leave prison,' he said.

'What offence did you commit?' Jukan asked.

'A murder,' confessed Jukan's new neighbour, and after that, they were both quiet.

After a while, Jukan interrupted the quiet. 'Tell me, how hard is it to be in this well-known Zenica prison that everyone is afraid of?'

'The conditions are better there than in many Bosnian houses. They have everything that a person could need. You can even study a trade there,' the man answered.

'What about lice? Do they have them there too?' Jukan wanted to know.

'What are you talking about? We regularly have a bath, everyone gets a haircut and shave regularly, also we have clean beds. The food is good, and we have very little to complain about,' the man answered.

'Are you simply joking or trying to trick me?' Jukan asked.

'What would be the point in my lying to you?' the man asked.

'Then why do they try to scare us with stories about the prison?' Jukan wondered.

'I don't know,' the man answered. 'You have to remember to obey all the rules at work and in the room. Certainly, there a lot of different people in jail, both good and bad. The main thing is that you don't get under the influence of bad people. With wolves, you must behave like a wolf and not show that you are afraid of them.

But they usually don't touch us kraeshniks because they know that we always have a weapon with us and that we're not afraid to use them.'

Over the course of the day, the two had many conversations, and Jukan tried to remember everything. Now he wasn't afraid of the thought of Zenica prison. And he wasn't afraid of his neighbour and thought of him more as a family member. Jukan noticed that during their conversations, the man was constantly rubbing his left foot. Jukan asked, 'What happened to your foot?'

'You had better try to remember this story, it may come in handy for you. In Zenica, there are plenty of punishments for guilty people, and this is the result of one of them. As punishment for one big fight, they took me into a room and closed the door behind me. I tried to look around, but it was too dark. At that moment, I got a crushing blow to my shoulder and was thrown against the wall. I could hardly stay on my feet, but then there was another blow to my shoulder, and I tumbled to the floor. Now I was hit on the floor, and my foot was twisted. Then I understood that I was not being hit by a man but by some heavy object. I tried to stand up to wait for the next blow. I felt the pain in my foot, it was difficult to control. This time, the object hit me from the back, and again I tumbled off my feet. I fell on the floor, the bone in my leg cracked with the most terrible pain. After that, I could no longer move or resist. The heavy object found me a few more times and hit me against the wall, and then there was silence. The lights came on, and I saw that this room was completely round. In the middle was an enormous bag hung from a wooden pole. In this room, there was no place to hide, especially in the dark. To lie on the floor was impossible, because the bag almost reached the floor.'

'It's amazing what people will make,' said Jukan, surprised. 'And what could you do against that?'

'I don't know, but you could try one thing. Stay against the wall and wait for the bag and then jump on it. Don't forget this,' the man advised Jukan.

For the next two days, the two spent a lot of time in these conversations, though it seemed more like advice for Jukan's future life in Zenica. Now that he was in the isolation chamber, his aunt could no longer send him food. Jukan hardly ate anything. Prison food didn't create any appetite in Jukan, and the smell of mould and decay made it even worse. But even in this smelly darkness, Jukan felt better than in the upstairs room. On the third day, they were woken by a siren. Officers came into the cellar, and seven people, including Jukan, were taken from their cages. They were connected in pairs, just Jukan didn't have a partner. Then they were connected around their waists by a very long chain, and they were walked out. It became clear that they were going to be taken now to Zenica. They silently went down the corridor, accompanied by two young handsome officers, obviously unspoiled by the dirt of prison life. The main gate opened with a creak, and they came out onto the square. The gate creaked behind them as if to say 'goodbye'.

It was still very early, and no one was about. Some snow was lying on the ground between puddles of mud; cold grey clouds threatening rain floated across the sky. One policeman walked in front of the chained men, and the second one closing the procession behind them. They crossed the square and came into the railway station building. Here, there were already a lot of people. Busy locomotives passed the platform, throwing up clouds of steam. One train was collecting carriages; all the railway men had whistles with which to communicate to the train drivers. They whistled; the train let out a puff of steam and then a cloud of soot as if they were talking. The prisoners whiled away the time watching these activities. At last, the train was ready, and the policemen were told where to sit their prisoners. The policemen unlocked the chains from around the men's waists; they moved into the carriages and sat down in pairs. They were locked then to special rings, and now they looked like pigs, each in its own pen. When Jukan thought about it, he burst out laughing, which surprised the policeman. 'What are you laughing about? You should be crying when you think about where you are going!' he said. Jukan didn't try to explain but turned to the window. Just then, the whistle blew, and the train began to move slowly, to the men's uncertain future.

The journey to Zenica took a couple of hours, but it seemed longer to Jukan, as the men were not allowed to talk. From all directions, Zenica was surrounded by mountains covered in snow, but the prisoners were not given a chance to admire the scenery. Straight from the station, they men were rushed to a covered truck and only came out of the truck when they had reached the prison courtyard. Now it was possible to look around. The courtyard was big, surrounded by a fence about five metres high. The sun was shining, and Jukan closed his eyes and relaxed. They remained there for about an hour before someone came for them. They were escorted by two security guards, who took them to the ground floor and into a big room with high ceilings. Straw had been laid on wooden planks, the kind that Jukan had slept on before. The first pleasant surprise was when they brought in dinner . . . first was a soup, followed by stuffed cabbage and then compote. Jukan had not had such good food even in his own home, and he slept well, dreamlessly, that night.

The next morning, they were woken by a siren, and then security guards came and took them to the toilets and to wash. Conditions were better here than at home, Jukan thought. Then they were brought back to the room and given breakfast. After that, they didn't know what to do with themselves, but suddenly Jukan remembered that here in Zenica was a prisoner, Shukar, from Chukovo. He was famous because he had been lame from birth and was a really wild character. He had been jailed for killing his two brothers; they had joked about a girl he was in love with, so he grabbed a knife and killed them both. One brother had tried to escape, but Shukar had caught up with him and killed him. Incredible stories were told about this wild character. Jukan had seen him once and now wanted to see him again.

In the room, there was a window facing the courtyard, but it was about two metres high and was impossible to look out of. The men had been told that it was absolutely forbidden to look out and that they would be punished. But Jukan, being pulled by the devil itself, persuaded his neighbours to help him climb onto the window. They agreed, and two lifted him by his arms, and another let him stand on his shoulders. Jukan grabbed the bars and looked out. Below, in a courtyard, were about twenty men walking in a circle, one behind the other. Their hands and legs were locked by chains, and they were only able to take small steps with great difficulty. For one of them, it was even harder because one leg was shorter than the other; Jukan immediately recognised him as Shukar. He watched a bit longer and then jumped down before he was seen by the guards.

At about noon, the door to the room opened, and the guards walked in. One of them ordered the men to quickly get all their things and follow him out into the corridor. There was practically nothing to collect, and it took only a minute or two to get all the men outside. They went down a floor into a waiting room with a long bench next to the wall. 'Take off your clothes!' one of the guards ordered, and everyone began quickly to undress. All the men kept their underpants on until the guard shouted again, 'The order was to undress!' They took off their underpants and stood covering their private parts with their hands. Jukan felt like a sheep going to be sheared. The security guard gave each man a small piece of soap and a washer. 'Now go and get washed,' he ordered. The bathroom was hot and full of steam. Jukan had never seen a bathroom like this in his whole life. He turned on the shower and stood under the hot water, which streamed over his body, giving him immense pleasure. He put a lot of soap on his head and began to rub it in. He scrubbed himself with the same energy as a sailor cleaning a deck! Soon, his body squeaked with cleanliness! After that, they were taken away to the barber, where, for the sake of hygiene, they were shaved bald, not only their heads but all body hair as well. Then they were examined by a doctor, and when he was sure there was no infection, they were allowed to get dressed. When they came back to the waiting room, they saw that their clothes had gone. Here, they were given a new prison uniform with wide black and white stripes. Jukan liked his new clothes except for the cap he had to wear on his head.

Then the men were taken to different rooms; four of his companions were taken to a shared room, but as Jukan was a dangerous criminal charged with murder, he was given a separate room. It was on the second floor behind a locked partition. The room amazed Jukan with its spaciousness and cleanliness. The ceilings were four metres high, and in one corner was an iron bed, with a chair beside it. On the wall over a table was hung a list of prison rules. Light came into the room through a small barred window close to the ceiling. In the far corner was the toilet . . . in the cement floor was a hole for basic needs, and to flush the toilet, he had to pull an iron chain which hung down from the ceiling. The water pressure was so strong and noisy that Jukan thought it could flush him as well.

Jukan felt that here he was real gentleman; never in his life had he lived in such conditions. For two days, Jukan studied the prison rules and schedule. Having received the advice from his neighbour in Bihach jail, he knew to learn it by heart, and now his rights and duties were clear to him. He had three meals a day, not worse than in the army, and most importantly, he had a good, long night's sleep, which allowed him to feel well rested and full of energy. No one came near him for two weeks, and he thought he would go crazy being so idle. No one gave him a job; he was full of energy and had to use it up somehow. He began to dance the Kolo right there in his cell; the smooth concrete floor was ideal for this purpose. In the beginning, he danced quietly but then became more frenzied, and he even sang. The security guards watched him with interest through the viewing hole, and sometimes laughed.

On the fifteenth day, they gave him some work. They brought a big bag of feathers; he had to separate the down from the bone part by hand. This work was tiresome and unpleasant, but it helped the time go faster. The important thing was not to move quickly and not to sneeze at all. But one day, he just could not help himself . . . the down got into his nose, and he sneezed. The separated down rose up to the ceiling and would not fall to the floor. If the security guards saw this through their spyhole, Jukan would be in trouble. He took his chair and propped it against the door handle. After a while, the spyhole opened, and the guard looked in. Immediately he heard the sound of the key turning in the lock as someone tried to get in. The chair withstood the first pressure, but soon another guard joined the first, and they broke through the door. The down fell like snow on their heads! For this offence, Jukan was sent for three days in the punishment cell on bread and water.

Everyday made Jukan more experienced about prison life. The guards saw that he was trying to do the right thing, and they respected him for that. With the beginning of spring, work was started on a vegetable garden, where they had to dig up the soil and then plant seedlings and keep them clear of weeds. As Jukan was the most skilled peasant, he was made head of the young prisoners. In his group, there were five people; all of them were a bit older than he was, and they did not like to be supervised by him. Especially resistant was a pickpocket named Stevo. He constantly tried to do the opposite of what he was asked, and every day the conflict between the two got deeper. Once when they were weeding, Jukan saw Stevo pull out some lettuces with the weeds.

'What are you doing?' demanded Jukan.

'I'm working! And why are you spying on me?' Stevo answered.

'Because you pulled out the lettuce!' Jukan said.

'It's not your business, village bastard!' Stevo abused Jukan, and Jukan rushed at him with his fists raised. Stevo was rather a big man, but Jukan's determination took him by surprise. Jukan managed to hit Stevo on the nose and few times, but then Stevo managed to grab hold of him, and they fell to the ground, still exchanging blows. The guards heard the noise and tried to separate them, but they were like bulldogs and would not let go. This noise then caused the chief of the prison to come out, and he ordered Jukan be punished. The guards grabbed him by his arms and took him down a long corridor, which got darker with each step that they took. Then they opened a door, pushed him into a dark room, and closed the door.

Jukan immediately remembered the advice given to him by his neighbour in the Bihach prison. He pressed his back against the wall and waited. He didn't have long to wait. Unexpectedly, something heavy knocked him sideways. But Jukan was ready, and he jumped onto the bag. The bag was big, and it carried Jukan around in circles, sometimes hitting him against the wall, hurting his legs. But it was necessary to put up with that pain, and he strengthened his grip. The bag flew around like this for a few minutes, knocking Jukan against the wall, ripping the skin from his legs, but at last the bag stopped and a dim light was turned on. Jukan heard the noise of a key in the lock and quickly jumped off the bag, trying to smile. When the guard saw Jukan, safe and smiling, he was stunned.

'Why are you smiling? What happened here?' he demanded.

'It's just that when you closed me in the dark room, I became alert and listened. At the moment when I thought someone had knocked me sideways, I jumped on the offender. It turns out it was just a bag,' Jukan answered him.

'Don't lie, who taught you this?' the guard wanted to know.

'I'm telling you, nobody!' Jukan insisted. The guard wasn't too happy about this, but it was in Zenica's rules that no one could be punished twice for the same infringement. Now Jukan's life entered a stable and predictable period. The conditions at the jail were good, and he liked them. He even had time to read the newspapers or books, sitting at his table. Now he just had to wait for the amnesty.

———— ✦✦✦✦✦ ————

That spring, Mishka graduated from school and passed his exams successfully. Right after that, he decided to go to Odessa to enrol at the military college. His father didn't want him to go, but he didn't want to stand in the way of his son's happiness either. His mother helped him get his things ready and saw him off on the road, crying. Mishka put on his most decent trousers, his father gave him some worn boots, and his mother made him a shirt. He put all his papers into an old military-like case, said goodbye to everyone, and headed for Tsebrikovo. It seemed to him that he wasn't just walking but was flying on newly developed wings towards this huge unknown world that was waiting for him. In Odessa, he took a tram to see his aunt, but the most important thing for him was, would he see Klara? He wondered what she looked like now. He had never been in a big city before, and he was amazed and a bit scared. Just in one carriage of the tram, there were more people than in the whole of Frieberg altogether. It was noisy and stuffy inside the carriage, even though the windows were opened. It was hard for Mishka to find the right stop to get out at, and then he spent another ten minutes finding the street and house. He came into a courtyard, and there he saw Aunt Zelda hanging out the washing. He had seen her once many years ago, but somehow he recognised her at once.

'Hello, Aunty,' he called out.

Zelda turned to look at him, a puzzled look on her face. 'Who are you?' she asked.

'I'm your nephew, Naum's son, from Freiburg,' he answered.

Zelda's face broke into a smile, and she opened her arms to embrace him. 'Oy, Mishenka, how you have grown up.' She bombarded him with questions, and he told her all the news. At last, she remembered to ask, 'What brings you here?'

'I came to enrol at the military college. Also, I came to visit you, hoping to see Klara,' he said.

'She doesn't live here anymore. She lives now with her husband and practically never comes here. I will give you her address, and you could visit her there. She lives in Otrada, not far from the bus stop,' Zelda said.

'I don't know when I could visit her. I need to be at the military college on Monday morning.'

'Tomorrow, you could visit her. Stay the night here with us. We don't have much space, but we will squeeze you somewhere.'

But the next day, all their plans were overturned. At midday, all the loudspeakers in the city were transmitting the same message. This morning, Klara had gone to the shop to buy bread. When she came near the shop, she saw an enormous crowd listening to the message from the loudspeaker. The crowd stood silently, many with open mouths and tears in their eyes. Klara stood to listen too. The message was read by Levitan, and his voice was so dramatic that it made Klara's hair stand on end. 'What has happened?' Klara asked a man, pulling at his jumper.

He pulled away from her hand and said, 'The war has begun!' These words hit Klara hard, and she began to cry knowing that from this time on, her life would be terribly changed. She listened to the end of the announcement and ran home, forgetting the bread. At home, everyone had already heard the news and were sitting around the table. Only Dima couldn't understand what was happening around him. He was just two years old but was talking like a much older boy. He tried to ask questions, but no one had time for him. Ljova wasn't at home; since the previous week, he had been on a business trip and was expected back the following week. An announcement came back on the radio that all men of military age should register at their local recruiting centres; otherwise, they would be treated as deserters.

Odessa was bombed on the first day. It seemed that the Germans wanted to destroy the military hospital, but the bomb fell on a neighbour's house just across the road. The explosion was so powerful that Klara thought that the walls of her house would fall in. There was a small cellar in the house, and the whole family rushed down there. The bombardment lasted about ten minutes, but it seemed to go on forever. When the planes had gone, everyone rushed out to look where the bombs had fallen. They found that a bomb had fallen on house number five on Pirogovsky Street, and the firemen were already there. Nobody knew just what to do, but everyone was certain that the war would not last long and that the Red Army would quickly defeat the treacherous German fascist aggressors. The next morning, Klara went to recruitment centre and registered Ljova.

Mishka was up early the next morning and went to the military college. It was very crowded with people everywhere. He joined a queue for registration. When his turn came, the captain sitting at the table asked him, 'What is your surname?'

'Kleiner Michael Naumovich,' he answered.

'How keen you are,' the captain said, grinning, 'I only asked for your surname. Where are you from?'

'I'm from Freiburg,' Mishka answered.

'Where is that, somewhere in Germany?' the captain asked.

'No, it's here, a German farm not far from Tscebrikovo.'

'So you are German?' the captain asked suspiciously.

'No, I'm a Jew.'

'That's good! What other languages do you speak?' the captain asked again.

'I can speak German,' Mishka answered.

'Where did you learn it?' the captain was curious.

'I graduated from a German school,' Mishka said.

'How well do you speak German?'

'As well as I speak Russian,' Mishka insisted.

'Then you are perfect for us!' The captain was delighted. 'Wait here, I'll be right back,' he said. He left the room and was gone for about five minutes. When he came back, everything was like a whirlwind around Mishka. He was taken as an interpreter, and the following day, he was supposed to go with a general to the front line. Mishka had nobody to inform that was leaving for the front line, so he just said that he was ready to go straightaway.

In the next few hours, he was shaved and given a uniform, boots, and hat. It took him a long time to fasten the foot cloths, the material that is wrapped around the feet to prevent blisters before putting on boots, but at last with the sergeant's help, he was dressed. Mishka was very surprised when he saw himself in the mirror, and at first, he didn't even recognise himself. Then he was introduced to General Shvabrin. He was a very serious fellow, not talkative and seemed nervous. He said to Mishka, 'Well, Private Kleiner, you have a very important job. You will be the interpreter when we manage to take an enemy soldier as a prisoner of war. You will translate accurately and only what I tell you. Is that clear?'

'Yes, absolutely, Comrade General!' he replied sharply.

'Excellent! We leave for the front line tomorrow at dawn. You can go now and rest. Someone will show you where you sleep.' Mishka turned around and left. The next morning, he and six others, including the general, left by car.

The closer they got to the front line, the more chaotic the situation became. On the roads coming towards them were crowds of people leaving their homes, moving with their cattle. Carts and cars were filled with family belongings. Cars with wounded soldiers raced past. Periodically, German planes attacked them, and everyone rushed to hide in bushes or under trees. The Germans didn't care what they were bombing, military or civilian. Here, for the first time, Mishka faced death. A second lieutenant who had been travelling in the car with them was killed in one of the raids. An explosion tore off his foot, and he was wounded in the stomach. He bled profusely and screamed in pain. Thank God, it did not last for long, and he died in Mishka's hands; the sound of his screams lasted a long time in Mishka's ears. Later, two tanks joined them. The general was in a rush to get to his troops as soon as possible, but in all the confusion, it was difficult to move. At midday on the following day, the car stopped for a few minutes so the men could take a short break and have some food. Mishka opened a tin of cooked pork and ate it with bread. Then he lay down on the ground and went to sleep.

He woke up to hear the low roar of a car motor and shouts in German. He stood up and saw that lines of motorcyclists wearing German uniforms were coming from all directions. He saw the general stand up and take out his pistol, but then, understanding the impossibility of resistance, he raised his hands. Everyone else followed his example and raised their hands as well. Germans surrounded them quickly and moved them to a nearby settlement. Here, they joined other prisoners of war, sitting near the wall of a piggery. Many of them were wounded and smeared with blood. Soon, a truck approached them, and a group of submachine gunners jumped out, led by a large red-headed officer who called out in German, 'Shprehen zi Deutsch?'

Mishka took a step forward and answered in German, 'I can speak German!'

The officer looked at him in surprise and ordered, 'Tell all officers, communists, and Jews to move to one side.' With a quivering voice, Mishka translated the order, keeping his eyes on the ground. The general got up first, and following his example again, a few other officers and other people got up to join him. The German officer gave the order for the submachine gunners to take the group outside and shoot them. Mishka couldn't believe his own ears, but his eyes didn't allow for any doubt. The gunners pushed the group to a wall with the butts of their guns and, in the presence of the others, shot them.

The red-headed officer then called to Mishka and asked, 'Who are you? Where did you learn to speak German?'

'I am German,' Mishka lied.

'That can't be true. How did you get here?'

'I was born on a German farm in Freiburg. There I lived and graduated from a German school. That's why they used me as an interpreter.'

The officer was doubtful and studied Mishka closely, but then his face broke out in a smile. 'Then that means that you are one of us! How far is your Freiburg?'

'Probably more than 100 kilometres from here,' Mishka answered.

'Now you can get a food ration, and you can go home. Tell everyone in your village that we are coming,' and he gestured for a soldier to bring him a ration. The soldier came back with a package, gave it to Mishka, and told him he could go.

Mishka turned and started to walk. He had trouble getting his feet to move. He couldn't believe that he was released and thought that they would finish him off with a shot in the back, but he decided not to run. He walked more than 100 metres, and still no one shot at him. He walked up a small hillock and began to walk back down, and still no shots came. He quickened his pace as he walked towards a small forest. His whole body was trembling with the pressure, and he began to run. He ran into the woods, and after a few steps, he fell on the ground and began to sob. He punched the ground with his fists and shouted, 'Criminal bastards, how I hate you!' At last, he calmed down, stood up again, and brushed the dirt off. Then he picked the ration box up from the ground and angrily threw it deeper into the woods. 'Guzzle your rations yourself, you damned fascists!' He decided not to go home. He knew the Germans would be there before him, and his father had good German friends who should help him. But Klara should definitely be warned. She had a small son, and she needed to get away from Odessa. Once he had collected his thoughts, Mishka decided in which direction he should walk and then walked off, fast.

Now the Germans bombed Odessa every day, but the people had no doubts that soon the Red Army would defeat the fascists. Ljova returned to Odessa two days after the war had started, and Klara told him that she had registered him at the local enlistment office. 'You didn't have to do that; I have protection from serving in the army. But now I have to go,' he told Klara. In the morning, he went to the enlistment office and came back already dressed in his lieutenant uniform. Next day, he would be sent to the front line. When Ljova's mother heard this, she sobbed and glared at Klara, but Ljova calmed her down. 'Stop blaming yourself, you did the right thing. I would have gone there myself. The main thing is for you to look after Dima. The war will end soon, and I will come back. Then we should be happy for many years together.'

Little Dima ran around his father, shouting, 'Hurray, my father is going to war!'

But the next day, Dima was already quiet and crying. Ljova took him by the hands and said, 'Well, Dima, say for me *riba,* which is "fish".'

Dima still couldn't pronounce the letter *r,* but being very cunning, he looked into his father's eyes and said, 'Pike!' and everyone burst out laughing. Before he left, Ljova said goodbye to his parents and then went to Klara. He took her in his arms and kissed her lips. Tears filled in his eyes, but he wiped them with the sleeve of his uniform. He turned and walked quickly out of the house.

--------------------◆◆◆◆◆◆--------------------

Every morning, they waited for the news that the fascists had been stopped. But the reports coming from the front line were only negative. More and more cities were being emptied, and the enemy was getting closer to Odessa. But no one had any doubt that the Red Army would prevent the fall of Odessa. City bombing was becoming more and more regular, and as soon as the sirens sounded, people ran into the nearest shelters. At night, no one switched on their lights, and the curtains were closed. It was not safe to go walking on the streets anymore.

One morning, a young man knocked at the door of Klara's house. His clothes were full of holes and were very dirty. He looked nervous and lost. At first, Klara didn't recognise him at all and asked, 'Forgive me, but who are you?'

'Klara, don't you recognise me? I'm Naum's son, from Freiburg.'

'Mishka.' She was delighted. 'What are you doing here?'

'I came for just one reason—to warn you!' Mishka started, but Klara interrupted him.

'First of all, go and have a wash. I'll give you something to eat, and then you will tell me everything.'

'I don't have a minute to wait,' Mishka said. 'I should go to the registry office. I won't come into the house and bring dirt inside.' Klara forced him into the courtyard and gave him some soap and a bucket of water, and he began to wash. As he got cleaner, Klara could see the familiar lines of his face. Then she brought from the house a piece of bread and sausage. At first, he refused, but then he began to eat so quickly that Klara could see that he was hungry. As he ate, he talked. 'Klara, you must evacuate at once.'

'No, why? The Red Army will never hand over Odessa.'

'Listen, you know nothing! Believe me, there is no one to defend the city. Everywhere it is just chaos and panic! The Germans are killing all communists and Jews, even children!' Mishka said.

'How do you know this?' Klara wanted to know.

'I was taken prisoner and saw it with my own eyes. Believe me, they are killing all the Jews!' Mishka insisted.

'How did you escape?' Klara asked.

'I told them I was German. You know everyone in our village spoke German. They believed me and let me go,' Mishka explained.

'Where would I go?' Klara asked. 'I don't have anyone in Russia, and Ljova has been sent to the front line with the army.'

'Even better! You go to the registry office, and they will give you letters for evacuation as the wife of an army officer,' Mishka said.

'Mishka, you are exaggerating. Everything will be all right,' Klara said.

'Believe me, it will not be all right! When I was crossing the river, it was impossible to see the water, just blood and corpses. You have no time to waste, rescue yourself and your child.' Mishka was extremely agitated; his hands were shaking, and his eyes were filled with tears.

Suddenly, Klara believed him and feared for herself and her child. 'What about your family, did you warn them?' she asked.

'I didn't have time. The Germans would certainly be there now, I think. From Odessa, you can go by car or train,' he said.

'Where are you going now?' she asked him.

'I'm going to the enlistment centre to ask them to send me straight back to the front line. I want to fight these animals. It doesn't matter if I die, I'll take as many with me as possible!' Klara looked at him and couldn't believe how this kind boy had changed so much and now was full of hate and confidence. He stayed for just a quarter of an hour, and Klara promised him that she would evacuate from Odessa.

As soon as Mishka had gone, Klara went to the office, where they gave her a letter with permission for four people to evacuate to Saratov. After that, she went to her mother's house and repeated everything that Mishka had told her. 'Mother, I have permission for four people to evacuate. Please come with me. I won't survive without you.'

'It does not look good, and I can't leave you alone. Go home now, and I'll come tomorrow. Do you want to take someone else with you?' Zelda said.

'I want to suggest your niece Rose. She is pregnant, and we should rescue her,' Klara said.

'You're right. Go to her and tell her to hurry. But how will we get away?' Zelda asked.

'Tomorrow at midday, we have to be at the passenger terminal at the port to board the steamship *Abkhazia* and to sail to Herson.'

Klara said goodbye and took a train to see Rose, who was already five months pregnant. But it was impossible to persuade her. Rose was absolutely sure 'Odessa will never fall to the enemy. And even if it does, my father's best friend is German. He will help us. Thank you for caring, but we will stay here.' Klara hurried home, and here she gave another of her friends, Riva, the chance to go with them. Riva gladly accepted the offer and began at once to pack. Klara had very little to pack; all Dima's and her belongings fitted in just one suitcase.

In the morning, the steamship *Abkhazia* was lined up against the pier, and on board was real human chaos. The crowds of people were like bees in a beehive. There were those with permission to evacuate and those who had come to see them off. There were people who had no documents but were trying to get on board by any means. From near the stairs, there was the constant shouting that only those with permission were allowed on board. Finally, it was Klara's turn. She showed her papers, and Klara, Riva, their mothers, and babies went up to the deck. When they got to their places, Riva's mother remembered that she had left a bag on shore and began to run downstairs. Riva asked Klara, 'Can you look after my Shurik? I will go and look for Mother.' Klara took the boy by the hand.

No sooner had Riva gotten off the ship than German planes appeared in the sky and began to shoot. Anti-aircraft guns placed in the port area opened up, returning fire. On board and on the pier, people began to panic. They tried to hide wherever they could, and the captain of the vessel gave orders to sail away from the coast. Sailors quickly raised the gangplank, and the *Abkhazia* began to move away from the pier. Klara asked her mother to look after Dima, and she ran with Shurik to the gangway. The steamship was already about fifty metres from the pier, where Riva was running around madly. Klara rushed to the captain, who was standing nearby. 'Comrade Captain, I beg you to stop the vessel!' she cried.

'What are you talking about? They are bombing us! Go back to your place!' he ordered.

'I can't. This is not my child, but he belongs to that woman running around on the pier,' she told him.

'I can't do anything. I can't go back to the pier to be a sitting target for the planes. You will have to look after the child,' the captain said.

'I have my own child; I couldn't cope with two!' Klara sobbed.

The captain looked at her kindly and said, 'You are just a child yourself. Wait, and when this attack is finished, I will send a boat to shore to pick up your friend.'

'Oh, thank you, Comrade Captain,' Klara said and went back to her place.

The attack didn't last long, and as soon as the situation had calmed down, the captain sent a boat to pick Riva and her mother up. When they came on board, Klara gave Shurik to his mother and went to look for her own mother and Dima. She didn't need a lot of time; her mother was walking towards her but without Dima. 'Mumma, where is Dimochka?' she asked in a frightened voice.

'I left him with good people who promised to look after him, and I came to look for you,' her mother said.

They went up to the next deck, but there was no sign of Dima. Klara and her mother began to run around the vessel, calling out his name. At last, they came across a big crowd of people, all talking about something, and when Klara made her way in, she saw a desperate Dima lying on the deck, crying. She picked him up and started to kiss him, but the crowd was angry with her. 'What a silly woman, forgetting all about your baby! What kind of mother is she? She is still a child herself,' people were saying. But Dima had already stopped crying and was smiling happily at Klara. Soon, the crowd dispersed, worrying about their own problems, and *Abkhazia* was going at full speed to Herson.

Thankfully, the planes didn't come back, and after twelve hours, they reached their destination. From here, they were to walk to the train station and get the train to Rostov. Because they had so little luggage, they were one of the first to reach the station. Here, they were to spend the night. Little Dima was so tired that despite all the moving around, he fell asleep every chance he got. Zelda was exhausted and could barely walk. Only Klara was still full of energy. It seemed that difficult situations made her more alert. And now she had a chance to think of where they were to go next. After listening to the advice of other people, she understood that she needed to cross the River Volga, where the Germans were unlikely to reach. Also, it was better not to go to Siberia, where they might die of cold, since they didn't have any winter clothes with them. It would be better, then, to go south, and so they decided to go to Saratov and decide on the rest later. To decide was one thing; to get tickets was quite a different matter.

Around them were crowds of people, some trying to get tickets, others trying to find a place to get a sleep or rest to gain valuable strength. It was practically impossible to get near the ticket office, so Klara decided to find a different way. She left her mother with the luggage and went to the chief station officer. Near his door, there was another noisy crowd, where everyone thought they had a reason to get a ticket without queuing up. Klara began to wait. Suddenly, the office door opened, and out stepped the chief officer and his subordinate. Klara grabbed hold of Dima and ran to block their way.

'Comrade Stationmaster, please help me to get a ticket. My husband is a Red Army officer and is now on the front line. I'm here with a small child and a sick mother!' she said.

'You are not the only one, everyone here is in the same situation,' he answered coldly and was ready to leave.

But just then, Dima began to cry and asked, 'But dear Uncle, please help us.'

The stationmaster's heart melted at this, and he ordered his subordinate, 'Well, Vasily, go and help them!'

A few hours after that, they were standing on the platform. The train consisted only of freight cars. There was no place to sleep, and people made themselves as comfortable as they could on the floor. They were to travel like this all the way to Rostov. Near them was a man of uncertain age who was trying to settle down. He was dressed as an old man, but his face looked quite young. His back was so sore that he could hardly move at all, and each of his movements was accompanied by loud groans. It was dreadful to listen to, and it was simply impossible for Klara to sleep. Klara and her mother spread their clothes under Dima, making him more comfortable, and they tried to sleep leaning their heads against each other. Klara had just managed to fall asleep when German planes attacked the train. The planes flew low over the train, and bombs fell nearby. The train stopped, and the people jumped out from the carriages to hide in bushes or under trees. The invalid was out of the carriage first and seemed to completely forget about his back pain. Klara was carrying Dima in her arms, with her mother running behind. Planes targeted the running people; machine gun fire passed just a metre in front of Klara and hit a woman running nearby. She fell to the ground without a sound, blood staining her back. At last, they reached the edge of the forest and rushed under the trees.

The planes came by a few more times, shooting at the people still running, but at last they flew away. There was a brief silence, and then came the shouts and groans. People tried to find their families, and at last Klara heard her mother. All this time, Dima sat like a little monkey on Klara's back, holding tightly to her shoulders. His brown eyes were full of fear but at the same time shining with curiosity. Now Klara put him down on the ground to readjust her clothing. People began to come out of the forest and bushes. The wounded were lying on the ground, groaning, and the dead lay as they fell. A medical orderly began to help the wounded and then collected the dead, putting them in the last carriage. People began to return to their places on the train, and the man who was suffering from back pain came back, hobbling slowly and holding his back, but he wasn't groaning anymore.

'Do you feel a bit better?' Klara asked him.

'It seems that one more attack like that and I will be fully recovered,' he joked.

After a few minutes, the train got under way again. There were no more bombings, and Klara managed to fall asleep, exhausted. The next morning, they reached Rostov. The further they got from Odessa, the deeper were the feelings of confusion and indecisiveness about what to do next. Each time Klara closed her eyes, she hoped that when she opened them again, she would be back home and all the nightmares would have disappeared. But when she opened them again, she saw only the crowds of confused people around her. She felt that there was no more energy in her body, and she wanted to scream for help, but then she looked at little Dima and her even more confused mother, and she understood that all responsibility lay with her. All her confidence and the feeling of power came back to her.

They didn't stay long in Rostov; the train for Saratov was departing in just a few hours. Again, they had to travel in freight cars, but this time there was a thin layer of straw on the floor, and so they managed to sleep better. On the stops along the way, Klara tried to buy food with her limited amount of money. Sometimes she managed to get some milk or cheese, and almost all of that went to Dima. They travelled for a day and a half to reach Saratov and arrived there in the evening. It was getting dark, and as they had nowhere to go, they decided to spend the night at the station. But it was impossible to find somewhere to sleep. Every seat was taken by people sleeping, and even on the floor of the most secluded places, there was no place to sit. Dima had fallen asleep, and Klara and Zelda were taking turns to carry him. Klara didn't know where to go, and because of sleep deprivation, her legs were not working properly and she walked as though she was drunk. When she was passing a column in the middle of the station, she stepped on the foot of a woman in a beautiful dress. The woman turned and angrily pushed her away; Klara couldn't keep her balance and fell to the floor. Dima burst into tears and ran to her.

Unexpectedly, the woman turned and bent over Klara and asked, 'I'm sorry, are you badly hurt?'

'That's all right, it was my fault too,' Klara said.

The woman's face became anxious. 'What are you doing here?' she wanted to know.

'My mother, my son, and I are evacuating from Odessa,' Klara explained.

'And where are you going?' the woman asked again.

'They sent us to Saratov,' Klara said.

'Do you have anyone here?' she asked.

'No, we have no one here, and, at present, we don't know what to do,' Klara replied.

'Where are you going to live?' the woman went on.

'We don't know. Tomorrow, we will start to look for a place, but we will try to spend this night here,' Klara answered.

'On a station with a little child? Get your things and come with me!' she ordered.

'We have practically nothing, and it is all with us,' Klara said.

'What were you thinking about? How are you going to survive? But enough for now, let's go!'

Klara returned to her mother and said, 'Mumma, this woman has invited us to spend the night at her house. Should we go?'

'And what if they rob us?' Her mother had her doubts.

'Mumma, what are you talking about? We have nothing to take!' Klara said. Her mother agreed with this point, and they started out after the woman.

They all left the station together. It was already very dark, and there were few street lights on. They crossed the square and walked half a block until they came to a three-storeyed house, where they went into a dark corridor. Their new acquaintance took a box of matches and struck one match. 'Look carefully where you walk. In this corridor, the devil himself could break his legs,' the woman warned them. They quietly followed her. Outside one door, she searched through her bag for a key, and at last, she opened the door and switched on the light in the hall. 'You must be quiet,' she warned them again. 'My neighbours grumble!' They walked through a corridor to a tall door, and with another key, the woman opened it and turned on the light. From the middle of the room, a single light bulb with an orange lamp shade lit up. The room was quite spacious; in the middle was a round table with four chairs, next to one wall was a big wardrobe with a mirror, and then a dressing table with a mirror and stool, and then near the window was a big bed. 'Come in, please,' the woman invited them, and when they were inside the room, she closed the door. 'Well, let's get acquainted. My name is Larisa. My apartment is very small, so I won't be able to keep you here for very long. But you can stay for a while. I work at nights, and so I'm not at home, and you can sleep here. But in the afternoon, I have to rest, so in the morning, you should leave. But tomorrow evening at six, you can come here again.'

Klara wrung her hands. 'But I have nothing to thank you with. You are simply an angel.'

'I'm very far from being an angel,' Larisa said. 'But now I must leave quickly. You go to bed now, and before nine o'clock, you will leave, closing the door behind you.' She waved goodbye and left, leaving Klara and Zelda standing, confused.

At last, Zelda broke the silence. 'I can't believe such people still exist! She saw us for only a few minutes, and now she leaves us here in her own house, unsupervised.'

'Precisely, Mumma, it's as if God himself sent her to us,' Klara agreed.

'But let's get to bed quickly. We have to be up early in the morning. Look, Dima has fallen asleep on the chair.' They lay down on the coverlet without taking off their clothes and put Dima between them. For the first time since leaving Odessa, they slept on a bed. They fell asleep immediately without any tossing and turning.

In the morning, Zelda woke up first and woke her daughter and grandson. They didn't want to get up, but she insisted. 'Let's get up and get washed. Larissa will be back soon.' Reluctantly, Klara got up and carried Dima out, looking for the toilet. In the corridor, she came face to face with a small elderly woman who looked at them suspiciously.

'Excuse me, where is the toilet?' Klara asked.

'Who are you, and how did you get here?' the woman asked.

'We are evacuees from Odessa,' Klara explained. 'Larisa invited us to stay here for the night, while she went to work.'

'Don't tell me she went to work,' the woman burst out laughing. 'Your Larisa doesn't work anywhere. She earns her money at the station as a prostitute!'

'That can't be true. You are lying,' Klara objected.

'Believe what you want!' the neighbour said, taking offence, and disappeared into her room.

Larisa came back before they left. She looked dreadfully tired; it seemed that this was not an easy way to make money. But she still smiled and even gave Dima a sweet. 'Thank you so much for your kindness,' Klara said. By this time, they were completely ready and simply left the house.

On the doorstep, Larisa said to them, 'If you don't find anywhere else to sleep, come back in the evening, at six o'clock.'

All morning long, they wandered along the streets, not knowing where to go. The mood in the city was dreadful; with loud speakers reporting from the front line and the news about how many cities were fallen made the mood even worse. Around them were refugees, just like them, and everyone looked unhappy and desperate. At last, they managed to sit down on a bench in a small public garden. Here, they had a chance to have a rest and try to work out what to do. Unexpectedly, Klara saw a sign above the door of a building, 'Meat and Dairy Factory'. 'Mumma, wait here for me with Dima. I will go and see if they have some kind of job for me,' she said and went to the industrial complex.

At the checkpoint, she explained that she would like to speak to the director, and she was let in. The director was not a young man and was unshaven. He looked very tired, and his eyes were red as though he hadn't slept properly for a long time. When he saw Klara, he cheered up a little. 'Girl, what are you doing here?'

'I'm looking for any sort of work,' Klara explained.

'We have nothing available,' he said. Klara turned to go through the door, but the director stopped her. 'Where are you from?' he asked.

'I've evacuated from Odessa with my mother and two-year-old son,' she answered.

'Alone, without any men?' he asked her.

'My husband is on the front line,' she explained.

'When did you last eat? You are painfully thin, just skin and bones. What can you do?' he asked her.

'I'm a bookkeeper,' she said.

'A bookkeeper, that's perfect!' he said. 'But you and your child will not survive here. The war will last a long time, and you should settle nearer to food. I will send you to one of my friends in regional Dergachi. He is the director of a dairy farm. Over there, you and the child will always have milk. Go there. His name is Drozdov Nikolay Ivanovich. I will write a letter to him. It will help you. Do you agree?'

'Of course, I agree!' Klara said. 'Thank you for your care, after all, you don't know me at all.'

'I simply feel sorry for you,' the director said. 'Come tomorrow morning and I will prepare the letter for you. But now you must go.'

Klara hurried back to the park where her mother and son were waiting for her. Dima was crying because he was very hungry, and when he saw Klara, he ran to her. 'Mumma, I'm hungry!'

'Then we will go now and get something to eat,' she said, calming him down, but Zelda interrupted her.

'Klara, we should save our money. We don't know how long we are going to have to live like this.'

'I think that tomorrow everything will change. The director has promised me a job on a dairy farm from where we will not die of hunger,' Klara said.

'Oh, what great news!' Zelda got excited. 'Where is it?'

'It doesn't matter where it is. The main thing is we will have food and somewhere to sleep,' Klara said.

They went to the market and bought smoked speck and bread, and for Dima, some cottage cheese. The rest of the day they spent in the city, and at six o'clock they went back to Larisa's place. 'Aha, you came back. Please come in.' She greeted them with a smile.

'It's just for one more night,' Klara explained.

'And tomorrow?' Larisa asked.

'I have found a job for myself, and we will go to Dergachi.'

'I know this place. It's not far from here. What a person you are! You've found yourself a job already, and you absolutely look like a child! Now, lie down and rest, and I will see you tomorrow,' said Larisa and left.

That night, Klara was thinking about Larisa a lot. Prostitute. Before this, she would never have stayed for a second near this woman. But this woman's heart had softened at the sight of these unfortunate refugees. She had taken them into her home, given them her bed. It meant that she was not worse but better than other people, and Klara felt sorry that she had always thought so badly about them. In the morning, she again thanked Larisa from the bottom of her heart, for her hospitality and kindness. Larisa pulled a chocolate from her handbag and gave it to Dima. 'That's for you, from this quite useless woman. I always wanted to have a boy like you, but life changed all my plans, and now the war has turned everything upside down.'

The director of the factory had kept his promise about everything. He explained to Klara how to get to Dergachi and gave her a letter for the director of the farm factory. He even gave them a dry food ration. Klara didn't know how to thank him, but he simply explained to her, 'Don't worry, girl, after all, someone had to help you. Just go and take care of yourself. These troubles are only just starting, and we will all need a lot of strength to pass all these tests.'

They arrived at Dergachi by noon. It wasn't hard to find the dairy factory; it was the biggest building in the settlement. At the checkpoint, they were stopped by the security guard. 'Excuse me, who are you looking for?' Klara was asked.

'I have a letter for the director of the factory,' she answered him.

'Then you must go through these doors,' the guard said, pointing. The office door was closed, and Klara knocked on it.

'Come in,' a pleasant voice responded.

With some hesitation, Klara entered the room. She saw two men, one dressed in a soldier's shirt, the other in a rumpled grey shirt. The man in the soldier's shirt asked, 'What kind of business brought you here?'

'I'm looking for Director Comrade Drozdov,' answered Klara.

The man stood up and introduced himself. 'I'm Drozdov, and who are you?'

'I was sent to you by your friend Comrade Belkin. He gave me a letter to give you,' she explained and gave him the envelope.

Without hurrying, he opened the letter and read it carefully. As he read, a smile began to appear on his face. Then he put the letter down and said to the other man, 'Makarov, meet our new bookkeeper. She will go to the Red Dawn farm. What is your name, girl?' he asked her.

'My name is Klara,' she introduced herself.

'And what is your full name?' he asked again.

'Miroshnik Klara Davidovna.'

'Excellent, and I'm Drozdov Nikolay Ivanovich, and this is my assistant, Makarov Victor Alekseevich. He will go with you to the farm and help find accommodation.'

'And what will I do there?' Klara wanted to know.

'Your task, Klara Davidovna, will be to keep all the accounts, and once a week you will come here with the report. You, Makarov, make sure that they give her clean premises where the three of them can live, and find her a two-wheeled cart by which she can bring her reports here.'

'Comrade Drozdov, where will I place them?' Makarov wanted to know, trying to resist.

'How you find them a place is up to you, but you must do it. Also make sure that they always have milk and cottage cheese. Besides that, find them some fabric and cotton wool so that they can make blankets and pillows for themselves. Do you understand me?'

'Of course, I understand you!' Makarov muttered and threw a baleful glance at Klara.

'Then go and prepare the lorry to take them to the village, and, meanwhile, we will fill in all the necessary papers,' Drozdov said.

When Makarov left, Klara began to thank the director. 'Thank you very much for everything that you are doing for me. I didn't expect that at all.' But Drozdov stopped her.

'Girl, what are you talking about? Someone has to help you because your husband is fighting for our native land.'

One hour later, they were driving across the steppes towards the farm. Makarov, Zelda, and Dima were sitting in the cabin of a lorry, but Klara had to sit in the back. The road was dreadful, and sometimes Klara felt that she would simply fall out. But, fortunately, they didn't have to drive for more than half an hour. They couldn't find any place in any of the houses for them, and Makarov decided to set them up in one of the classrooms in the local school, in a room with a Russian furnace. When they were left alone, Klara began to believe, for the first time, that they would survive this awful evacuation. She sat down on a bench and felt that all her strength was leaving her. She relaxed finally and began to cry.

Next morning, Klara was already at work. In the main central room was the director's office. Next to him was the room of the chief veterinarian and agriculturalist. In the Accounts Department was the table of the economist and Klara's table as bookkeeper and then the tables of the norm setter and tally keeper. About 100 people worked at the factory, and the other workers were scattered around the surrounding state farms. There were practically no men working in the factory, because most of them were fighting on the front line. Here, there was just one old man; the rest were all women, most of whom were Kazakhs. All of them treated Klara with respect and love. Many of them had children who had been sent to the war and were now sending back letters. Many of the old Kazakhs could neither read nor write, and they asked Klara to read their letters to them. She couldn't refuse them and sometimes even wrote back their answers for them. But not all relationships were going well. Here in the factory was an ex-serviceman by the name of Zaharov, who had been sent to exile in Siberia. He was a very grim man who only smiled when he was listening to reports from the front line from where there were only distressing reports coming. He repeated with pleasure the names of all the cities which the Soviet army had left to the Germans. Occasionally he showed Klara the list of surnames he had written down and said, 'Very good! The Germans will come soon, and I will show them all you damned Jews and communists. Oh, how I hate you!'

He really was threatening, and finally Klara decided to complain to Drozdov. He listened to her and said, 'Don't worry, Klara. If the Germans come, I will take you with me, and I will shoot this bastard myself.' These assurances calmed Klara a little, and life settled into a routine.

Every morning, Klara went off to work, leaving Dima with her mother. Zelda tried to be economical and to look after her grandson. She darned their clothes and washed them, prepared the food, and took Dima for walks. Klara came home in the evenings very tired. They didn't starve but ate very little, and so Klara had hardly enough energy for the whole day. She tried to find her husband and wrote him letters, but she never received any reply from him. It was easy to assume that Ljova simply couldn't find them or that he was not alive anymore. Dima by this time was talking as an adult and constantly asked the same question, 'When will my father arrive?'

Meanwhile, autumn and the first of the cold weather had arrived. But Klara didn't have any winter clothes, and she went to work in summer shoes.

The orange disk of the sun slowly went down behind the hill, and night came very quickly. Mishka closed the collar of his soldier's shirt and threw his overcoat over his shoulders. The evenings and nights were getting very cold, and there was no place to get warm. He had already spent two days in this trench, and by now he was used to it. By evening, it was usual for the German attacks to ease off, and then it was possible to rest a little. He took off his helmet and shook the dust from his hair. His hair was so dirty, it seemed it was made of rock. He had already forgotten the last time he had taken a bath, and there was only one time in the morning when he could wash his face. Two months had passed now since he had said goodbye to Klara in Odessa. In this time, he had become a skilled soldier. In Odessa, he had again gone to the recruitment centre. He hadn't told the true story of how he had been released by the Germans but simply explained how they had been surrounded by Germans and, by some miracle, he had simply escaped. They believed him and again sent him to the front line as an interpreter.

This time, he was in the intelligence division and was almost always on the front line. Now, Mishka had almost no fear. He had witnessed German brutality, and now only hatred moved him. He wasn't afraid of death anymore; he had faced death on the first day of the war. He wanted to get into the action, but almost all the time they were retreating. It was almost impossible to counter the German tanks and heavy fire. Now, in this unusually quiet time, it was possible for Mishka to relax. He pulled a tobacco pouch filled with makhorka from his pocket, took a pinch of tobacco, and put it on a paper. With movement born of habit, he twisted a roll-up cigarette and lit it. The smoke made him a little tipsy, and at once he remembered his own family. He had absolutely no idea what had happened to them and frequently blamed himself that he hadn't warned them. But he knew that he couldn't have gotten there before the Germans. Mishka's only hope was that they had evacuated, though he knew that his father would never leave his farm. His other hope was that the local Germans were good friends and would not give them away. But he had absolutely no news.

Next to Mishka, leaning on their elbows, two friends, Seryoga and Vadim, were sitting on the trench wall. Mishka had been fighting side by side with them now for about a month, and today they had lived through another long, mad day. They had become like brothers and could rely on each other. Many people had disappeared in this meat grinder: small and tall, thin and fat, cheerful and gloomy, all disappeared under its relentless pressure. Some of them had been blown to pieces, some fell silently as if they had fallen asleep, and others shouted and screamed for help from their pain. So far, Mishka and the other two had been lucky, but how long their luck would last, no one knew.

'Private soldier Kleiner,' Mishka heard the lieutenant's voice.

'I'm here, Comrade Lieutenant,' answered Mishka, standing to attention.

'Come to the captain, he has news for you,' the lieutenant ordered.

'Yes,' Mishka responded and went to a covered section of the trench where the officers met. There he was met by Captain Veselov; he had the same exhausted look as his soldiers.

'We have a letter for you,' the captain informed him.

'From whom?' Mishka asked.

'Look for yourself,' the captain said, handing him a small envelope.

Mishka took the envelope and returned to the trench. He pulled out a small stump of a candle, lit it, and began to read. The letter was from his sister, Riva, and started with the words 'Hello, my dear brother Mishka. I write this letter in the hope that you are alive and it will find you. You are the only family now who remains in my life.' Having read these opening words, Mishka's heart was full of dread, but he made himself read on: 'As soon as you left, the war began. Germans came to our farm just some weeks after the start. Our father didn't want to run away and leave the house. He was sure that his German friends would help him, but everything turned out very differently. On the day the Germans arrived, I was grazing a goat not far away from the farm. When I decided to return home, I spotted an officer in a fascist uniform and hid in some bushes. From there, I could even hear what they were saying. Together with Father's friend Markus, they went to our house. Markus pointed his finger at Mother and Father and said that they were Jews. I don't want to describe the horror of all that happened because it could break your heart. I will only tell you that they lined all our family up against the wall of the house and shot them with machine guns. In horror, I fell to the ground and fainted. When I recovered, I slowly moved into the forest because I knew I wasn't able to help anyone. I managed to run away, and after a few days, I managed to reach free territory. I don't know how I am living these days, I seemed to have lost my mind. In my head I see all the time the picture of the execution, and at night it is hard to fall asleep. Now I am going to evacuate, but I don't know where. Dear Mishenka, if you are alive and receive this letter, please try to find me. I don't have anyone in this world except you. I kiss you lovingly, your sister Riva.'

Mishka finished reading the letter, clasped his head in both hands, and began to sob like a little child, crying, 'Why, why, why?' And what wrong had they committed? They had lost their lives because they were Jews, and he hadn't been able to warn them. He sobbed without noticing the captain had come out and was looking at him with pity. He didn't see how Seryoga tried to approach him but was kept away. Mishka sobbed, and together with his tears, the pain left him. He didn't know for how long he cried, but gradually he grew calmer, and he fell asleep, leaning his elbows on the trench wall.

Mishka woke up suddenly because the ground was shaking and the air was rumbling. He opened his eyes and saw that it was already bright and his friends were on their feet. Mishka looked out of the trench and saw four field tanks across the field, followed by German infantry. The tanks fired a volley, and a shell whistled just over them, hitting a low hillock behind them, and from the explosion, they all got covered in dirt. At that moment, the guns from the next trench opened fire but missed their target. The tanks continued to press on but were still too far away. 'Don't shoot,' the captain ordered. 'Let them come closer!' The tanks again fired a volley. One of the shells hit the gun on the right of them, and it was overturned. Soldiers standing nearby fell like nuts from a tree. Despite that, Mishka did not feel frightened; he wanted only one thing—to have revenge for the death of his family. He felt for the two grenades and two limonka on his belt 'Get ready, fire!' ordered the captain, and they opened fire. Two German soldiers fell on the ground, but the others bent down and moved closer to the cover of the armoured vehicle. The remaining two guns were shooting without any visible success, but at last one shell hit a tank and it began to burn. Two men jumped from the tank, and it began to spin on the ground. The remaining three tanks stopped for a moment and then moved forward again. This time, a shell exploded much closer to them. Mishka fell to the bottom of the trench, and for some time he couldn't hear anything. When he looked up, he saw the lieutenant was lying on the ground, writhing in pain. Vadim was standing nearby, shooting from his machine gun. Mishka stood up next to him and looked out from the trench. The Germans were now so close that he could see their faces. He started to shoot, and the Germans fell to the ground. But the tanks continued to move.

About ten metres in front of the trench was a bush, and Mishka decided to use this as cover. He crept out of the trench and found a small shell crater and slipped in. Bullets whistled over his head but missed him. The path of the tank was very close. He put his hand grenades in front of him and looked out of the crater. The tank was no more than ten metres away; the infantry was close behind. Mishka threw one grenade and lay down again. He heard a powerful explosion, and the tank finally stopped. He took another grenade, pulled out the ring, and threw it. There was another explosion, and again Mishka looked out. The tank was on fire, and turning on the spot, its track was broken off and it had no mobility. There were a couple of dead bodies lying on the ground, but the others, along with the other two tanks, began to withdraw.

Just then, Mishka heard a rumbling behind him, and when he looked back, he saw three Soviet tanks sent in to counter-attack. Behind the tanks, the infantry was moving. Chasing the enemy, they passed by him, and only at that moment, Mishka felt a pain in his shoulder, and feeling dizzy, he lay down. After that, everything was like in a dream. The captain ran to him and clapped him on the shoulder, saying, 'Well done, Kleiner! You have shown real heroism, and for that I will recommend you for a decoration. But it seems that you have been wounded in your shoulder.'

A nurse ran out to examine his shoulder and put a bandage on it. The wound wasn't serious; simply a splinter scratched his shoulder. They gave him a few sips of spirits, and Sergeant Kvashnin, winking at the other soldiers, said, 'Well, who ever said that Jews were not good fighters? Look at our Kleiner, he is simply a hero!'

As a result of the fight, they managed to take four German soldiers and one officer as prisoners. They reported to army headquarters, and the next morning, the order came to bring in the five captured Germans. Mishka and one other soldier were sent as a guard and interpreter to accompany them. Mishka didn't want to be saddled with them and asked his commander, 'Comrade Captain, I'm asking you not to send me with them.'

'Why is that?' the commander was surprised.

'I can't look at these bastards. They killed my family,' he replied.

'I can't do anything, Kleiner. I've been ordered to send you as an interpreter, and that's why you have to go.'

Early the next morning, the five German soldiers, with their hands tied, took their seats in a covered lorry, and they got under way. As soon as they drove off, artillery bombardment on their unit's position began, but they didn't see that. A few minutes later, they were under fire from German planes. Shells were exploding around them, and the driver was turning sharply around hills and fields, trying to avoid being hit. Their lorry was shaking so hard, they thought they would be sick. Finally, a bomb blew up in front of them; the lorry was thrown up in the air and stopped.

Mishka ordered the Germans to get out of the lorry and ran to the driver. He was lying motionless on the steering wheel, blood flowing from his head. Mishka opened the door, wanting to pull the driver out, but his body tilted and fell noiselessly to the ground. He was dead. Mishka ordered the Germans to stand up and run to a ravine; they obeyed reluctantly . . . it wasn't easy to run with tied hands. They took cover in the ravine and waited until the end of the attack. The planes bombed the road and shot from machine guns for a little longer, but finally they were gone. All the survivors began to leave their hideouts. Mishka and Private Rjaboshtan ordered the Germans from their shelter. Mishka had watched the captured men closely and saw how hopefully they had looked at the planes.

'Bloody fascist swine! Did you see how they looked at the planes?' he asked Private Rjaboshtan.

'I hate them too, but an order is an order, and we have to take them in alive!' he answered.

They made the prisoners stand up and walk to army headquarters. Going in the same direction were hundreds of people, all trying to escape from the fascists. The captured men continued to walk with their hands tied by rope, so they couldn't render any resistance. When they arrived at the place where headquarters were supposed to be, they found that it had moved somewhere else, and Mishka had to take the Germans further from the front line. During this retreat, Mishka was constantly thinking about his family, and quite often the horrible thought crossed his mind that maybe one of these captured soldiers had shot his family, and then his hands searched for his gun.

All day long, they tried to find headquarters but couldn't find a single trace. They had completely run out of food and the tired bound Germans refused to go any further. They had to be pushed constantly. Nevertheless, night found them on the road, and they had to spend the night in a dilapidated hut. They were so tired that they were simply falling off their feet, but Mishka and Private Rjaboshtan had to take turns to sleep because they couldn't leave the Germans unguarded. The Germans slept next to a wall and destroyed oven, but Mishka and Vasily settled down near the exit from the hut. Rjaboshtan was the first to sleep, and they were supposed to change guard every two hours. Soon, everyone was sleeping like the dead, and only Mishka was walking, holding a machine gun, trying not to fall asleep. Sometimes he felt as though he was falling asleep, and he would go outside to get refreshed in the wind. The night was cold, and in the deep black sky, cold stars and a new moon were shining. After struggling for two long hours, Mishka began to wake Rjaboshtan, but it wasn't easy . . . he did not want to wake up. At last, he opened his eyes and looked at Mishka without any understanding. 'What do you want?' he asked.

'Stand up, Vasily, now it's your turn to be on duty.' Vasily reluctantly stood up, still rubbing his eyes like a small child.

Trying to get as much sleep as possible, Mishka lay down on his place and fell asleep straightaway. His sleep was deep but very disturbing. He dreamed his father and mother were calling to him. But when he tried to stretch his hands to them, Marcus, their neighbour, dressed in German uniform, kept getting between them. Then he saw Klara running with a small child across the field, being chased by Markus on a German tank. He woke with a bad feeling and saw Rjaboshtan sitting asleep with the machine gun in his hands. Right next to him, the Germans were quietly trying to undo their ropes. Mishka jumped to his feet, grabbed his machine gun, and screamed in German, 'Sit still, bastards!' They were frightened and froze.

Vasily woke up and pointed his gun at them too. 'What happened?' he asked.

'It happened that you fell asleep, and they nearly escaped!' Mishka answered him.

'No, I didn't fall asleep. I simply closed my eyes for a minute!' he tried to excuse himself.

They didn't have much time to set out on their way; the noise from the front line was so loud that it seemed to be chasing their heels. They hardly managed to get out on the road when the rumble of planes and explosions from bombs started again. They rushed under the trees for shelter, but this time there was a huge explosion and the sound of trees splintering. Mishka fell to the ground, covering his head with his hands. Then he heard two more explosions and then silence. He raised his head and looked around. The five captured soldiers were lying nearby, covered in soil, and what was once possible to call Private Rjaboshtan was lying further down. His body had been separated from his legs, and on his face was frozen a strange grimace as though he had seen something terrible. Mishka tried to raise him but understood that there was nothing he could do to help him. Mishka knelt down on his knees on the ground, holding his head in his hands. He sat that way for some time. At last, he turned to look at the Germans.

The prisoners sat on the ground, speaking about something, and it seemed that they were smiling. He didn't know anymore what to do with them, and he had no one to consult with. He knew he couldn't leave them there. He hated them so badly and couldn't forgive their smiles. He stood up, grabbed the machine gun, and went up to them. 'Stand up!' he screamed in German. They began to stand, but he continued. 'What are you laughing about? Hoping that you will get free? No, that will not happen! Who invited you here, and who gave you the right to kill us? Oh, how I hate you! Damn you, bastards!' He pointed the machine gun on them and began to shoot. All five fell to the ground, but he continued to shoot at their already motionless bodies, and even when the magazine was empty, his hands continued to shake. At last, he opened his hands, and the gun fell down. Mishka sat on the ground and began to sob. Now, he look at the blood-stained bodies with their already frozen faces, but on the other hand, he felt easier in his soul, and the need for revenge was gone. He stood up, put the machine gun on his back, and quickly and without looking back went to find the receding army.

In the morning, after breakfast, Jukan was sitting in his cell, waiting for when they would be sent to work in the fields. He heard a strange sound from the street; it was getting louder and louder, and Jukan couldn't understand what kind of motor would make that sound. The noise was then accompanied by a loud whistle and then an explosion of such force that Jukan thought his eardrums would burst. This explosion was followed by others; the chamber walls shivered, and Jukan hid behind a thick wall. Now he understood everything . . . the war had started, and the Germans were bombing the jail. The next explosion was so strong that he stopped thinking about anything, falling on the floor and expecting to die, but death avoided him. He lifted his head and saw that the room was full of dust and fallen plaster. The door was wide open, opened by the explosion in the corridor. He got up and left the room. Here, too, the air was full of dust, there were no security guards to be seen, and all the other doors were still closed. The bombardment continued, and Jukan began to go down the stairs. He didn't see anyone, neither on the second floor or the first floor. Then he ran out into the empty prison yard, crossed it, and walked down into a cellar. Here, in the dark shelter, all the guards were sitting, covering their heads with their hands. Jukan quietly sat down on the bench next to them and waited for the bombardment to end.

It ended as suddenly as it had started. Then the security guard who was sitting next to Jukan lifted his head and was surprised to see Jukan sitting next to him. 'What are you doing here?' he asked.

'I'm hiding from the bombardment,' Jukan said.

'Who let you out of your room?' the guard asked again.

'No one! The door was knocked out by the explosion,' Jukan explained. The other security guards were sitting quietly as though nothing was bothering them. They stayed in the shelter for a few more minutes, and only when all the noise had definitely stopped, they began to walk up the stairs. Nobody paid him any attention, but Jukan obediently trudged behind them, listening to what they were saying. And the conversation was that the war had started, but they hadn't yet had any instructions about what to do with the prisoners, and they had no idea. At last, Jukan decided to attract the attention of one of the guards.

'What am I supposed to do?' he asked.

'Go back to you room,' the guard told him and prepared to leave.

'But it has no door, it was blown out!' Jukan objected.

'I don't know what to do. Go to your room and stay there, even without a door,' the guard said and went into his office.

Jukan obediently went upstairs. Near all the bars, prisoners were crowded, asking him what was happening. 'The war has begun, and nobody knows what to do,' he explained to them.

For quite a long time, Jukan's position in the prison was strange. Recently the coronation of the new king had taken place, and in its honour, the amnesty had been introduced. Jukan was included in this amnesty and only waited for the official paperwork. War had changed all these plans. Inside the prison, it was complete anarchy, and there was no sign of any security guards. The following day, the prisoners were all fed just once, and this meal was more like a pig slop. By evening, it was clear that most of the security guards had run away. The next morning, the prisoners were woken by an unfamiliar and terrible noise. Jukan climbed onto the window; he was no longer afraid of being punished for that. Here from the third floor, he could see all the street, and the first thing he saw was the enormous, heavy tanks crunching their tracks on the road. He couldn't see any people on the street, but suddenly, from the corner of a house, a handsome Royal Army officer stepped out, a sabre in his hand. He proudly straightened himself and bravely walked to the enormous tank. The tank crew did not expect this surprise. The officer extended his hand with the sabre, like a toreador, and stopped, ready to give a resolute blow. But the blow did not come; the machine gun fire from the tank almost cut the officer in half, and his lifeless body fell on the road. The tank got under way again, going around the shapeless blood-stained body, and slowly continued on its way. Jukan was frozen by this shocking scene!

The remaining security guards let all the prisoners with German origins out of their rooms and began to operate with their help. Now, nobody went out for exercise, and nor was food distributed. When night came, there was still order in the prison, but by morning, everyone was demanding to be let out of their cells. The noise was so loud that it was impossible to hear anything. At last, one security guard came, demanded silence, and began to deliver a speech in a loud voice. He explained that he could let them all out, but then they would be officially considered as runaways from the prison, and then they could all be punished. He promised that within a few days, all of them would get the right documents and then they would be able to go home. Everyone came to the conclusion that this would be the best way and agreed to wait. But now, they were taken from single rooms and locked up in groups. There was practically no more order, and almost everyone played cards. No one knew where the money and alcohol came from, but the games became more and more serious. Some were winning, some losing, someone was accused of cheating. Fight broke out, and at last someone pulled out a knife. That night, there were two murders, and Jukan decided that he had to leave this place.

Jukan organised a group of young men who had been released under the amnesty, and they began to plan their escape. There were no more security guards inside the jail; they were behind bars with barbed wire, protecting the exits from the jail. Whether the prison was protected from the outside, no one knew. They needed to check this out. All the next day, they tried to find ropes and to make metal hooks. At the same time, Jukan organised with one of the guards and got handwritten documents saying that they were released by the amnesty. Now, he and his companions kept in their group; they didn't want to be attacked by any of the groups of angry criminals who now ruled the jail. But no one tried to attack Jukan; they all knew that he had committed murder. The card games continued, and from time to time, fights broke out, so Jukan and his friends decided not to wait any longer. All day long, two of the most skilled thieves were making a master key from the room, and others tried not to attract attention to what they were doing.

As soon as it got dark, they opened the door, got out into the courtyard, and hid in a dark corner. Here, they took out the ropes and hooks and began to throw them up onto the wall. They managed to get just one of the hooks to grab the top of the wall, and while his friends tried to fix two more ropes, Jukan began to clamber up the wall. When he reached the top, he was blocked by barbed wire. For this, Jukan had cutters, and holding the wall with one hand, he tried to cut the wire. At last, with a huge effort, he managed to do this. Now, a couple of his friends had also managed to climb onto the wall, and Jukan began to climb down the wall on the other rope. Here, he looked around, couldn't see any security guards, and gave the signal to the others. In a few minutes, everyone was on the other side of the wall, and they slowly walked through the kitchen gardens, making their way to the forest. Most of them had worked in the kitchen gardens before and were familiar with the landscape. It seemed that no one had noticed their escape and most likely would only discover it the next morning. So when they got to the forest, they decided to have a rest and think about what to do next.

The group decided to walk together to a town called Jaice, and then everyone would walk home by themselves. For safety, they walked only at night and would sleep and rest in the afternoon. The biggest problem was that no one knew which road to take, and they randomly chose to go in the direction of Travnik. None of them could swim, so even the smallest river was for them an insuperable barrier, and they could only cross at bridges. But every bridge was guarded, and their documents were checked, and seventeen young men of conscription age caused special suspicion. They were arrested the next morning when they crossed a bridge next to a village where Croats and Muslims lived. The local police didn't understand the situation yet and were acting more on intuition. When Jukan showed them his documents, confirming that they had been released from prison, the policeman calmed down, gave them a pack of cigarettes, and released them. They were arrested the next evening in Travnik and were kept in prison most of the next day.

It was difficult to move and remain unnoticed in such a big group, and they decided to break up. Four people from Serbia separated from them and continued on their own. They didn't have any food but had money. If they were passing a Muslim village, they would send a Muslim in to buy food, and if it was a Serbian village, they would send a Serb. But sometimes even that didn't help, and they were arrested again. In Predor, they were kept under arrest for two days and then were released again. Now they all went their separate ways. Jukan had only Nusred from Bosanki Petrovats with him. They never got lost because they knew the area so well.

The last time they got arrested, in Crupa, where the police were particularly aggressive and wanted to send them to Germany for labour. But even here, good luck was with Jukan. Unexpectedly, a tall and very handsome Italian officer walked into the room. He went up to the policeman and began to talk, but suddenly he caught sight of Jukan behind the bars of the cell. He slowly walked up to the bars and said, 'Are you Jukan Vignevich by any chance?'

'Yes, I am,' confirmed Jukan. 'Where do you know me from?'

'So you don't remember me, but I stopped many times at your house, selling wine to your grandfather.'

Jukan looked more carefully, and really this man was similar to that Italian, just the uniform changed his appearance. 'I haven't been home for a long time,' Jukan said.

'Where have you been, and how did you get here?' the Italian wanted to know.

'I was in jail when the war broke out and was released to go home. But these policemen arrested us and want to send us to Germany.' He pointed to the police.

'Wait, I will talk to them,' said the Italian and went to one of the policeman and took him outside. They were back in a few minutes.

The policeman came to the room, opened the door, and called Jukan. 'You can go. Just because this man knows you. We release you under his responsibility.'

Jukan thanked the policeman and went out with the Italian officer.

'Where will you go now?' he asked Jukan.

'Definitely home!' Jukan answered him.

'It is not so simple. It's not safe to be a Serb at the moment. You should avoid any contact with Croats and Germans. Don't walk on roads, only through the forests. Now we will go to the shop. I want to buy some tobacco for your grandfather. Tell him I remember him well. With God's help, the war will end soon, and we will meet again at your house.' After that, they came to a kafana, which was located on the very edge of the city. Here, they drank coffee, and Jukan had a slice of pita. They sat on the veranda from where they had a good view of the river, but the descent to it was very steep. 'From here, we will go in different directions; I will go back to the city, and you will jump from the veranda and run down to the river and walk through the forest.'

'What do you mean?' Jukan objected. 'Here, it would be very easy to break my leg, and I can't swim!'

'I told you what you will do, there will be no more discussion!' the Italian said. 'Stand up and go!'

Jukan reluctantly stood up, stepped over the handrail, jumped down, and ran to the river. But in his head, there was just one thought, *Will he really shoot?* But there was no shot, and he successfully got to the river and entered the forest.

Now it was clear that the Germans had already passed through Bosnia, and there was no sign of them in the small cities and towns. But now there appeared the Ustachi, who were German allies and some Muslims who were supporting them. They hated Serbs and their kingdom and now were using any way to get revenge. The life of every Serb was in danger. On the seventh day, Jukan arrived in Begovats. Here, there were really only Serbs, so there was no one to be afraid of. Radko, the owner of a local kafana, was very pleased to see Jukan. He gave him food and offered a horse and cart, but Jukan refused, explaining that it was not safe to travel on the roads. At an exit from the village, he met a peasant who was carrying a few guns on his shoulder.

'Where are you taking them?' Jukan asked.

'To the police station,' the peasant answered.

'What for?' Jukan wanted to know.

'What you don't know is that there was an order to hand over all weapons that are in the houses to be destroyed!' the peasant explained.

'And aren't you sorry to be handing them over?' Jukan asked.

'Yes, I feel sorry, but what can you do? They can shoot you for having a weapon!'

'Well, at least give me this carbine?' Jukan asked. 'It's a pity to demolish such a beauty. Where did you get so many of them?'

'When our Royal Amy retreated, they abandoned everything, even the machine guns,' the peasant answered.

'Pity I wasn't there. I would definitely have picked up a machine gun,' Jukan sounded disappointed.

'All right,' agreed the peasant and gave Jukan the carbine. Jukan hung it over his shoulder and continued on his way home, feeling much more confident.

The day was warm and sunny. The May sun was burning now like in summer, and Jukan was sweating. Finally, he climbed the last hill, and right there before him was the most treasured landscape . . . he was just above the Maniat's house, the Mandich house was on his right, and his own Vignevich house was visible on his left. His heart tightened in his chest, and he quickened his pace. He couldn't see anyone at first, but as he got closer to the fence, he saw his mother running out to meet him. They embraced for a long time, not noticing that other people had come out, everyone except grandfather. Then it was time to greet his father. Like real men, they shook hands and then embraced. Then all the others, everyone came to greet him. By the way they behaved towards him, it was clear that they considered him now a real man, and Rade and Mirko looked away when he spoke to them. Then they went into the house where Grandfather was sitting proudly and alone. Everyone stopped at the doorway, but with a gesture, Grandfather called Jukan to the table. Jukan went closer a little hesitantly.

'Here you have returned, my grandson? This time, not like the last with a collar around your neck, but now with a carbine over your shoulder,' Grandfather said bitterly.

'But look what is happening around. It's time to stand up for ourselves,' Jukan tried to justify himself.

'Not only is your head too hot, you always act first and think later. Because of that, you are always in trouble and bring trouble into our house,' Grandfather said.

'What can I do if it is true?' Jukan asked.

'Yes, it is difficult to say what to do. Unfortunately, it seems that in our family, blood runs so hot that from any injustice, we light up like matches. But it's fine. Take off the carbine and let's sit down and eat.'

'Wait, Grandfather, I brought a gift for you from your Italian friend who sold us wine. He rescued me from the police in Kupinovo and from being sent to Germany to work. He sent this tobacco in gratitude for your friendship,' Jukan said, giving Grandfather the tobacco.

'Well, let's start from that,' said Grandfather. 'It seems that you have learnt how to bring gifts and pleasant news as well!' At these words, everyone burst out laughing and began to take their seats around the table. At first, they asked about life in prison and then how he managed to get home. Then they began to discuss what they needed to do now, and at that point, opinions were divided. Grandfather and Grandmother said it was necessary to do what the authorities ordered; Jukan, Mirko, and Rade suggested not to obey, but the middle generation wasn't sure what to do.

Next day, Jukan visited some neighbours to talk to the young men. Altogether he counted about thirty of them, and when they were all gathered together, he felt a lot more confident. Almost all of them had guns and were not going to submit to anyone. There were rumours reaching Lipa that the Germans were arresting Serbs and simply shooting them, but people weren't sure what to believe. Jukan and his two close friends, Milovan and Sayo, decided to go down to Bihach and to find out what was really happening. They left early the next morning and went towards Ripach. As soon as they reached Ripachky Klanac, they met a thin Muslim dressed in a student's uniform walking in their direction.

'Boys, where are you going?' he asked.

'To Bihach, to find out what's happening,' Milovan said.

'You'd be better to ask me, and I will tell you,' the young man said.

'But we don't know who you are or whether we can trust you,' Jukan objected.

'I'm Ibragim Pashich, from Belaj. I was a student in Belgrade, but when the Germans took over, they offered me a place as a clerk in Bihach. But now I've run away, and I want to participate in the resistance,' he said.

'We also want to resist, but we don't know how to do it. That's why we wanted to look at what's happening in the city,' Jukan said.

'No, you don't have to go there. Everyone could see that you are Serbs, and you would be arrested and maybe even shot,' the young man said.

'Then what will we do?' asked Milovan.

'Go back to your village and tell everyone not to listen to the propaganda and not to go to the police station. Tell any men and boys older than ten to hide in the forest, but it would be even better if everyone left. People have to arm themselves. I still have a few places to visit, and then I will come to you. We have to make people stand up and act, not just in one village but all across Bosnia.'

'Well, we will do what you said and wait for you, but look, don't deceive us!' Jukan warned.

After that, they went in different directions, and when they got back home, they repeated to everyone what Ibragim had told them. Some believed the story; others didn't. People of the older generation still thought it was necessary to obey the authorities; Grandfather absolutely refused to leave his home. 'You do what you want. For me, it's not necessary to leave. I'm an old man, and they don't need me.'

All the young men decided that from this day they would not sleep at home. Only Rade and Mirko didn't want to go too far from the house and wanted to sleep in a small extension shelter. 'Are you crazy?' Jukan was indignant. 'They will find you there at once!'

'Who will look for us among the sheep?' they disagreed.

And then Jukan took the carbine from his shoulder and angrily said, 'If you won't come with us, believe me, I will shoot you!'

By evening, all the men had left the house, leaving only Grandfather, all the women, and the younger brother, Pepo. It was already the beginning of June, and to hide in the forest or in wood nut bushes or even in corn was very easy. The corn that year grew as tall as a man. Now would be the time to mow the grass, but the war had destroyed all the plans. Instead, all the men were hiding in the woods. But no time was wasted. The power was taken over by the older men who had served in the army before. They took away all the weapons from the young men, including Jukan's carbine, which he didn't want to give away.

'Why should I hand it over?' he asked indignantly.

'Because your head is too hot, and you don't have any military discipline. Because of your temper, everyone could suffer!' his father explained.

'Then give me back the pistol that my uncle gave me, otherwise I won't agree,' Jukan said.

Father looked into the bag and took out a package tied with rope. He undid the rope, and there inside lay a beautiful pistol, its metal sides shining. 'Take that, and give away your carbine,' Father said. Reluctantly, Jukan handed over the carbine, took the pistol in his hand, and gently stroked it. But with only a pistol, he didn't feel like a real fighter, so he snatched grandfather's old hunting gun.

Nobody knew what to do next, but just to be busy, they cleaned all the guns and made grenades. In every country house, there was always a stock of dynamite and gunpowder, which they used in stone quarries, but now they were being used to make bombs. They filled ceramic water pipes with dynamite, inserted a detonator, and connected cords. In a couple of days, they had a solid stock of grenades. Jukan's father was leading the older men, and the younger men were led by the fast and fearless Sayo Grbich. He was five years older than Jukan, the same age as Rade and Milovan. Though Jukan was younger, his stormy past and time spent in prison, as well as his well-known hot temper, put him level with them. He was also close to Milovanom because he was in love with Jukan's favourite cousin, Zorka, from the Mandich house.

The police came unexpectedly a few days later. It was early in the morning, just after sunrise. The police searched through all three houses and the small shed where Rade and Mirko had planned to hide. They didn't find anyone except Grandfather, the women, and Milan. Then they ordered Grandfather to dress and follow them. They also picked up the old men from the Zorich and Manjats houses. All the other men were hiding in the forest, trying to agree what to do next. Usually the women brought them dinner, but this day, Milka came much earlier and told them what had happened. Jukan's father was so shocked that he stood as though paralysed. Jukan grabbed a gun and shouted, 'Why are you just standing there?' and ran home, followed by Rade, Mirko, and Pepo.

They found no one at home except the women, who were crying, and then they ran on to Begovats. On the way, they met an old friend of Father's, who told Jukan there was no point in running as the police had already taken all the arrested men to Bihach. Jukan understood that there was no point in keeping going and decided to go back.

Near the house, his friends were waiting for him. 'Well, what's the news?' they asked.

'They've been transported away to Bihach,' he answered.

'What bastards!' someone said. 'How long can we tolerate this?'

'I think we've had enough! We have to attack the police station, disarm the police, and burn down the barracks so that they don't have a place here,' proposed Jukan, and everyone supported him with joyful shouts.

But this time, Jukan's father interrupted the conversation. 'Nothing should be done with a hot head. Perhaps tomorrow they will let them go and everything will calm down again. We need to send someone to find out what is actually happening,' he said, and the older men went to have another meeting.

A soon as they had gone, the younger men had their own meeting. Sayo took the initiative. 'We will never get to do anything with them. Let them discuss it, and we will act on our own!' Almost everyone supported him, and they began to gather quickly. Now they were not hiding anymore and were ready to fight back against anybody. The blood pounded through their veins, and sometimes someone shot into the air. They almost ran, with Jukan and Milovanom right in front.

Begovats was silent, even around the police station. They lay down on the ground and began to shoot at windows, but no one shot back at them. Then they gave a few grenades to Rade, who was the strongest, and he began to throw them at the station. After the explosions, they lifted their heads and saw that one of the walls had fallen in. After a few more shots, they ceased to fire and carefully went into the building. Jukan glanced through one of the broken windows and saw nobody inside. The door wasn't closed, and they carefully entered. There were no people, just a dreadful mess. It was clear that the police had left in a panic, leaving behind papers and empty boxes.

'Bastards, they've already left!' said Milovan and spat on the floor.

'Let's burn this station down and destroy their spirit,' Jukan proposed and pulled out matches. He collected all the papers, put them in a heap, and put a chair and some wooden boxes on top. Then he struck the match and set fire to the papers. The flames caught and quickly grew bigger. The boys walked out the door and took a seat not far away from where they could watch how the fire destroyed the barracks. At first, it burnt slowly, but soon the roof began to smoke and the fire broke through. Then the boys were surprisingly cheerful watching this, and now they knew there was no way back. Their excitement was so great that they burnt two small beer places across the road where the police often spent their free time. Then they went back into the forest in a cheerful mood and saw Jukan's father and the other men coming out towards them.

'Where are you going now?' Sayo asked them.

'We've decided to attack the police station,' they answered.

'You can talk even longer now,' Sayo told them bitterly. 'There's no more police station, only ashes.'

'Why did you leave without telling us anything? We must have discipline!' Mile said angrily.

'If we wait for you, we would never dare to do anything. You can think about your homes and families, but we are young and have nothing to lose. We will do whatever we decide!' Sayo answered.

Every day, more and more people were coming into the forest. In all the neighbouring villages, the people had driven out all the police and were getting ready for resistance. But in the cities, Ustachi began to get organised, and a new army was created named Domobran. They began to arrest Serbs and kill them. Stories about it were reaching Lipa now too. One morning, they brought Jukan's small cousin Kosa from Petrovats. Her parents had managed to send her to the village, but Uncle Toma and his wife were arrested the next day and were shot. Any hopes that with time everything would get better finally disappeared. For everyone, it became clear that to survive it was necessary to take up arms.

By the end of June, there were almost no Germans in Bosnia. They were moving in long divisions to the east. Now the Ustachi and Domobran were dictating the rules. Muslims, too, became more active, and one day, Jukan and his friends spotted a group of men from Chukovo moving in the direction of Lipa. There were about 100 of them, and their intentions were obviously aggressive, but at the same time, it was clear that they were not very confident. They kept looking around, frightened. Though there were more of them, Jukan's friends could not allow them to attack their village. So Sayo suggested shooting at them, and despite the distance between them, they began to shoot. As soon as the Muslims heard the shooting, they stopped and looked around. Then Sayo ordered them to get closer and to shoot more accurately. After several more shots where the bullets landed much closer, the Muslims fell to the ground and started to crawl away. Then, after a short discussion, they decided to retreat, at first slowly, and then they began to run.

Every day, more people arrived. The more brutally the Ustachi behaved, the more people were moving to the forest. Now there were hundreds of them, and they began to divide themselves into divisions: each ten people made a branch, three branches a platoon, and four platoons made a 'cheta'. Milovan Pilipovich was nominated the commander of Jukan's branch, and Sayo Grbich became the commander of the first platoon. Each platoon was attached to several houses, which supplied them with food and drink. Military discipline was established, and the men who had already served in the army began to share their military arts with the young. But they were not doing just serious things in the forest . . . they found time to snack and drink and to play cards as well. They played cards now every day, and Jukan, having experience in jail, enjoyed his authority and won a lot. They played 'Ajnts'; the game wasn't difficult but required a good memory. It needed the players to take some risks and, most importantly, to trust your luck and, when you had it, not to let it get away. Soon, Jukan had so much money that he couldn't carry it anymore in his pockets. After a month, he hid the money in a pillowcase, and stories about his luck spread very quickly.

At the end of June, the news arrived that Hitler had attacked the Soviet Union.

Though the news was unpleasant, many thought that now Russia would destroy the fascist army and help free Yugoslavia. But news from the east was not good . . . the Soviet armies were retreating in panic, losing many, either killed or wounded. People trusted this news very little or simply didn't want to believe it. Meanwhile, the Ustachi ruled in the cities but so far had not shown up in the mountains and forests. But one morning, a young man ran to them, all the way from Vrtoch, and brought with him bad news that 600 Ustachi soldiers with newly recruited Domobran had arrived from Petrovats and that they had built a big camp next to a church and had plans to run fast attacks on the neighbouring villages.

Representatives from all the platoons gathered to decide what to do next. They couldn't afford to sit in the woods and wait for the Ustachi to begin to hunt for them or to clean out the villages. Now there were more than a thousand armed men, all of them in a fighting mood. Therefore, it was decided to attack the camp the next night. They spent the rest of the day discussing their plan of attack, and as darkness approached, they started to move to Vrtoch. They walked in silence; no one said a word, and no one noticed them. The camp was surrounded by a stone wall, but nobody guarded it. The Ustachi were so confident that they hadn't posted a guard. The campsite was beyond their expectations; here, there were obviously more than 600 people, but the platoons did not change their plans. Each platoon knew their task and silently began to take their positions. Everybody waited for the agreed signal, and although they knew the operation was dangerous, no one showed any fear. At last, Sayo raised his hand, and they prepared for the attack. 'Fire!' Sayo screamed, and grenades and home-made bombs flew towards the camp. Explosions roared non-stop! The tents quickly caught fire, and the silhouettes of half-naked soldiers could be seen running out. Fire from every kind of gun opened up.

The camp was in complete panic, and they didn't put up any resistance. Jukan was shooting at the panicking figures and felt no pity for any of them. He was paying back for his grandfather, for Uncle Toma and his family, for all those who had been taken away and shot. The battle didn't last long and gradually stopped. Some Ustachi managed to hide in the church and were shooting from there. But they couldn't put up resistance for too long. The church was showered with grenades, and then, having crept closer, they began to throw grenades in through the broken windows. At last, the church began to burn, and heavy smoke began to appear through the roof. Two soldiers managed to crawl out, stood up, and raised their hands. 'Don't shoot, we surrender!' one of them cried out, but it didn't save him! A few shots rang out, and the two fell to the ground.

Everything was finished very quickly. The camp had been turned into a cemetery. Bodies covered in blood were lying around, and there were terrible groans from the wounded. Now the time came to collect trophies and to count the dead. It came out that there were a lot more of them than they expected . . . more than a thousand men. It turned out that in the evening, their camp was reinforced with an extra 400 men. Now they were all lying here together. They had been going to introduce new order in Krajina, but now they were all lying on the ground in crooked poses, and none of them were going anywhere in a hurry anymore. The night attack had taken them by surprise. All kinds of weapons were now lying around the camp: carbines, pistols, cartridges, grenades, mines, and even machine guns, and all of them almost new. From that day, Jukan and his friends weren't short of guns anymore.

From the first day of the occupation in Odessa, the arrests had begun. All Jews had to be registered. Tanja Klyanchkina was now Tanja Pencheva, married to a Bulgarian, and because Bulgaria was a German ally, nobody touched them. She tried not to go outdoors, even to walk with her child and husband, Shurik. Tanja's mother-in-law became very irritable and shouted at Tanja all the time. One day in late autumn, someone quietly knocked on their window. Tanja put a scarf over her head and went outside. At first, she couldn't see anyone and was turning to go back inside when she heard a quiet female voice. She turned around, and there in front of her was a dirty beggar.

'Who are you looking for?' Tanja asked.

'Tanja, don't you recognise me? It's your sister, Zina.'

Then Tanja looked more closely, and she only recognised her sister by her eyes, which were shining with fear. 'What happened to you, Zinochka?' Tanja hugged her frightened sister.

Zina began to shake, and tears streamed down her face. 'Tanja, they killed all of them!' Zina sobbed.

'What do you mean "all"? Calm down and speak more slowly,' Tanja said.

'They shot all of us, in the park, me, our father, and all of our neighbours. They lie there, near the bog . . .'

Tanja examined Zina and now could see that her clothes were covered in soil and blood, and she understood that Zina was telling the truth. 'How did you manage to escape?' she wanted to know.

'I don't know. They lined us up near a big hole and started to shoot, and when people began to fall, I fainted and fell into this grave as well. I came to myself only to hear that they were shooting the wounded, so I tried not to breathe. Then they began to cover us with soil. I was lying near the top, and they covered me just a little. It seemed that they were in a hurry, and it was getting very dark. When they left, I was able to dig my way out and to come here. Please save me, Tanjusha.' And her body began to shake with crying.

'Zina, keep it quiet. We don't need to be seen by my mother-in-law. She hardly tolerates me. Go quickly and hide in the shed. I will bring you some clean clothes.'

But Zina couldn't be quiet. 'I can't understand why they hate us. What have we done to them? They praise Moses but damn us, his children. How could they love Christ and hate us, the people who brought him to this world?'

'It's hard to explain,' interrupted Tanja, 'but now we don't have time for that,' and she left Zina in the shed and ran into the house.

Shurik was sitting on the bed, an angry look on his face. 'Where have you been?' he asked.

'Shurik, Zina has come. She is in a terrible state. She says that the Germans were shooting them. Can you imagine, they killed my father!' Tanja said.

'Well, and what are you going to do?' he asked her.

'She is covered in blood; I will take her some clean clothes,' Tanja explained.

'Tanja, she can't stay here with us. She will definitely get us into trouble,' Shurik said.

'If that is so, then I will leave with her,' Tanja answered him.

'How can you say that? We have a son, have you thought of him?' he asked.

'I can't leave her in this state!' Tanja said.

Shurik clutched his head and began to think. At last, he came up with a suggestion. 'All right, let her stay here for the night. Tomorrow, I will take her away to the catacombs, where she could hide.'

The rest of that night, Tanja didn't sleep at all. She took clothes and a blanket to Zina. Tanja had to undress her because Zina was in such a dreadful state. Then Tanja put a blanket down on the floor and made a bed. As soon as Zina lay down, her eyes closed, and she fell into unconsciousness.

The next day, the weather was dreadful; from early morning, cold rain fell non-stop, and the streets were almost deserted. It suited them, though, and helped them to get to the sea cliffs without being noticed and without any problems. They walked down the slope by a slippery but firm footpath and then stopped.

'Well, here we are, we've come to the place,' Shurik told Zina.

'Where are we?' Zina asked.

Shurik stepped behind a tree and slipped between two thick bushes. 'Follow me,' Shurik called, and Zina followed him. Here, she saw how he climbed through a small hole and indicated that she should follow him. She climbed through and found herself in complete darkness. 'Wait, I will light a candle,' Shurik said and then struck a match and lit a candle.

Zina looked around and saw that they were in a stone grotto the size of a small room. 'Where are we?' she asked.

'At the entrance to the catacombs, only it's filled with rocks,' Shurik said.

'And I should live here, on my own?' Zina asked, her voice filled with fear.

'We don't have any other choice,' Shurik explained. 'You can't stay with us at home. If they find you, we are all finished. So you have to live here for the time being.'

'But what if they find me here?' Zina asked.

'No one will find you here. Only two people know about this cave, me and my school friend Grisha. But now he is not here, he is at war on the front line. This cave is our greatest secret. Look what we have here!' he said and proudly showed her a wooden box in a corner. In it were two small pillows and a blanket.

'How can I sleep here? I'm sure there will be a lot of rats!' Zina complained.

'I don't know, I've never seen any. But, even if there are, you have no other choice. You have to stay here until we find another solution. I will leave you a few candles and some food. Tomorrow, I will bring you some more. I'll whistle as I approach. It's better that you don't go out during the day unless to hide in the bushes, but you could go out carefully at night.' After giving her these instructions, Shurik said goodbye and went home, where he expected an unpleasant conversation with his mother.

His mother sat at the table, a stern look on her face. 'Shurik, I have to talk to you,' she began.

'What about, Mother?' he asked.

'Who was here last night?' she asked him.

'I don't know,' he lied.

'Don't lie! I know perfectly well that Tanja's sister was here yesterday. I simply didn't want to get involved. But remember, she is a Jew, and those that hide Jews could be shot. Tanja is a Jew too, but she is your wife; her Jewish sister is not supposed to cross our doorway anymore.'

Shurik could do nothing but swallow this bitter pill, but relationships in the house changed for the worst. Every day, Tanja's mother-in-law got more and more angry, often swearing at Tanja. She constantly repeated that one day all of them would be killed because of Tanja. Tanja tried not to leave her room at all, even to walk with her little Zenya. But then she was accused of doing nothing at home. Eventually, she declared to Shurik that if Tanja didn't leave the house, she would tell the police. Shurik responded that if Tanja was leaving the house, he would leave too, and that if she were to die, he would die too. These answers made his mother quiet for a while, but not for long.

The next show of interest in Tanja came from a proud Ukrainian neighbour whose husband had been subjected to suppression some years before the war. She began to ask where Tanja was and whether she was afraid to leave the house because of her nationality. After that conversation, Shurik's mother came home in fear and panic and immediately began her attack. 'No, I can't live anymore under this stress. I've just met our neighbour, and she was asking me about Tanja. This bitch will report us to the police as revenge for her husband. Listen, Tanja, do you really want to ruin all our lives, even the life of your small son?'

'What do you want me to do?' Tanja asked her.

'Simply go somewhere and hide! We will look after your son, Zenya. I beg you!' she said.

'Mother, please be silent,' Shurik began, but Tanja stopped him.

'No, it can't go on like this any longer. I will leave tomorrow,' Tanja said and went to her room.

Shurik rushed after her. 'Where will you go?' he asked.

'You will take me to be with Zina,' she said.

'How will the two of you live together in that small cave? Winter is coming,' he said.

'We will manage somehow. I don't want to expose you and Zenya to any more danger.'

All evening, they discussed plans, and Shurik decided to try to make contact with people from the Odessa catacombs. Early next morning, they left the house, taking with them some food and warm clothes. The streets were still empty, so they arrived at the cliff side unnoticed. Carefully they crept to the cave entrance. Here, Shurik whistled twice as was his agreement with Zina, and they squeezed inside. It was dark in the cave.

'Zina, where are you?' he whispered.

'Shurik, you are not alone?' They heard Zina's voice.

'I came with Tanja,' he answered and struck a match to light the candle. The two sisters saw one another and hugged each other. From then on, Tanja and Zina lived like rats, sitting practically all the time in the dark cave, and though their eyes got used to the gloom, to be there like that was real torture. So, late in the afternoons, they crept out of the shelter to look at the sunshine and to get some fresh air. Shurik visited them every other day, pretending to be going fishing. He brought them not only food, water, and candles but also the bad news that the Red Army was retreating further back under the blows of the fascist army. At night, the sisters were confident enough to take small walks and to sleep more in the day.

With time, Tanja began to miss her son, Zenya, so much so that she dared to get closer to home and watch him walking with his grandmother. During one of these visits, she was stopped by the police. 'Stop, don't move! Where are you going?' shouted the senior policeman.

'Are you talking to me?' Tanja asked in a surprised tone, trying not to show how frightened she was.

'Of course, you! Where are you going? Show your documents!' he demanded.

'I have no documents with me. I'm simply going to the buy milk for my child,' she said.

'She is lying, and it seems to me that she is Jewish,' the younger police officer interrupted.

'I'm not Jewish but Russian, and my husband is Bulgarian,' she lied.

The older policeman looked at her carefully and said, 'Well, if you are Russian, cross yourself and say a prayer!'

Tanja was confused for a second but then crossed herself and began to pray. 'My God . . .' She began uncertainly, but at this time, it seemed that someone from above began to prompt her, and she was just repeating the words . . . 'Amen.'

She was finished, and the policeman smiled at her and said, 'All right, you can go!'

She turned and began to walk away, but her feet barely obeyed her as though they were made of lead. At last, she turned the corner and began to feel better. Only now did she realise what had happened. How could she have said a prayer? She had never known one, and no one had ever taught her. She had only been in a church once, to attend a wedding ceremony. This had been a miracle, and it shook her. From this point on, she absolutely was certain that God existed and that he was watching over her. This made her feel warmer in her heart, and everything that had lost its meaning became important to her again. It was now clear to her that with divine help, she could endure all the hardships that had befallen her.

Part 5

Klara woke up early to feed Dima and then went to the office. Drozdov was coming, and she didn't want to be late. She went outside and was struck by the cold. A freezing wind blew through her; she rolled up her scarf and ran to the office. Drozdov wasn't there yet, but in the room, Makarov was looking grim. 'Damn! The freezing weather has arrived, the cowsheds are cold, and we have no more forage left! How we will get through the winter, God only knows. If the cattle start to die, we will be punished. Now the country needs food more than ever.'

Just then, the door opened, and Drozdov came in. He looked at Klara and smiled. 'Well, are you used to it here now?' he asked.

'We are very well, and it is all thanks to you,' she said.

Drozdov looked at her carefully and said, 'Look how you are dressed! There's a frost outside and you are dressed in just light shoes and a scarf. And what do you think about this, Makarov? Your employee could die of cold!'

'What am I supposed to do? I don't have any clothes here!' he said.

'I don't care where you find them, but make sure that by tomorrow she has felt boots and a short fur coat. Break your neck, but make sure you get them. Do you understand me?' Drozdov answered.

'Well, and if I don't find them?' Makarov asked.

'Then you will give her your own' was the reply.

'Yes, I understand, Comrade Director!' Makarov muttered and left. Klara and Drozdov began to sort out the documents.

Makarov came back a few hours later, bearing in his arms a sheepskin coat and felt boots. With a wry smile, he threw them on the table. 'There, you see, you found them, and you were telling us that you don't have any,' smiled Drozdov. 'Try them on, Klara!'

'What's the point of talking with you when you don't listen?' responded Makarov, waving his hands desperately.

Klara took the felt boots in her hands and saw that one of them was white and the other black. 'Why are they different colours?' She was surprised.

'Because there were no others left,' he said.

Klara took off her shoes and put on the felt boots. The left one went on very easily, but the right one was more difficult. And then she made another discovery. 'They are both for the left foot!' she exclaimed.

'I told you that's all we have, so you will just have to wear them like that!' Makarov said.

Klara looked at Drozdov, but he just shrugged his shoulders. She put on both the boots, got to her feet, and although it was difficult to walk, she felt much warmer. Then Klara tried on the sheepskin coat. It wasn't new and was very heavy, but she put it one and did up all the buttons. Drozdov and Makarov looked at her and burst out laughing. 'That's it! Now you look like a real milkmaid. Now you are just the same as us!' Really, she did look awful, but she was warm.

With her black and white boots, she was easily recognised by all the collective farm workers; they could spot her from a distance and used to say, 'There goes our accountant!'

Once a week, Klara had to report to Drozdov, and for this purpose, a tilt cart with a horse was given to her, and in the winter, she was given a sled. The farm had practically run out of food, and so the horse could barely shuffle its feet. Sometimes the horse just refused to go, and then Klara was supposed to use a whip. When winter arrived and the steppe was covered in deep snow, the road to the industrial complex was much more dangerous. On the way, not only was it possible to get stuck but also there were hungry wolves in the area, and their howls made Klara's blood turn to ice. Usually, she travelled to the centre with Makarov, and he drove the horse. One day, he had too much to do and told Klara that she should go alone. 'How can I do it, I can't even drive a horse!' she begged.

'You don't need to know anything; the horse knows the road, and she will take you. Sometimes, if the horse is obstinate, you have to hit it with the whip and shout, "Ach!" and she will run.' As proof, he lightly hit the horse with the whip, shouted 'Ach!' and the horse got under way. He gave the whip back to Klara and went into the office.

Klara followed all the instructions, and the horse unwillingly moved forward. The horse knew the road home well but was hardly moving its feet. They had gone a few kilometres when snow began to fall. The wind was blowing into her face, and the horse began to walk more and more slowly and then completely refused to move and lay down in the snow. Klara grabbed the whip and began to wave it and at the same time was calling out, 'Ach!' However, the horse didn't pay any attention to her. Then Klara started to hit her harder, but she didn't get any results. Then she sat down and started to cry!

Unexpectedly, Klara heard a noise and raised her head. About 200 metres away was a cart with two people on it. She got to her feet and cried loudly, 'Help!' The cart turned and started to move in her direction. When it got level with her, the driver stopped the cart, and the two young men, mechanics from a neighbouring farm, jumped down.

'Why are you screaming?' the taller one asked.

'Dear boys, please help me. This useless horse refuses to move. I will freeze or be eaten by wolves,' she answered him.

'Give me the whip,' the second mechanic said. He took the whip and raised his hand. The horse didn't wait to find out what happened next and rose at once. 'She will not stop anymore,' he promised her. Klara again sat down in the cart, and the horse began to move. The mechanics took their places in their own cart and started off in the opposite direction. But a minute later, the horse again lay down in the snow and refused to move.

Klara jumped off the cart and ran after the others. 'Please, boys, don't leave me alone. The horse again refuses to move!'

The cart turned and came back. 'Well, what will we do with you?' the tall mechanic asked her.

'Please take me home!' she begged.

'Yes, but then we have to make a two-kilometre loop,' he said.

'Don't leave me here alone; I will definitely die here,' she cried.

'What should we do, Seryoga?' the other mechanic asked.

'We probably have to take this accountant back home,' Seryoga said and sat with Klara in her tilt cart.

As soon as he raised the whip, the horse began to walk, and the second cart followed them. Without any further mishaps, they arrived at the farm, and Klara arrived home. She invited them in for some tea, but it was getting dark, and they hurried home.

The next morning, everything was covered in snow so deep that it was difficult to get to work. So winter had arrived, but Klara wasn't afraid of it anymore. They had a warm corner and some winter clothes, but the most important thing was that they had something to eat. Every day on the farm, she was getting milk and sometimes butter. On the small amount of money she earned, they could buy bread, soap, and other necessities. Now they waited for spring and some good news from the front line. But the good news was still far away, and from her husband, there was no news at all. From her brother, Simeon, there would be no news anymore. Right after the war had started, he had been sent to the front line in a battalion recruited from criminals. He was fighting near Leningrad and lost his life. No one knew if he had been killed by a bullet facing the enemy or a shot in the back by the commissar. Nobody found his grave, and nobody was looking for it.

✦✦✦✦✦

Winter arrived early, and the snowfalls in Bosnia were like those in Siberia. It was difficult to move between settlements, and to get to Lipa from Bihach was almost impossible. In late autumn, the road through Ripachki Klanats had been blown up and mined by the Drvar 'cheta' under the command of the Royal Army officer Mane Rokvich. The enemy could now only come from the Petrovats direction, but there the roads were exposed to the fire of guerrillas too. Before in Bosnia, Serbs, Croats, and Muslims live happily together, but now all minority groups ran away from the settlements, and their houses were burnt. At first, only Croats attacked Serbs, but now rumours were going around that Muslims were burning down Serbian houses and Orthodox churches, and there were frequent cases of violence against Serbian women. In response, they didn't have long to wait; all 'jamijas' in the district were burnt, and Muslims had to run to Chukovo.

However, it wasn't always fighting. A lot of time was spent on gambling. Many of them played cards. Their circle was rather big, about twenty people played, and each of them had a nickname. Jukan's nickname was 'Chiko', Milovan was 'the peasant from Zagreb', though he had never been to Zagreb, and Sayo Grbich had the totally unexpected name of 'Stalin'! Jukan's prison experience gave him a significant advantage; his impudence and ability to take a risk at the right time influenced his opponents more than sorcery! Rumours about his luck spread quickly. They played for money and cigarettes, sometimes for food and alcohol, and sometime even for rings and watches. Jukan felt that good luck was always with him and seldom left him. Once, he played against a man called Lazo. He was ten years older than Jukan and had a wife and two children. Small but very pushy, Lazo was also famous for his own good luck, and this time they were facing each other in a game that each of them wanted to win at any cost.

At first, good luck smiled on Lazo, and he won some games. Jukan was hurt but didn't want to concede and continued to raise his stakes. The bank grew to a very serious size, and Lazo started to fidget in his seat. Jukan took another risk, and this time good luck smiled on him. 'Aints!' he declared and, throwing his cards on the table, began to collect his money.

Lazo's face got longer, and his eyes sparkled spitefully. 'I will double the bank,' he said.

Jukan thought for a while and then said, 'Why? It's already too big.'

'Are you scared?' Lazo teased.

'No, I'm not scared! Put your money on the table and deal the cards,' Jukan said.

Lazo put his hand in his pocket and brought out the necessary sum of money and put it on the table. But now it was clear that he had run out of money. Jukan put the same amount of money on the table. The crowd around them grew silent. Lazo handed Jukan two cards. Jukan looked at them and asked for one more. Lazo threw a card on the table; Jukan carefully looked at it, covering it from the spectators' eyes, and asked for one more. Jukan again looked at the card from the bottom, put them all on the table, and said, 'Deal for yourself!'

Lazo opened his cards; he had an eight and a seven. He maliciously spat on the floor and took one more card and smiled. It was a king. 'Nineteen is enough for me, what have you got?'

'Twenty!' answered Jukan and threw his cards down on the table. He began again to collect the money.

'Wait, we will still play!' protested Lazo.

'Do you still have any money?' Jukan asked.

'Let's play on credit. I will give you the money tomorrow,' Lazo said.

'No, I don't play on credit, especially cards,' Jukan refused, 'and especially because you have a wife and children!'

'No, you can't stop a game like that! You should give me a chance to recoup!' Lazo shouted and grabbed Jukan's hands.

'I agree to give you a chance, but you don't have any money!'

'All right, to hell with you. I put up my watch!' Lazo said, rolling up his sleeve and removing a beautiful watch. Jukan took it in his hands and listened to see how it worked. 'What are you looking for? It's a Swiss watch,' Lazo said. Indeed, it was an excellent watch, and Jukan agreed.

'All right, put it on the table!' Jukan agreed.

They again took their seats at the table, and the spectators grew quiet. With shaking hands, Lazo began to shuffle the cards and put the pack down in front of Jukan. The first card was seven and then two. He asked for a third, and it was a ten. He decided to stop. 'Enough, deal for yourself!'

Lazo turned the first card; it was a nine, the second one an eight. He became thoughtful, carefully looking at Jukan, but he gave an indifferent smile. Lazo rubbed his temples and hesitated and then dealt a third card. It was a six of spades! He threw the cards on the table and shouted, 'God damn it! Too much!'

'Then we are finished,' announced Jukan.

'No, let's play more!' Lazo begged.

'I told you, that's it,' he said and was ready to take his win, but at that moment, Lazo quickly grabbed the watch and put it in his mouth. His eyes were almost popping out.

'Put it back on the table,' Jukan warned, but Lazo only shook his head. Blood ran fast in Jukan's head. 'For the last time, I am warning you, put the watch back, or I don't know what I will do to you!' he repeated.

But Lazo wasn't prepared to give anything back and stood up in a defensive pose. Jukan grabbed him by the shoulder, and a fight began. Lazo wasn't able to put up much resistance, and in a few seconds, Jukan was on top of him. 'Spit out the watch!' but Lazo shook his head and tried to throw Jukan off. That made Jukan wild; he hit Lazo on the jaw. Lazo knocked his head against a wall and fainted. Jukan tapped him on the cheek, but there was no response. Then he opened Lazo's mouth and checked it with his finger, but surprisingly there was nothing there. 'He has swallowed the watch!' Jukan said to the surrounding witnesses and got to his feet. 'Never play with such bastards who don't keep their word!' He spat and went out through the door. But as it happens in cards, good luck does not last forever, and to hold on to it is a tricky business. And it seemed that Lazo had swallowed his good luck together with his watch. After that, Jukan's luck also went away, though no one could say he became a loser.

Guerrilla life was difficult. Most of the time they slept in hastily put together timber barracks where they slept together on the floor. Sometimes it was necessary to sleep in the open air. They didn't get food every day and often went hungry for a few days. The food they did get came from local homes, sometimes delivered by local peasants.

One day, Jukan and Milovan were invited to the house of one of his mother's friends from Gorvets. They were so happy with the offer that they totally forgot about precautions and went into the house without checking around. They had just started to eat when shells began to explode close to the house. It was the Ustachi, who had spotted the boys from the top of the road and had opened fire. The women began to wail and rushed out on the street, but Jukan and Milovan were so hungry that they couldn't leave the food on their plates. One of the shells exploded in the shed next to the house; the boys exchanged glances and continued laughing and pushing food into their mouths. The next shell hit the house, and dust fell from the roof. By this time, their mouths were full and the dishes were empty. They didn't have time to chew their food but rushed out of the house and took shelter behind a small hillock. Milovan had served in the army and knew how to move by crawling, but Jukan's bottom stuck out of their hiding place, and Milovan cursed God and ordered Jukan to lie down. 'Get closer to the ground and crawl after me,' he ordered.

Milovan crawled, holding his carbine in his hands in front of him. Jukan had his grandfather's heavy old gun and dragged it behind him on his belt. Unexpectedly, the trigger of the gun hit a stone and shot. The bullet narrowly missed Milovan's head.

'Are you losing your mind?' he shouted. 'You want to kill me?'

'I did it accidentally,' Jukan said.

'We will die here, or they will take us prisoners, which would be even worse. Let's run to the edge of the forest. Go!' screamed Milovan, and he jumped to his feet and ran. Jukan rushed after him. Traces of machine gun bullets followed them and sometimes nearly beat the dirt from under their shoes. They ran and continued to laugh loudly as if being so close to death amused them. They ran like hares, coming closer to the edge of the forest, and at last found the shelter of the trees. After running a few more steps, they stopped and look at each other. Yes, today they had managed to eat and laugh, but not die!

Not only the lack of food made life difficult, but also the absence of hygiene was an even bigger factor. They slept in groups entirely dressed. The lack of water made washing almost impossible. In these conditions, lice attacked them. At first, only a few people had them, but soon all of them were scratching. At last, they got to Jukan too. He tried everything, but nothing helped. Pimples covered his body, and he was scratching like a madman. One small cut on his foot, caused by a rusty nail, at first reddened and then got inflamed. Then the foot began to decay. He tried to disinfect it with rakija, but that didn't help. After a while, he noticed that his foot began to get thinner, and he began to limp. Now he asked to be shown to a doctor; they placed him in the hospital for the wounded and sick. The hospital was a big barracks in the forest where the patients lay on the floor.

But there was a doctor and some medicines. They disinfected his wound and put on bandages, but it didn't help. The foot continued to decay and decrease in size. The muscle dried up, and the skin wrinkled like that of an old man. It was impossible to move his foot.

On night, when everyone was sleeping, he heard a conversation between a doctor and a nurse. The doctor was whispering, 'I feel sorry for this man, Jukan. His foot is already in such a bad state that we can't help him. Lice have carried the infection all over his body!'

'What are you going to do?' the nurse asked.

'We have to amputate the leg tomorrow, otherwise we will lose him.'

The nurse was appalled. 'What a pity, he is such a young, handsome man, and he will become an invalid!'

The two of them passed by, but Jukan pretended to be sleeping. When the hospital was quiet, he collected his things and went outside. Here, behind the barracks, he quickly dressed and began to walk home, limping badly. On the way, he found a suitable stick, and with the help of his knife, he made himself a shtap. Now it was easier to walk, but to cover these few kilometres, he had to walk for the rest of the night and all the next day. When he got home, it was almost night-time, and as usually happened, the first person he met was his mother. She saw him limping and rushed to help.

'Oh, dear, what has happened to you, my son?'

'My foot has decayed, and the doctor wanted to amputate it,' he said and explained the situation.

'Oh, God! Please don't let us down!' She was terrified. 'Let's go into the house.'

Soon, all the household members were around them: Father, Rade, his wife, and Nana. They examined his foot and were horrified. Mother told them, 'We have to wash him and change his clothes, and you, Mile, go and bring back the old woman called Dara, whom everyone thinks of as a witch. She knows old secrets and can even drive out the devil. Do you remember where she lives?' Father nodded. 'So go right now!' she said with such a voice she had never used when speaking before to Father, but he just nodded and left.

While they boiled water in the largest pot, Jukan was given some food. Despite his weariness, he ate greedily, hardly even chewing the food. Then he took off his clothes and sat in a big barrel, and Mother began to pour the water from a bowl. An almost forgotten feeling of pleasure filled him while his mother washed his head, chest, and back. Then he himself washed his healthy foot, and Mother carefully washed his wound and disinfected it with rakija, while Jukan howled like a wolf! After that, he was given clothes that were so big, he almost sunk into them.

'Where are my clothes?' he asked.

'I gave them to Nana to burn . . . for now, wear Rade's clothes,' she said.

They put him on the bed in a very quiet corner of the house and left him alone. Here, weariness did its job, and he fell into a deep sleep. He regained consciousness when he heard a conversation next to him. He opened his eyes and saw in front of him the deeply wrinkled and furrowed face of an old woman. She was reading some spells over him, and behind her back, he could see his mother. The procedure didn't last long, and he couldn't understand any of it. But when she was finished, she addressed Jukan. 'It's a nasty infection in your body, and you have to kick it out. You were right not to let them chop your foot off. But now, you should pour your own urine over the leg!' Jukan's face showed his astonishment. 'Don't doubt it . . . nothing but your own urine will rescue you. Each time you need to pee, collect the urine and pour it over your foot. In a few weeks, you will see that the infection will go away. Do you understand me?' Jukan nodded, and the witch and his mother left the room.

Right after they left, Jukan collected his urine in the selected jar and began to pour it over the wound. The warm urine burnt his foot, but he put up with the pain. Right after that, he lay down on the bed and quickly fell back to sleep. He continued to do this a few times each day, and changes slowly started to show. At first, the colour of his foot changed and the inflammation cleared up. The skin began to regain its usual look. The itching ended, and the muscular weight began to increase. He stayed at home for two weeks, and in this time, his foot completely healed and he could walk almost without limping. Thanks to his mother, he got rid of the lice and got new clothes. But, unfortunately, it wasn't safe to stay at home, and soon he returned to the forest.

⋅✦✦✦✦✦⋅

It seemed that this terrible winter would never end. On the steppes, it was very difficult to hide from the cold wind. But humans can get used to almost everything, and Klara got used to the cold too. On the way to work, she wore her sheepskin coat and her multicoloured valenki, and in the evenings, they whiled away their time sitting next to the hot oven. Zelda tried to look after the house and little Dima. Her grandson bombarded her with questions, and she couldn't always answer him. Life was monotonous and boring, but who could complain when the country was fighting a terrible damned war? After long and frightening reports from the front line, when cities were left to the enemy, the Germans now seemed to be exhausted. And if before Zaharov had been constantly frightening Klara by saying that he would give all the Jews and communists to the Germans, causing her such constant fear, now he calmed down. But when unexpectedly, near Moscow, the Soviet Army hit back, Zaharov completely shut down. Now people began to hope for a fast victory. But soon again, the Germans started to push the Soviet Army to the Volga and the Caucasus. When winter was over and spring had begun, bad news from the front line again saddened their lives, and Zaharov again began to chase and threaten Klara. Again, she complained to Drozdov.

'Don't pay any attention to him,' he advised her. 'Sometimes I think I can understand him. Even though he was a "kulak", they were too cruel to him. He lost his wife and two children . . . after that, anyone would become embittered.'

By the end of March, the cold had receded, and the snow started to melt. The roads were like slush, and to get to the central village was very difficult. Klara finally got used to her position and coped with all her duties without any problems. Despite her youth, everybody respected her and even asked her for advice. Local Kazakhs were especially kind to her, because she often wrote letters to their sons on the front line. They quite often brought her presents and asked her to visit them in their homes.

One day, together with Drozdov, she went to another collective farm, where they invited her to the yurt of the farm director. In their honour, he had killed a young lamb and had prepared pilaff. It smelled so good that Klara's mouth filled with saliva. Drozdov and Klara took their places next to the owner, and the rest took their seat around. It was warm in the yurt, and they took off their winter clothes. They had to eat with their fingers from a big kazan. Klara had never eaten with her fingers before and looked around for a spoon or fork. Drozdov leant over to her and whispered in her ear, 'Stop your city manners! Do not offend people and eat like everyone else, with your fingers!' and he gave her such a hard stare that she stretched her hand to the kazan and took a pinch of pilaff. It was hot and very greasy. Klara took some and put it in her mouth, and the pilaff simply began to melt. She was about to take another pinch when she noticed the dirty hand of a boy who was trying to reach the pilaff. She looked at the others' hands, and they were not much cleaner, and her appetite disappeared.

Then the owner began a speech. 'Our accountant is an excellent woman. We love you very much, and today you are our honourable guest.' He rolled up his sleeve, baring a not-very-clean elbow, took from the kazan a big pinch of pilaff, and rolled it between his hand and his elbow. Then he moved it closer to Klara's mouth and said, 'Eat!'

She was completely shocked and was afraid that she would throw up at the very thought of having to eat it. She seemed to turn to stone. But then, Drozdov unexpectedly came to her rescue. He bent over and took the plov from the elbow of the owner and then turned it into a joke. 'Why do you offer everything to her? After all, I'm the boss, not her, and I'm your guest as well!'

The joke went over well, and everyone burst out laughing, even Klara. But she didn't want to stay much longer in this house to be offered something else again. She put her hand on her forehead, put a look of pain on her face, and said, 'Nikolay Ivanovich, I'm not feeling very well today. Can we go home? My head is spinning, and I feel as though I'm about to fall. I think I have a high temperature. Also, my son is sick, and my mother can't look after him properly.'

Drozdov hadn't had enough to eat and wasn't too happy about leaving but didn't object. 'Yes, certainly it's time to go. I have heaps of work to do in the office,' he agreed, and they began to put on their outside clothing.

When they got to the cart, Drozdov attacked Klara. 'Couldn't you control yourself somehow? This man invited us into his house, slaughtered a lamb, and prepared pilaff. He allows you to eat from his elbow, a sign of deep respect. And because you are squeamish, you nearly offended him.'

'I didn't want to offend him,' she objected, close to tears. 'I couldn't eat it, and I was scared even to look at it. I thought I would vomit right there in the middle of the yurt.'

'Well, it's fine now, calm down.' Drozdov changed his tone. 'I can understand you, but you have to remember that if you offend a person here, you can become an enemy for life!' Klara remembered this lesson well and never again visited anyone's home.

Before the snow had fallen, there remained almost no forage, and the cows had become skinny, and some of them had no strength at all. To help them stand on their legs, they were tied by ropes to the beams. They produced practically no milk, but the farm was still supposed to provide food for the front line. Drozdov and Makarov became so nervous that it was almost impossible to talk to them. But, by some miracle, they managed to survive. And with the coming of the new grass, they began to take the cows to the meadows. The pressure eased, and Klara began to pay more attention to her family. No news arrived from the front line, and she couldn't answer Dima's question, 'When will my father be coming back?'

One day, her new girlfriend Katja came running into the office very excited and rushed to tell Klara her important news. 'Klara, today we should go together!'

'Where to?' Klara asked.

'Yesterday, I was taken to a Kazakh, who was predicting the future by stones. You won't believe me, but he told me the complete truth!'

'Don't be silly, Katja. You are a city girl, and you still believe such nonsense?'

'You are silly yourself. Everyone has a destiny, and some people can read it. You don't know anything about your husband, but maybe he could tell you that.'

At first, Klara didn't trust her, but eventually curiosity got the better of her, and the next evening they went to visit what Klara thought of as the Kazakh charlatan. He lived on the edge of the village in his brother's yurt. As they approached the yurt, Klara remembered her last bitter experience and said, 'I don't want to go inside. You go and ask him if he could predict my future out here, and I will pay him.' Katja shrugged her shoulders and went in to negotiate. In a few minutes, she came back out, and behind her was the man.

When they came closer, Klara looked at the man's face and at once understood that he was not a charlatan. The Kazakh had a beautiful face, and his eyes were shining with something like a child's innocence. He carefully looked at her and then called them aside to where a small fire was burning. They took seats around the fire, and the Kazakh pulled some stones from his pocket and began to study them. Then he selected a few, put them in his hat, and asked Klara, 'About whom do you want a prediction?'

'My husband,' she replied.

'Then think about him,' the Kazakh told her. He shook the hat a few times and then threw the stones onto the ground. Then he started to carefully examine the pattern. At last, he lifted one stone and said, 'It looks bad!'

'What do you mean by bad?' Klara cried.

'I can't see him among the living, nor among the dead, but he will not return home,' he said quietly.

'I don't trust you; it can't be like that!'

She continued to cry, but he looked at her indifferently and asked, 'Do you want me to continue or not?'

Katja touched Klara's hand, and she calmed down. 'Please continue,' she said.

'You have one son, and with him, you will survive the war.' Klara breathed deeply with relief. 'You'll meet another man, not from this country, and with him you will have two more children. You will do a lot of travelling, but one of your children will die before you.'

Klara couldn't take any more. 'I can't listen to this nonsense anymore! Let's go, Katja. How much will I pay you?'

'If you don't like my prediction, you don't have to pay. Just go, young woman,' he finished and began to collect the stones.

On the way home, Klara couldn't calm down. 'He is just not normal; such nonsense he foretold me. I don't trust a single word,' she cried.

'Don't be so sure, Klara. We will live and see.' Katja calmed her. But as the months passed, more and more doubts began to creep into her soul, because still there was no news from Ljova. She began to write letters to the military enlistment office, requesting that they help her find her husband, but again there were no results.

＋＋＋＋＋＋

After his illness, Jukan became much more careful. He tried to watch his hygiene. Lice were spreading infections, and that year a lot of people were lost to typhus. To beat the lice, they decided to boil their clothes, but it didn't help. At last, they made an iron boiler, and inside they used overheated steam to disinfect their clothes and blankets. Gradually the lice receded and their illnesses stopped. Now they were well organised and didn't hide like animals in the forest but were constantly looking for a chance to attack the enemy. They attacked transport convoys with weapons and attacked small groups of Ustachi and Domobran. With the Ustachi, they had very strict rules; those who were taken prisoner were shot in the same way, as there was no mercy shown by them to Serbs. The Domobrans

146

were a different matter. They had been sent to the army unwillingly, not as volunteers. So, when they were taken prisoners, their weapons and uniforms were taken, and they were allowed to go home.

The partisans didn't have any uniforms and were dressed in anything they had. But now, they had as many weapons as they wanted: rifles and carbines, grenades and mortars, machine guns, and even some artillery. But the main thing they had now was discipline, and they were led by communists. They weren't allowed to play cards anymore, and Jukan had to forget his hobby. From an innocent boy, he became a skilled partisan who understood each situation. They weren't located near Lipa anymore but were coming down to Ripach. They even attacked Bihach and actually had it surrounded. But the enemy had the advantage with arms, and particularly artillery. So the partisans tried not to get involved in open battles, but they were much braver and more adventurous. They succeeded because of their unpredictability and the risks they took.

Jukan felt particular pleasure when they attacked the enemy's food stocks. He usually used the cover of fog or rain to creep to a herd of cows or sheep, and take them away. Once, he even managed to steal an enemy mobile kitchen, and the quality of their meals improved greatly. His supplying abilities were noticed, and he was made the quartermaster of the platoon. In one attack, he managed to get himself a horse . . . not just an ordinary horse but a pure beauty. His grandfather always had kept beautiful horses, hard-working and with strong muscles. But this one was different. It was coloured bay, with thin but muscular legs, lean, and fast as lightning. You couldn't do any ploughing on such a horse, and it would have been foolish to even think about that, but to ride it was sheer pleasure. Jukan used all his ability to find a common language with his horse. He began by talking to him in a low voice, coming closer, and then stretching a hand and took the bridle. But the horse didn't even try to escape; it seemed he was frightened by the loneliness and shooting and accepted the friendship offered by Jukan. Jukan called him Dorat. They became inseparable at once, and Dorat didn't obey anyone else. The secret was that Jukan quite often indulged him with sugar. Many tried to ride Dorat, but it always ended the same way, with the would-be rider on the ground.

But a more essential skill was that Dorat could feel the enemy, even from a distance. It was difficult to explain how he did it, but he would stop suddenly, move his ears slightly, and snort softly. This meant that the enemy was nearby. He recognised the special scent of the Germans and Ustachi, and the most important thing was that he was quiet. So it happened at the end of spring near Ripach, Jukan and Dorat were coming back late at night and came across a big group of Ustachi. Dorat again warned him in time, but there was no place to hide. They were forced to get into the River Una and hide under a tree. It's quite hard to stay in Una even in the summer months when the water temperature hardly gets over ten degrees. In the spring, it's even colder, and to stay there for even a few minutes is hard.

Though the Ustachi hadn't noticed them, but it seemed that they were not going to leave quickly. The Ustachi were having a long talk, and poor Dorat stood silently in the cold water, not making a sound. They were forced to stay there for more than half an hour, but at last the Ustachi left. Shivering from cold, they got out of the water, and Jukan hugged his horse and gratefully clapped him on the neck, and Dorat playfully butted him back on his shoulder.

The next month, they got into more trouble. That rainy day, their cheta was relocating to a new position, and Jukan and Dorat were walking slowly in a line with all the others. All of them were thoroughly wet from the pouring rain, and everyone had the same wish—just to arrive at their new position where they could get out of the rain. Visibility was dreadful no more than about 100 metres. Suddenly, Jukan heard the sound of a bell, which is usually carried by the leading sheep in a herd. He listened more carefully and again heard the sound. Inside his enterprising brain, a new idea was born! He told his friends he would catch up with them further down the road, and he turned his horse and followed the sound. He was going down the hill, and the rain was getting heavier and heavier. He pulled down his hat so that the star on the brim was almost in his eyes. The bell sound was getting louder, but it seemed that it was not moving. At last, Jukan saw in front of him an empty wooden cattle stall, but there was nothing inside but a long stick on which was hung a bell occasionally ringing with the wind. Having understood his mistake, Jukan turned his horse around and rushed to catch up with his cheta. The rain whipped his face, and it was difficult to find his directions; even Dorat was puzzled and a little nervous.

Soon, Jukan realised that he was lost. He thought for a while and remembered that the river flowed from his right side and decided to move in that direction and then get to the bridge that they were supposed to cross. As he was hoping, after a short time, he came to a little break and saw the bridge with his cheta crossing it. Jukan rushed to the bridge, but by this time, the rain was so heavy that it was almost impossible to see anything at all. He had ridden into a column but soon understood his mistake . . . it was a column of Ustachi and Domobrans. To his luck, everyone was trying to hide from the rain under their clothes and nobody noticed him. This wasn't easy to do, because the partisans had no uniforms, only trophy ones. Jukan was wearing the same outfit as the Domobra, except for his hat, a pilotka with a star on the front. Jukan quickly turned the star to the back and hid it under his collar. He pulled back his neck, trying his best to hide his face so that only his eyes were visible.

The bridge wasn't long, but Jukan felt that it went on for an eternity. Thank God, nobody paid him any attention, and at last they reached the other side. Here, the hill started, with the forest at the top. Suddenly, the commander dismounted, and everyone got down from their horses. Jukan used his spurs and sent Dorat up the hill; it was wet, and Dorat's hooves were sliding, but he sensed the danger, and with this, he dug them into the ground, and they finally reached the top. They were not far into the forest when the Ustachi realised what had happened and began to shoot. Bullets whistled around Jukan and Dorat, but none of them hit their target, and in a few seconds, they reached the trees. Here, it was possible to take a breath, but Jukan continued to whip the horse, and Dorat carried him further away from danger. Nobody rushed to catch up with them, and it seemed in such dreadful weather, people had no desire to fight. He didnt find his cheta that night and had to sleep in a small grotto in the forest. He found them the next morning.

Now, he seldom visited his home. The front line, with the Germans and Ustachi, was too far away from Lipa, so it was too hard for Jukan to get there. His father and Rade stayed with the women and children. They tried to run the household in the same way as before, and now that Jukan's brother, Pepo, was almost an adult, he helped them. Every house supplied the partisans with food and sometimes with shelter. All Bosanska Krajina helped the partisans, and here they felt at home. The Germans and Ustachi felt like they were in a minefield. As soon as they had decided on some military action against the partisans, the locals immediately notified the partisans, and they avoided any contact. To fight the Germans, who had tanks and heavy artillery, in the open spaces was almost impossible. But it was quite another matter on narrow roads and gorges. Here, the partisans attacked them with such ferocity that it was difficult to escape and survive. Nobody felt sorry for the enemy, because in practically every house, someone had been lost or wounded. That is why nobody took prisoners. The once frightening feeling that you could kill someone wasn't scary anymore. To shoot at the enemy became a habit, and some even got drunk on the feeling. In war, it's necessary to be fast, because if you don't shoot first, the enemy will, and then you don't have the chance to press the trigger.

But in some cases, people who had already seen a lot of horrors were still shocked by war's cruelty. Such a thing happened that summer, not far from Banja Luka, where Jukan's brigade was fighting. That day, they tracked down a group of Ustachi and Domobran. They were moving along the woods, not expecting any trouble. They were walking up a long, gentle, and entirely open slope. At the top of it, though, the partisans with two machine guns were waiting for them. They allowed the enemy to get to a distance of fifty metres and then opened fire. Taken by surprise, the Ustachi and Domobran turned and ran down the hill, but the machine guns continued to mow them down. What happened next would stay in Jukan's memory for the rest of his life. It was not clear how, but a burst of machine gun fire cut the head off one of the Domobran, and it fell to his feet and rolled down the hill. The body seemed not to understand the situation and, on reflex, continued to run after the head. People who had seen a lot in this war were frozen, and the firing stopped. Everyone looked on in horror. The body refused to fall. It seemed to last a long time, like a slow-motion film. The head rolled down a couple of more metres, with the body running behind. At last, on flat ground, the body took a few more steps and fell down, and the head, as if realising that the pursuit was over, finally stopped. The pause in fighting continued for some time, but then it broke out again, but not with nearly the same intensity.

✦ ✦ ✦ ✦ ✦ ✦

After Germany's defeat near Moscow, many people thought that the war would now go differently, that the fascist army would be thrown off Russian land and the people's moods improved. But when summer came, Hitler's army restarted its offensive. They moved to the Volga and Caucasus. Saratov lay in their way. The enemy was now very close, and the fear for their future didn't leave Klara for a minute. Zaharov again began threatening that he would give the name of every Jew and communist to the Germans. He waited on purpose for Klara in a place where no one could see them, and stepping out in front of her, he spoke with hatred. 'Well, damned Jew, we won't have to wait much longer. I will expose all of you!'

'Why do you hate Jews so much? What have they done to you?' Klara asked angrily.

'Because you sold this land to the communists, and I hate you for it. You ruined my life!' he answered.

'What connection do I and my small son have to this?' Klara asked again.

'You are all the same!' he said and took a step towards Klara. At that moment, she could not contain herself and pushed him away with her two hands. Zaharov's legs gave way, and he fell down clumsily. Klara ran to the office.

The next day, she decided to again complain to Drozdov and told him everything that had happened. 'What a scoundrel,' he said angrily. 'One day, I will kill him with my bare hands, but you don't have to worry about him, he's a sick man.'

'How can I not worry? The Germans are now so close!' Klara said.

'They will not get here; I am almost sure of that. But, believe me, if that does happen, I will not leave your family. I will take you together with my family,' Drozdov assured her. Drozdov's words gave her hope, and Zaharov's threats didn't frighten her anymore.

She never lost faith that her Ljova was still alive and would soon find them. She wrote to all possible military departments but received no answers. Then, unexpectedly, she received a letter from Ljova's brother, Sasha. He and his family and two sisters were evacuated to Tashkent, where he was working as a doctor in a military hospital. He asked her to write back as soon as she received his letter. Klara didn't delay and sent him a letter the same week. So with expectation of a response, the summer ended and autumn began. The Germans got even closer; they were expected to get to the Volga, and the fight for Stalingrad had already started. At night, the sounds of explosions were heard from the front line. Once a week, on her trips to the Central, Klara learnt the latest news. Fresh troops were sent to the front line, and wounded troops were sent back. There was a feeling that the final battle was about to start, and whichever side won this would win the war. Klara didn't believe in God, but these days she prayed for victory.

A very harsh winter had arrived, the second winter of their evacuation. But now they had their warm corner and were experienced in how to survive. Everyone held their breath, waiting for good news. One November night, the noise from the front line grew even louder, and the horizon was lit up by the explosions. Horrified, Klara thought that the Germans had broken through the front line, but the radio soon gave them the great news that the Soviet Army had surrounded the enemy, and under Paul's command, they were preparing to destroy the enemy. Never in her life had Klara shouted so loudly, but she wasn't embarrassed, because no one tried to constrain their emotions and didn't want to! Only the bookkeeper, Zaharov, didn't look happy; he became quiet and tried to keep out of sight.

That winter, hunger was more severe. Food was needed for the front line; the peasants didn't have enough food for themselves. Forage for the cows was practically non-existent. The cattle were hungry and could not stand on their feet. Cows were tied up in stalls to prevent them from falling. But, despite all that, Klara and her mother and Dima didn't starve. They always had some milk. Drozdov provided them with little lumps of sugar. Dima ate the sugar with such pleasure that Klara took him to the doctor from the industrial complex. 'Doctor, surely it's abnormal for a child to eat so much sugar?' she asked him.

'Entirely normal,' he calmed her down. 'A child's brain develops at this age, and it needs a lot of food. For this, sugar is one of the best foods. He is a happy child that he has it. It would be worse if he doesn't.' And Dima was growing to be a very smart boy. His brown eyes burnt with curiosity, and the number of questions he asked would make a professor demented.

One more long winter, which seemed to freeze the whole world, passed. Klara only went to work and back to her mother and Dima. It seemed that normal life had stopped and that the war would never end. However, the sun again gained strength and started to melt the snow, the ice broke up from the streamlets and rivers, and, at last, soft green grass again broke through. In spring, a camel that Klara rode onto the main office gave birth to a very clumsy and lanky but at the same time pretty male calf. Dima was enthralled by him and tried to stroke it whenever possible. But this joy didn't last long. The little calf simply disappeared, and his mother began to call out, trying to get him back. Her cries were so heartbreaking that Klara ran to find out what had happened to the young one. She found that a local Kazakh had slaughtered him that morning. Nothing could be done, and Klara calmed down, but the mother continued to suffer. It was most terrible at night; she groaned so badly that Klara thought she would have a heart attack.

One some days, the conditions became intolerable, and Klara decided that they needed to leave this place. Right at this time, Klara received a letter from her husband's brother. Sasha had always treated her better than any of the other relatives from the Miroshnik family, and he had loved Dima as though he was his own son. In the letter, he rejoiced that he had been able to find them. He told her that he had no news from Ljova. He suggested that Klara move to be with his sister, Nadia, who lived in Tashkent. His letter ended with the words 'Get over to Tashkent. Life there is much easier, and after the war, Ljova or I will find you there.' This strengthened her belief in a better future, and for the first time in two years, she had the feeling that life had not yet come to an end and that there were new adventures ahead of her. Now she was ready to meet them! They didn't need much time to collect their belongings . . . they were all kept in one suitcase.

The hardest thing was to break this news to Drozdov, because he had always treated her as a daughter. She found the right moment to speak to him. 'Comrade Drozdov, I have to speak with you,' she said.

'Don't worry, speak up. You look so serious that I think this will be a difficult conversation.'

'I came to tell you that I am going to leave.' She squeezed out the words, shifting from one foot to the other.

'Where do you want to go to?' he asked. 'Odessa is still under German occupation.'

'I'm not going to Odessa but to Tashkent, where my husband's sister and her family live. They have asked me to go,' she said.

'What is it that you don't like here, or has someone offended you?' he asked her.

'What are you talking about? I owe you my life! You rescued me. I feel badly even talking about this,' she said.

'All right, if you have found relatives, of course, you must go. I would prefer you to stay, though. I've gotten used to you, and you do your job so well, but, so what?'

'What are you saying?' Klara asked.

'You have only one life, and you must decide what is best for you,' he said.

'As long as you don't hold anything against me, then I will go,' Klara answered confidently.

The local Kazakhs for whom she had read and written letters learnt about her departure and came with gifts. All of them wished her a happy journey, and some even cried. Drozdov took them by car to the station and waited for the train to arrive. At last, he said, 'Look, Klara, if you are not comfortable over there, come back. We will not let you down.'

'Thank you for everything,' Klara said and kissed him on the cheek. He was embarrassed and blushed.

They had to travel by both passenger carriage and cargo carriage as when they arrived in Saratov, but this time, there was straw on the ground. And now they had padded jackets and didn't suffer from the cold as much. Now they had food as well, given to them by the locals. They had only one problem—they didn't have water, and Klara had to run to find it each time the train stopped. At one of the big stations, she grabbed a jar and went to search for a tap. Meanwhile, the train had been moved to another platform. The water queue was long, and Klara lost ten minutes. With her full jar, she had to run to the train, and here she saw a woman in railway uniform. 'Where is the train to Tashkent?' she asked, and the woman pointed to carriages standing on another platform. As she got closer, she saw that on the cars was written 'Tashkent–Saratov'. She grabbed the sleeve of a railway worker and cried, 'Where is the train to Tashkent?'

'What's wrong with you, girl? It's on the opposite side, on platform nine!' and he pointed in the opposite direction.

Klara didn't have time to listen to the rest; she rushed in the direction the man had pointed to. She ran with every last bit of her strength; she felt her heart pounding in her chest but kept on running. At last, she saw their carriages; an engine was already attached to the cars, with steam billowing, ready to move. She heard the whistle, and the train started to move. The train was speeding up in her direction; she waved her hands, but no one noticed. The engine passed her, pulling the carriages behind. They gained speed, and she couldn't wait any longer. She threw away the jar, and with the last bit of strength, she reached for the handle and tried to jump onto the footboard. But her feet wouldn't obey her any longer . . . she stumbled and hung on with her hands. Her feet dragged along the ground, and Klara thought that the end had come. Suddenly, the screech of brakes sounded, and the train stopped. She let go with her hands and fell to the ground, knocking her head on a cross tie. She lay on the ground with her eyes closed. People surrounded her and helped her to her feet.

'Have you broken anything?' some asked her caringly, while others were swearing at her.

'What a silly woman, she nearly killed herself, and now, because of her, the train has had to stop!'

Then she was taken to her carriage, where she was met by her mother's loud cries and the crying of a frightened Dima. But Klara noticed nothing and didn't talk. She got to the corner and fell on the straw. She lay there for two days, not even getting up to drink water. The day before they arrived in Tashkent, she started to regain her senses and began to talk again.

The trip to Tashkent took eight days. The city met them with bright colours. As soon as they got off the train, they were struck by the heat. They were surrounded by beautifully dressed, smiling people. Laughter could be heard everywhere. They gave the impression that nobody knew about the war. Klara, with her mother and small son, looked like beggars. On the platform, Ljova's sister, Nadia, and her husband, Simeon, were there to meet them. Klara recognised her at once and hailed her. Nadia didn't recognise her at first. Obviously, she did not expect to see them in such a bad condition, and Simeon had a nasty look on his face. But he quickly realised his mistake and hugged Klara, while Nadia even took Dima's hand and gave him a big kiss on the cheek. 'Look how you have grown. A real handsome man now!' she said. Then she put Dima down on the ground. Simeon grabbed the suitcase, and together they walked out of the station. They took a small bus from the hospital where Simeon worked as a doctor and Nadia as a nurse. They lived in a big three-roomed apartment near the hospital and a big, colourful market.

The next morning, Klara went to the market. She still had some money and wanted to buy something for Dima. The market amazed her, with its abundance of fruit and vegetables that she had never seen before: dried apricots, dates, figs, raisins, and melons. Klara was so distracted that she came back home empty-handed. Early in the morning, Simeon and Nadia had left for work, and Klara began to wash their clothes with her mother. They had to change clothes because it was so hot, but now they didn't have any summer clothes. Dima had outgrown all his clothes, and they urgently needed to buy new ones. Zelda had only one skirt made of chiffon and one black blouse. Klara still had one silk dress that she used to wear in Odessa. Now she took it from the suitcase, ironed it, and put it on. She felt like a tsarevna, a princess, the frog who had thrown off her frog skin. When Dima saw her, he laughed happily and clapped his hands.

Somewhere around noon, Simeon arrived to pick up some documents. He looked at Klara in her summer dress and went into the other room. After a while, he called her in. 'Listen, Klara, can you help me to find a red folder? I'll search in the case, and you rummage in that chest,' he said and pointed to the corner.

Klara opened the chest, sat down, and began to look through its contents. Unexpectedly, she felt a hand on her hip, and she jumped as though she's been stung. 'Simeon, are you crazy?' she asked.

'Keep quiet. Look what a queen you are!' he said.

'Don't come any closer to me!' she warned, taking a step back.

'Don't be silly, no one will find out,' he said, taking another step closer, but Klara dodged around him and went to the room where her mother was sitting on a chair, putting a new shirt on Dima. Simeon came out after her and went straight to the door. 'I'll be back this evening,' he said, slamming the door behind him.

Klara knew that it was impossible to stay there much longer and decided that she needed to get a job quickly. The next morning, she began her search and didn't have to look for long. She went to a big textile industrial complex and decided to try her luck there. At the checkpoint, she found out where the Accounting Department was. She found it in a big brick building with windows covered in iron bars. She walked upstairs and along a corridor, reading the signs on the doors. In the hallway, people were rushing about with paperwork; they were busy, and nobody noticed Klara. At last, she came to a door with the sign 'Chief Accountant'. Klara quietly knocked at the door, but there was no answer. She pushed the door, and it opened with a scratchy sound. A grey-headed man with thick glasses was sitting behind the table. He seemed very busy and asked angrily, 'What are you looking for, girl?'

'I'm looking for the chief accountant,' Klara said.

'Why?' the man asked her.

'I'm looking for a job,' she said.

'Then you need to go to the Staffing Department, my darling,' he answered her.

'But I'm an accountant.' Klara refused to give up.

The man looked up and burst out laughing. 'How can you be an accountant? You are still a young girl. Don't distract me, I have important things to do.' Klara hung her head and walked towards the door, but he called to her. 'Who are you, and where are you from?'

'I was evacuated from Odessa with my mother and small son. We spent two winters in Saratov and have just arrived in Tashkent. We are staying at my husband's sister's house, but we can't stay there long. I have to find some work,' Klara explained.

'Oi! We are from the same city. If you are from Odessa, that changes everything. What's your name?' the man asked.

'Klara!'

'I'm Speransky Arcady Semyonovich. So, Klara, tomorrow you can start your new job.' He lifted the telephone and called. Someone answered, and after a few minutes, a chubby bald man in over-sleeves came into the room.

'You called me, Arcady Semyonovich?'

'Sorokin, this is our new accountant, Klara. She will work in the Supply Department. It is very important that by tomorrow you find her a decent room. And she is not alone. She is with her mother and little child. Try to do it as if you are doing it for me,' Speransky said.

'I understand. We will find something,' Sorokin said.

'That's it, then. Tomorrow morning, I will be waiting for you, and now you can go home.'

'Thank you for your kindness! I have been so lucky with kind people,' Klara said and left the office.

Now Klara wasn't in a rush anymore. Deep in her heart, she felt warm and relaxed. Now she had a job and a place to live, so these worries had been overcome. Klara decided to go the market again and to buy something for Dima. Knowing his love of sweets, she bought a little bit of dried melon and apricot. This present made a big impression on Dima; he first twisted a slice of dried melon in his fingers and then carefully bit it. Then his big, bright eyes lit up with astonishment and delight. 'Oi, how tasty,' he cried. 'What is it?' Klara told him that it was dried melon, and Dima asked for more.

'Just one more slice, and we will leave the rest for tomorrow,' Klara told him. Dima ate the second slice slowly, closing his eyes with pleasure.

'Why have you suddenly decided to spoil him when we have hardly any money left?' Zelda asked.

'Don't worry, Mama, now we will have everything. I have a job!' Klara reassured her.

In the evening, when Nadia and Simeon came back from work, all of them sat around the table to have supper. They had sausage, tomatoes, cucumbers, and grey bread. Klara was hungry but tried to restrain herself, but Dima ate greedily, especially loving the crackling cucumbers.

'Well, how was your day?' Nadia asked.

'I went to search for work,' Klara told her.

'What do you think, how long will it take you to find a job?' Simeon asked with a smile.

'I found one already,' Klara answered. Simeon almost choked!

'Where, if it's not a secret?' he wanted to know.

'At the textile factory as an accountant. They even promised me a flat,' she replied.

'We will see what they give you, probably some kennel in a hostel,' he said. But his sarcasm was not warranted.

The next morning, Speransky took her to a new apartment, almost opposite the factory. The supply manager opened the door, and letting Klara go first, he asked, 'How do you like it?'

Klara didn't know how to answer. What she saw surpassed all her expectations. It was a real one-roomed apartment with a kitchen. It had three beds and a wardrobe. 'Thank you. I didn't expect anything like this,' Klara confessed.

'That's perfect, then! Today you move in, and tomorrow you start work!'

Klara went back to Nadia's place to pick up her mother and Dima. The rest of the day, they were occupied arranging the new apartment. Zelda was cleaning and constantly thanking God for such good luck, and Dima was just happy that he had a bed. So their life in Tashkent began successfully. The textile factory was huge and produced shyphon, a thick woollen cloth. Hundreds of people worked there, and the Accounts Department was big. On the first day, Klara made friends with a charming girl called Anja. She was the same age as Klara, lovely and cheerful. They became friends quickly and often went together to the cinema after work. Yes, Klara had a job and was regularly paid a salary, but it was difficult to support her mother and Dima on one wage. But life continued to find Klara a saviour! This time, it was the director of the dining room, Victor Nazarovich. As part of her work, Klara had to go to the dining room daily to check the accounts. Each day she went there, the director offered her a free dinner and quite often gave her food to take home. On the money she saved, she could buy some clothes, and now they didn't look like ragamuffins anymore!

Jukan tried not to fall asleep while sitting near the fire where almost all the brigade had gathered. Already snow was falling continuously, a strong wind was blowing, and it was unusually cold. People froze to death almost every day. Many died while sitting near a fire, trying to have a little rest, but falling asleep. The partisans were dressed in any clothes that they could find, but the most important problem was that they didn't have footwear. Everyone dressed in what they could take from the dead Germans and Ustachi, but Jukan didn't like to, because his father had told him since childhood not to take anything from the dead. This winter, he couldn't resist and broke his father's order. After one fight, he saw the beautiful boots of a dead German officer. They were made of fine, shiny leather. At first, he hesitated, but then he removed the boots as quickly as he could so no one would notice and hid them in his bag. They were just his size, incredibly comfortable and light. But the most important thing was that his feet weren't frozen anymore, though he only had thin socks.

The German army was retreating. Only three months ago, it looked as though all of Yugoslavia would be free again. Throughout 1942, the partisan movement gained strength, and by autumn they had taken back Bihach and proclaimed the Bihach Republic. The Ustachi tried to hold it to the last bullet, and almost all of them died. The Domobrans were a weak support for them. At the first sign of danger, they put down their weapons and surrendered. The partisans let them go home, but many of them were recruited by force back into the army again, and some of them were taken prisoner a few times. The Supreme Army headquarters, led by Tito, was based in Bihach, but Jukan's brigade didn't stay long and moved towards Zagreb. They had only 100 kilometres to go but were met by well-prepared Germans. They were better armed, with unlimited ammunition, but more importantly they had tanks, cars, motorcycles, and artillery. In the beginning, the partisans showed serious resistance, but gradually they ran out of ammunition and had to retreat.

Winter had set in, and snow was falling all the time. In the open, it was still possible to move, but in the ravines, the snow gathered in high drifts, making their retreat difficult. The Germans had the advantage because they could move on skis, and the partisans had to carry their wounded. The Germans felt more confident in the open spaces and preferred to avoid the forests. Their motor vehicles could only move on the roads, and aircraft wasn't used in the snow. In the forests, the partisans felt much more confident, though walking in deep snow was extremely hard. They had no front line and attacked the enemy when they least expected it. These surprise attacks put heavy losses on the enemy, and after an attack, they would get a few days of calm. After the liberation of Bihach, Jukan became the platoon quartermaster. His job was to supply foodstuffs for the platoon and establish contacts with the local population. The Serbs considered them defenders, but in the Croatian and Muslim settlements, the provisions were collected by threats and force. Jukan had a talent for organising and forging relationships with the locals, and during one of the calm days, near Krupa, he became a member of the communist party and quartermaster of the brigade.

The winter continued to test everyone. God seemed to be angry with mankind and covered them with snow. People were exhausted; they ran out of ammunition and food. They threw away the machine guns and carbines, for which they had no more cartridges, and began to eat the horses, for which they didn't have food. Jukan had some lumps of sugar, and thanks to that, he still had enough energy to bear arms. His friends weakened from hunger and could barely drag their feet. He fed the most helpless with lumps of sugar. Near Krupa, they faced a German division that was pursuing them. They were on opposite sides of a gorge, filled by snow too deep to walk on. The day passed in constant firing, without visible success from either party. The situation was made worse because of the newly wounded, who became a burden. The snow continued to fall, and by the end of the day, the Germans and partisans ran out of energy to keep fighting. Then something happened that nobody would believe. Each party dispersed in different directions, walking on two narrow tracks made by their feet, just a few metres from each other. They carried their weapons overhead, and nobody fired a shot. The snow was at shoulder level, and they could only see the heads of the enemy. They walked silently, looking into the eyes of their enemy, but on that day, there was no hatred in their eyes but more like understanding. The partisans moved towards Petrovats, the Germans in the opposite direction.

The Germans continued to receive supplies regularly, but the partisans were starving. The number of wounded was huge, but no one ever thought to leave them behind, though they slowed them down. Therefore, it was decided that the main force would retreat towards Drvar, but Jukan's first brigade had to cover the withdrawal by taking the brunt of the fighting. They entrenched themselves in the frozen ground. They were tiring the enemy by using their cunning, arranging ambushes in unexpected places. They often attacked the enemy and made them run. But there is a limit to any persistence, and they had to retreat further into the mountains, taking the enemy with them. They split into groups and continued to flee in different direction. Sixteen people remained in Jukan's group. They had practically no bullets and only a few grenades. They were surrounded on all sides and had to climb the densely wooded mountain. The snow here was so thick, they were almost swimming, leaving a clear track. Near the top of the mountain, the forest unexpectedly finished, and they found themselves in a big stony glade, clear of snow, but open to a strong wind. From here, there was nowhere to go.

'So there is nothing more we can do but die here,' said Milovan, making a helpless gesture.

Everyone silently agreed. Only Jukan had one small offering. 'Let's dance the last Kolo.' They gathered into a circle, put their hands on one another's shoulders, and slowly began to spin in the dance. Gradually they got into a rhythm, almost forgetting what was happening and wholly got caught up in the dance. They came back to reality when they heard an unfamiliar voice.

'What a strange place and time for dancing you have found!' They turned towards the voice and saw an old peasant dressed in a shabby sheepskin coat.

'Father, how did you get here?' Milovan asked.

'I live here, but what are you doing here?' the man asked.

'We can do nothing. We are surrounded and will have to die here,' Jukan explained.

'Well, probably it is still too early to die. Just follow me,' he said with a smile, and they silently followed him. They entered the woods and walked for about twenty metres and came to the edge of a break. The thickly falling snow didn't allow them to see for more than about 100 metres, and the rest of it was just a white haze. The old man brought them to the edge and showed them a hole almost full of snow. 'Jump one by one in here,' he said.

'Are you crazy?' asked Milovan.

'It's a pipe that the woodcutters use to get the chopped wood to the lowlands,' the man explained.

'You want us to jump in there and die?' Milovan asked again.

'Do you have a better solution? What is the difference how you die? Follow me.'

The old man came to the hole and carefully sat down with his feet outstretched and pushed. His body almost silently slid down. The group exchanged glances and shrugged their shoulders.

'To hell with it, I'm going to follow him,' said Jukan and repeated the old man's movements and slid down. The first few seconds, he flew through almost total darkness, trying to give his body a streamlined shape. Despite that, he hit an ice wall and came into the light seeing how he had to shape himself to slide. But now he could see the dangerous places and tried to soften the blows. It was hard to tell how long the slide lasted, but it ended when Jukan was thrown into a thick snowdrift and stopped.

'Stand up quickly and come here before someone hits you,' the grandfather shouted from under a tree where he was standing. Jukan quickly got to his feet and ran, and almost the same second, Milovan slid into the snowdrift. One after another they slid from the mountain and got off with just a few bruises. So, without a shot being fired, they got to the other side of the mountain, where they didn't see a single person. They didn't know how to thank their saviour, but he gave the impression that he didn't know why they praised him. So, unexpectedly, the battle on Shator Planina was over, but later the verse was created:

> Niko ne zna shta je tezko,
> ko Shator Planinu nije prochao peshke.
> (Nobody knows what is hard torment,
> who didn't cross Shator Planina on foot.)

They were now far away from military action and began to move towards Bihach. Hunger exhausted them, and they tried to move without attracting

159

attention. Next morning, they came to a lonely house standing on a hill. Smoke was coming out of the chimney, and nobody was around. Observing all the precautions, Jukan went into the house, where he found one old lady. She was the owner of the house, and her two sons were serving in the Ustachi.

'Listen, Mother, for me, it doesn't matter who your sons are. We don't want to hurt you. We only need some food, and we will leave you alone.'

'What kind of food are you talking about when I'm as hungry as a wolf?' she asked bitterly, and she sounded convincing.

But Jukan had a strong feeling that this wasn't the truth, and he ordered a search of the house. All his soldiers were peasants and knew very well where it was possible to hide food, and they started the search. But an hour later, they had still found nothing. Jukan refused to give up, however. He took the old woman outside, rolled up his sleeve, showed her the big compass, and lied. 'Listen, Mother, this device will show me precisely where your storage is, so give us a little, or we will take it all.'

The woman was obviously frightened but tried not to show it and continued to resist. 'Where is my storage? I have nothing to eat myself' she cried.

Jukan, pretending to look at the compass, began to walk around, trying to watch her eyes. Sometimes he stopped, peering into the distance, secretly looking at her. At last, when he began to peer at the valley filled with deep snow, the old woman turned pale and began to bite her lip. 'Here it is,' said Jukan, pointing his finger, and the old woman began to wail. They took shovels and went down the hill and began to dig. Soon, they found four large barrels of cheese, laid in salty cottage cheese for preservation. There were more than 100 cheeses, but they didn't want to take them all. Everyone took one cheese, and the rest they left for the old lady. Now they could relax . . . with cheese, they could survive.

———————— ✦✦✦✦✦ ————————

The severe winter passed, but many had not survived. The spring quickly melted the snowdrifts. But with it came an epidemic of typhoid. More people were dying every day, and the old men were especially vulnerable. In May 1943, Jukan's father died unexpectedly from typhoid, but he only heard about it after the funeral. The Vignevich house had lost its head, and now all the pressure lay on Rade's shoulders. Jukan's young brother, Pepo, joined the partisans as well and served in a machine-gun platoon under the command of Sayo Grbich. In Jukan's life, a lot of changes had happened. The name 'Chiko' now stuck with him permanently, and he became the division quartermaster. No one of his age occupied such a high position. His duties included supplying provisions for more than 6,000 people. In territory freed by the partisans, he represented the law. This position was far from safe. The previous quartermaster was skinned by rebellious peasants who put salt on his body and left him to die in torment.

Jukan had quite good organising abilities and a talent to find a common language with people. It was necessary, though, to feed the army at any cost, and sometimes he had to use unpopular methods. In friendly Serbian territory, the partisans were considered defenders, and people gave voluntarily. But even here, unpleasant conflicts could happen. When they were in the areas of the Ustachi sympathisers, it was necessary to use force. But he never blamed children for their parents' actions and never left a house with children without a cow and some food, and never took everything. If sometimes he felt he had gone too far because of a difficult situation, the next time he had an extra cow or sheep, he gave it back to those victims. And it must be said that the rumour was spreading that he was a firm but fair quartermaster, so he often went into villages without protection.

His new position went with a new uniform and good boots, and now he looked like a dandy, drawing attention from the opposite sex! He also had a new horse, given to him by a peasant. His old horse, Dorat, had been lost in the fighting on Shator Planina. His new horse was a black beauty, tall and slender, never used to pull a plough. Jukan now usually slept in a bed in houses and felt uncomfortable looking into the eyes of the partisans that he had served with before. But what could he do? He hadn't appointed himself to that position, and no one could blame him.

With time, the partisans gained more strength and control over more territories. Finally, they reached Banja Luca and surrounded the city. There were a considerable number of Ustachi and Domobran troops in the city, but they couldn't hold out for long. The partisans expected any day to get the order to attack the city. In the evening, Jukan went to visit Sayo Grbich's brigade, where his younger brother was serving as a machine gunner. At first, he didn't recognise Pepo, as he had changed so much since they had last been together. Pepo had become a real man, though his eyes still had that child's spark in them. Because of the age difference, Jukan and Pepo had never spoken much. When Jukan had left the house, Pepo was still a child, and they saw one another only during Jukan's rare visits home. Now Pepo was taller than him, slim and handsome. They hugged one another and sat down on fallen tree trunk.

'Well, how is your life, little brother?' Jukan asked.

'Pretty good,' Pepo answered.

'Wasn't it too early for you to join the partisans? You left Mother alone at home with a little son,' Jukan asked again.

'No, it wasn't too early. Nobody could blame me for leaving,' Pepo said.

Jukan had to accept this, but he refused to give up. 'Sayo praises you to me and said that you are very courageous and, in a fight, you don't know fear.'

'He exaggerates! Everyone has fears, and no one wants to die,' he said.

'Listen, I could move you to my brigade, and we could fight together,' Jukan suggested.

'No, Jukitsa, I can't do that. I've become used to my fellows and would feel uncomfortable to leave them at such a crucial time,' Pepo said.

'But have you thought about Mother, and what she would do if something happened to you?' Jukan tried one last trick.

'There's no need to mention Mother,' Pepo stopped him. 'I'm not going to run into bullets foolishly.'

Jukan couldn't persuade Pepo, and after a long conversation, they hugged and left. He didn't expect that to be their last conversation. The next day, the Ustachi decided to try to break through the encirclement and attacked. They knew they had no other option than to break through or die. They fought with extraordinary frenzy, bringing down an avalanche of bullets on the partisans. Very few of them managed to break through, but the partisans suffered severe losses too. Pepo died, together with two friends from the same platoon, because the most substantial attack came in their direction. Jukan learnt about it a few days after they had buried his body. So this war had destroyed the lives of his three dearest men: his grandfather, his father, and now his brother.

Another year had passed, and spring came. Now, very few people doubted that the Germans would be defeated. From Ljova, there was still no news, and it became clear that he was either dead or was a prisoner. If he was alive, it wouldn't be difficult for him to find them. All the Miroshnik family knew where they lived. Klara practically lost all hope of seeing Ljova again. Everything turned out the way the Kazakh had predicted. He was no more among the living, because there had been no news, nor was he among the dead, because they hadn't received a death certificate. Even Dima asked less often, 'Where is my father?' There was only one wish—that now this war would come to an end and they would be able to go back home. At last, on April 22, there came the news over the radio that the Soviet armies had liberated Odessa. There was no limit to their joy! Klara and Anja decided to celebrate, bought a bottle of vodka, and went to Anja's hostel. Here, they were joined by two more of Anja's girlfriends, who were also from Odessa. They quickly organised some snacks on the table and sat down to celebrate. They drank vodka from small glasses and snacked on pickled cucumbers. Klara had never drunk alcohol before, and the first glass knocked her at once. She went red and started to feel hot, and after the second glass, she became so cheerful that she couldn't stop laughing.

They then began to sing, and Klara, only when it was night-time, realised that she urgently needed to get home; she knew her mother would be going mad! She got to her feet and found out that she could hardly keep her balance. She became even more happy, continuing to laugh and teetering like a drunk. The girls couldn't let her go home alone, so they all went together with her. Despite the late hour, there were still many people on the streets celebrating the liberation of Odessa. On the way home, Klara almost became sober again, but she still couldn't stop laughing. Her mother was waiting for her near the apartment, and she looked very worried. 'Why aren't you asleep?' Klara asked her.

'I'm waiting for you! Where have you been until this hour?' Zelda said.

'Listen, Muma, don't you know that Odessa has been liberated?' Klara tried to explain.

'I know it all, but that's no reason to come home drunk!' Zelda told her. 'Thank God that Dima fell asleep and didn't see this disgrace!'

'Don't talk nonsense, Muma. On this occasion, it's compulsory for everyone to get drunk! That's it, soon we will go home!' Klara said.

'And what if the Germans return?' Zelda wanted to know.

'They will not return, but just in case, we will wait for a couple of months,' Klara said.

The difficulty was that the war was still in progress, and before returning to Odessa, it was necessary to get an invitation from a relative living in the city. Klara had had no contact with any relative since the beginning of the war and no one to invite her. They had to wait for more than a year. They spent Victory Day in Tashkent. Everybody celebrated this day; people cried with joy, and never had there been so many tears! Other people cried, remembering those who had died in the human grinding machine that the war had been, and still others cried for those that were missing, that they would be found alive and could come back home.

Speransky ordered the chief of the warehouse to bring food and a couple of litres of spirits. They laid the food on tables in the middle of the Accounts Department, and they celebrated until late evening. In the warehouse, they even found an old record player and a few records, and after a few drinks, they were singing, and some even tried to dance. Next to Klara was the chief of the Staffing Department, Zynaida Vasilevna. She, too, was a bit drunk, and she and Klara wailed out the songs together. Unexpectedly, she put her arm around Klara's shoulder.

'Well, what are you planning to do now?' she asked.

'We want to return to Odessa, but we don't have an invitation, and there's nobody to ask,' Klara explained.

'Don't get upset that you don't have an invitation. You don't need it. You go for a holiday to Odessa and you simply don't come back. I can help you with that,' she said with a wink to Klara.

The idea was brilliant, and within the month, Klara and her family went on a holiday. They had to travel again in heated cargo carriages, with long train changes and constant inconveniences, but nothing could cloud the joy of returning home. Odessa met them with the heat of summer, bustling streets, and loud laughter. There wasn't the feeling that until just recently there had been a war, though around them were many destroyed houses. There were still many people in uniform, but next to them were people in bright clothes, with smiles on their faces. The Romanian occupation had burst into Odessa, and the streets and markets were full of different goods. From the station, they went to the Miroshnik house. The house had been plundered and was occupied now by the Krichanov family, a mother, her daughter, and granddaughter. It looked as though they had taken part in the plunder, because some of the Miroshnik family plates were on their dresser. The Krichanov family house had been destroyed by German bombs, and they had settled in this empty house. They allowed Klara only onto the threshold but didn't let her inside.

Klara was upset and went to the military registration and enlistment office. Her only hope was the certificate that her husband, Lev Miroshnik, was a lieutenant in the Soviet army and had died fighting near Stalingrad that she had been issued. These offices were almost across the road. In the courtyard were crowds of people, soldiers and officers, wounded and invalids, women and children. Klara left her mother and Dima on a bench and went inside, which seemed to be even more crowded. She went up to a window where a woman in uniform was sitting.

'Could I see the commanding officer?' Klara asked.

'He is busy and can't see anyone now,' she was told.

'It's urgent, I must see him,' Klara insisted.

'I've already told you, he can't see anyone right now,' the woman said angrily. 'Please go away from this window.'

But the bitter experiences of their evacuation had made Klara determined. 'Don't be rude to me. I've just returned from evacuation and have no place to live!'

'What's all this shouting about, girl?' Klara heard a pleasant voice behind her and turned to see a tall, handsome captain with a charming smile.

'I'm not a girl but a widow,' Klara said.

'Then let's go into my office,' he said, and Klara followed him.

'Sit down and tell me your story,' he said.

'My name is Klara Miroshnik. My husband, Lev Miroshnik, lost his life in the battle for Stalingrad. Here is his death certificate. Today, we returned from our evacuation to find that our house is occupied by other people.'

'Who are they, and who allowed them to settle there?' the captain asked.

'Their surname is Krichanov. Their house was destroyed by the bombing,' Klara answered.

'That doesn't matter, the house belongs to you and your husband, who was a Soviet officer. Don't worry, we will help you,' he said, calming her down.

'Thank you very much, but when will this happen? We have no place to sleep, and I have my mother and small child with me,' Klara asked him.

'Where is your house?' he wanted to know.

'Opposite your office, on Proletarian Boulevard,' Klara said.

'Then I will send my assistant with you. He will help you to fix the problem.'

'I don't know how to thank you,' Klara said.

'It's too early to thank me,' he said.

And it was too early for rejoicing! As it happened, the Krichanov family had been settled in this house by the same military registration and enlistment office because her son was on the front line and they had nowhere to live either. As a result, the decision was made that the house belonged to Klara, but until they could find somewhere else, the Krichanov family could live in the house as well. The decision was very vague because the house had only two rooms suitable for living in. The rest of the house was dilapidated, with broken windows and full of rubble. Klara had to stay a few days in Ljova's brother's house. After a couple of days, Klara was approached by a well-dressed woman with a very stylish hairstyle.

'My name is Tamara Petrovna, and I have a very exciting proposal for you.' Klara wanted to know what this proposal was. 'I was told about the difficulty with your house, and I have an offer for you. Your home is in a dilapidated condition, and to fix it, you will need a lot of money, and you don't have it. But I do have money. I work as a director of the London Hotel. I have an excellent two-roomed apartment on Pirogovsky Street and can offer it you as an exchange. I will give you one day to consider this. Tomorrow, you can give me your answer. I'll be here the same time as today.'

Tamara walked away, leaving Klara standing, open-mouthed, and undecided what to do. She waited a little longer and then ran back to get her mother's advice. Zelda was tired of wandering all over the world without a place of her own, and she gladly accepted the offer.

'Why are you even thinking about this? She offered you an apartment where we can live like normal people. If you don't want to think about me, think about your son. This year, he has to go to school,' Zelda said.

'But don't you understand, it's the whole house she's taking?' Klara said.

'It's this house, where other people live as well, and we don't know for sure whether we will get it at all. Don't be silly. Just agree!' Klara decided to accept the offer.

The next morning, the woman arrived precisely on time. 'Well, have you decided?' she asked.

'I agree, but we have another family living in our house, and they can't move until they get another place to live,' Klara explained.

'That's not my business. I offered you everything I could, and I have nothing more.'

'So, what am I supposed to do?' Klara asked.

'I don't know. Let them live in one room, and you live in the other until they get a flat,' she suggested.

'I will have to discuss it with them. Can you show us the apartment?' Klara said.

'Why not, I will do that with pleasure.'

They didn't have to persuade the Krichanov family for long, and they agreed to go and have a look at the apartment together. It was just opposite the military hospital on Progovsky Street. The building was in excellent shape, in spite of the fact that bombs had almost destroyed the building next door. The building had a cosy enclosed courtyard. They climbed to the second floor, and Tamara opened the door. From the first look, even from the corridor, it was clear that the apartment was big and clean. Klara had forgotten when she last lived in such conditions. Both rooms were spacious with high windows, and there was a bathroom and a toilet. But most important for Klara was that it was the right size with a clean kitchen.

The Krichanovs were happy too and agreed to settle into the smaller room. Now the main thing was to do all the paperwork accurately, and Tamara promised to organise everything. In under one week, Klara's family and the Krichanov family moved into their new apartment. Klara enjoyed the beautiful spacious room, and her mother shone with happiness. Sometimes Klara regretted giving away the house, which had been beautifully restored by the new owner and looked like a doll's house. The Krichanovs never did get a unit for themselves and stayed living in the second room. But life moved on, and on the first of September, Dima went to school, into the first class, and Klara found a job in the military aviation unit, which had just returned from Germany and was now disbanded in Odessa.

·+♦♦♦+·

Mishka hadn't slept so well for a long time. He had become so used sleeping in the continually rattling explosions and automatic gunfire that he could sleep anywhere. This night, it was almost silent. Yesterday, German's capitulation was declared, and the end of the war had come. The day had finally arrived, but it was difficult to believe. After a wild celebration, shooting into the air, and heavy drinking at a party in honour of victory day, Mishka had a very sore head and he had gone to bed. Now he had a huge headache, like the one he had after he had been wounded in the head in the fight for Leningrad. After being evacuated from Crimea, Mishka had gone all the way from Stalingrad to Berlin. He wasn't a naïve fellow anymore but a wise fighter who had been in savage battles. He had learnt how to survive this enormous man-meat grinder without hiding behind his comrades' backs and to show his bravery when it was needed. He had two medals and a Red Star award on his chest. Most of his family had perished, and his hate of the fascists had no limits. And it became even stronger as they began to liberate cities from the Germans. He also discovered how the Germans treated the Jews. Mass executions and sending trainloads of people to Germany had been normal. When they began to liberate Poland and enter Germany, he had seen the concentration camps, heaps of human bodies, and high chimneys of the crematoriums. This made him even more irreconcilable, and he swore to take revenge for this terrible injustice. Working with the Germans as a translator, often his hands itched to grab a pistol and just shoot them and send them to hell. But on the other side, in his eyes was the image of those Germans he had shot in Crimea.

Now, Mishka wiped his eyes and turned his head. Near him lay his best friend, Shamil Rahmatuev, with whom he had fought for the last two years. Shamil had pulled him out, wounded, from a trench, and put him into the hands of hospital attendants. A bit further down was Sergey Pivovarov, a reckless, merry fellow, ready to joke even within minutes of the danger of death. It seemed that the sun had risen a long time ago, and Mishka needed to wake his friends, even though he wanted to let them sleep.

'Wake up!' he ordered and nudged Shamil with his elbow. The men began to move and open their eyes.

'Couldn't we start the first day of peace differently?' croaked Sergey.

'And how would you like to start the day?' Mishka asked.

'I would like you to bring us a hundred grams of vodka for our hangover.'

'Would you like a salty cucumber as well?' Mishka asked.

'Yes, but I don't believe we will ever get it from you.' Sergey hopelessly waved his hand and closed his eyes.

'I've already told you to get up,' repeated Mishka, and the boys got up.

They went into the courtyard and over to the tap. Sergey took off his soldier's shirt, turned on the tap, and began to splash himself with water. It was still cool, and Mishka and Shamil jumped aside to avoid getting wet. Suddenly, they heard a shot. Sergey froze, and they saw a bloody hole in his back. Mishka and Shamil fell to the ground and looked around. It was only possible that the shot came from a chapel located behind the fence. Mishka grabbed a machine gun and shouted to Shamil, 'Stay here and help Sergey!' He ran out onto the street; it was about 100 metres to the chapel, and in a minute, he was next to it. Just then, a thin young man in a military uniform ran out of the doors, holding a rifle in his hands. When he saw Mishka, he raised his gun, but it was already too late. Mishka had already pulled the trigger, and the bullets pierced his skinny body. The German fell, but Mishka continued to shoot. At last, he stopped and went closer to the body. He pushed it with his foot and turned it over. In front of him was the body of a very young man, maybe even a schoolboy. But it wasn't important anymore . . . now it was just a corpse with open eyes that had no more life in them. He remembered Sergey and ran back. Here, he saw a few people surrounding Shamil, with the breathless corpse of Sergey on his knees. Everyone was shocked by this event. People were used to death and seeing it almost every day, but they still couldn't accept Sergey's death after a victory celebration.

But Mishka felt worse. He couldn't forgive himself for having woken Sergey up and sent him to wash. He almost felt like a murderer himself, and the rest of the day he spent alone.

'Stop blaming yourself. It won't help anyone, and you are guilty of nothing.' Shamil tried to reason with him.

'How am I not guilty when I started a not-needed wake-up exercise? If I hadn't, Sergey would probably still be alive,' Mishka said.

'Nonsense! It was destiny, and you can't do anything about it,' Shamil said.

'All the same, it hurts to feel that you are a part of this fate,' Mishka muttered.

———————— ✦✦✦✦✦ ————————

About a month after the victory celebrations, the troops began to be demobilised, and Mishka and Shamil were part of a division going home. They had decided that they would go to Tashkent together, to where Shamil's relatives lived, and to start a new life. But before that, Mishka wanted to go back to Freiburg to find out what had happened to their house and to perhaps meet some family members who were still alive. But the most important thing for him . . . he wanted revenge for the death of his family. From the letter from his sister Riva in 1941, he knew that his father's best friend Markus had betrayed them to the Germans, and now Mishka thought that he should answer for that.

They went to Minsk together, and from there, Mishka went by himself. He went by train to Vesely Kut, and from there he went on foot. He didn't want anyone to notice him and went through fields and bushes and arrived in Freiburg after sunset. He got closer to his house and saw that nothing but two walls remained. Carefully, trying to remain unnoticed, he entered the house and searched through the ruins, trying to find anything that would remind him of his past life, but the home had been utterly destroyed. Pre-war memories about parents, brothers, and sisters rushed over him. He clasped his head in his hands and quietly began to cry. Then Mishka began his plan. From his bag, he pulled a trophy Browning, carefully wrapped in cloth. He put the holster back in the bag. He had been afraid that Markus would recognise him, so he hadn't shaved in more than two weeks and he wore civilian clothes, and the big grey cap made him almost unrecognisable. Mishka had decided to pretend to be a German soldier who had escaped from a prisoner-of-war camp, and he knew that his German language would help him.

When he got to Markus's house, it was already dark, but a dim light was burning inside. The owners weren't asleep yet. He quietly knocked at the door and waited, but from inside the house, there was complete silence, and after a while, the candle was extinguished. Having waited a little time, he knocked again, this time more persistently. Behind the door there was still silence, but at last a low voice asked in Russian, 'Who is there?'

Mishka recognised Markus's voice and replied in German, 'Open, please.'

After a long silence, somebody began to whisper, and at last he heard the sound of the lock. The door opened slightly, and Markus's head showed. Mishka recognised him at once; with time, he had grown thinner and a lot older, but animal fright burnt in his eyes.

'Who are you, and what do you need from us?' he asked in German.

'My name is Walter. I escaped from a prisoner-of-war camp and am trying to get home. I know that Freiburg is a German farm, and I'm asking for your help.'

Markus carefully examined him from head to foot, and after a short pause, he said, 'I can't hide you in the house. We are under constant surveillance. They will simply shoot us.'

'Don't hide me in the house. I only want to take a rest and have something to eat. I'll leave tomorrow night. As a German, you should help me,' Mishka said.

'I have a hay shed near the forest. You can spend the night there, and early in the morning, I will bring you something to eat.'

'I agree. Can you take me there?' Mishka asked.

'Follow me,' agreed Markus and set off quickly with Mishka following. At the shed, Markus stopped and opened the door. 'You can stay here, don't go out anywhere. I'll come in the morning,' he said.

'No, you wait,' Mishka stopped him in Russian and pulled the pistol out of his pocket.

Markus's eyes filled with fear, and his mouth dropped open. 'I don't understand. Who are you?' he croaked.

'You don't recognise me, you swine!'

Markus looked with horror and then understood what was happening. 'Is that you, Mishka?'

'Yes, it's me. Tell me, what happened to my parents?' Mishka said.

'I didn't do anything to them, on my word of honour, I did nothing to them,' Markus cried.

'Shut up, swine!' Mishka bellowed. 'Riva told me everything, how you led the Germans to them, and they were shot right in front of you!'

'They threatened to shoot anyone who hid Jews,' Markus sobbed.

'So you sacrificed their lives for your right to live? Then die now, swine!' Mishka pointed the pistol at Markus's head.

'Forgive me, Mishka, spare my family!' Markus begged, falling to his knees.

'For forgiveness, you can ask God. You will see him soon,' said Mishka and pulled the trigger.

He shot three times, and the lifeless body of Markus fell to the ground. Mishka had fulfilled his task, but his soul felt no better. He had only killed one villain, but how many others like Markus still walked the earth with impunity? He decided that he would not allow them to live in peace. Over the next three months, he went, without any clear plan, through small towns and villages, pretending that he was looking for work and asking the locals about the occupation and who had cooperated with the fascists. Then he waited until night-time and carried out his punishment. In this time, he killed six traitors, but it didn't bring him any satisfaction. He began to feel that he was behaving like a sociopath, stuck in a corridor without an exit. The end came quickly. He was arrested at Berdichev station. He didn't have to wait long for his judgement. He was sentenced to eight years' imprisonment, but it was reduced because of his military record. He was to serve his sentence in Kazakhstan, and on the way to jail, his only regret was that he hadn't seen Klara.

———— ✦✦✦✦✦ ————

Jukan finished his dinner with pleasure and pushed away his plate. Militsa, the owner of the house, took away the dishes and left the kitchen. Jukan remained alone and looked around the room. Now he didn't need to sleep in forests under trees or take part in any fighting. His duty was to establish rules in the liberated territories. In every small settlement, there was a chairman of the community, chosen by the peasants or appointed by Jukan. In one village, he had offered this position to the most prosperous peasant, but the man refused it.

'How could I be chairman when all my sons are Chetnik?' he asked.

'But it's him who is Chetnik, not you,' Jukan objected.

'No, I couldn't do it anyway, because in your opinion, I'm a Kulak.'

'Well, my grandfather was also a Kulak but worked all his life. How could I trust this position to a ragamuffin who can't even support himself? And you are well respected by others. So we really need people like you,' Jukan insisted. They argued for about an hour, and at last, Jukan made him agree. After that, Jukan never had a problem with this village. Everyone knew exactly what quantity of grain, beans, cabbage, eggs, and milk they should deliver to Jukan.

In each platoon, there was a housekeeper engaged in supply and a main housekeeper for the cheta. There were quartermasters for the battalions and brigades, and all of them reported to the quartermaster of the division. Everywhere he went, Jukan was accompanied by about thirty people, and the locals gave them what they demanded. They were still dressed in any uniform they could find, but Jukan didn't like the military uniform and wore civilian dress. Sometimes he had to recruit young men who had reached army age into the partisans, and he tried to do it without looking if they were his relatives or not. Only one exception was made for his cousin Rade, because he was too big and clumsy and would be an easy target for the enemy. Rade also had a grumbling wife, Stana, and a son, and if Rade died, Jukan would be responsible for them.

Now, Jukan's office was based in Travnik, and he lived in the house of the local forest warden, who had been appointed by Jukan as chairman of the local community. Jukan had a clean room and ate with the warden and his wife, Militsa, his two sons, Micho and Pero, and their older daughter, Radojka, a long-legged, graceful, and gorgeous girl. Just looking at her made his heart beat faster. However, in Bosnia, you had to be very careful how you dealt with a girl;

otherwise, you could suddenly become a head shorter! Radojka was chairman of the local Komsomol organisation. She wore a leather jacket, and a pistol hung at her side. She didn't like the way Jukan did his job, and in the evenings, there were often sharp disputes, which ended when her mother sent Radojka to her bedroom. Gradually he began to feel that she was showing more interest in him, and her remarks were less biting.

Jukan had always been successful with women, but this time, his feelings were very strong. They suited each other very well; she could flash like fire, and the local boys avoided her, afraid of her fiery character. But also, Jukan, or Chiko, had the reputation of a person who had been through fire and water, and few of them got in his way. All of his friends had important positions too. Sayo Grbich, or Stalin, became brigade comanander; and Milovan, or Seljak from Zagreb, became the brigade commissar. Milovan's cousin Branko was nicknamed 'the Mister' because he looked so impressive and became the assistant to the commander of a division, though before the war he had been a policeman. Once at the very beginning of the resistance movement, they had played cards together. Now they seldom met and fought in different brigades. Jukan spent about half a year in Travnik, and his life was very comfortable. He was given another beautiful horse as a present; this one had been a circus horse. It was so graceful, it made everyone jealous. It understood everything that Jukan told it and was able to dance as if in an arena. Jukan always had treats for it, and when he rode his horse, Jukan felt like a prince.

Jukan's relationship with Radojka was getting warmer, though they still argued. One evening, when no one else was around, he unexpectedly drew her to him and kissed her. Radojka stepped aside and grabbed her holster and then lowered her hand and smiled.

'Chiko, why did you do that?' she asked.

'Because I love you,' Jukan answered.

Then she stepped closer, and, looking him in the eyes, she said, 'I love you too!' So began the biggest love story of his life.

It was 1945. There was a feeling that the war was coming to an end. The Soviet army had freed all Soviet territory and was pursuing Hitler's army on European soil. On the other side, the German army was being pressed by Allied armies, who opened a second front in France, instead of the Balkans, as the British and Americans would have preferred, but Tito rejected that and said that a second front on Balkans already exists.

The partisans freed more territory, and Jukan was sent to a new division, based in Kakanj, where the manager of the local community had been killed. Jukan didn't want to leave Radojka, but these orders were not to be questioned. Radojka was to stay and hold her Komsomol secretary position. Despite the fact that the war was getting to an end, the fighting became even harder, and more people died than in all the previous years. The Germans fought with desperation, trying to make their way from Greece and Yugoslavia to Austria. Fighting with them was the Evgeni division, made exclusively from Germans living in Banat. This unit was well armed and had spent the war fighting against the partisans. They had no pity for either partisans or civilians. Where they had been, rivers of blood flowed, and the partisans had old scores to settle with them. In Kakanj, they were encircled, and despite persistent German attempts to break through, the partisans held on. Almost all the enemy were killed, and about 500 were taken prisoner.

Slobodan Voinovich was a courageous and very talented officer and the commander of the division where Jukan served. He was one of the few genuinely professional officers. Before the war, he had graduated from the military college and was captain of the Royal Army. His experience was highly valued. Every partisan, including Slobodan, had an account to settle with this German division. Partisans examined all the captured Germans, who were lined up to get their orders. Ahead of them was a handsome elderly general decorated with many awards and medals. Slobodan went up to him and asked, 'How is it that your breast is covered with so many awards? Is it for the blood of the Serbian people?'

'I'm an old officer, and all of these awards were given to me for bravery. These are German awards, but if I had served in your army, my breast would be covered in your awards,' answered the general proudly.

Slobodan called up an officer and ordered, 'Take the general away and lock him in a shed.'

'And what about the others?' he was asked.

'Shoot them all!' he replied.

'How?' the officer asked, surprised.

'The same way that they shot our people,' Slobodan replied and turned and went to tally the head count.

The order was carried out straight away. All, except for the one general, were shot near a small forest and buried in a common grave. Almost all the partisans approved this decision, but executing the captured was illegal, and Slobodan faced a lot of trouble for doing it.

After they took Kakanj, Jukan's brigade moved on to Sarajevo. The Germans were leaving their positions without a fight, trying to get to Austria as soon as possible. They had only one way . . . by railway. It was possible to go by sea, but almost all the Dalmatian population had risen up against the fascists. When Jukan's brigade reached Sarajevo, it had already been liberated by other divisions, and the Germans had left to try to reach Slovenia. In May, spring arrived. The partisans had pursued the Germans almost on their heels, exposing them to more losses. The day that they arrived in the village of Zidani Most was a beautiful day, and for the second day in a row, there were no sounds of shots. Jukan took off his shirt and lay down on the grass to sunbathe. The sun felt lovely, burning his body, and he closed his eyes in pleasure. Suddenly, automatic gunfire and loud shouts filled the air. He quickly raised his head and looked around. Shots were coming from everywhere, but nobody was hiding. On the contrary, everyone was running around waving their hands and laughing. It turned out that the Soviet army had taken Berlin, fascist Germany had surrendered, and the war was over. They had waited almost every day for this news, and now it had arrived. People celebrated like children, shot in the air, drank, and danced the Kolo.

Jukan celebrated as well. He had been a part of this war from the first day to the last. How many people around him had been lost, how many made cripple, and here he was, alive and well. But on the other hand, there was one disturbing thought . . . for all these years, he had become used to war, and he had completely forgotten how to live in peacetime. The most important thing, though, was that he had changed. Before the war, he had been a simple, rural boy. And now he was the quartermaster of a division commanding hundreds of people. He had no idea what he would do in peacetime, but for sure he knew he would not be going back to his native Lipa.

They stayed in Zidani Most for about a week. Jukan was living in a rich Slovene house where a big family lived. Everybody continued to celebrate the end of the war with such passion, it seemed everyone had gone mad. Three sisters live in this house; it would be hard to say that they were beauties, but they were magnificently well built, and all of them loved Jukan very much and seemed prepared to tear him to pieces. It seemed they had no shame and were having sex with him, one by one and sometimes together. At first, he indulged in these games with pleasure, but soon he began to feel exhausted. But the sisters continued to demand more sex, though two of them were married. It was clear that this young and successful Bosnian man was a big attraction. Meanwhile, he had to supply the army with goods, and he was ready to drop with weariness. At last, his division was sent on redeployment to the Adriatic Sea. Jukan left Slovenia not only with some regret but also with relief, because he felt that he would simply die, caught up in the endless love hop!

His division was now sent to the Dalmatian coast, to Split, Zadar, and Dubrovnik, and Jukan's office was in Croatia Novi, in warehouses taken from the Germans. From here, he had to personally accompany all the shipments of food stuffs, because in the mountains there were still plenty of Chetniks threatening the transports. Now everything was transported by car, not horse, though Jukan still kept his favourite horse, Druze, and rode him with pleasure. They understood each other perfectly, Druze knew all the commands, and there was no need to use a bridle. Jukan understood all his snorting and head and body movements. Jukan had never had such an understanding with any other horse, and no other horse was as spoilt.

The long summer passed in these post-war tasks, and Jukan had not had time to even visit his mother. He had such a huge financial responsibility that he couldn't leave his post for even a day. His predecessor, who was leaving the warehouse to him for a higher position in Belgrade, warned him, 'Look, Chiko, I'm giving you an extremely valuable post. But I feel sorry for you, because you are too young to control it all, and you will definitely end up in jail.' In this warehouse, there was everything that anyone could need, and many people in a ruined post-war country would have wanted to profit from it. Jukan wasn't afraid of anything and was prepared to accept responsibility. On the other hand, during the war, he had selected his staff himself and had a good feeling about whom to trust and never forgave even small thefts. All his subordinates were older than him but unconditionally took orders from him. Between them was a former lawyer and bookkeeper, but most had grown wise through life experiences. So everything was well accounted for, and very seldom did anything go missing. However, this routine job finally became too boring for Jukan, and he asked to be sent to study.

Jukan's division was on the Adriatic Coast all summer long and into autumn. Then the order came that they were to relocate to the city of Valjevo, in Serbia. Jukan had to provide food and accommodation for all divisions during the move. And though it was now peacetime, it was not an easy task to provide 6,000 personnel with everything they needed. Before their departure, he went with his old friend Sayo Grbich, nicknamed Stalin, and now the commander of a brigade, to visit Travnik and to see Radojka. She was so happy to see him that she left her job for the day and went to her home to change her clothes. She came out in a beautiful dress and high-heeled shoes. Radojka looked great, even in her uniform, but now she looked like a real city girl, and Jukan had never seen anyone like her. Sayo was impressed as well. He nudged Jukan with his elbow and quietly whispered in his ear, 'What a lucky man you are. Look at the beauty you have found for yourself. Only don't be a fool, you can't lose a girl like this.'

They walked across the city, arm in arm, and she often put her head on his shoulder. Jukan felt that he was in seventh heaven, and it seemed as though everyone was looking at them. After dinner at a restaurant, Radojka went with them to the station, and on the platform, they kissed for the last time. 'When will we meet again?' she asked him.

'Goodness knows, maybe never' was Jukan's unexpected reply, and he stepped onto the footboard of the departing train.

The redeployment in Serbia went very smoothly. There were no problems with accommodation and food supplies, and for that, Jukan received official gratitude from command head office. Soon after that, he was promoted to a new position; he was appointed deputy chief of an artillery brigade, which contained four battalions: heavy artillery, anti-tank, anti-aircraft, and light artillery. Now, under his control were three and a half thousand people and a hundred units of military machines, including trucks, tractors, big guns, and all kinds of shells.

He owned a vehicle but preferred to travel on his favourite horse. The brigade headquarters were in the centre of Valjevo, on the Klubery River bank, in a big three-storey house with its own restaurant. Jukan rented an apartment right across the street. His life was gaining speed. In his twenty-four years, he had advanced to a colonel's position, with a salary of 6,600 dinars. This was big money, and when he received it the first time, he simply didn't know what to do with it. There was practically nothing to spend it on!

Jukan's food was brought to him by the owner of the restaurant. She was about thirty-five years old, and very attractive. When giving Jukan his tray of food, she always bent low to show her big white breasts, and when leaving, she showed her playful bottom, making it impossible for him not to notice her charms. Jukan successfully fought with his own desires and didn't give in to her tricks. He didn't want any new gossip, and so he pretended not to notice her beauty. For all the hardships he had experienced during the war, now he felt like a cheese in warm butter. But he still asked to be sent to study. It was clear to him that he didn't have enough education, and without this, he would never achieve new heights.

Jukan rejected the first offer of study in Sarajevo, but in October, he had an offer to go and study at the military academy in the Soviet Union. His joy had no bounds . . . after all their victories, this was now possible, thanks to the Soviet Army, led by the great Stalin. To go to study in a country where communism had won was a great honour for him, as a young communist, and he willingly prepared the warehouse transfer to another officer who had just arrived. He was a captain and had already grown the grey hair of the wise. Jukan showed him everything in the warehouse, trying not to miss anything. In the evening, when they arrived back to the staff office, the captain looked at him and said, 'I look at you and I can't believe my eyes. Do you really want to leave all this?'

'What's so surprising?' Jukan asked, shrugging his shoulders.

'It's simply madness to leave such a position. How do you know what is waiting for you in faraway and cold Russia?' the captain asked.

'Only time will tell!' Jukan evaded answering, but everyone was asking the same question. All his subordinates begged him to stay and not to leave such a successful career. However, it was well known that the biggest part of this Bosnian's character was his stubbornness, and at the beginning of November, with four other young officers from his division, he left for the small town of Churuk in Banat, where they were joined by other officers. Altogether, there were 300 of them, all young, self-confident people.

They were accommodated in rich local houses, where they were on full provisions. All of them continued to get their full wages for doing almost nothing. Their only task was to study the Russian language, which was taught to them by a priest from the local church, but it turned out that he wasn't good at it. They learnt some words, which they could hardly connect into simple sentences. The rest of the time, they drank, went to dances in the local club, and tried to satisfy the healthy demand and curiosity of the local female population. Jukan's salary was enough for everything, and he decided to buy himself some new clothes. He bought two pairs of smart shoes, a suit, and a magnificent long leather coat. He looked like a real city dandy! He lived in a house with Officer Gioko Negovan, from Lika, who was always smiling and joking. They became inseparable friends. Soon, Gioko's cousin Milan Ribar and a few other future cadets joined them. In this carefree way, the winter passed, and at the end of February, they were ready to leave. They were sent from Kikinda station with honours and an orchestra. Kind parting words and wishes for successful study were spoken. They would go back home as well-educated officers who would become the elite of the Yugoslavian army.

They were all very excited, anticipating future adventures, though many felt fear in the pits of their stomachs at the thought of possible difficulties. They travelled in a first-class compartment where litres of rakija were drunk, and the fun didn't stop for a minute. The next day in Romania, they had to change from their compartment to a cargo train. The mood of many of them soured, but these men had endured five years of war and were ready for everything. They still had stocks of cheeses, ham and prshut, string beans, and salty cabbage. So soon they started singing and even tried to dance and didn't notice that one of their fellow students, Ivo Zdravkovich, was left at the station. Now, for the first time in their lives, they were abroad, and they felt not just like fellow students but like relatives. The train continued to carry them away further into the deep snowdrifts of Russia.

They spent three days in the cars, rushing past small towns and villages, through big stations to the faraway city of Volsk, located in the Saratov region. It was very cold in the carriages, despite the ovens that were installed, and the men tried to keep warm with alcohol and to have fun playing cards. No one was equal to Jukan in this business, and he won a solid amount of money. However, soon very few were willing to play with him. Sometimes he looked out of the small window at the landscape rushing by, but the only thing he saw was snow, snow, and more snow. Fir trees were covered in snow, and the small houses had sunk to their roofs in snow. On the fourth day, the train stopped, and the doors were swung open. Before them appeared boundless plains covered by deep snow. Not far away, they saw three four-storeyed buildings. It was their Infantry Academy.

The station was called Privolsk, and here the railway lines came to an end. The men all got out of the train and lined up and then went to the school along a narrow path cleared of snow, above which walls of snowdrift towered. They entered the school territory near a bath. By this time, they were all feeling frozen, and their faces were not so happy anymore. Then they were ordered to go down to the basement, which appeared to be a huge bathroom. Their next order was to undress and to hand over their personal things. No one liked this order, but they didn't challenge it. The new cadets stripped to their skin, they were given a washbasin and a wisp (a small bundle of straw), and with these they entered the bathroom. It was not very clean to look at, but here it was warm, even hot. The mood changed again, and even some laughter was heard. Nobody really knew how to use the washbasin and wisp properly, so basins were often dropped with a terrible noise, causing gales of laughter. Even more fun was when someone stepped on the soap and fell, and even funnier, when someone fell together with their basin.

Everyone finished bathing and went to the waiting room, where instead of their Yugoslav uniform, they were given the military cadet uniform. It was sewn badly and looked terrible, but at least it was new and clean. Then they were taken to their barracks, on the third floor of the next building. All 300 people lived in the one room that occupied the whole floor. Everyone had just a bed and bedside table, and it was clear that Jukan should forget about his luxury lifestyle for a while. But, on the other hand, it wasn't that difficult, because as partisans, they had been used to living in a forest under a fir tree. An even greater disappointment was waiting for them in the dining room. The food they were given for dinner was hardly edible. The first course was Russian cabbage soup, made of salty cabbage, which reminded Jukan of slightly coloured water with a few leaves floating in it. Jukan tried a few spoonsful with black bread that reminded him of dirt. But that was just the beginning. The second dish was meatballs with pearl barley porridge. The meatballs were brown and didn't smell like meat, while the pearl barley porridge was like elastic and slid off their teeth. Their bodies refused to swallow it, causing some vomiting reflexes, and Jukan stopped trying and pushed his plate away. The only thing he managed to eat was compote, even though the fruit in it wasn't fresh.

So their new life started unpromisingly. Their mornings began early, and with marching and singing, they learnt Russian soldier's songs. Loud orders had them falling on the cold ground, running in full regimental dress, and they were wrung out. Nobody cared that they were all officers. Everyone gave them orders, and this annoyed them. They silently put up with all this, and when it was time to study, they tried not to miss a word that the teachers spoke, though their Russian was far from perfect. Unexpectedly, after about a month, Ivo Zdravkovich showed up. The most surprising thing was that in this time he had learnt to speak Russian and Romanian. He was a strange man; during the war, he had been wounded in the head, and as a result, he had lost the ability to sleep normally. He was often not able to sleep for weeks before falling into a death-like deep sleep for a few days or a week, and it was impossible to wake him. His memory was phenomenal; he remembered literally everything that his teachers said and what he read in books. He had a photographic memory, and it started to irritate his teachers, whom he quite often corrected, finding errors in their lectures. Some teacher didn't know how to react to this, but unexpectedly it all came to an end. After a month of sleepless nights, Ivo fell into a deep sleep and slept for almost a week. When he did wake up, he had forgotten everything and had to start again. But he remembered everything again very quickly and soon overtook everyone again. The teachers decided that it was impossible for him to stay in the school, and with two other seriously sick cadets, he was sent back to Yugoslavia.

All the rest continued to study, living in very harsh conditions. The temperature in the barracks was very low, in spite of the fact that there were furnaces. The food was still terrible, and their stomachs refused to get used to it. The truth was that the Russians couldn't survive on such food either. It was possible to get food in the market, but they didn't have any money. They were only given six roubles and sixty kopecks a month, and that was to buy polish for their boots. The cadets tolerated these conditions for a few months, but gradually the feeling of discontent began to grow, and they decided to start a hunger strike. After the wake-up siren and gymnastics, they were taken to the dining room. They all took their seats, and the plates of food were put on the tables, but none of them picked up their spoons. They simply sat there, sitting quietly and stupidly looking ahead. The sergeants started to worry at first, running between the tables and shouting, 'Eat! Why aren't you eating?'

But nobody paid them any attention. Then the officers were called in, but the cadets refused to speak to them too. Then they were taken to the classroom, and the lessons went normally and the teachers calmed down. But at lunchtime, everything was repeated. Though the meals were of slightly better quality, and despite the rumblings of their own stomachs, they didn't touch the food. Then the head of the school came to the dining room. He was a wonderful man, and the cadets all loved him. Colonel Tsurilo was gypsy by origin, with curly brown hair starting to turn grey at the temples. They gave him their list of requirements, and they wanted a representative from the Yugoslavian embassy to visit them. They didn't have long to wait, and in less than a week, the military attaché arrived from Moscow. The meeting took place in the assembly hall. Firstly, he recognised their military merits, but then he began the attack.

'The party has entrusted you and sent you to study, and instead of that, you dishonour your country and call a hunger strike.'

But they didn't want to be quiet. 'We are officers, and they treat us worse than soldiers. We are not getting any money, and the food is so terrible that you can't put it in your mouth. We can't eat the porridge, and we demand at least sometimes to have beans.'

'The officers tell me that you have normal food!' the attaché said.

'Stay here for a week, and then you will see!' they told him.

'I don't have time for that. I need to get back to Moscow urgently,' he said. When he said this, everyone took off their caps and began to throw them onto the stage. The military attaché and officers quickly retreated through a back exit.

After this departure, the changes for the better started almost immediately. Now there were a lot less drills, the soup became thicker, and they were given string beans instead of pearl barley. The most important thing was that they began to receive a salary of 120 roubles, and on this money, they could buy food from the kiosk or the market. The protests stopped, and life got back on track. Sometimes they were allowed to go out, but Privolsk was such a distance and had so few places for leisure. They studied in this top infantry school for exactly one year, and after passing their examinations, they were transferred to Odessa. This news was met with enthusiasm; at last, they could get away from this godforsaken place.

Part 6

They arrived in Odessa in September, in the middle of an Indian summer. Jukan sent a postcard home to his grandma Marija, where he wrote,

> My dear Baka, I have finally arrived at the last point of your damnation on the Black Sea. But it's not as black and terrible as you said. On the contrary it is beautiful. Kiss you with much love,
>
> Your useless grandson, Jukitsa

The men loved the beautiful, noisy city of Odessa at first glance. After spending a year in the godforsaken, far-off city of Privolsk, Odessa was paradise. But this was just in the beginning. The infantry academy opened its doors for the first time that year, and it was obvious that it wasn't ready. Its buildings had suffered from the bombardments of the war, the windows were not glazed properly, and many of them were simply boarded up with plywood. The central heating didn't work, and there were no stoves in the barracks, so it was dreadfully cold. The food was awful, and on top of that, they were told that they would again be studying the first-year curriculum. The cadets weren't prepared to accept this and spoke to the authorities. The teachers tried to break their spirit with enforced discipline. That day, from early morning after breakfast, they had to march on the parade ground before class in full regimental dress, in incessant rain. The commands 'lie down' and 'stand up' sounded all the time. Jukan had never been known for his patience and was even famous for his hot-tempered nature . . . he couldn't hold himself in this time. Having risen once again, he kept standing when the next command came to lie down.

The sergeant was surprised by his insubordination and continued to issue orders, but on the following order, a few more people didn't lie down, and on the next order, no one lay down. The sergeant got closer to Jukan and screamed, 'Private Soldier Vignevich, lie down!'

'I will not lie down,' Jukan answered loudly and threw his gun on the ground. 'Enough, we don't need this education any longer, send us home!'

All the cadets put their guns on the ground and started to shout, 'We want to go home!'

They all walked to the barracks and began to discuss their plan of action. Everybody felt determined and ready to defend themselves with weapons. Many of them, despite customs inspections, had managed to bring in their pistols and continued to hide them. The academy authorities sent a representative. He listened to their demands and told them that these would be considered, but for now, they should stop their strike and get back to study. But everyone was united and refused to obey. 'Then you will get into a lot of trouble,' the major threatened and left the premises. That evening, Jukan wrote out a list of their twelve demands:

1. To recognise all ranks received during the war
2. To return the uniforms of the Yugoslavian army
3. To return all awards
4. To pay them their salary according to rank
5. To allow them to go into the city after class
6. To stop all unnecessary drills and to treat them as officers
7. To glaze all windows in the building
8. To connect the central heating
9. To transfer them to the second year of their education
10. To provide normal food
11. To replace pearl barley porridge with string beans
12. If they can't do these things, then send them back to Yugoslavia.

Next morning, they were asked to choose ten representatives to do the negotiations, and as Jukan was the instigator, he was one of them. At noon, a small bus with little windows rolled into the courtyard, followed by some cars. Jukan and his companions were to go by bus, and they reluctantly agreed. The teaching staff was to travel by 'Gaziks'. Everyone was on alert; many had the impression that they were to be taken to an open field and shot! But the bus was going towards the city. At last, they arrived at a big building on which was written 'Staff of the Odessa Military District'. Everyone knew that the commander of this district was the legendary Marshal Zhukov, the conqueror of fascist Germany, who was no longer in Stalin's favour and had been sent far away from Moscow to warm Odessa. They were told to get out of the bus and to follow a young lieutenant. They climbed a wide set of marble stairs to the fourth floor, walked along a corridor, and found themselves in a spacious reception room, where they were met by a well-dressed, handsome captain. He asked them all to sit down and went back into the office. After a while, he returned and ordered them to line up parallel to the wall, with their backs to the door. They were surprised, but the captain said, 'Don't argue, follow your orders!' They obediently waited in line.

It was not clear exactly how, but unexpectedly, the wall slid open, and there in front of them was Marshal Zhukov, the conqueror of Hitler's army, about whom they had heard so much. They had sung songs about Tito and Stalin, but Zhukov was a legendary figure. And now he stood in front of them. There was no doubt about who he was, and everyone stiffened, as if bewitched. Not only were the cadets amazed, but also the academy staff turned pale with fear.

'Hello, Comrade Cadets!' he greeted them.

'Zdravija zelaem, Comrade Marshal!' they all responded.

He approached them and greeted them all with a handshake and then said, 'Let's all move to the next room.' In the room was a big table covered in a bright green cloth. 'Well, sit down, Comrades,' he said. They all took their seats, and Jukan was on the corner. Zhukov took his seat next to Jukan and began to speak. 'Tell me, my friends, why are you striking?' and his face took on a serious expression. Cadet Koprivitsa, who spoke Russian the best, stood up and began, but his voice broke down, and he got confused.

The pause became painful, but then Jukan stood and started to speak. 'Comrade Zhukov, we came to the Soviet Union to study. We are all officers who fought four years in the war, and many of us have the highest awards. What sense is it to drill us like ordinary soldiers? We want our uniforms back and to be paid the salaries according to our rank. In the building where we live, there is no glass in the windows, and the rooms are not heated. It's impossible to study in such conditions. The food we get is awful, and because we have no money, we can't buy anything at the markets. We studied for a year in Privolsk Infantry School, and now again they want to instruct us on our first year's studies. I don't know why they need to make us suffer and waste time. I wrote a list of our requirements, here it is. I ask you, Comrade Marshal, to consider them, and if it is not possible to fix it, then we ask that you send us back to Yugoslavia.' He put the note in front of Zhukov.

As Zhukov listened to Jukan, his face became more and more serious. As Jukan took his seat again, silence filled the room. It was so tense that no one knew how it would end. At last, Zhukov turned to the chief of the academy and asked, 'Is this true?'

'Partly, but not everything . . .' started the colonel, but Zhukov lost interest and turned back to Jukan and his friends. Now, he had a cheeky smile on his face.

'Well, Comrade Officers, I have heard what you have to say. I have to tell you that, with the utmost respect, I followed the way you resisted the fascist armies, led by Tito. Therefore, I will try to contact Comrade Stalin and probably Tito too. We will try to solve your problem. You can go now, and you, young man,' he said, turning to Jukan, 'can come at any time to my office, and I will always be happy to see you.'

They all left the office, but the teachers were asked to stay. As soon as Jukan and his friends got out into the corridor, their tension disappeared, and they began to laugh. They were taken by the same bus back to school, and on their arrival, their friends bombarded them with questions. When they told them that they had met with the legendary Zhukov, the barracks went crazy. Then they began to discuss what to do next, and they all came to the conclusion that the next day, they would begin to study again. In the morning, after exercise and a considerably better breakfast, they walked to the classroom, singing. None of them knew that at that moment, they were being watched from the window by Zhukov. He had kept his promise and was at once engaged in fixing their problems. Jukan never took up the marshal's invitation to visit him. The next day, changes began to appear in abundance. All the academy heads were dismissed. Early in the morning, in the barracks rooms, tradesmen began fitting the windows, and soon they were fixed. The central heating couldn't be fixed quickly, but instead, heaters made from iron barrels were installed, and the smoke flew directly through the windows and out to the street. There was a lot of smoke, but it was warm. In the dining room, the food improved greatly. They started to get potatoes, macaroni, and even string beans.

But the most important thing was that on the second day, some tailors arrived and measured everyone. Soon, they were given the uniforms of the Yugoslavian army officers, only the epaulets were Russian. They started to receive a salary at the rate corresponding to their rank, and Jukan was getting the highest one. Now they could buy everything they wanted, and after class, they were allowed to go to the city without permission. Also, they were transferred to the second-year curriculum, so all their demands had been met. These exciting events helped them to believe in themselves again and made them even closer. The academy head office realised that there was no need to have bad relationships with the cadets, and life became easier for everyone.

After class, they were free to go to the city, and Odessa accepted them with pleasure. The girls were instantly attracted to them. They visited clubs and dances regularly. The never went alone and were always ready to stand up for themselves. At dance parties, they quite often had to face the local hooligans. In post-war years, Odessa was terrorised by the 'Black Cat Bandits'. The whole city was afraid of them, but what could they do against a group of well-organised officers who had fought every day of the war, looking death in the eye? Once, the Black Cat Bandits came in a big group to a dance in Djukovsky Park. They started a brawl in the middle of the dance, pulling out knives, with a group of young boys who tried to object to them. When Jukan and his friends walked in, they found themselves face to face with the bandits and decided to support the very frightened young men. The bandits, armed with their knives, refused to back down, but after a short and very unsuccessful fight, they had to give in. The result was very impressive . . . leaving the dance party, Jukan and his friends hung the bandits up by the belts of their trousers on the peaked iron fence, making them look like Christmas tree decorations. After that, the bandits tried to avoid meeting them.

+ + ✦ ✦ + +

Life in Odessa entered into a peaceful flow. Any hopes of Ljova returning back home from the war had faded away, and only little Dima trembled with hope when he saw any officer passing by the house, thinking that it might be his father. Dima had grown up quickly and had turned out to be a clever madcap, and it became difficult for his grandmother Zelda to look after him. Klara spent almost all of her day at work in the military aviation squadron. She brought home a modest salary, which, together with her widow's pension, was barely enough to live on. Many people hinted that as chief accountant, she could live much better, but she always pretended that she didn't understand their hints and continued to work for her salary. Dima, with the other local children, climbed on the ruins left by the bombardments, where it was possible to find very dangerous toys, such as bullets, grenades, and even bombs. Quite often, it was possible to hear the sounds of explosions around.

Klara came home from work one day and had just entered the courtyard when a neighbouring boy passed her and said, 'Your Dima shot himself!'

'What nonsense are you talking?' Klara asked angrily and tried to grab hold of the boy, but he slipped past her around the corner and disappeared. Her heart almost stopped, and she rushed into the house. At the doorway, she saw a group of neighbouring scandalmongers led by Varvara Vasilevna. When they saw Klara, they all became silent. 'What has happened?' she asked, frightened.

'Your Dima is wounded,' she was told, and not waiting to listen to any more, she rushed into the room. Here in the middle of the room sat Dima with a bandage on his foot. His black curly hair was in disarray, and his eyes were bright with guilt and fear. Next to him was a frightened Zelda, her hair also in disarray.

Klara fell to her knees and cried, 'What happened?' and she began to touch his leg. Zelda and Dima both began eagerly to explain what had occurred.

That day, Dima and his friends had been climbing on the ruins of a house that had been destroyed in the bombing, looking for war trophies. They had been lucky and found some cartridges. They started a fire and threw the cartridges in it and hid around the corner. The fire began to burn down, but the cartridges still hadn't exploded. At last, the fire went out, and the boys decided to leave their shelter. When they got closer to the fire, two cartridges blew up, and Dima felt a burning pain in his leg. He fell to the ground, and, at first, the other children all ran away but then returned to help him. They carried him to the military hospital, which was just across the road. Then one of the boys ran back to get Zelda. She screamed and ran to the hospital, and the news of Dima's wound spread quickly through the courtyard and beyond. But, as it turned out, the wound wasn't all that bad; the bullet had passed through the soft tissue without touching the bone. The doctors quickly checked Dima and stitched up his wound so well that he came out with a big loss of blood and a small scar, which remained with him for life. Klara listened to this story while hugging Dima's knees, and by the end, Dima had begun to smile a little. Then Klara got to her feet and cried, 'When will all this end finally!' and gave him a sharp slap over the head. From this time, all adventures ended, and Dima was much more obedient.

Time passed. One afternoon, Klara was going to the bank when she was caught in a torrential downpour of rain. Not having an umbrella, she took shelter inside the first gate. Here, she tried to shake the water from her hair, but just at that moment, a young woman ran in and almost knocked Klara over. 'Please be more careful,' Klara said.

'I do apologise,' the young woman started but then stopped. 'Klara, is that you?' Now Klara looked more carefully and recognised the stranger to be her old school friend Tanja Klyachkina. They hugged each other and then began asking one another about what had happened to them during the war. Klara heard about the atrocities committed during the occupation, about the executions in the park, about Tanja's sister who had turned grey and was a bit mad from fear, how she was tossed out of her mother-in-law's house, and how poor Shurik had hidden them in the catacombs.

For Klara, it seemed impossible that they could have survived all these torments, and it seemed to her that her own war adventures were very easy ones. Klara told Tanja about her husband and brother who had been killed and the difficulties of her last evacuation. Carefully she looked at her old friend and noticed an orthodox cross around her neck.

'Tanja, what is this?' she asked.

'It's a cross, Klara. I converted to Christianity right after the war. On that day when the Germans forced me to pray to prove that I was Russian, I said a whole prayer, even though I had never been to church before. At that moment, I felt that it was the Lord who put the words into my mouth. From that day, I believe in him, and that is why I accepted Christianity,' Tanja explained.

For Klara, who had never gone to synagogue or church, it meant very little. 'Where do you live now?' Klara asked her.

'I live with Shurik and Zhenkoj in Tenistaja Street, in Arcadia, and where are you?' Tanja said.

'I live with my mother and Dima in an apartment on Pirogovsky Street, just opposite the military hospital,' Klara answered.

'It's so great to have met again. Now let's not lose one another anymore, and we will meet soon,' offered Tanja, and they went their separate ways.

A couple of weeks later, just in front of her apartment, Klara noticed a colonel with a big bunch of red roses, which he handed to Klara. She recognised her old admirer, Lyonka Rjaboy, and he was shining with happiness. 'Klara, how glad I am that I meet you again,' he said.

'How did you find me?' she asked.

'Tanja Klyachkina gave me your address,' he told her.

'What a chatterbox she is!' Klara laughed.

'Why, are you not glad to see me?' he asked disappointedly.

'What are you saying, Lyonka? We are very good friends,' she said calmingly.

'No, not friends! Klara, I have loved you all my life, and now Tanja tells me that you have lost your husband. I have come to make you an offer. Marry me, and we will go to Moscow together. I have a wonderful apartment and a very important job. If you agree, you will live without wanting anything,' he promised.

'But I am not alone. I have my mother and a son, Dima, who is going to school this year. I can't leave them!' she said.

'You don't have to leave anyone. Take them with you. I have enough space for everyone,' he said.

Klara became silent. Even though the thought of marrying Lyonka was disgusting to her, she didn't want to offend him. After all, he had always loved her and had never done anything to hurt her. She needed to come up with an idea, and then a wonderful thought occurred to her. 'Listen, Lyonka, Tanja didn't tell you the whole story . . . it has only been one year since I received my husband's death certificate. I have promised myself to wait for him for not less than two years. There are so many cases where people who were thought to be dead have returned home. At least for Dima's sake, I should wait that long. That's why I can't accept your offer.'

'You have decided that for sure?' Lyonka asked.

'Yes,' she replied.

'If that is so, give me your word that when I arrive in one year's time, you will agree,' he said.

'Let's not get too far ahead. You come in a year's time, and then we will see.' Lyonka accepted this compromise without enthusiasm. In the evening, they went to a restaurant, and the next morning, Lyonka returned to Moscow, promising to return in a year. After the war, one more of Klara's friends, Mishka Tabachnikov, had become one of the most popular Soviet composers. He was the one who had accompanied the girls on the grand piano at the Tram Driver's Club. He was now in Moscow too.

Klara continued to work as the chief accountant for the military aviation division. Under her supervision was a book keeper, Lena Perjevaja, with whom she became good friends. Lena had spent the whole war in this division and was in an intimate relationship with Colonel Rybakov. He was madly in love with Lena and was always ready to give her gifts. His division had been billeted in Germany for more than year after the war, and there they had expropriated hundreds of valuable items. However, the colonel was married before the war and had a wife and two children. Now she was demanding that he return to his family. The colonel was called to the district staff office, where they had a long discussion, after which he came back as gloomy as death. He called Lena into his office and locked the door. Lena wasn't expecting anything and had run happily to the meeting. They spent more than an hour behind the locked door; through the door, it was possible to hear Lena shouting and crying, followed by the apologetic voice of the colonel. But the conditions laid out to him in the staff office made the situation desperate. After a long conversation, Lena left the office in tears and came to Klara. She explained that their joint life was over. Rybakov was to return to his family, and she was to go back to her native Kherson City.

To make up for this, Rybakov gave Lena many expensive gifts. Among them were four silver fox furs and one Royal fur coat made of ermine, boxes of crystal, vases and plates, watches, and jewellery. Klara was simply shocked when she saw all these luxury items. Lena was packing things in boxes, and she was very irritated.

'I don't know where I am going to put all this stuff, and whether I need all these things at all,' she complained.

'What things are you talking about?' Klara asked.

'This vase, for example!' Lena said, putting on the table a beautiful vase decorated around the edge with colourful fruits.

Klara had never seen such a beautiful thing in her life. 'My god, what a beauty!' was all she could say.

'Yes, I like it very much too, but where will I put all this? And it could break on the way. And where will I put it in my house? It would be better if you bought it from me,' Lena said.

'I would buy it, but I don't have very much money,' Klara replied.

'How much do you have?' Lena asked.

Klara opened her purse. 'Only thirty roubles,' she said.

'OK, give me thirty,' Lena agreed, but for Klara, thirty roubles was a lot of money, and it was important to her.

'Let's go to the commission shop and let them value it,' she said.

'Let's do that,' Lena agreed, and they carefully put the vase in a big bag and went to the nearest commission shop. When the shop owner saw the vase, he couldn't hide his delight, and his eyes flashed greedily. He began to examine it more carefully.

'Well, how much will you give me for it?' Lena asked impatiently.

He turned and looked at her directly and said, 'I'll give you 2,000 roubles. Do you agree?' Both of them were shocked by this price, and Lena accepted it at once. The money was put into her hands almost at once, and no receipts were given. Later they came to the conclusion that Lena had sold it cheaply and that it was much more expensive than that. They came back shocked and silent, and Klara cursed herself for her stupidity.

—————❖❖❖❖❖❖—————

The window of Klara's house faced the backyard, and the house next door was in ruins. At that time in Odessa, there were many captured German soldiers working on the city ruins, trying by hand to clean up the destruction that they had caused. They were taken to the ruins early in the morning and worked until three o'clock, with a lunch break. They looked very unhappy dressed in worn-out uniforms, and their bony figures showed through the holes. They tried not to look at the eyes of people and pretended not to hear the malicious sneers of boys and not to see the spittle of the old women. They patiently bore this burden and tried to make up for their sins. They worked slowly, knowing that it would not change anything. Only at dinner time could they take a little rest. The food they were given would be regarded as rubbish, even in prison, but they patiently ate the soup with a small piece of bread. Such a meal was not enough for an adult male. For a long time, Zelda watched them with hatred; perhaps one of them had killed her son or Klara's husband. But gradually her hatred for these unfortunate people disappeared, and only pity was left. One of them reminded her of her son, and once during dinner, she went up to him and offered him a piece of bread. He jumped aside in shock but then took the bread and ate it greedily. Since then, Zelda regularly fed the Germans. Some of their neighbours noticed this and mentioned it to Klara.

'Mumma, why are you doing this?' Klara asked her mother.

'What are you talking about?' Zelda responded.

'Why are you feeding these fascists?' Klara wanted to know.

'They are hungry and miserable, and I feel sorry for them,' Zelda replied.

'How can you feel sorry for them, after all they did to us? I simply feel ashamed in front of our neighbours,' Klara said. But deep inside, Klara didn't condemn her mother; she understood her.

Just after they had returned to Odessa, Zelda had written a letter to her sister in America and soon received back a very detailed answer. They were glad that Zelda, Klara, and Dima had managed to survive the war, though their men had been lost. The war hadn't touched their American relatives, and even more than that, they had made very good money. Elsa had married a very successful dental technician whose business grew every day. They had two children, Kenny and John. Oll had a shop and was married to a very beautiful woman called Irma. They had one boy, whom they had named Michael, and Irma was pregnant with their second child. It would seem that at this time, the family knew only peace and stability. But Oll was very energetic and full of ideas. Unexpectedly, Uncle Robert, who had left to open a business in Florida, sent him a letter. Florida had always seemed like paradise to Oll, so when Uncle Robert invited him to Miami for a business talk, he accepted. He didn't say much to Irma, only promising that he would be back soon.

After two weeks, he came back delighted . . . he and his uncle had bought a whole hotel, so now they had to sell the shop and forget about their well-established lifestyle and travel to Florida. For Irma, pregnant and with small Michael on her hands, it was a terrifying prospect, but she couldn't discourage Oll, and, anyway, it was already too late. In Miami, there was an unusually bad heatwave, and there was just one escape—the beach! But this place horrified Irma the most . . . on house walls was written 'No Jews'. Fortunately, at that time, the military fleet was based in Miami, and the seamen filled the hotel. They were overwhelmed by the work, but the hotel began to make very good money. Irma, although pregnant, worked as hard as everyone else; she cleaned rooms, did the laundry, cooked meals, and looked after her son. But it was clear already that the risk they had taken and the money that they had invested into the business was bearing fruit. The hotel was doing better and better, and plans for their future were getting more and more optimistic. They didn't forget, though, about Zelda and Klara. They sent them a parcel of clothes! When Klara brought the parcel from the post office and opened it, she screamed with delight and surprise. She had never seen such beautiful clothes in all her life. There were dresses, hats with a veil, high-heeled shoes, high-quality nylon stockings, and some shirts and trousers for Dima. When Klara put on one of the dresses and the shoes, she looked in the mirror and saw a beautiful stranger, and for the first time in her life, she loved what she saw.

⁜⁜⁜⁜⁜

In January, Jukan, together with the other cadets, graduated from their second-year scholarship, and now only one more year remained. For their vacation period, they were sent for two months to Yugoslavia. Jukan was sent to an infantry regiment located in a small Croatian town, Otochats. After arriving at the base, Jukan at once went to see the commanding officer, who turned out to be his good war friend Mirko Beslan. When he saw Jukan, he ran, and they hugged each other.

'Chiko, what are you doing here?' he asked, astonished.

'I was sent to your regiment, directly from the Soviet Union, for practical experience. Tell me what I have to do,' Jukan said.

'Hey, stop this ridiculous conversation,' said Mirko. 'We've had a lot of experience together, so I will make sure you have a room of your own. But now, go and have a bath, change your clothes, and we'll go to a restaurant to celebrate your arrival.' Jukan quickly made himself ready and went back to Mirko's office. The work day was finished, and they went to the restaurant, but, first, they took a short walk around the little town.

'Tell me, what is your life like over there?' Mirko asked.

'I can't say that I like it,' Jukan answered.

'So, why did you go to Russia?'

'I simply wanted to get an education, but now I can see that there is practically nothing to study there,' Jukan told Mirko.

'You didn't really need it. You held such a good position here, and by now, you could be in Belgrade,' Mirko said.

'Nothing we can do about it now,' Jukan said. 'The choice was made, and now I just have to finish this school.'

'Yes, now you can't change anything. Let's go and have some fun and remember our war adventures,' agreed Mirko.

The 'Old Town Kafana' was the best in the city, and its owners were ready to do anything for Mirko. They were given a table right in front of a small stage where a group of musicians was playing. They started the first song, and the first snacks appeared on the table, together with a bottle of shlivovica. They poured each a glass, and slowly the party started and gained speed. The music got louder, and the accordion player stood next to Jukan. Rakija went down the throat easily, and the baked mutton seemed very tasty, compared to the pearl barley porridge. Soon, some local beauties turned up, and pretty soon they were sitting and hugging them. Then the dances started and lasted late into the night. Their heads were getting heavier and their purses lighter. After the restaurant, they went to see the girls off and got home early in the morning.

The next day, Jukan woke with a dreadful headache and desire to kill his hangover. It was already noon, and he pulled himself together and went looking for Mirko. Jukan found him in his office in a very bad state. When he saw Jukan, he tried to put a smile on his face.

'How do you feel, Chiko?' he asked.

'Couldn't be worse! We need some treatment immediately,' Jukan said.

'We will, but, first, I need to leave a few orders,' Mirko said and called in his deputy and explained the situation. 'Listen, as you see, my old war friend is here, and we want to spend some time together. Therefore, please replace me, and call me only if there is a special emergency. For a couple of days, you have to be here without me.'

'No problem,' his deputy agreed, and Mirko and Jukan went off to find a cure.

But a couple of days wasn't enough for them! Their hellbender continued for more than a week. They spent every evening in the restaurant, and the owner greeted them as relatives. The restaurant became a centre for entertainment, and many more people came. The orchestra tried their best; they even invited a violin player to join them. Rivers of rakija continued to flow, baked ruznici, chevapchichi, and pleskavici disappeared from the table with amazing speed. Locals and beautiful girls often sat at their table. The girls always loved Jukan, and he felt like a movie star. The hellbenders went on until late into the night and usually came to an end with a rough love scene. They woke up about noon, every day more and more exhausted, and their monetary stock considerably diminished. Jukan even had to sell a camera that he had bought in Odessa.

In the middle of the second week, the desire to go out had considerably decreased, and Mirko said to Jukan, 'Listen to me, Chiko. I'm really glad to see you, but it's time for us to calm down. I have plenty of work to do, and our parties have to stop.'

'I completely agree with you. You do your job, and I will continue my practical experience,' said Jukan.

190

'No, you don't need any practice . . . you go home, and I will fill out the necessary paperwork. Today, we will celebrate for the last time, and tomorrow you leave!' said Mirko. And they had one more party, and this last time was wild!

The next day, Mirko took Jukan to the railway station and put him on the train travelling to Bihach. In Bihach, Jukan stopped for one day to see some relatives and friends. Once this city had seemed big and noisy to him, but now it looked like a very small provincial town. Besides that, more than half of his relatives had perished in the war, and he walked around a town that was like a big cemetery. He didn't have any desire to stay longer; he bought some gifts for home, and the next morning, he left for his native Lipa. The overloaded bus clambered slowly along the bumpy road to Ripachki Klanats, which they had destroyed to prevent the Germans getting to Lipa. Now this road had been cleared of mines and roughly fixed, but it wasn't a pleasant journey, travelling over potholes. He got off the bus at Begovats and slowly walked home over the Milkin Mount. The day was magnificent, the sun was pleasantly warm, and Jukan started to sweat, but it didn't bother him at all. He breathed in the native air, and he was constantly looking out for something familiar. When he got closer to the house, he saw a small flock of sheep being grazed by a boy on the opposite slope. Most likely it was his younger brother, Milan, but Jukan decided not to stop and went directly to the house.

He was coming to the house from the back, so no one saw him. He entered the courtyard and at once saw his mother. She was taking water from the well, and he went closer to her, trying not to frighten her, and called to her, 'Hello, Mother.'

She turned, saw him, and clutched her head. 'My god, Jukitsa, my son! Where have you been for so long?'

'Don't ask me. Where haven't I been?' He hugged her, and she began to cry. They stood like that for a few minutes and then went into the house.

Right at the entrance, he saw Nana sitting next to the oven, making dinner, and a bit further inside, sitting on a chair, was his baka Marija, who recognised him at once. 'Look, our wanderer has returned. Come closer and let me look at you.' Jukan went closer. 'Look how skinny you have become in this Russia,' she said.

'It's all right, I'll put on some weight. And I bought you a gift from Russia,' Jukan said, taking a scarf from his suitcase and putting it on her knees.

'It's a good scarf, and very soft,' she said, putting it to her cheek. 'At last, even from you, I have a long-awaited gift.'

Jukan turned to Nana. She stood silently nearby, waiting for her turn. Over the years, she had become even smaller, had grown thin, and was a little stooped. He hugged her and asked, 'How are you doing, my Nana?'

'Things are pretty normal, only it would be much better if you were here.'

'Well, look who has arrived back to us.' Jukan heard an unpleasant, loud, rough voice; it was Stana's voice; she alone spoke this way.

He turned and saw her in the doorway. 'Hello, Stana, where is your Rade?' he asked.

'He is working; now he is the only man in the house and has more and more to care about,' and she showed him her belly. Only then did he notice that she was pregnant.

'But this means that soon there will plenty of helpers,' he laughed, trying to make a joke.

'Why don't you speak about you, my dear? Aren't you going to stay here now?' his mother asked with sadness in her voice.

'No, Mother, that's impossible. In a month, I will go back to study in the Soviet Union, and after that, I will serve in the army. So I'm only here for a week,' he answered.

By dinner time, Rade's son, Ilya, and Jukan's younger brother had driven home a herd of sheep and cows. Jukan hadn't seen Milan for more than two years and had almost forgotten what he looked like. He had turned ten already, and now he was a skinny, snub-nosed boy with surprisingly clever black eyes and a constant smile. He looked curiously at his older brother but didn't know what to say to him. In the evening, Rade came home. In the last two years, he had grown older and had become even skinnier. He was tall but didn't look huge. His son, Ilya, was only nine, but he was quite large and a well-developed boy. Next to him, the small dark-haired Milan looked like a dwarf. While the women were preparing dinner, Jukan and Rade drank a few wine glasses full of rakija, and Mother prepared coffee for them. Then they all took their places at the big round table on which there was an oil lamp, and they started to eat. When they were all sitting at the table, it was cosy and cheerful. In the years of war, almost all the men had been lost, and now there remained just the two. But they tried not to notice this, and they bombarded Jukan with questions about Russia, its dreadfully cold weather, and if he had seen Stalin.

'No, I didn't see Stalin, but I did talk with Zhukov,' he answered and began to tell how that had happened. They all sat there with open mouths and listened attentively. Sometimes he invented a little bit and coloured the story so it seemed even more cheerful. And his little brother, Milan, listened spellbound, trying to catch every word.

The next day, Jukan and his mother went to the Mandich house, where his mother had been born and from where she had been stolen by his father. Here, they spent the whole day, ate and drank, and remembered the war and the last years. They returned home in the evening, happy that they had spent all day together, the first time in more than ten years. A new day came, and Jukan was tired of being idle. He decided to go to their nearest neighbours, the Zorichs, and there he spent most of the day. In the evening, they had dinner almost in the dark, and he answered all the same questions. The absence of light and a radio drove him mad, and every day was just long hours of doing nothing. After life in the big city, it became annoying here, and he decided to go to Bihach, and from there to Belgrade. In this big city, there were cars, buses and trams, and shop windows full of beautiful things. In the evenings at the restaurants, music played, and along the wide streets, there were lamps shining. The main thing was that the city was full of beautiful women. He took to life here like a duck to water. He stayed again with Stric Nikola. His fellow student cadets were very glad to see him again. Hellbenders went on every day until night-time, and they left for the Odessa academy reluctantly, with considerably worse health. Before they left, each of them was given a new leather coat. Two of their class had not turned up in Belgrade, and they left without them. They went through Romania, and in Bucharest, they were invited as honoured guests to stand with Chaushesku at the May Day Parade. To refuse such an honour was impossible, and Jukan, as senior in rank, headed the delegation, but the majority of his friends decided to visit the local brothel.

——————— ·◆◆◆◆◆· ———————

They were studying again. It was their third and last year, but the special drive to study was not there. After lectures, the cadets would go to the city, and almost all of his friends had girlfriends. But Jukan had no desire to enter into a serious relationship. He had noticed, though, a quite beautiful, well-dressed girl who was working in the military aviation unit located across the road. One of his companions had met a girl by the name of Zenja at a dance, and it was from here that the love story began. Zenja worked with Klara, under her supervision as a bookkeeper, and they were also good friends. One day, Zenja began to tell Klara excitedly, 'Listen, Klara, I have met a Yugoslavian officer, and he's very interesting, and he looks after me well. But he's not the one I want to talk to you about. He has a friend who is very handsome. He saw you and would like to meet you.'

'You must be crazy! I won't go anywhere,' Klara cut her off, but Zenja did not give up, and every day she insisted that Klara meet this officer.

'You are so silly. Why not just meet him? How many times can I lie and say that you are very busy?'

'Very well, then,' Klara agreed. 'I don't want to meet him particularly, but on Tuesday I am going as usual to my English language course. If he waits for me at the bus stop near Kulikova Square, then I will meet him.'

'Agreed. What time?' Zenja asked.

'Eight o'clock,' said Klara.

On Tuesday as agreed, Klara went to her course. Unexpectedly, the lights went out, and the class had to end. When they went outside, they saw that the whole city was without lights. Klara waited for a while near the bus stop, but no one came, so she had to walk through the dark Kulikova Square, constantly looking back, afraid that she was being followed. Finally, she reached home without any mishaps, and just then the lights came back on. Her mother and Dima were at home. They sat down at the table, where there was a pan of chicken broth and home-made noodles. They didn't have time to even pour the broth into their bowls when there was a knock at the door.

Zelda opened the door, and Zenja came into the room with a young officer in a foreign uniform, looking marvellously elegant, with unusually beautiful eyes. 'Klara, you have visitors,' Zelda said. Dima, having seen the uniform, jumped from his chair and ran up to the officer.

'George (as they called Jukan in Odessa), this is Klara.'

'Hello, Klara,' he said with his lovely accent.

'This is my mother, Zelda, and my son, Dima,' Klara introduced them, and here Zelda took the initiative.

'Come and sit down with us and eat. There isn't a lot at our table, but you are welcome to share what we have.' George and Zenja accepted the offer and sat at the table on stools that Klara brought out. Klara poured them both some broth.

'This is really tasty,' George said.

'You still have to try the chicken neck,' Zelda said, flattered by his praise. George accepted a piece of chicken; the taste was unusual but very pleasant, but the most interesting thing was that there were no bones.

'Where are the bones?' he asked, surprised.

Everyone laughed, and Zelda joked, 'They simply dissolved!'

'But the wings didn't dissolve?' He continued to be surprised, and everyone laughed again, and the mood at the table became very easy. Dima laughed too, and George winked at him.

After dinner, they sat for about an hour, and when they were ready to leave, George asked, 'Would it be possible for me to come again tomorrow? I liked your chicken.'

'Certainly it's possible. It was a pleasure for us to meet you,' Zelda said, and from that day, George became a regular visitor. Their relationship developed very quickly, and within a week, they were going to the cinema and theatre. Klara really liked him, and he was very cheerful. Even his strong accent made her smile.

Soon, all the military cadets were sent to a camp located in Permomisk. Here, they learnt military doctrine and spent a lot of time at the shooting range. It was terribly hot, and they didn't feel like doing anything. It was even hard to think. But it became necessary to think very quickly when something very unpleasant happened. One morning, the radio informed them that Tito had betrayed the ideas of the proletariat movement and had sent Yugoslavia on a contradictory course to the idea of communism. This message came like a bolt from the blue, and no one knew what to do next. They changed the radio wave to Belgrade radio and began to listen to the news from there. And it was even worse! Moscow and Belgrade were going in different directions, and the main thing was that the cadets, having studied in the Soviet Union, were now named openly as traitors of their country. They could not accept that. The majority of them had fought as partisans all through the war and had not been afraid to die for the ideals of Stalin and Tito. All of them had awards, and some, like Jukan, had the highest award of Yugoslavia, 'Spomenitsa'—organiser of the guerrilla movement.

And now they were guilty because their country had sent them to study in the Soviet Union. There were incessant arguments. Some said that they should go immediately to Yugoslavia. Others thought they should contact the military attaché in Moscow and follow his advice. Still, others said they should finish their studies, as the arguments between Stalin and Tito would quickly end and everything would get back to normal. But nobody from the Yugoslav embassy arrived, they had been forgotten, and the disagreements grew worse. Jukan was with those who thought that to go back home, where they had been declared traitors, was a stupid idea. He wanted to wait until things cleared up. But in his heart, Jukan had a very unpleasant feeling that his whole military career had come to an end and nobody could help him anymore. Every day passed in intense political debate, sometimes almost reaching a fight.

On his return to Odessa, Klara noticed the change in him; he had become grey, and his smile had disappeared.

'George, what has happened to you?' she asked.

'I don't know what to do. I do not want to go home as a traitor, but also I love you,' he said.

It was wonderful for Klara to hear these words, but she covered his mouth with her hand. 'Do not think of me. In Yugoslavia, you have a mother and brother. It is your native land, and you will not be happy anywhere else. Go back and forget about me and find another woman for yourself,' she said.

'Does that mean that you don't love me?' he asked.

'I do love you, but I don't want you to be unhappy because of me,' Klara said.

George hugged her to him and kissed her lips deeply. 'To hell with it all. I love you, and I do not want to lose you,' he concluded, and they continued to meet.

Soon, though, unexpected obstacles arose. One morning when she arrived at work, Klara was called into the office by the chief officer, Colonel Romanovsky. Elegant and always tidy, he had always treated Klara kindly.

'Michael Vasilevich, did you call me?' she asked.

'Yes, Klara Davidovna. Sit down here.' Klara sat down obediently, and he continued. 'Klara Davidovna, I don't know how to begin. We all respect you very much and are happy with your work, but we have a problem.'

'What is it?' She was surprised.

'Tell me, why are you meeting with this Turk?' he asked.

'Which Turk are you speaking about?' Klara asked.

'The cadet from the academy with whom you are going out,' Michael said.

'He's not a Turk. He's from Yugoslavia.' Klara was specific.

'I'm simply warning you that you should stop these meetings,' he said.

'I'm in love with him, and I am not going to leave him.' Klara was adamant.

'Then I should warn you that you will be dismissed, though I would do it with great reluctance,' he said.

'Do as you want,' she answered sharply and went out of the office. This conversation spoiled her mood, but she couldn't conceive of breaking up with George. She knew perfectly well that it was never encouraged to meet foreigners in the Soviet Union and it was often punished. But right now, she wanted to support George and decided to stick with him.

George came to the house every day now, and Zelda was happy. Dima was so attached to George that he followed on his heels constantly. It was lovely for him to see a man in the house, an officer and a war hero. Klara knew that she could be dismissed from her work, but in her heart, she hoped that there would be no more threats. She didn't have long to wait for the follow-up to her conversation with her boss. After a few weeks, she was called into the staff office and was told that she had been sacked. In her resume, there was a new line that she was dismissed without the possibility of further employment. She decided not to tell George. He hardly noticed, as his thoughts were on whether to stay or leave. As a result, there were two groups formed by the cadets. The first decided that, in spite of the fact that they would be called traitors, they would go back to Yugoslavia. The second group decided to wait in the USSR and wait for relations to improve. In the first group, there were about 150 people, and in the second group, there were 52 people, including Jukan. At the beginning of August, permission was given for the group to go home. The farewell was gloomy; everyone was sad.

After this departure, the group staying had to think about what to do in Odessa. All of them had met local girls and wanted to get married, but it was forbidden for a Soviet citizen to marry a foreigner. At last, the authorities came to the decision that they would have to become Soviet citizens. But George and his friends did not want to lose their citizenship of Yugoslavia, and then a compromise was reached. They were offered temporary citizenship, and with heavy hearts, they agreed to this. Now there were no obstacles to their marrying Soviet girls. On 25 August, George and Klara went to the registry office and registered their marriage. They celebrated very modestly. George bought a bottle of champagne, and Zelda made dinner. Their witnesses were George's friend Zhivkovich and his girlfriend, Galja. They drank wine and ate stuffed fish, and George and his friend were again amazed that there were no bones in the fish. The guests did not stay long, and Jukan stayed for the night.

Study at the academy had finished, and all of them were given the rank of officers in the Soviet army, equivalent to their previous rank in the Yugoslav army. All fifty-two of them were sent to the South Ural military district to settle down in the city of Chkalov. Klara went with George as an officer's wife, leaving a very concerned Dima with his grandmother in Odessa, where he was going to school in the fourth class. And though, at first, Dima had liked George, now he was afraid.

'Mama, I want to go with you too,' he began to ask.

'We can't take you with us because we do not know where we are going and where we will live at the moment.' She tried to convince him, but Dima continued.

'But I will be together with you.'

'No, you should study, and as soon as we are settled, we will bring you there.'

'Is that the truth?' he asked, looking at George.

George confirmed. 'As soon as we can, we will send for you and your grandmother.' At these words, even Zelda brightened.

Klara and George gathered what they needed, but there was nothing much to collect. They had clothing in two suitcases, and in a box, they had some dishes, two sets of bedclothes, and two pillows. They had to travel more than two days by train, and George's best friend, Gojko Negovan, and his young wife, a cheerful brunette called Zoya, were in their apartment. The women settled on the bottom bunks and the men on the top. In that way, they often played cards and ran out at stops to buy wine or beer. There was almost constant laughter in compartment. Occasionally, one pair went to the restaurant so that the other pair could indulge in lovemaking, and after that, the other pair. By the time they reached Chkalov, they were all a bit tired and got out of the carriage very happily. They were billeted in one of the local barracks located on the riverbank. A small room had been given over to each young family, but the toilet and kitchen were communal, and the food was prepared by some of the women.

On the second day, the men went to the Staff of the South Ural Military District, where they were divided into groups. George was appointed to the post of commander of the mortar brigade and was sent directly to the Grahovetsky military camp, located under Gorky. The camp occupied a huge area, and there were shooting ranges everywhere and settlements for the employees. George and some of his friends were settled in small wooden houses, one for each family. In each, there was a small kitchen with an oven and a storage room. There was also a bowl over an iron washstand for washing. In the mornings, the water was very cold. The wooden toilet was on the street and even more inconvenient. To get there, they had to walk about seven metres in cold or rainy weather, which was why they only used it in emergencies! Within a week, George had taken over the affairs from his predecessor, and Klara went to the local shops and markets, buying provisions. She cleaned the house and made the supper. By the time George arrived in the evenings, the furnace had been lit and the house was hot. They had supper together and then indulged in love games, and life in this little wooden house seemed like paradise.

Winter arrived early that year. Frosts struck in October, and the rivers were soon frozen. A column moved slowly along the road, covered in snow. George travelled in one "gazik" car, together with the commander of the division, Maltsev. The colonel could see that George was still not used to Russian frosts and constantly played tricks on him. The colonel ordered everyone to get out of the cars. They passed some passages. At last, Maltsev turned to George and said, 'Well, George Milenovich, do you know what you're standing on?'

'Certainly I know,' answered George.

'Well, and what is under you?'

'The ground, Comrade Colonel' he answered again.

Then the colonel burst out laughing. 'Under your feet is the greatest Russian river Volga.'

This worried George; after all, in Bosnia, even the mountain river, Una, had never frozen over, and here, the great River Volga was completely frozen over, and you could walk on it. He looked around and decided that he would play the game too, not wanting to disappoint them. He carefully tapped on the ice with his foot. 'So, Comrade Colonel, you can stay here and I will go to the shore.' And he started to run towards the shore, and behind him, everyone was in gales of laughter.

They began to follow him, shouting, 'Where are you running, Captain? Today on this ice, even tanks would be moved across!'

The joke had gone over well, and now, at every opportunity, they tried to play a trick on him. George did not take offence, and on the contrary, he noticed that his relationship with them was very much improved. So, gradually, they got used to their life in this new camp; his role as a Soviet officer was very different to that of life in Yugoslavia. Here, they all followed the charter, whether they understood it or not. Klara and George stayed in the Grahovetsky camp for about two months, and from there, George was sent to Gorky for further training. They were settled in a hotel for military men, "Ketch". The hotel was warm and cosy, and their room was decently furnished, and the most important thing was a big bed, bigger than they had ever seen before, and they spent almost all their free time on it. They were absolutely happy and grew deeper and deeper in love. Here in this bed, their first son was conceived, in 13 Zalomova Street.

The hotel didn't have baths, and it was necessary to bathe in the public baths, which were in the city centre, in Mayakovsky Street. At the desk sat a large brunette in a padded black jacket.

'Is it possible to buy tickets for a bath?' Klara asked.

'What session?' the cashier asked. George and Klara shrugged their shoulders.

'We have come to the baths, not to the cinema,' Klara said.

'I still ask you, what session do you want to go to?' the cashier asked again.

'Well, what sessions are there?'

'Each lasts quarter of an hour, and the next session that's free is at 4 p.m.'

'Then please give us tickets for 4 p.m.,' Klara said.

They waited in separate places, Klara in the female and George in the male sections. Before the session, they were warned that they would have ten minutes, and in this time, they would need to wash. 'All undress,' the command sounded, and people began to take off their clothes and put them into a locker. Not everyone was as quick, and some lagged behind. Soon, everyone was naked. Some were embarrassed and shifted from foot to foot; others were not afraid of the intimate parts of their bodies. They were all given a towel, and they entered the shower where each person had a cubicle. 'Everybody ready? Your time has started,' came the announcement, and everyone began to wash carefully. In ten minutes, they had to wash and rinse their hair and then their body. 'Your time is coming to an end,' the voice said. 'Now wash off the soap, because I'm turning the water off!'

'Wait, I'm not ready yet,' someone called out.

'I can't help that,' the bath woman was insistent. 'In fifteen minutes, there is another session. Wash off or stay soaped!' So they hardly had time to finish washing. Klara decided not to go there again.

Every morning, George went to work, and Klara wanted something to do as well. She managed to find a job as an assistant to the chief accountant in the house-building industrial complex. Her boss was happy that he had found someone he could trust to do the work. However, after three months, George was moved to a new position to the capital of Bashkiria, Ufa. When Klara told her boss this news, he was horrified and waved his hand in the air.

'I will not release you. We need you here,' he said.

'It's not possible. My husband is being sent to Ufa,' Klara explained.

'Let him go, and you stay here,' he said.

'You must see that's impossible. I have a young child waiting for me as well,' Klara said.

'All right, I understand, but you must understand that now I have no one to help me with the work,' he said and reluctantly signed her release and wished her a happy journey.

They arrived in Ufa at the beginning of February. The snow fell, and the houses were up to their roofs in snow. In comparison to Gorky, Ufa seemed small and provincial, even though it was the capital of the Bashkir Autonomous Republic. They were accommodated at the Hotel "Ketch", on the corner of Lenin and Stalin Streets. By this time, Klara was in her fourth month of pregnancy and had a small stomach, which no one but George noticed. Her pregnancy had been accompanied with dizziness and vomiting. George was excited to think that he would have a successor; Klara felt old and was not looking forward to giving birth to the child. At that time, people who were thirty did not feel young! George was disgusted by this nonsense but began to watch her with mistrust. He was afraid she would have an abortion. One evening, Klara wanted something sour. She wanted a lemon, and she wanted it so badly that she thought she would die.

'Dzhordzhik, I beg you, go and get me some lemons,' she said.

'Where will I get them? The streets are already dark, and all the shops already closed,' George asked her.

'If you won't get them, I will surely die,' she begged again.

George put on an overcoat and boots and left the house. The city was covered in snow, and he rushed around in search of lemons. He combed all the shops that were open; he went into cafes and restaurants, but there were no lemons anywhere. But he did not give up. At last, he got to the Hotel "Bashkiria", and the restaurant was almost empty. 'Listen, would you have a couple of lemons?' he asked the director.

'This is a restaurant, not a food shop,' the man answered.

'My pregnant wife craves lemons,' George began to explain emotionally, and his accent got even stronger. But it was all for nothing; the director left. George was about to leave but was called back by a waiter, who told him to wait behind the door. After some minutes, the waiter came back with a package in his hands.

'Here are two lemons,' he said.

'Oh, thank you, how much?' George asked.

'Give me ten roubles and go!' was the answer.

George paid the ten roubles and ran home, holding tightly to his precious parcel. Klara was waiting for him, sitting on the bed, and when George came in, she jumped off the bed and rushed to meet him. 'My god, Dzhordzhik, where were you? I was so afraid, I thought I'd go crazy.'

'And I was going crazy, running around the city, searching for lemons!' George answered her.

'Well, did you get some?' Klara asked again. He held out the two lemons; Klara seized them, washed them quickly with water from the jug, and began to eat them, skin and all. She ate so greedily that she had a sore mouth. 'I'm sorry that I sent you out at night to search for these lemons,' Klara said when she had finished, 'but, believe me, if you hadn't brought them, I would definitely have died!' Having said that, she lay down on the bed and fell instantly asleep. The pregnancy went normally, except for the one time she almost killed herself. She had craved tea from a samovar and went to the neighbour living above them. On her way back, her foot slipped on the rug, and she slid on her bottom all the way down the steps. When she had recovered, she sat still for a long time, afraid that she might have lost the baby. But everything was fine, and she tried to be more careful after that.

At the beginning of spring, they received a room in a communal flat, a big room with a niche for the bed. In the second room lived another Yugoslav officer, Branko Radetich, with his young wife, Tamara. She and Klara did not get on very well. She was young, beautiful, and very self-confident, and Branko gave her everything that she wanted. Klara noticed that time and time again, as soon as Branko had left for work, Tamara went for a walk, usually around the corner to where a young man waited. Klara thought that she behaved like a prostitute, but she didn't mention it to anyone.

The spring ended. The hot sun melted the snow and icicles hanging down in enormous blocks from the roofs. Some of them broke under their own weight and fell to the ground with a roar. It wasn't safe to walk under the roofs. The top layer of snow on the round began to thaw, and the water cut channels for itself, and it was possible to fall in. George forbade Klara from walking in the street, as her stomach had grown, and their future child began to move more often. In the evenings, George liked to put his ear to her stomach, trying to hear what he was certain was his son. He sometimes even muttered something to him in Serbian.

'What are you saying?' Klara would ask.

George laughed it off. 'It is man-to-man talk,' he said.

They decided to go to Odessa, where Klara could be helped by her mother. So, at the end of May, George took a vacation and took his wife to Odessa. The trip took two and a half days, and when they arrived in Odessa, it was a beautiful summer day. Their arrival was like a bolt from the blue for Dima and Zelda. After nine months away, Dima had grown up and matured, and Zelda had grown old and thin. And though she had a good relationship with Dima, it was very hard to keep up with him. So when she saw Klara and George, Zelda was delighted. Dima met them uncertainly. He kissed his mother and offered his hand to George. George dispelled all their suspicions. 'It is necessary for Klara to give birth here, and right after that, we will take you to Ufa. We are one family and should all live together.' These words warmed Dima, and Zelda simply burst into tears.

The weather was very good, so George, Klara, and Dima went to Atrada Beach, and to get to the sea, it was necessary to climb down a steep path. Klara said it was too dangerous for a pregnant woman, but George insisted that it would do her good. Klara did not swim; the water was still very cold, and she just got her feet wet. But George swam constantly, and though at first he was frightened by the waves, he gradually got used to them and learnt to float. Sometimes they went by tram to Arcadia Beach, where the path to the sea was less steep and Klara was not afraid of falling. It was easier to learn to swim here; the waves were smaller, and he learnt to float on his back. The fear of water and sinking left him, and by moving his hands, he learnt to swim. By the end of the holiday, he was well rested, and Klara was even rounder. The time came for George to leave, and Klara was afraid. She had only now begun again to feel happy, and now they had to be separated again. George left in the middle of June and told Klara to give birth to a son.

+ + + + + +

When George arrived in Ufa, he was assigned as a commander of a train of new recruits who were supposed to start duty on the far east of the country. The train was made up of fifty-three cars in which were twenty recruits and one sergeant. There was a car for the officers, the doctor and hospital attendant, and one car was the kitchen. George was responsible for getting them safely to their destination without mishap and to hand them over safe and healthy to their future commanders. In wartime, he had learnt to care for soldiers, and in peace, it should have been an easier job. They went in cargo car' in summer, it did not need heating. The cook was excellent. It was not easy to supervise this group; they were still very young, full of energy and enthusiasm and often heading in a dangerous direction. It was one thing to deal with a few people, another to look after a thousand people. Here, there already was a social group involved. Quite often in the evenings, the recruits went on food and alcohol binges, and they presented a danger to the local women, though some women were very glad to see such a big group of sexually obsessed youths who did not care about appearance or age. But some of the decent girls suffered; on one station, when the officers weren't around, they pulled some young girls into the wagon and raped them. Some rapists were caught and were condemned to service in a penal battalion.

They travelled for twenty-eight days and stopped in Novosibirsk, Irkutsk, and Birobidzhan. Sometimes they had to stop because of floods on the great Siberian rivers. The final stop was Peter the Great Bay. When George saw it, he could not believe his eyes; it was so beautiful. The enormous gulf, surrounded by hills, defied his imagination. The military camp was settled down under these hills, and they were named after the commanders of those units. Within five days, George delivered all the recruits to their divisions. Although in the camp it was calm, the feeling beyond was disturbing. Day and night, explosions were heard. It was a bloody war between North and South Korea, which was basically a struggle between communism and imperialism, a war between two ideologies. Although the conditions were disturbing, George knew this was not his war, and he travelled safely in a compartment of the train, and in eight days, he arrived back in Ufa.

Klara remained with Zelda and Dima. She didn't go to the beach anymore and stayed at home more and more, helping Zelda. Her stomach by now was enormous, and it was heavy to carry, as the child inside was very restless and turned often. On 11 July, Klara went to the maternity hospital located opposite Kulikovo Square. However, on her arrival, her labour pains stopped! She spent the night in the hospital room, and she didn't sleep at all. Then the next day, 12 July, she was sure that she would give birth that day. She didn't want her child born on the thirteenth. A young doctor, Victor Vasilevich, whom they lovingly named 'our Vitenka,' took charge of the ward that afternoon. When he went up to Klara, she seized him by the sleeve and said, 'Help me give birth today. I don't want my son born on the thirteenth.'

'Stop worrying, lie easy, breathe, and when the time comes, strain and help the baby to leave,' he said.

'All right, and please stay nearby to help. I should give birth today,' Klara pleaded. The long day passed with useless attempts, and then evening came.

The doctor repeated, 'It's all in your hands. Please try!' Klara hoped that she would have time to give birth before midnight, but it was not to be. Just before midnight, there was a change of doctors, and before leaving, Victor Vasilevich said, 'Well, here, I must leave you. We will meet tomorrow.'

The doctor left, and almost at once, the serious pains began. But now she didn't want to give birth and decided to wait until the next day. However, you cannot dictate to God, and at twenty minutes past midnight, on 13 July, a baby boy was born, fifty-four centimetres in length and 3.4 kilos. The birth was without complications; he was washed, wrapped in blankets, and shown to his mother. After that, the exhausted Klara was taken to the room next door, where the midwife had left, and she was left, weakened, and forgotten in the small dark room. Luckily, it was July and the weather was warm. She tried to call for help, but no one came.

At daybreak, the midwife returned. 'Why are you still here?' she asked indignantly. 'And no one has helped you?' Klara shook her head. But it was already too late, Klara's uterus had chilled, and she suffered for a long time because of that. The two of them left the hospital a week later and were met by Zelda and Dima. Dima had mixed feelings now that his mother had a new son, who might take away his mother's love for him, but, on the other hand, he was glad that now he had a little brother. Having stayed in Odessa for another month, the family left together. It was a pity to leave the apartment in sunny, bright Odessa, and Dima had to leave all his friends. But to live in Odessa on one pension wasn't possible. Everyone hoped that their life in Ufa would be happy. They quickly sold all their furniture and left for their new life.

When the family arrived in Ufa, George separated the niche where their bed was by a small screen. He bought an iron bed for his mother-in-law and a folding bed for Dima. Now everyone had a bed, except their new baby, whom they called Milan, in honour of George's brother. For the first couple of months, he had to sleep in a large suitcase, adapted for this purpose, with the cover propped up with a stick. But the stick wasn't always enough, and sometimes when Milan moved, the stick fell, the suitcase slammed, followed by general panic. The birth of his son gave new meaning to George's life. It seemed to be impossible to get a child's bed in Ufa, so George went to Odessa to get one. If you had the money, it was possible to get anything in Odessa, even a nuclear bomb! The trip was successful, and George came back with a small wooden bed. Now everyone had somewhere to sleep, but it was very crowded in just one room. But in spite of this difficulty, the new family lived in peace and friendship. George went to work early in the mornings, and Klara found a job as a bookkeeper in the Ministry of Education. Dima went to new school, and Zelda watched her small grandson and prepared the food. It was certainly hard to live in just the one room, and with only one kitchen, they had to put up with Tamara.

All the small incidents could be smoothed away, but one evening, when Klara was in the bathroom, she overheard a conversation between Tamara and Branko.

'Did you see my underpants?' he asked.

'They were washed and hung on the radiator in the corridor. Didn't you take them?' Tamara answered.

'No, but I need them,' Branko said.

'Then go and look if they're on the bottom shelf,' Tamara suggested.

Branko went out but was soon back. 'I couldn't find them,' he said.

'That means her son Dima has stolen them,' Tamara said.

At that, Klara rushed out into the corridor as if bitten by a snake. 'What kind of rubbish are you speaking?' she asked.

'I say for certain your Dima took them. There's no one else.'

Klara sprung at Tamara, seizing her hair and tumbling onto the floor. Klara knocked Tamara's head on the floor, and Tamara yelled for help. Branko and George, both back from work, began to separate the women, and at last they went to their rooms. Here, George tried to understand what had happened.

'What got into you? Why did you attack her?' he asked.

'He called my Dima a thief, and for that I could kill her!' Klara said.

'You must make up with her!' George ordered.

The next day, the whole building knew about the fight and were talking about it. Colonel Poljakov, the political enforcer in the army, called Klara into his office, and Klara was expecting trouble. He met her very coolly and asked her to sit at the table. 'Sit down, Klara Davidovna,' he said. She obediently sat down, but the colonel's tone changed, and he said in a soft voice, 'Klara Davidovna, you are a beautiful, intelligent young woman. What made you start a fight?'

'I am ashamed, but she really offended me. She called my son a thief. My son never took anything, and why would he take her husband's smelly old underpants? I was simply ready to kill her,' she explained.

The colonel rose quickly and walked away from the table. 'I haven't heard anything that you said just now, but I agree, your neighbour was certainly wrong to blame your son. She had no right to do that,' he said. 'We will move her and give the room to someone else.'

'Please, Comrade Colonel,' Klara interrupted him, 'why can't we occupy both rooms? We have five people living together in the one room—me, my husband, my mother, our baby, and my older son, Dima. The poor child has nowhere to do his homework.'

'Why didn't you tell me this at the beginning? I think that both rooms must be given to you. But I can't make this decision myself. You go home and I will let you know the decision.' Having thanked the colonel, Klara rushed home with an easy heart, and in the morning of the next day, they were informed that they could occupy the whole apartment. Their joys knew no bounds. Klara, George, and their new son remained in the big room, and Zelda and Dima moved to the other room with the table, where Dima could do his homework.

But if in one hand they were given this gift, it was taken away in the other. In November, the division went on military exercises to Alkino. George's duties were to take the personnel in one car and the food in a separate car. That day, the snow was falling as if it was a solid wall. The train left Ufa slowly and could hardly move because of the snow on the rails. Sometimes the train had to stop, and the soldiers had to clear their way with shovels. It must be said that these soldiers were not regular soldiers. Among them were former criminals who were sent to the army at the end of the war. They had been sent to penal battalions, and after their sentences were finished, they were sent to the regular army to continue their service. Even though they were in soldier's uniforms, they looked very dangerous, and George didn't take his eyes off them. But about four kilometres from Alkino, the train stopped. Someone had to go to Alkino for help, and George decided to go. Visibility was no more than five metres, and George had to be guided by the cable posts running along the railway line.

The snow became a blizzard. In the open spaces where the wind raged, there was less snow because the wind blew it away, but on the lower places, the snow drifts were so deep that he was falling into them. Sometimes he had to make a detour, and George had no idea how long he had been going. His hands were freezing, and he could feel moisture in his boots. He began to feel tired and really wanted to sit down and rest, but he knew that he couldn't do this; to sit down meant to freeze to death. So he determinedly went on. When he had almost given up, directly in front of him, he saw the station. He went up to a small house near the station and pushed open the door. There was the lovely smell of heat and cigarette smoke, and he saw a small inspector. When the inspector saw George's condition, he invited him at once into the room and had him sit near the stove. 'Take off your boots and wait until I get back,' he said. When he returned, he had a bottle in his hands. He took a dirty glass from a shelf and poured about 150 grams of transparent liquid into it. 'Drink!' he ordered.

George obediently tossed the liquid down his throat. At first, he felt nothing, but then his throat burnt and the flame rushed to his stomach. It was pure alcohol, and George had never drunk anything like it. 'Water!' He began to wheeze, waving his hands.

'You don't need water, wait. Give me your hands.' He poured some of the liquid onto a piece of cloth and began rubbing George's hands and then his feet.

Gradually, George felt his hands and feet begin to warm up, and his body heat spread. 'Listen, our division is stuck in snow several kilometres from here. We need help urgently,' he said.

'Wait, first of all, we need to help you,' the inspector said.

'Do you have a phone?' George asked.

'Yes!'

'Then make a call, that is an order!' George said.

Slightly offended, the inspector went to the phone and lifted the receiver. In about fifteen minutes, a young lieutenant entered the room and saluted. 'The captain ordered me to come to you,' he said. George put on his boots again, put on an overcoat, and went outside, where it was already getting dark. On the cross-country vehicle, they came to a place where they met Lieutenant Colonel Medvedev. George described the situation and asked him to send help to clear the road. But the lieutenant Colonel explained that it was impossible to do anything more that day, it was too dark, but that help would be given the next morning.

'Now, you have to rest,' he ordered. 'You have done more than enough for today.'

The next morning, the snowstorm had eased, and the sun shone from a blue sky. George, with a group of soldiers armed with shovels, started to clear away the snow, and an hour later, they met soldiers from the division clearing the snow in the other direction. So it ended successfully. But during George's absence, someone had broken the locks on the food car and had stolen bags of sugar, canned food, tea, and other products. It wasn't possible to find out exactly who took it, but it was clear that the former criminals had taken it. The full extent of the theft was more than 5,000 roubles, and George was ordered to repay the loss from his salary; he kept just 10 per cent over two years. Poor Klara, she wept bitterly. After all, they had hardly enough money to live on.

Here in Ufa, their family relations became stronger, as well as friendships with other Yugoslav families who had just arrived. There were Gojko and Zola Negovan, Bruno and Lida Mrak, Anton and Zina Yanesh, and others. Only tall, thin, and handsome Milan Ribar, a cousin of Gojko, who spent time with them, could not find a girl. On free evenings, they gathered, played chess and cards, moulded pelmeni, fried beljashi and chebureks, sang songs, and drank. And if before they didn't like vodka, now they were used to it and drank with pleasure. They also snacked on herring, which they couldn't put in their mouths before. In the Ural Mountains, fresh fruit and vegetables were not easy to get in winter, so each apartment had a shed where all these products were stored for the winter. Every summer, they bought cabbage, tomatoes, and cucumbers from the collective farms and salted them. In the summer, they tried to make jam from cherries, strawberries, raspberries, and gooseberries. They did all these things when all the families were together. Zelda constantly amazed George with her cooking; the cutlets were aromatic and juicy; the meatballs in sauce were faultless and went well with any garnish. The broth and chicken necks never ceased to amaze him. And the stuffed fish was simply superb!

When George ate, Zelda watched with pleasure and was happy when he praised her cooking. She loved her son-in-law and always took his side when he and Klara argued. During winter, they often cooked 'holodets' from beef and pork legs. After the legs were completely cooked and cooled down, everyone sat at the table to separate the meat from the bones. This was not easy work but gratifying, and after cleaning the bones, they could lick and gnaw the bones from the meat that was left. Dima was especially keen on this work. He was always hungry and wanting something to eat. In Ufa, Dima had to find new friends, and soon he had a set. He was going to school happily, he studied hard, and when Klara and George went to class meetings, they heard nothing but praise. Dima and George had a good relationship. However, Dima always felt a bit of envy when he saw George holding Milan with a blissful smile on his face.

＊＋＋＋＋＋

Milan grew quickly, though he was a very frail boy. Fortunately, Klara had a very good family doctor, Voronov Pavel Ivanovich; his wife, Polina Grigorevna, worked with Klara in the Ministry of Education. Klara only had to call to say that there was something wrong with Milan, and Pavel Ivanovich would come immediately. But, despite his illnesses, Milan gave his parents a lot of pleasure. George ran home from work each day and then did not let his son go. Klara, when she came home from work, would feed the child, clean the flat, and then, when she wanted so badly to sleep, Milanchik would cry and often wake her up. George was used to sleeping under the noise of bombs, and he continued to sleep. So Klara was always the one to get up. After some months, she had grown very thin and pale. She sometimes fell asleep sitting at her desk!

Time passed quickly. Milan grew and began to crawl very quickly on the floor and even tried to stand up. When he was barely nine months old, George brought a rope from work and tied it along the sofa so that his son could learn to stand, holding on to it. Milan made his way along the rope, amusing his parents and neighbours. Their neighbour Kirilova Nadezhda Petrovna, who lived on their floor, once warned them, 'You shouldn't do that. If the child starts to walk too early before his bones get strong, he will have curved legs for the rest of his life.' Klara was frightened by this, but George continued, and it must be said that Milan's feet did not suffer as a result.

At about two years old, Milan was talking well and asked such ridiculous questions that Nadezhda Petrovna often said to Klara, 'Klara, please call Milanchik.'

'Milan!' Klara would call.

Milan always answered with 'Mama, do I need you?' This always made Nadezhda Petrovna laugh.

For New Year, Klara and George decided to give everyone a surprise and put up a fir tree. George drove to the woods and cut down a really beautiful fir tree. To bring it home was not easy! They did not want to put the tree up while Milan was awake, and finally Klara got him to sleep. The fir tree was too tall, and its top branches brushed the ceiling. They had to shorten it, and at last they placed it in the corner opposite Milan's bed. The fir tree was magnificent, even without decorations. Then they added ornaments. They had to work quietly so as not to wake Milan. They worked on the tree until three o'clock in the morning and put Ded Moroz, Santa Claus, under it and then put out the gifts. They were completely exhausted after that and went to sleep at once. But their efforts were well rewarded . . . when Milan woke up in the morning, he shouted with delight, 'Mama, Papa, what is this?'

'It's from Santa Claus. He has brought you a fir tree,' Klara said.

'When did Santa Claus come?'

'He came last night and said that you are a very good boy and that you deserve a fir tree,' Klara said.

'Why didn't you wake me up?' Milan asked.

'Santa Claus says that children should sleep at night. He has brought you a present,' Klara said.

'Santa Claus brought me a present, it can't be!'

'Yes, because you were such a good boy!' Klara said again.

Milan clutched his head and ran to the neighbours. 'You won't believe it, Vera Petrovna, go and see what Santa Claus brought me!' Klara and George got great pleasure watching the reaction of their son!

Ufa, once thought to be so far away, was now their home city. They got used to this new life in the capital of the Bashkir Republic, and the sounds of 'kuray' and the melodies of 'Bishmarmak,' the taste of Kumiss (horse milk), and the smell of horse sausage. Milan had grown up here and was now in kindergarten. But, here, there were problems. He did not want to sleep and refused to eat. The director of the kindergarten, Gesha Haleevna constantly complained to Klara. Then Klara had a cunning idea. Picking Milan up from kindergarten one day, she said, 'This morning, they broadcast on the radio that you ate badly again today.'

'How does the radio know?' Milan asked.

'The radio knows everything,' Klara answered. After that, Milan started to eat. A few days later, Klara decided to test him again. 'Well, so you ate badly again?'

'Who told you that?' Milan wanted to know.

'It was on the radio again,' she said.

'What a liar your radio is. I have eaten well today,' Milan said, and the officer standing near them burst out laughing.

Dima graduated from year eight and went to year nine. He had turned into a very thoughtful young man who liked mathematics and physics. He often went to the dumps and looked for parts of radios. He also liked aeroplanes and went to the glider group that had opened in the Pioneer Palace. Above all, he loved to read, especially the American authors Theodore Dreiser and Mark Twain. He read day and night, and when Klara turned off the lights, he read with a small lamp under the blankets. Klara hid the books and the lamp, but his love of books did not go away; it became stronger.

That winter, the city faced an epidemic of diphtheria, and Milan picked up the infection. At that time, this illness was considered extremely serious and often ended in death. Pavel Ivanovich helped Klara to be in the hospital with Milan, though it was very difficult. The room was big and filled with beds. Next to them was a bed of very beautifull girl Svetochka. The children in the beds coughed ceaselessly. The doctors were very busy, and Klara helped all she could. On the second night, Klara was very tired and had taken a little nap, sitting by Milan. She had a most disturbing dream and began to sweat with fear. She opened her eyes and looked at Milan. He had turned blue and was not breathing. Klara grabbed him and ran to the window and held him outside. The icy air broke through to Milan's lungs, and he began to breath and then to cry.

A nurse rushed in and shouted, 'What have you done? Close that window at once.'

'My child had stopped breathing,' Klara explained. 'I exposed him to the air.'

'And did it help?' the nurse asked.

'Now he is breathing, and he isn't crying,' she said.

'You have saved his life, then,' the nurse said. 'Now the crisis has passed.'

And she was right. In the morning, Milan felt much better and even smiled. When George arrived to visit them, Klara and Milan were by the window, and both of them waved happily when they saw him standing under the window. (This was one of the earliest memories that Milan had seeing the image of his father under the window.) In a few days, Klara and Milan were discharged from hospital, but the girl Svetochka wasn't; she died that night.

The next summer, the family decided to go to Odessa so that Milan could get stronger, bathing in the sea and eating fresh fruit and vegetables. They were met Klara's cousin Semyon and his wife, Klara. Semyon and Klara rented a big summer house in Chernomorka, and they invited George, Klara, and Milan to stay there with them. Semyon was a master of all trades, mainly mechanical and blacksmithing, but he could turn his hand to any work. He could fix any car, and so he earned well and his family lived well. They had one daughter, Asja, who was a year older than Dima. Asja was a very cheerful, boisterous girl. Klara was the most picturesque person in Semyon's family. She was very beautiful but very stout, with an unusually kind face on which there was always a smile. She cooked all the food, went to the market to shop, and cleaned the summer house. Klara and George tried to help her, but she always stopped them. 'Klara, I don't need your help. You should be resting. You are just skin and bone, and George is not much better. And, well, Milan is simply a small skeleton. You need to eat, rest, and gain some weight. Milan needs to drink milk!' So each morning, Klara went to the collective farm that was next to the summer house and got fresh milk for Milan to drink.

Both Klara's were good friends; they understood one another, and when they could, they bathed in the sea and sunbathed together. Semyon and George became friends and, in the evenings, often drank the local wine, which they had in abundance. After a good rest, Klara and George decided to go to Kishinev and to visit cousin Lyonja and his wife, Eve. In Kishinev, there was no warm sea, but there were more fruits. Lyonja and Eve had two daughters, twelve and five years old, and they included Milan in all their games. Lyonja and George soon found a common language; they talked about their military adventures and plans for the future. Of an evening, they drank litres of Moldavian wine, which was much better than the wine in Odessa. Lyonja's house was on the very edge of the city, and behind it was a field of flowering red poppies.

On one of the evenings, after Milan was in bed, George and Klara went for a walk along the road. An enormous full moon hung over the horizon, lighting up the vast fields of red poppies. George and Klara looked at one another, joined hands, and ran. They fell onto the grass and indulged in long, rough acts of love. They returned home satisfied and happy, and the next day they kept finding blades of grass in their hair. The outcome of this night was not long in presenting itself. Already, on returning to Ufa, Klara knew that she was pregnant and told George about it. He was thrilled to hear this news.

'Now you will give birth to one more son for me,' he said.

'Nonsense! I do not want any more babies. I am not so young anymore,' Klara answered him.

'But after the night we had, you have to give birth to one more son, a handsome man of the future.'

'How will we feed him? We hardly make ends meet now.' Klara worried.

'One more mouth will not make a big difference. You give birth, and let me take care of the rest.' George was adamant.

In May, George's division was sent on a special task. That year, under the city of Totsky, there would be tests of a secret weapon. For this experiment, special buildings had to be built to study the destructive force of the new weapon. The trees for the construction were cut from the woods near Perm. The amount of wood needed was enormous. Soldiers cut and sawed trees from morning until evening, and George's work included supplying them with food and sending the timber by troops to Totsky. As they later found out, the nuclear bomb was the secret weapon being tested there. The task was so important that George was not allowed any leave and could not be present at the birth of his second child. But he had left Klara exact instructions . . . to give birth to another son! Klara listened to the instructions but gave birth to a girl, and a very pretty one at that. She was born with long black hair and black eyes. They were taken from the maternity hospital by Zelda, Dima, and Milan. George had bought a small carriage especially for the new baby. Milan was very proud that he had a younger sister and wanted to wheel the carriage himself, but Dima also helped. George returned only after all the timber cutting had been finished; he had grown thin, was suntanned, and came with gifts for everyone.

But returning home had not been easy. The commander of the division, Colonel Gromov, said to him, 'My friend, Vignevich, you and I will go together to Totsky and participate in the nuclear tests!'

However, George did not want to take part in these tests because he expected that nothing good would come of them and protested. 'You promised me that I would be able to go on holiday after this part. Now you can keep your promise. My daughter was born, and I want to be with my wife.' So this was agreed, and George managed to avoid the tests. As it happened, the tests produced catastrophic result for the people involved; three of George's Yugoslav friends from the chemical divisions were very ill and soon died of radiation.

So George arrived home with gifts, and the most amazing thing that he brought was an enormous striped Astrakhan watermelon. Milan saw it standing on the table and was stunned. He got a stool and climbed onto the table. The watermelon was taller than him and looked extremely juicy and sweet. The sliced red pulp looked like crystals and melted in the mouth. But George, first of all, ran to see his daughter. And though a girl was not what he had wished for, as soon as he looked at her, he fell in love. She was small and beautiful, like a doll, with a tiny birthmark on her cheek in the exact place as Klara. After some discussion, they named her Larisa; even Milan liked this name. But Milan's delight quickly began to dissipate when he saw all the attention that his parents were giving to her. Besides, she often cried so loudly that it was impossible to sleep. Milan sometimes escaped to Dima's room, who was also bothered by the crying.

'What do you think? Do we need her? It was much quieter without her,' Milan said.

'Yes, it was better without her,' Dima agreed. So Milan began to make long and involved plans for getting rid of this little girl who bothered them and made their mother tired with big bruises under her eyes. But an unexpected incident prevented the realisation of any plan.

That day, Klara and Zelda were sitting on a bench in the courtyard, with little Larisa sleeping peacefully in her pram. Generally, she slept better in the afternoons than at night. It was a hot summer's day; swallows and dragonflies flew in the sky, and colourful butterflies and bees were gathering pollen. Milan suddenly remembered that his favourite tricycle that his father had brought him was at home. He ran to his mother and demanded that they go and get his tricycle. 'Mama, stay here with the baby. I'll be right back,' Klara said and followed Milan, who had run ahead. It was gloomy in the corridor after the sunny courtyard, and Milan stumbled and hit his head on the fourth step and fainted. When Klara came in, she saw him lying motionless on the steps. She rushed to him and turned him over and was horrified to see a gash in his forehead, which was bleeding profusely. Klara yelled so loudly that all the neighbours and everyone sitting in the courtyard heard her shouting and ran to help. Some were giving advice; others ran to get first aid supplies, and Zelda ran home and got a wet towel to put on Milan's head. But the towel was dirty, and Klara threw it on the floor. Their neighbour Kirsanov came running with a bandage and cotton wool.

The ambulance arrived quickly, and Milan was rushed to hospital. All the way, the frightened Milan screamed in pain, and Klara sobbed. In the hospital, Milan was taken to the theatre, where the doctors wanted to operate. But Milan's screaming and Klara's sobbing made it impossible for the doctors to concentrate, so the doctors asked Klara to leave and wait outside. But Milan begged the doctors, 'Please don't make my mother leave. I won't cry anymore, I promise.' The doctors agreed reluctantly, and despite the pain, Milan did not cry anymore. The doctors closed the wound and rolled a bandage around his head. When they were leaving, the doctor told Klara that Milan had missed his temple by less than a centimetre; any closer, and the result would have been very sad! Home from the hospital, Milan hung on to Dima, who had been very frightened for his young brother's life. The scar on Milan's forehead remained and is still visible to this day.

But after a while, Milan's attempts to get rid of his sister were renewed. Once, when she cried, he threw a pillow and blanket over her. Larisa nearly choked, but luckily Klara came into the room just then and rescued her. Milan was severely punished for this, and his father personally hit him with his belt; Milan's bottom reminded him of his offence for a long time. In the winter, when it was already very cold and snow was lying on the ground, Klara began a serious conversation with Milan.

'Why don't you love your sister?' she asked him.

'You love her more than me,' Milan said.

'That is not true!' Klara objected.

'She cries all the time, and no one can sleep,' Milan added.

'So, because you do not love her, she should be thrown out,' Klara challenged him.

'Yes, throw her out!' Milan was happy. Klara opened the 'fortachka', a small part of the window, and the icy wind blew into the apartment. 'Well, then, I will throw her out,' Klara said and put Larisa's head out through the hole. Suddenly, Milan felt sorry for his little sister, who was doomed to freeze to death in the street. He grabbed Klara by the skirt and said, 'All right, Mama, you don't have to throw her out. After all, she is ours.'

'You won't hurt her anymore?' Klara asked.

'I will not!' Milan said.

'You promise?'

'I promise,' Milan answered, and so the long conflict was over, and Milan even began to love his sister.

After a couple of years in Ufa, almost all the Yugoslavian families had children. The Negovan family had a son born a year after Milan, and now they played together under the table, shooting one another with toy pistols. Milan Ribar had searched for a long time for a suitable wife and finally had chosen the young and beautiful Kapitalina. They had a daughter, whom they named Lena. Anton Janesh had lived for two years with his beautiful wife, Zina, who insisted that she had a needle stuck under her heart and any sudden movement could kill her. So she did not do any housework, and it was all done by Anton after work. He washed, cleaned, prepared the food, and washed the floors. It is necessary to say that Ufa was the capital of Bashkiria, and the main religion there was Muslim. It was not acceptable there for a man to do housework; it was essentially women's work. They lived in a semi-basement apartment with windows almost at street level.

One day, while passing by, Klara noticed a crowd of laughing men looking into their window. Klara went up closer and looked in. There in the room was Zina lying on the sofa in a smart dressing gown, while Anton washed the floor with a cloth. The local muzhiks could not contain their laughter, and soon stories that Anton crawls in front of Zina with a cloth in his hands, spread around the building, and people openly sneered at him. Anton suffered at this, but once, during a party, Zina got drunk and danced wildly to the music of an accordion. Anton became suspicious, and soon they were divorced. Anton quickly married a very lovely girl, and a year later, their daughter was born, and they named her Lena. The only childless couple was Bruno and Lida Mrak.

When people gathered now for a party in someone's house, it was full of the noise of children shouting. But this didn't prevent the men from spending their time together happily while the women prepared the food. In the winter, they ate beljashi and pelmeni, and in summer they had vareniki with cherries or potatoes. The men warmed themselves in winter with vodka, which they had become used to, and usually beer in summer. They also often played chess. The evenings usually finished with games, lotto, or cards, or the well-known Russian game 'Fool'. Gojko Negovan was always the ringleader; he often cheated, winking or kicking his partner under the table, which caused much laughter.

This was all accompanied by hot political debates. They all hoped that Yugoslavia and the USSR would reconcile. And even though Stalin's death had shaken them all, little had changed. In Russia, the death of this small moustached man shook everyone. People cried on the streets and in their homes; the impression was that doomsday was coming. George and his friends were shaken too; all these years of war had been in Stalin's name. After the war, still in the USSR, Stalin looked down at them from practically every wall and had told them how to live. Klara met a friend on the street crying because of Stalin's death.

'Why are you so sad, Polina?' she asked.

'What will be do without him?' Polina sobbed.

'We will live as we have always lived, maybe even better,' Klara said. At these words, Polina froze and stopped crying. And it was true, the world had not stopped turning, and soon rumour of Stalin's excesses began to circulate.

Polina's husband, Voronov Pavel Ivanovich, was the doctor of the Ufa psychiatric hospital. They were a well-educated couple and liked very much to go to the theatre. Somehow, Pavel Ivanovich had obtained tickets to a performance of the Moscow Theatre that had arrived on tour. Polina got ready and waited for Pavel Ivanovich to arrive home from work. But for some reason, that day he was late. Polina began to get worried. There was an hour before the performance, and then half an hour and then she knew that they were late! Polina's worry became anger as she waited for her husband. Pavel Ivanovich, having drunk a little at lunchtime, had forgotten all about the performance. After work, he went to a bar in a hotel and had drunk some Armenian cognac and had bought two packs of eggs, which were in very short supply. He was very happy with his purchase and hoped that his wife would also be delighted! He opened the door of the house and said, smiling broadly, 'Polinochka, I've brought you some eggs!'

Polina took the eggs from his hands and asked, 'Well, and what about the theatre?'

Pavel Ivanovich suddenly remembered everything. 'I'm so sorry,' he pleaded, but it was too late. One of the packs of eggs came down on his head, the broken eggs slowly dripping down his hair, his jacket, and his white shirt. Polina was struck by the devil and began to throw eggs from the second pack, laughing wildly. Pavel Ivanovich ran into the bathroom and closed the door. Polina threw more eggs at the closed door and then lay down on the sofa and began to cry. For a long time, Pavel Ivanovich tried to erase his guilt, and Polina, when she told this story to Klara, laughed so much that Klara laughed with her with all their hearts.

When Nikita Sergeevich Khrushchev became the secretary general of the Central Committee of the CPSU, he was very keen on a food programme, and all the country marched in step with the leader. Across all Kazakhstan, the boundless steppes were ploughed and sown with grain crops, and George had been sent with his division to develop this virgin land "tscelina". They had to live in tents in an open field, where the field kitchen and dining tents were placed. The soldiers worked hard from morning until evening, and at night they had to be watched that they didn't get drunk and do stupid things. But to follow all of them was impossible, and one morning, while working in the fields, a tractor ran over two soldiers who had slept in the field after a rough night. This caused a lot of trouble, and the public prosecutor arrived from Moscow.

Sometimes, in the steppes, a strong wind would pick up the dry earth, and a dust storm would begin. It was impossible to hide from the dust, and the dust was everywhere, even in your mouth. Many tents collapsed in the wind and were carried away over the steppe, so George ordered the soldiers to cut off layers of turf and to secure the unstable tents from different directions. He was right; the tents were no longer blown away. But it was hard to please everyone, and one day there was an inspection led by a lieutenant colonel from the Moscow Military Academy. He didn't like that the tents were secured by turf, and he called George.

'Captain, what is this for?' he asked.

'To strengthen the tents against the wind,' George answered.

'That is nonsense, and I order you to clean up this disgraceful mess,' he said.

George could hardly restrain himself and answered, 'You, Comrade Lieutenant Colonel, cannot give me an order. For this, we have a commander. If he orders me, I will carry it out.' The lieutenant colonel's face reddened, and he left. George didn't see him again.

Harvesting the wheat was done by combine harvesters; the virgin soil had produced enormous quantities of grain. Sometimes in the mornings, George passed endless fields of wheat, and coming back in the evening, he could see no sign of it; it had all been collected. The grain was loaded onto trucks to be carried to the silos, but the roads were made of turf, and this meant that the trucks stalled and broke down in the fields. The shortage of silos was obvious, and the grain could not be stored. So the grain was unloaded in the fields, directly onto the ground, covered with a canvas against the rain, and it decayed. Sometimes these wheat mountains started to rot and the grain caught on fire and could not be extinguished, even by fire engines.

After the harvest season, George came back with gifts for everyone. He brought Larisa a beautiful big doll with eyes that closed, and for Milan, a two-wheeled bicycle. George was sent back to 'tscelina' two more times and was awarded a medal, 'For Virgin Soil Development'. From his last trip, he brought back a piano, 'Belarus', which Milan was to learn to play. By then, Larisa was one year old, but she still wasn't walking, only crawling quickly over the floor. Milan had started to walk very early on the rope along the sofa, but when Larissa was put on her feet, she quickly sat back down on her bottom. One day, George came home early from work, and Klara met him in the corridor, with Larisa in her arms. When she saw her father, Larisa was so excited that she escaped from her mother's arms, jumped up off the floor, and ran to her father. All the family was delighted, and George picked her up and kissed her. So without any training, Larisa learnt to walk.

———— ◆◆◆◆ ————

In 1956, Dima left school and prepared for admission to the aviation institute, which was just across the road from their house. Klara went to see his teacher, and she said, 'Klara Davidovna, your Dima is a talented boy, and he could study on level five, the best marks, but he will only get three for work education and four for German language.'

'So, how can I help him?' Klara asked.

'He needs to take these subjects more seriously,' his teacher said.

'I will talk to him,' Klara promised.

When she spoke to Dima, he said, 'Mama, do not worry, I will get into the institute. I have all the knowledge I need. I do not want to learn German—after all, those bastards killed my father.' With that, the conversation ended. Dima left school with mostly excellent marks, with a four for German and a three for work education. The admissions exams began, and Dima prepared for them diligently. The mathematics exam was the last and the hardest. He passed it and received the level five he needed to enrol in the first course.

After some months, there was a meeting in the Ministry of Education, where Klara worked. Klara met Dima's professor; they sat together in the auditorium and started talking together in the break.

'You know, my son is studying at your institute,' Klara said.

'What is his name?' he asked.

'Miroshnik.'

He looked at Klara carefully and said, 'Did you know that I examined your son in mathematics? We had a huge competition for one place, and to be honest, I tried to get your son to fail. But he answered all my questions, and I had to give him the top mark. He is a talented young man.' This praise was very wonderful for Klara to hear, and she went home in a great mood.

Dima was very happy going to the institute. However, he soon fell ill. It began with Milan, who got ill quite often, and infected everyone in the house. That year, Milan had picked up in kindergarten mumps and was ill for three days before passing it on to Larisa. Her glands were badly swollen, and she had a high temperature. She was sick for a week before passing it on to Dima. Mumps is a childhood disease, and they fight it much easier than adults. Dima got very sick and, as a result, came down with very bad complications that ended in meningitis. He was taken to the hospital where he stayed for fifteen days. All the family was very worried, because one of the side effects of meningitis is brain injury. Fortunately, he overcame his illness but left the hospital very tired. The dean of the institute suggested that he take an academic break, but Dima refused and decided to keep up with his work. It wasn't easy, but he persisted, studied hard, and finished the year successfully, having failed just one exam on resistance materials.

Over the summer vacation, Dima needed to have a rest. So, after breakfast, he often went with friends for a swim in the White River, or Ufimka River. He went with his neighbour Velerka Mester on one of these trips. Valerka was not a good swimmer, so he stayed near the shore. But Dima, as a true native of Odessa, thought himself a good swimmer and swam across the river. Ufimka was a small river but fast, and often there were whirlpools. Dima reached the other side, got out of the river, and walked for a while among the bulrushes. Then he jumped back into the river to swim back. He didn't notice that a whirlpool had formed near him. He only noticed the whirlpool when it began to form a funnel. At first, he tried to get out of it by swimming hard, but gradually his strength left him, and the whirlpool got a firmer grip on him. Just then, Dima remembered something that he had read in one of his books—that if you are in the grip of a whirlpool, you need to stop resisting, let the whirlpool drag you down, and from there try to swim out. Dima took a deep breath, and after looking at the world one last time, he went to the bottom. He twirled and lost his orientation but suddenly felt the bottom of the river under his feet. He pushed from the bottom and floated sideways and up. He reached the surface just as he thought his lungs would burst and inhaled deeply. Then he saw Valerka running along the riverside, frightened and shouting. Dima got out of the water, and Valerka ran up to him. 'Dima, you're alive! How did you manage to get out?' Dima explained what he had done, and Valerka listened, open-mouthed. After that, Dima was more careful in the water.

Larisa grew fast. She ran non-stop, but unlike Milan, who always fell on his head, Larisa always fell on her bottom. It seemed her centre of gravity was on a soft spot, and after each fall, she would get up and run again as if nothing had happened. She had difficulty in pronouncing some sounds, and if a word began with the sound 'r', she simply wouldn't say it. Just before they were getting ready to take her to a speech therapist, she suddenly began to say it. But now, having tried so hard with the sound 'r', she almost completely forgot how to make the sound 'l'. Now she drank 'mirk', not milk, ate 'cutrets' instead of cutlets, and she called Milan 'Miran'. When she was three years old, she went to the same kindergarten where Milan proudly showed her the sour cherry tree and where the gooseberries were growing. Already, on 1 September, Milan had gone into first class. The school was just two blocks from their home, and the children were seen off by their family. Milan was dressed in his school uniform, and he had the school peaked cap on his head. Klara and George looked at their child and could hardly hold back their tears.

Standing next to them was their neighbour, the family Radashkevich, who were looking at their child, Sashka. Sashka stood next to Milan while speeches were made, and then the first bell rang, and the children went into class. The children were seated by their teacher, Tatyana Borisovna, and Milan sat next to Sashka. After that, the teacher began to read the surnames of the pupils, and the children would rise and answer the teacher's questions. Tatyana Borisovna was a large, very nice, and kind teacher. She easily related to the children, and they loved her. When she called Milan, she asked him, 'Milan, that is a strange name. Who gave you that name?'

'My father,' he answered, a bit embarrassed.

'What is his nationality?' she asked.

'Serb!' Milan answered.

'But what nationality?' she asked again.

'He is from Yugoslavia,' Milan explained, confused.

'Clearly it is a very beautiful name, well suited even to a girl,' she said, and all the children burst out laughing.

The teacher went on, and among the children, there were many beautiful names: Sashi, Mashi, Valeri, and Natasha, and even one named Mars. Milan went home upset. When she saw him, his mother asked him, 'Milan, where is your bag?' Milan was horrified, clutched his head, and realised that he had left his bag, with all his books, at school. They ran back to the classroom, and there at the door was Tatyana Borisovna with his bag.

'Milan, it is your first day at school and you've forgotten your bag already!' She laughed.

'What kind of bungler are you?' Klara asked him.

'Don't be cross with him. He's a very good boy,' the teacher said. So the first day ended, but for a long time, he reproached his parents for giving him such an unusual name.

On the second day, there was one more incident. It was in a lesson when Tatyana Borisovna asked them to make lines in their writing books using a ruler. Milan and Sashka grabbed the same ruler. 'Don't touch it, it's mine,' Sashka objected, and they began to pull the ruler. At last, Milan got hold of the ruler, and Sashka spat at him. Milan spat back, and Sashka spat again; again, Milan spat back.

They were so busy that they didn't notice Tatyana Borisovna was standing near them, and she asked, 'What are those two camels doing in this class? This is not a zoo!' The other children burst out laughing.

'This is my ruler,' Sashka insisted.

'That's a lie. It's my ruler,' Milan said indignantly.

'Whose ruler is that on the floor?' the teacher asked. They both looked under the school desk and saw a ruler on the floor. It all became clear to both boys. 'However,' the teacher continued, 'since you can't sit together, we will move you.' Milan was moved next to a very nice girl, Lilej Sajfundilinoj, and he kept glancing at her lovely profile. So the troubles ended and work began.

Milan studied well, though his teacher complained of his carelessness. Klara and Tatyana Borisovna soon became friends. One day, Tatyana Borisovna took Klara by the elbow and said seriously, 'You know, Klara, we have a problem.'

'What is it?' Klara asked cautiously.

'Our Milan is not willing to die for our native land,' the teacher said.

'I don't want him to die either,' Klara said.

'I understand, but it's very important that people are ready to die for their native country,' Tatyana Borisovna said.

'What do you want me to do?' Klara asked.

'It's essential that he say it, even if he doesn't believe it,' she was told. That was easier said than done. Milan questioned almost all the Soviet values. He didn't understand the heroic acts of Matrosov and Gastello. Gaydar's books and morals did not answer any questions in his little head. So when he was sent to Pioneer Camp, he managed to stay there just one day before asking his mother to let him go home.

George faced similar problems himself. Sometimes he faced sneers about his accent and the foolish jokes of some of the officers, especially from Captain Filimonov, a huge, red-headed, healthy fellow with lots of freckles. He constantly told jokes that offended George and pushed him out of the way. Once, in the office of the assistant to the commander, he again made a sarcastic joke and pushed George. George's anger exploded; he seized Filimonov by the sleeve with one hand and grabbed his collar with the other and threw him across the room. Filimonov turned in the air and landed sideways on a table standing in the office. The table broke into pieces. Filimonov began to get up off the floor, groaning. But at that moment, the assistant to the commander of the division got between them and shouted, 'I order you to stop! I advise you both to forget about it, and it will be better for everyone.' The table was mysteriously replaced, and no one mentioned it again. No one found out about this incident, and George's service continued normally.

But there was no chance of advancing his military career. After the war, there was an incredible number of officers. There were not enough regiments for colonels; there were more officers than soldiers. A year later, George was sent to the building of the Baikal-Amur trunk railway. No, George did not have to lay the rails himself, but he was placed at the main railway junction in Chita. Here, there was so much work to do that there was hardly time to sleep. His responsibilities were great, but, surprisingly, there were no missing funds or thefts. He had an excellent relationship with the stationmaster, who demanded that George be given a higher rank based on his diligence, and a couple of months later, George was given the rank of major. Coming back from a business trip soon after, he bought Milan a children's bicycle that had just come out, the 'Schoolboy'. Milan managed the bicycle well, and his joy knew no bounds!

That year, some more of the comrade emigrants returned to Yugoslavia, but most decided to wait for the time when they would not be called traitors. This day never came, and it became necessary to accept that they would have to live far from their native land for quite a while. No one wrote to them from Yugoslavia, and they stopped writing too.

But Klara and Zelda sometimes had letters from America. Rahil's daughter, Elsa, wrote to them. She wrote about herself and other relatives. Elsa's husband was a dental technician, and his business prospered. Their income was so good that they were able to buy their own home with a pool. Klara could hardly believe it. Elsa's children, Kenny and John, were going to school and were already real Americans. For Oll and Irma, their business had developed even better. The hotel brought them in a good income, and they were able to buy another hotel. It was no longer necessary for Irma to work in the kitchen and clean; she just had to watch her workers. And Oll did not work with the same intensity, and they were able to travel together. In their letters, they didn't complain about their lives, and it became clear that they were all assured of a safe future. Rahil still thought of Zelda as his favourite sister, and understanding that it would be impossible for them to visit America, they tried to help them with parcels. These parcels helped very much; Klara and George's salaries were not enough to buy these nice clothes; there was hardly enough for food. So parcels from America were really welcomed. When Klara wore the dresses and shoes that they sent to her, she looked like a smart actress who had just left the screen. Civilian clothes weren't necessary for George; he always dressed in military uniform, and only when they went on holidays to Odessa did he wear anything else.

Part 7

By now, I have grown up, but I still remember these events that happened so long ago, and I can describe them as I remember them. What do I remember from my childhood? I remember that it was happy. After school, I would come home and be waited on by my grandmother Zenja . . . that is what I called her. Grey-haired and thin, she looked after us while our parents were at work. I remember as if it was yesterday; the taste of her chicken soup, the meat cutlets with roast potatoes, her doughnuts, the crunchy rhustiki, and the compote made from dried fruits. My grandmother was always ready to help us and never asked for anything in return. Her difficult life had made her able to cope with anything that turned up, and now she was living in an apartment with her daughter, her grandchildren, and her son-in-law, whom she loved. In the house, there was always food, and everything was calm.

My mother, Klara, was a surprisingly dynamic woman, and her work was always finished quickly. She organised everything in a loud voice, but this same voice could be surprisingly sweet when she sang, and singing was something she had love to do ever since she had been a child. I especially liked it when she sang songs from the film *Children of Captain Grant* or one of Paganel's songs, 'Once a Brave Captain Lived'. She loved to laugh, and her laughter was so infectious that it was hard to stop. She was a very devoted mother who loved her children intensely. In return, she demanded the same level of love back and said that children should love their mother above all. Our father, George, did not love us any less but did not demand any love back from us. I was always amazed by his big, strong, and also soft country hands. And though these hands sometimes (very seldom) punished me, I loved them and can still feel their warmth when he patted me on the head. These hands could make surprising things; he could cut a branch from a tree and make fiddlesticks, or make the Serbian wind instrument, the diple, a recorder, or make a pipe, or weave shoes from straw. He wasn't very talkative, but he never threw his words to the wind. He wasn't very tall, but his enemies never saw fear in his eyes, no matter what size they were.

My brother, Dima, was much older than me and was studying at the aviation institute. Every morning, when I woke up, I had to go from our room to the toilet, passing the place where Dima slept on a folding bed. I usually stopped to check what Dima was doing. He usually lay still with his eyes closed, giving the impression that he was sleeping. But I knew this wasn't true, and as soon as I tried to run past, he would very quickly pull out a pillow and throw it at me. Sometimes I was lucky enough to escape, but most of the time he would knock me off my feet and I would fall into the bathroom. Then Dima would run, pick me up off the floor, kiss me on the cheek, and say, 'See, Milashka, I got you again!'

I always knew that he loved me, but his love was a bit strange. If I argued with him, he punished me with 'smaska' . . . when he wet his fingers with saliva and rub my hair. It was quite painful, but most of all it was offensive. If I continued to argue, he would put me in 'salaski' . . . he would put me on the bed, bend my legs behind my head, and hold me in that position until I farted. Then he would laugh, kiss me again, and let me go.

Only later did I understand why he did this. Dima didn't remember his father at all and had grown up without him. My mother and grandmother loved him very much, but for a boy, it's important to feel a man's love. When George came to live with them, he started to believe that he would get this love. When I was born, he realised that my father's love for me was on a different scale, and it made him envy. Even I was confused by the difference. My father called me 'my knight', and I always felt how big his hands were, stroking my head. I have to admit that my childhood was full of love and care. We weren't rich, but we always had something to eat. I had everything that the other children had, skis and sledges, fads, and a bicycle, and I played with my friends around the streets and the park.

In summer, we went for picnics to the Belaja or Dema rivers, and sometimes to Ufimka, which was much faster and had dangerous whirlpools. In the city, we often visited Jakutova Park, where we could hire a boat and paddle around the lake, or take a ride on a steam locomotive, which was operated and driven by schoolchildren. In wintertime, we could skate or ski in the same park or ride down the hill on our sledges. So life was not dull, but it wasn't easy either. With the other boys from our courtyard, we explored neighbouring houses and garbage tips, which were alive with rats. Our adventures were greater during school holidays, when we were almost all on our own. Our parents, of course, wanted us to be involved more productively; for example, my father bought me a piano, and I was sent to music school. I can't say I didn't like playing the piano, but the streets were more appealing to my imagination, so my musical success was not very impressive.

My younger sister grew quickly and continued to go to kindergarten. Fast and determined, she was like a boy and played with me and all my friends. The majority of our games were war games; we were involved in real battles, fighting with wooden swords. In winter, we made snow fortresses and came home entirely wet.

Dima now was seldom at home. In the mornings, he went to study and then stayed at the college for classes, and in the evenings, he played basketball in the sports complex. He wasn't very tall but was very skilful and played the role of playmaker. He came home late at night, had some food, and immediately went to bed. But at one time, he found a new adventure. He started to date a girl called Galina. No one knew about it at home, just that he was coming home very rarely. One evening, he brought Galina home. She was a large girl with a thunderously loud voice, very self-confident and not very polite. She seemed to have been spoiled by her parents, because her father was the director of a big factory. That evening, Dima informed his parents that they were getting married. They had already decided on this with Galina's parents. They agreed on a date when the two sets of parents would meet. The meeting took place at the Puticavich home. Pavel Gregorjevich and Claudija Sergeevna met George and Klara very kindly but with the intent to show that they were much more important people. They lived in a four-roomed apartment with their two daughters and Pavel Gregorijevich's mother. The floors in the spacious rooms were laid in parquet and decorated with expensive furniture. The shelves held costly crystal glasses, shining in all the colours of the rainbow, hundreds of books lined the bookshelves, and beautiful pictures hung on the walls. But they had one more thing that very few people could dream about—they had a private car, Pobeda, as well as a car provided by the factory. According to their income, Galina's parents had allocated quite an amount of money for the wedding, and Klara and George felt like very poor relatives, and this feeling irritated them a lot.

The wedding took place in the Puticavich apartment. From Dima's side, there were just Mother, Father, Grandmother, Larissa, and me. All the other guests were from Galina's side, and there were a lot of them. The two biggest rooms were lined with tables and specially prepared benches. Toasts were made, vodka and wine flowed, and the tables groaned with snacks and food. Klara knew that she should be happy that her son would now live in such a prosperous house, but inside her soul, the 'cats' were scratching, and she didn't like her new relatives. After the wedding, Dima moved into the Puticavich house, where he and his wife had a separate room, and now he came home even more rarely. In half a year, they both graduated from the institute and were sent to the Perm Aviation Factory. Klara was worried for Dima, but on the other hand, she was happy that she didn't have to deal with Galina anymore.

After Dima's departure, events started to fall on their head in abundance. The new secretary of the Communist Party, Nikita Khrushchev, changed the party course. Relations with the army changed too. Since the war, the number of officers in the military was astronomical! There were more of them than positions available, and to get to a higher rank was almost impossible. In all these years, George had only been able to get to the rank of major, and his friends were doing no better. Finally, a decision was made—the army was to be cut by 1,200000 men, and George was included in that number. He became a pensioner at the age of forty because he had served enough years; four war years, multiplied by three, and sixteen post-war years was altogether twenty-eight years, more than enough to retire on. He could have asked to stay in the army, but he was tired of this dog-style living, with constant moves, and was happy for it to come to an end. Klara was even happier and dreamed about returning to Odessa.

They were offered a two-roomed flat in Kazan, but George categorically rejected that. 'No, Comrade Colonel, I don't want to move to Kazan!'

'And where do you want to go?' he was asked.

'To Odessa!' he answered.

'You want to go straight to a resort! What would happen if everyone wanted to go there? You need a good reason to go to Odessa,' the colonel said.

'First of all, I went into the army from Odessa, and, secondly, my wife was born there and lived most of her life there. She doesn't want to live anywhere else,' George said.

The colonel was silent for a while and then nodded and agreed. 'Well, we could send you to Odessa, but in Kazan we could provide you with a home. In Odessa, you have to get a home by yourselves.'

'Good!' agreed George, and a week later, he went to Odessa.

In Odessa, Semyon and Klara Podvisotsky met him as a brother, and he stayed in their apartment. The next day, he went to the city council to register and try to get a home to live in. But the queue of people waiting for a unit was so long that it was impossible to tell how long he would have to wait. George had to act as well as he could, and what helped was the friendly attitude towards all the Yugoslav officers. He decided to go and try to get help from the first secretary of the city, Gorispolkom. However, he had an unexpected change of plans. Early the next morning, he woke up with a terrible stomach ache. He first thought that he had food poisoning. He made a very strong cup of tea, drank it, and decided to go to the meeting. But he couldn't make it to the place; the stomach pains were so bad that he thought he would vomit and decided to go back to Semyon's house. When he got there, only his wife, Klara, was at home; she looked at him carefully and exclaimed, 'George, you look terrible, and you are so pale. Quickly lie down on the couch, and I will get a hot water bottle.' So Klara took over his treatment. When he started to feel better, Klara decided to go to the market to get food, and George stayed at home alone. The pain started to get worse, and the hot water bottle was cool by that time. To heat the water would take too long, so George heated up the iron and wrapped that in a towel and placed it on his stomach.

He was still like this when Uzik came back from work. 'What's happening here?' he asked.

'I have a terrible stomach ache,' George groaned.

'And you decided to cure yourself with a hot water bottle?' Uzik asked.

'But nothing else helped!' George said.

'Lie down on your back,' Uzik told him, and George did what he was told. Uzik confidently went closer to George and pressed very gently on George's stomach. He took his hand away quickly, but the sharp pain made George scream. 'It's clear that you have appendicitis, and we need to call an ambulance quickly.'

George didn't argue for too long, and within a couple of hours, he was in the military hospital. Uzik's diagnosis was correct and confirmed by a young woman doctor who examined George on his arrival. The pain was by now intolerable, and George was not sure how much longer he could put up with it. The surgery was to be done immediately, but right at that moment, there were no experienced doctors in the hospital except this young girl who had just recently graduated.

'You have to choose,' she said. 'Will you allow me to do the surgery, or will you wait for another doctor? Just remember, though, that every minute is working against you.'

'It's not much to choose from.' George grinned and even tried to make a joke. 'If I have to die, it's better to die in the hands of a beautiful woman.'

The young doctor blushed and said to the attendant, 'Get him ready for surgery!'

The surgery was carried out under general anaesthetic, and after coming to, the first thing that George saw was the face of the same young doctor. 'Well, George Milenovich, congratulations! Your surgery was successful. Do you want to see the appendix that nearly killed you?' George nodded in response; his tongue wouldn't obey him because his mouth was so dry. The doctor left and came back holding a small dish. With a pair of tweezers, she lifted a small stump about two or three centimetres long. 'Here it is!' she said.

'It's so small. How could I die from that?' he asked.

'I don't think you would have survived until tomorrow,' the doctor said. She left, and George fell asleep. A week later, they took out the stitches and discharged him from the hospital. The only reminder of this surgery was a small scar made by the inexperienced doctor.

And now, with renewed energy, George went for his appointment with the First Secretary of the Executive Committee of the People's Deputies. The man who met him was very kind and listened carefully to his story and then called in the office assistant in housing accommodation and gave her instructions: 'Tamara Petrovna, I would like to introduce you to George Milenovich. He is a political immigrant from Yugoslavia. He served in our army but now is retired and has come to settle in Odessa. By the way, his wife was born here and lived here most of her life. We must help them find accommodation!'

'But we have a complicated system with accommodation,' she tried to object. 'Some people have to wait for two years to get an apartment.'

But the secretary insisted. 'This is an exceptional case, and I ask you to do everything possible.'

After that, George dealt only with Tamara Petrovna, and in a couple of weeks, he had some good news. 'I have a surprise for you, Comrade Vignevich. You will get an apartment on the fifth station of "Big Fountains". But it will not be ready for a couple of months. Now you can go back to Ufa and get your family ready to move.'

George felt on top of the world. The very next day, he took the train back to Ufa, where bad news was waiting for him. At that time in Ufa, an epidemic of Botkin's disease, known commonly as yellow jaundice, was raging, and I caught it. In the evening, I started to feel sick and was vomiting. My mother made me some strong tea, made it drink it, and put me to bed. The next morning when she saw me, she was scared. My face had turned yellow; even my eyes were yellow! She understood that things were not good and called our doctor friend, Pavel Ivanovich. He arrived half an hour later. His diagnosis was clear—complicated case of hepatitis, and I was taken straight to hospital. Intensive treatment was begun; the injections of glucose in my legs were especially painful. They pumped glucose into me to help my liver; my legs were so swollen that it was hard to walk. Mother went to the market to get a lot of fresh fruit to help my recovery. I was getting better but very slowly. My father had arrived to take us to Odessa, but this unpredictable disease slowdown of his plans worried him, that he might lose the apartment. We had to move as quickly as possible, and they started to persuade the doctors. I was getting so many injections that my body was covered with very painful welts, but as a result, my yellowness was fading and my liver was getting smaller. I still needed some time before I would make a full recovery, but I was discharged on the condition of a very strict diet.

We left Ufa in August, and that morning, there was a heavy frost on the ground. This time, there were only five of us leaving, because Dima and his wife were living in Perm. Our trip lasted three days, and we were all very impatient to get to Odessa as soon as possible. At last, the train stopped, and we got out onto the platform, where we were met by Semyon and his wife, Klara. It was clear by the smiles on their faces that they were happy to see us. Semyon hugged his aunt Zelda and then Klara and then the rest of us.

'Congratulations on your return to Odessa,' he said.

'I feel very uncomfortable that we might be a stone around your necks,' Klara started.

But Semyon replied angrily, 'Nonsense!' He tapped George on the shoulder and said, 'Let's go home!'

'Thanks for your kindness, and I hope that we will not have to live at your place for too long. I think we'll get our apartment in a couple of weeks,' Klara said.

'Listen, Klara, you are part of our family, and we will do everything for you that we can. We should stop talking about this right now!' And with that, Semyon took Klara's hand and led them to his car. We weren't all able to get into the one car, so we took a taxi as well. Semyon and Klara lived in a big new building, situated next to a Newmarket and right above a "Friendship" cinema. The apartment was spacious with parquet floors, beautifully furnished, and with a big balcony overlooking Sadovaya Street.

We took our things, and Semyon told us to put them in a bedroom. In the kitchen, Semyon's wife, Klara, was heating up the dinner. Now there were two

Klaras in the house, and this caused some confusion. Both of them were busy in the kitchen, and the men opened a bottle of vodka, poured it into glasses, and had a shot. Just a few minutes later, the door opened, and Uzik, Asja, and their two children, Larisa and little Shurik, came into the room. They joined everyone around the table, and the party started. The feast lasted until the evening, and there were many toasts and plans for the future, and nobody doubted that the future would be great. At last, they decided that it was time to sleep.

'And where will we sleep?' Klara asked.

'You will sleep in our bedroom,' Semyon said.

'But where will you sleep?' she asked again.

'We will make a bed here on the floor,' Semyon answered.

'No! We won't agree to that,' Klara and George protested together, but Semyon stopped them.

'In this house, I decide who is sleeping where, and you will sleep in our room, where there is enough room for everyone.' The dispute was over, and they had to sleep where they were told.

George decided to go to Odessa City Soviet of People's Deputies Committee the next morning and to get his apartment as soon as possible. He was hoping for one thing, but when he got there, he was told that his apartment had been given to another family. 'But how is that possible? You promised it to me, and you told me to bring my family. Now you tell me that you have given the apartment to someone else!' He was very indignant, and his accent became even stronger.

Tamara Petrovna looked a little embarrassed but shrugged her shoulders and said, 'Please understand, we can't do anything about this unit anymore. We had to give it to a "Soviet war hero", because they get priority for their accommodation.'

'So, what am I supposed to do? We have no place to live, and we are staying with my wife's relatives for a short time. My son was just recently discharged from hospital and is still very weak.'

'We can't do anything about this apartment, and we can only wait for the next one. Believe me, the next one will definitely be yours. You just have to wait a little longer,' Tamara promised.

George left the office so upset that he didn't know where to go. He didn't know how he would break the news to Klara. He wandered around for a little while, had a beer to boost his confidence, and then went home. But when Klara saw him, she immediately knew what had happened.

'My god, George, you look terrible. What's happened? Didn't we get the apartment?' George shook his head. 'Why do we have such terrible misfortunes? How did they explain this?' She wanted to know.

'That apartment was given to a "Soviet war hero", but they promised that the next apartment will be ours,' George explained.

'But when will that happen, and where will it be?' Klara asked.

'They said nothing about that, just that it will happen soon,' George said.

'What will we do? We can't impose ourselves on Semyon and Klara.'

'Let's move to a hotel,' suggested George.

'We'll talk with Semyon first, though,' said Klara.

As soon as Semyon came home from work, they told him the unpleasant news. Semyon listened quietly, considering the situation. But Klara tried to reassure him. 'Don't worry, we will move to a hotel,' she said.

'You will go nowhere! We'll all stay and live here. During the war, we were cooped up in basements. Surely we can live for a few months in my big apartment.'

'But we don't want to impose on you,' Klara said.

'Then you want to offend me?' Semyon asked. It was impossible to argue with Semyon with his Odessa logic. So we all stayed in his place, and on 1 September, Larisa and I went to school. We were not very happy in this school. I couldn't get used to the game of Mayalka, which was popular with all the boys; neither did I like the strange hobby of collecting and exchanging labels from jars and bottles. It didn't matter how well Klara and Semyon treated us; we tried to behave as quietly and modestly as possible. Zelda and Klara went to the market and tried to buy some food for the house, but we were living solely on George's pension, and it clearly was not enough.

Every day, George went to the Odessa People's Deputy and to the Military Registration Office and tried to get an apartment sooner. At last, in October, he was told that they would receive a three-roomed apartment in a new building on Novoarkadievskaja Street. With this wonderful news, he almost ran home and told everyone who was at home. There was such a noisy reaction that the neighbours no doubt got frightened. And it wasn't clear just who was happier, the Vignevich or Podvisotsky families. Semyon and Uzik immediately wanted to toast this news, but Klara rejected that idea. She was afraid to jeopardise their good luck, so they all ended up going to bed early, to be sure that George could get back to the Deputy's Office the next morning. In these two months, George had quite annoyed them, but Tamara Petrovna sympathised with him. When he got to her office, she got up from her chair and smiled at him. 'I have to congratulate you, George Milenovich. I have a gift for you today.' She opened her hand, and there on her palm lay a small bunch of keys. 'Here are the keys to your unit, take them,' she said.

George took the valuable keys in his hand and felt happier than he had in a long time. He wanted somehow to show his gratitude to this woman . . . unusually for him, he kissed her hand, and she blushed deeply. 'So, I can go now?' he asked.

'Wait, I must give you the warrant for the apartment,' she said and took some papers from the table and gave them to George. He carefully folded them and put them in his pocket.

'When do you think we could move in?' he asked.

'You could do it even now, but today is Friday. Officially you can move in on Monday, so there's no need to rush.'

228

'That's good, but I have to run home now before my wife goes crazy. She's worried that something could go wrong again.'

'Everything will go well, don't worry,' Tamara said, shrugging her shoulders. 'But if you are so concerned, then run!'

He went out of the door and ran almost the whole way to the number 2 trolley bus stop. Then it was a long twenty-minute ride in the overcrowded trolley bus. He kept touching his pocket where the precious warrant for the apartment was. He flew up the stairs to the fourth floor to Semyon's apartment and knocked at the door. From inside, he could hear Klara's voice and the sound of her steps. Her face was flush with excitement, but there was fear in her eyes.

'Come on, tell me, did you get it?' she asked.

'Yes, I've got the keys,' George said, shaking the keys in front of her face. Klara grabbed them from him and kissed them a few times.

'Tell me, when can we move in?' she asked.

'On Monday,' George said.

'Oh, we have to wait so long. Can't we move in now?' she asked him.

'Tamara Petrovna said we could probably move in today, but officially it's Monday,' George said.

'No, I don't trust anyone anymore. We have to move in today, because I have an awful feeling that someone else will move in over the weekend before us!' Klara said. George didn't think that was necessary, but trying to stop Klara was like trying to stop a moving train, and he agreed. 'You go to school and get the children'—she gave him a job to do—'and we'll do everything we can to move into the unit today. Mama and I will pack everything that we need for the first couple of days, and the rest we will get later.'

George went to the school, and in the house, Klara and Zelda gathered together the most important things. A few hours later, the five of us took a taxi and travelled in the direction of Arcadia. We children were even more excited than our parents and kept asking them questions: how many rooms were in the apartment, would we have separate bedrooms, how far from the sea was it, and did it have a telephone?

The weather for moving wasn't the best; it was cold and damp, drizzle was falling, and a cold wind chilled us to our bones. We found that our home was the last on the street. The entrances were from the yard, and there were still no sidewalks, just puddles and heaps of dirt. We began to look for our entrance; we found it second from the left. Trying not to attract attention, we opened the door and started to walk up the stairs. At last, we were in front of our unit, and still no one had noticed us. George put the key in the lock, turned it twice, pushed open the door, and stepped into the corridor of our new unit. Larisa and I ran straight in after him, and then came Klara and Zelda, our grandmother Zenja, as we children called her. George closed the door behind them. Larisa and I ran around the unit, screaming loudly. Mother had to stop us, 'Stop screaming, otherwise they will throw us out of here!'

'Why? It's our unit now,' Larisa argued.

But Mother said, 'Because we are still not allowed to move in, not until Monday. That's why I'm asking you to whisper.' We reluctantly did as she asked.

Outside, it was starting to get dark, but the electricity had not been connected yet. We started to prepare our beds. From our bags, we pulled out two thick camel-hair blankets and put them on the floor, covered them with two bed sheets and put down four pillows and another two blankets. By that time, it was dark, and we lit candles, which we placed on a piece of paper. After that, Klara took out some bread and sausage, which we divided among us. Klara pulled out a thermos of hot tea and two metal mugs. George took from his coat pocket a bottle of vodka and three little metal glasses and put them all on the floor.

'Let's have a house-warming drink!' he suggested.

'What are you saying, George? You know I don't drink, especially vodka!' Klara reminded him.

Unexpectedly, Zelda said, 'I will have a drink with you. And I suggest that you have a drink too and not spoil the party!'

'All right, give me some vodka,' Klara agreed, and George happily poured vodka into the three glasses and gave one to his wife and the other to his mother-in-law.

'To our new home!' They happily clinked glasses, and with us with our teacups, and drank.

Unexpectedly, Klara reached out her glass to George and said, 'Pour more for me. I want to drink that nobody takes this apartment away from us. I still can't believe it's ours, but while I'm living, I'll never let anyone take it from us.'

'Believe me, no one will take it away from us,' George said, stroking the pocket where he kept the pistol he had brought from Bosnia.

After that, we all started to go to bed without undressing. We all tried to sleep, but no one succeeded because we were all too excited. Not even Larisa and I could sleep; we were whispering plans about what to do the next day. Outside, the rain continued to pour, but we were more comfortable sleeping on the floor of our new house than ever before.

The next morning, the rain had stopped. We woke early, washed our faces, and got ready for our jobs. George went to organise the container with our furniture, Klara went to the shops to get food, and Zelda stayed at home to look after us. Despite her protests, I put on my coat and went out into the street, where I came face to face with a boy the same age as me, Vovka Kompaneets, who had moved into a unit with his family on the same evening. Our friendship would last a long time, even to today. On Monday, the electricity was connected, and the central heating was switched on. On Tuesday, our very simple but much-needed furniture arrived. Now everyone had their own bed, and our everyday life got more and more comfortable.

That same week, Mother took us to our new school, N59, located on Pirogovsky Street. We were to travel by trolley bus N5. I wore a school uniform and pioneer tie, as we had to in Ufa. I was enrolled in class 5A, and we waited for the break after the first lesson. At last, the bell sounded, and the pupils ran out of the classroom into the corridor, shouting loudly. None of the pupils were wearing uniforms. When they saw me in my pioneer uniform, they attacked me like savages and pulled me out of my mother's arms. She screamed at them, 'Let him go immediately!'

With this shout, a very small man, the geography teacher, came out of the classroom. 'Stop this at once!' The pupils all stepped back and left me in the middle, utterly dumbfounded. My uniform was unbuttoned, my pioneer tie had disappeared, but I was smiling like a fool. I already like these children more than the children from the last school. I have to say that discipline in this school hardly existed, and the teachers had great difficulty controlling the pupils.

More families of Yugoslavian immigrants, discharged from the army, began to settle in Odessa. Near us, Milan Ribar settled with his wife, Kapa, and his children, Lena and Nikushka. Nikolay Gruich and his wife settled even closer. A little further up the road was Slavko Stojanovich's unit, where he lived with his wife, Rima, and two daughters, Larisa and Rita. The Achimovich family lived on Prospekt Gagarina. On Pirogovsky Street, the Velich family lived with their son, Slava, who went to the same school as me. The families met together pretty much every weekend, and we celebrated all the holidays together, from New Year, May Day, to November 7, the Day of the Great October Revolution, to any other insignificant holidays. They only needed a reason for a party, and birthdays were perfect for that. At those parties, the men usually drank, played chess, and argued about politics. The women prepared food, gossiped, and looked after the children. But the children were growing quickly and needed less and less of their parents' attention.

The building we were living in belonged to the Odessa Shipping Company. A majority of the units were occupied by seamen's families, some by families of the Odessa football team, "Chernomorets", and a few lucky other people. It was located just two blocks from the sea; our back windows faced a square across the road and a boggy area where the factory left their sewerage. All that was later turned into a park. On the right side of the building was the Champagne Factory, but the most important thing was that right across the fence in front of the building was the Odessa University Stadium, where I spent almost all of my very happy childhood. Here, I met my first friends, Jura Burshtein and Vova Olenin, who, for some reason, had the nickname Ljolik. In the same building with them lived Surik Kotljar and Mishka Zmeev. Unfortunately, there were not a lot of boys in our yard, so we were always in danger of attacks from boys from other yards.

It was impossible to live on my father's pension, and after we had settled in, he began to look for a job and was prepared to take anything at all. Klara was also looking everywhere, but she couldn't find anything. At first, people were ready to take her on, and then suddenly they refused her application. She was losing hope when, out of the blue, an opportunity opened up. She was offered the position as bookkeeper in Lespromhoze, with a salary of forty-five roubles. It was so small; she was ashamed to tell anyone. But she agreed because the financial position of the family was hopeless. It was a small salary for a lot of work; she hardly found time for a lunch break. Every day, she bought a bread roll for five kopecks, which she had with a glass of sour cream. Klara's only hope was that one day soon she would find a good job with a decent salary.

In searching for his job, George had to take into account one thing . . . that he was already a pensioner. His military pension was 120 roubles, and he was allowed to earn not more than 90 roubles, and he didn't want to work hard for that money. One day, in search of work, he came to the office of the director of human resources of the Black Sea Shipping Company. Comrade Bojko listened carefully about George's work experience in the army and said, 'You, Comrade Vignevich, must go and look for a job in our Mechanical-Experimental factory. They have a manager of the supply division, Pyzhov, but you can tell him you need a job, and I will call him too.' George took the address and went by bus to Peresip, where the factory was located. The Factory Administration and Accounting Departments were in the same building, on the second floor. Former lieutenant Colonel Pyzhov was a large man with a strong physique but not such a friendly face. He immediately felt threatened by George's appointment and protested that he didn't need any assistance in his office. But the order came from above, and George got the job.

From the very first day of work, George began to develop good relations with all the workers, except his immediate superior, who constantly tried to tell him how to do his work, though he was a useless specialist. All the factory administration was located in two big rooms. The director's office was divided by a partition into two spaces. The first was for the director and his assistant, and the second one for the Supply Department and chief engineer, Gerber Alexander Lvovich. Since the war years, George had been famous for his unique ability to supply his division, and he didn't lose this in civilian life. Without any major effort, he was able to get everything that the factory needed, and it was very much appreciated by everyone, including the director. However, his immediate boss didn't recognise that, and he kept on telling George how to do his job. Sometimes the instructions were too rough, and George would fight back.

'Why are you always telling me what to do? I used to supply the army of 40,000 men, not just a small factory. Please leave me in peace,' he complained.

'It doesn't matter to me what you were doing in Yugoslavia. Here, I am your boss, and you have to listen to me!' Pyzhov shouted in reply. All this happened quite often in front of the director or chief engineer. As a result, it became clear that the situation could not continue, and a solution had to be found. Thanks to the efforts of the director, Storozhev Anatoly Pavlovich, they managed to move Pizhov to the bigger ship repair factory, and George stayed with them as chief of the Supply Department, and from that day, he didn't experience any problems.

Winter passed and spring arrived. I graduated from the fifth year, and Larisa from the first year, and the holidays had begun. School N59 wasn't famous for its educational results; on the contrary, it was famous for its very bad discipline. Neither Klara nor George was happy with the school and decided to move us to another new school, N35, which was built on Prospekt Gagarina, next to the Odessa Film Studio. But we didn't have to go to school until September; now we had holidays, and I enjoyed them. In Ufa, I was always a frail boy and was hit by infections one after the other. Here in Odessa, the fresh air had a healthy influence on my body. With my friends, I played football in the stadium, and, without our parents knowing, we went to the sea, a fifteen-minute walk from our house. I got suntanned and became stronger and stronger, and even an awful fungus on my feet that I had picked up in the baths in Ufa, in the salt water, had become smaller and finally disappeared before the end of the year.

Almost everywhere in Odessa, there were fruit trees growing, cherries and apricots, and my friends and I were always attacking these trees. Everything in Odessa suited me well, especially the hot southern sun. Larisa was only eight years old and couldn't go to the sea yet; she spent a lot of time with our grandmother. On very little money, Zelda still was able to cook really tasty and decent meals. As a first course, she usually made soup or chicken broth with stuffed chicken neck. But quite often, she made red or green borsch, and sometimes rassolnik. Her cutlets were so tasty that our mouths watered even before we got into the unit. She made delicious goulash, but her stuffed fish was her specialty. She had learnt in Ufa how to roast bilashi, and to mould vareniki and pelmeni. She made sweet things for us as well, like hrustiki, which was made from dough and powdered sugar; they had a wonderful taste. That's what was on our menu!

The only thing that made us look different from our neighbours was our clothes, which weren't new. We lived in the buildings of the Odessa Shipping Company, and the seamen brought beautiful clothes from other countries. The majority of my friends' fathers were seamen, and Urka's father was a doctor, who got expensive presents from clients, so all my friends dressed better than me. Sometimes they let me dress in their clothes, and I was grateful for that, but my heart always felt heavy. Larisa was dressed no better than me and always wore Larisa Warshavsky's old clothes. This situation couldn't last too long, and Klara was always looking for a better-paid job. One day, she had some good news. At a meeting in a restaurant one day, George's friend from the shipping company asked him, 'George Milenovich, what is your wife's occupation?'

'She's an accountant,' George said.

'And does she need a job?' he asked.

'She certainly needs a job. In her present job, she is paid very poorly.'

'Well, then, tomorrow she should come in and see our chief accountant, Comrade Ivanov. He needs an accountant.' With this news, George went home and told Klara. At first, she couldn't believe her ears and then started to jump for joy. The next morning, she woke up early, washed, and put on her best clothes and went for her appointment.

Ivanov Valery Vasilijevich appeared to be a very kind man, and he met her with a smile. 'What is your name, dear?' he asked her.

'Klara Davidovna,' she answered.

'Tell me where you worked before and what you were doing,' he said. Klara told him about her employment experience. Valery Vasilijevich listened to her with interest, and in the end, he concluded, 'You will fit this position very well. Go now to the Staff Department and enrol yourself. I will give them a call now.'

Klara rushed off to the Staff Department, where she was met by a man with smoothly brushed hair and sharp eyes. 'Good morning, I was sent to you by Valery Vasilijevich,' she said.

'I know, he already called me,' he said. 'Give me your passport, and I will start to fill out the forms.' Comrade Zimin took a questionnaire and a pen and opened the passport. But he didn't write anything. His eyes rested on the first page, and the expression on his face changed. He sat still without moving for some time and then looked at his watch and said, 'You know, it's time for our lunch break. It would be better for you to come back here in an hour,' and he gave Klara her passport back. Klara was confused but took the passport and went out into the corridor. She realised that something was wrong. What this man hadn't liked was that she was Jewish. She decided not to jump to any premature conclusions and just to hope for the best.

She walked along the street but didn't buy any food, and after an hour, she went back to the Staff Department. Zimin met her with a sour expression on his face. 'Klara Davidovna, I have some bad news for you.'

'What is it?' she asked.

'The position is no longer available,' he said.

'Then why was I told that you needed an accountant?' she asked again.

'It's simply that we had a few candidates for this position, and preference was given to another person.'

'Don't make a fool of me!' Klara didn't believe him. 'I know perfectly well why you don't want to give me the job.'

'And why is that, if it's no secret?' he asked.

'Just because I'm a Jew,' Klara told him.

'I didn't say that to you, but you can think what you want,' he answered in an iron voice. Klara started to cry and ran out of the office. She ran along the corridor, not noticing anything around her. No one had ever so openly told her that she was rejected on the base of her nationality.

Klara had very seldom thought about being Jewish; she had grown up in a Soviet school, and it didn't make any difference to her, but in the last years, she had noticed a more and more negative attitude to Jews. But this time, it had been especially evident. Before leaving, Klara tried to see the chief accountant to talk to him, but she was told that he had left already on a business trip. She went home on the trolley bus and felt like a badly punished dog. When he went inside, she fell down on the sofa and started to cry. In the evening, she told George everything, and he tried to calm her down, but Klara couldn't forgive such an awful insult. 'If I'd had a gun right then, I would definitely have killed him!' she shouted. But very soon, and utterly unexpectedly, Klara was offered another job opportunity.

One day, at a lunch break, a young man approached her and said, 'Klara Davidovna, let me introduce myself. I'm Romanov Konstantin Sergeevich.'

'And how do you know me?' she asked.

'An employee at your industrial complex has recommended you to me and told me that you are a very skilled accountant.'

'Yes, I'm experienced, but do you have a job for me?' Klara asked him directly.

'The answer is yes, or, more correctly, I will have it. It would be better if I start at the beginning. I was recently called in to the city council and was told that Odessa doesn't even have a single Lombard, a pawnshop, and they would like to open one.'

'I was never involved in this kind of business before,' Klara said.

'Neither was I, but someone has to do it, and that will be us,' he replied.

'And how will we do something that we know nothing about?' asked Klara, confused.

'You and I will go to Kiev and Moscow to learn. We will see how other people are doing it, and then we'll employ the right people, find the premises, and then do even better than the others. And you would help me to do that,' he answered.

'Are you offering me a job?' Klara asked him. 'When will I start, and what kind of money will you pay me?'

'You start right now, and will the salary of 120 roubles suit you?' That was almost three times more than she was earning at the moment, and she didn't even have to think about it.

'Indeed, I agree,' Klara agreed.

'We need a person who would be able to provide all the correct accounting to make our pawnshop a profitable enterprise. They will watch us carefully, and we must not falter. Tomorrow, we will go together to the City Soviet of People's Deputies, and you will meet our director, Comrade Krutov. He doesn't understand a lot about our business, and he will be insulting, but you don't need to pay attention to that.' And, really, she often had to ignore Krutov. He was an ardent anti-Semite and often took out his rudeness on Klara, but she didn't ever hold her horses with him and always showed him her disgust. But with Romanov, she always had an amicable and productive relationship. He was a very gentle man, always tried to protect Klara from their boss's rudeness. They were sent together on a business trip to learn everything about Lombard's: what kind of premises they needed, how to organise security protection, what kind of assets they would accept, what percentage of interest they would charge, where to find the most experienced estimators, and how to run the accounting. They went to Kiev and Moscow for more than two weeks, and while Konstantin Sergeevich studied the more general organisational questions, Klara studied all the accounting issues. They came back to Odessa with a clear idea of how to run the business.

Premises were found not far away from where we lived, on the corner of Novoarkadievskaja Street and Prospekt Gagarina, in a beautiful building on a busy intersection, and they immediately began to convert it into a pawnshop. The first people they employed were estimators and the staff for the Accounting Department. Klara and Romanov were involved in all the organisation and legal details. She had to order all the necessary accounting books, all the receipt books, and to print all the instructions. The director had very little understanding of the business but still tried to get involved in everything. The two new estimators were Jewish, and his anti-Semitism couldn't tolerate that. 'Are you trying to establish a Zionist organisation here?' he demanded, accusing Klara. Sometimes he was so insulting that Klara even thought about quitting, but Romanov was always able to calm things down. Finally, they overcame Krutov's resistance; the two estimators were employed in spite of their nationality because they couldn't find anyone else. At last, after a couple of months, Lombard's was opened. A lot of people started to bring their valuables, and in spite of the long queues, everything was going smoothly. Occasionally, a few clients made a fuss when their items weren't accepted. But even in that case, the security guards quickly restored order and removed the offender from the shop. Klara was well respected in this job and was paid reasonably good money.

After getting the position of chief of the Supply Department, George started filling other positions. First of all, Milan Ribar was made his assistant, and then he employed Dmitry Velich, another Yugoslav immigrant who had graduated from the military college in Kiev. Now, in the office, they could speak Serbian. In the factory, no one minded; in fact, everyone loved it and often made friendly jokes about it. The Supply Department did its job very well, and the management was very happy with it. In his hunt for materials necessary for production, George rushed all over the city and sometimes went on business trips. He followed his rule, 'Never come back empty-handed,' and he had a bulldog grip. On these trips, he had to compete with other suppliers, but he had one significant advantage—he was Yugoslav! He often met former soldiers and officers who fought at the end of the war in Yugoslavia and who remembered well how the partisans had helped to beat the fascists. That's why George was often able to get results where others failed. Both his assistants, Milan and Dmitry were doing well too.

Quite often, to get results, George had to treat the other party to alcohol and to drink with them, and he was getting better at this too. In Ufa, he drank only occasionally, but now he was drinking almost every day. Klara didn't like it at all and would often scream at him. George didn't work all day long; often in summer, after lunch, he would spend a few hours on Lunzeron Beach, where he swam in the sea and sunbathed. His skin got so dark, it was almost black. It was hard to believe that this person who was born in the Bosnian mountains, where they didn't have enough water to drink, would become such a lover of the sea.

Here in Odessa, they usually met with Yugoslav friends, though some Russian friends met with them occasionally. Only in their close circle did they feel free to talk about any political subject. The topics were so difficult, and they argued so passionately that sometimes after these discussions, they didn't speak to one another for weeks. That year, they were joined by two other outstanding political refugees, Milan Kalafatich and Tule Milich. They were quite a bit older and more experienced. They had started their political activities before the war. Kalafatich was especially interesting; before the war, he had become a Comerton fighter and fought in the Spanish Civil War against the fascist Franco regime. After Franco's victory, he had been locked up in a high-security jail from where he made a very famous escape. The escape was very bold and made without a single bullet being shot. They had lured a prison guard into the cell, disarmed him, and taken the keys. Then they disarmed every guard, locked them into the cells, and ran away.

During the Second World War, he fought in Yugoslavia, held a high position in the Communist Party, and quite often met with Josef Bros Tito. But he was an outspoken Stalinist, and after the war, when Tito and Stalin's relationship broke down, he was sent to prison on Goli Otok Island. The jail was famous for its severe methods of corrective work. The island well deserved the name Goli, because not a single tree grew on it, and it was open to the scorching sun and sticky salty winds. The work was hard, but what made it most difficult was that it was senseless. One day, they would carry heavy stones by hand from one side of the island to the other, and the next day they would take them back again. And so it went on day by day. The food was terrible, the work exhausting, and anyone who protested was subjected to humiliating torture. But Milan was a tough nut and withstood everything. What was hardest for him was to be separated from his Russian wife, Zenja, and his daughter, Tanja. In the end, he managed to escape, and he ran away to the Soviet Union without saying anything to his wife and daughter. They joined him a year later. Now he lectured at the Odessa State University in the faculty of Party History. Among his new friends, he was an active debater, with great self-confidence, and he had good reason for that. He was well educated and had such enormous life experience that it was difficult to argue with him. But George found it easy to find a common language with him and to have his own opinions. It was harder for Klara to find a common language with his wife, Zenja, who considered herself to be a very sophisticated lady and tried to show it to others. Klara would never allow anyone to treat her as second class, so they often had regrettable arguments.

⋅⋅⋅⋅⋅⋅⋅

Since Khrushchev had come to power, the relationship between the USSR and Yugoslavia had become warmer, and there was a feeling of hope in the air. At last, in 1963, they were informed that Yugoslav immigrants and their families could apply for a holiday trip to Yugoslavia, and they quickly began to collect all the necessary documents. Never before had Klara had to deal with the OVIR and had no idea how difficult it all was going to be. They had to collect many documents and to fill out a questionnaire, only one of which was given to each person and could not be corrected. It cost them not only a lot of money but also a lot of stress. On the appointed day, lots of people gathered in the corridors of OVIR, and its employees were trying hard to spoil the lives of anyone going abroad. They demanded new documents or additional information about a relative. They always made grimaces when they asked Klara about her nationality. George had an easier time with them, probably because of some special instructions. All this was happening in work hours, so their bosses were not too happy about it all. At last, at the end of May, they were permitted to go and were given their international passports. They still had to wait, though, for the school holidays to begin.

By now, they were trying to borrow money for the trip, tickets, and money to exchange to dinars; they were only allowed ninety roubles per head. But there was also the chance to do some business, and they were given plenty of advice. Living close to seamen, they were told what to buy and where to sell. A number of valuable goods were included—black caviar, table silver, watches, and cameras. For all that, they needed more money, but more importantly, they needed to find these goods that were scarce, even in Odessa. Besides that, they had to buy gifts for George's relatives, and that became Klara's job. George got involved with making contact with his mother, his brother, Milan, and sister, Kosa. In all these years, he wrote to his mother very seldom and had never had a letter back because she could not write. Once, he received a letter from Lipa, where they explained that Milan had gone to live in Zagreb, where Kosa lived, and after that, Milka had joined them. They also gave him Kosa's address in Zagreb, and he wrote to her. He received an answer about a month later. Kosa explained that his mother was living with them in Zagreb and that they were all waiting for our arrival with impatience.

At last, summer arrived, we children finished school, and everything was ready for our trip. I didn't want to go because everything that I had heard about

Yugoslavia was negative. I imagined Yugoslavia to be a poor agricultural country with a bloody dictator. I preferred to stay home and play football with my friends in the stadium than to visit some dirty pit hole. But despite my protests, no one would agree to leave me at home. Larisa was still too young to expect anything, and Klara was shaking, thinking how George's relatives would meet her. George himself was thinking mostly about meeting his mother again and how his war friends would accept him.

The first stop we made was in Lvov, where Sasha, Tanja Pencheva's brother, lived. He showed us around the city, while he and Klara remembered happy old school years. In the evening, he and his wife took us the railway station, where we boarded the Moscow to Belgrade train. The carriages on this train were much cleaner and better fitted out than the ordinary trains. We had some tea and then went to bed, because the trip was supposed to be difficult. Early the next morning, we arrived in Chop, where all the wheels were to be changed for the narrow track. We had to leave the train and walk around the small town. There was absolutely nothing to do in Chop, and we soon went back to the station and continued on our trip. After that, it was a border, knocks on doors, checking of documents, and visits from customs. We had to open our cases and answer many questions. We all had the feeling that we were doing something illegal.

After that, the train moved on again, and soon we could see the Hungarian landscape, with small stations and little towns, and at last, after five hours, we arrived in Budapest. We stopped there for five hours, so we decided to go to the city. At the station, we were only allowed to exchange twenty roubles, so we decided to walk. None of us except Father had been abroad before, so we were all expecting trouble. But while no one touched us, it was clear that Hungarians didn't like people who spoke Russian. Anytime we tried to ask them a question, they pretended that they didn't understand us and walked away. Budapest was a vast and gloomy city, and we left it without any regrets. We got back to the station and continued our journey. Again we looked at the landscape through the windows, and periodically a border officer would knock on our door.

The next morning, we arrived in Belgrade, and we looked out of the windows with great excitement. The landscape was similar to Hungary, but the cars on the roads were very different; we had never seen anything like them before. At last, the train came into the city; the first high-rise buildings had appeared, and we had never seen anything like them in Odessa. The train slowly rolled into the station and stopped, and we stepped out onto the platform. We left our suitcases in the luggage room and left the station. Father decided that we would take a taxi to go to his aunt Strina Sofia. We came out of the station, and instead of the hole that I had expected, in front of us was a big, beautiful, noisy city. There were many beautiful cars on the roads; the people were dressed nicely and smiled. But the most amazing thing was the shop windows. In the Soviet Union, we usually saw advertisements and only a few products. Here, they were bursting with stylish goods. Even more impressive were the windows of the delicatessen shops, where there were products we didn't even know what to call. At first, I couldn't believe it, but with time, the truth became clear, that the stories told to us in Russia about Yugoslavia were simply lies.

We were a total surprise to Strina Sofia. Jukan had always managed to surprise her before the war, and he was doing it again now. Sofia was a very kind woman, a smile always on her face. She met us with joy and at once found a name for us, 'Moi Rusi' (my Russians), and because I was so skinny, she called me 'Komarac', or mosquito. She lived in the middle of Belgrade, but her house was in the same condition as it was twenty years ago. She had two rooms, and two adult children, Sveto and Nada, who still lived with her. Sveto lived in a wooden extension in a courtyard, with a bed, a little table, a couple of chairs, a radio, and a TV. Sveto was a cheerful, strong man who practiced daily with weights and was proud of his muscles. There was always music that we had never heard before coming from his room. Her daughter, Nada, was a bit older. She didn't engage in any sport but loved to eat a lot, so she was very fat. We were invited to stay the night, but there weren't enough beds, so Klara slept with Larissa, George slept in a folding armchair, and I slept on a folding bed under the stairs. It was not very comfortable, but at least we were not on the street. Strina was a generous woman, but, unfortunately, she had very little to share. She had raised her two children alone. They always had barely enough money in the house, and they lived very modestly. We didn't want to impose on them, so the next day we left for Zagreb.

On the station in Zagreb, we were met by Kosa and her huge and very handsome husband, Nicola. Kosa was very excited because Jukan had saved her life during the war, when he had taken her from her parents in Lipa a few days before they were all executed. Now she ran to Jukan and put her head on his chest. 'Dear Jukitsa, how happy we are that you've finally arrived.' After that, she turned to Klara. 'Let me see who Jukan swapped us all for,' and they exchanged kisses. And after that, she greeted Larisa and me. We went in two cars to their home. We were in a taxi because Nicola and Kosa were driving their small beetle-like car, the Fiat 750, known as the 'Ficho'. They lived with their one-year-old daughter, Sanja, in a new three-roomed apartment. With them lived Jukan's mother, who opened the door for us and looked at Jukan in astonishment. 'Oh, my Jukitsa, you're almost bald.' He went up to her and carefully hugged her by her shoulders, and they both began to cry. They stayed like that for a few minutes, and no one wanted to disturb them.

At last, Kosa did it. 'Listen, Nina, he didn't arrive alone. Here are your daughter-in-law and their children.' (In this household, Milka was known as Nina.)

Milka went up to Klara and said, 'So that's what you look like.' They exchanged kisses, and then it was my turn. My grandmother looked at me and then covered her mouth with her hand. 'My god, he looks exactly like my Pepo' (the son who had been killed during the war), and she hugged and kissed me.

'And this is my daughter, Larisa,' said George and pushed her forward.

'That's not a Serbian name. We'll call her Loritsa.' And from that time on, everyone in Yugoslavia called her that. For us, it was very difficult to get used to our new grandmother. She was so different from our grandmother in Odessa, who usually dressed in colourful dresses. Nina always wore black with a widow's black scarf on her head. She had a very scratchy voice, and she looked really like a peasant. But in time, we got used to her, and every year we got closer and closer.

Milan, Jukan's brother, arrived last, and he had left work early. Last time Jukan had seen him, Milan had been only ten years old; he was very small and very thin, and they had very little in common at all. Now he had changed a lot and was a very handsome young man, with incredibly bright brown eyes and a big smile. His eyes were always happy and warm, and it seemed that he was always in a good mood. We stayed in Zagreb for a week. In this time, we visited a favourite cousin of Father's, Zorka, who was married to his old war friend Milovan Pilipovich, who was now a colonel. They had three grown-up children: Sveto, a very modest and hardworking man; Micho, a handsome and cheerful son; and Milanka, an even more beautiful daughter, a student at the Medical University. We were made very welcome in their home, but it was clear that Milovan was afraid of what the UDBA (the Yugoslav KGB) would think about these meetings. Jukan was disappointed that some of his war friends refused to meet him at all. He was trying to give the impression that it didn't worry him, but it wasn't easy. With Milovan, he often had difficult political debates where they couldn't find a compromise.

At last, all the family, including Milka and Milan, went to see Lipa. We went by bus to Bihach and had planned to see a few of our relatives. I had the impression that it didn't matter where Milka went; she could knock on any door, and anyone who opened the door would invite us in and put rakija and kava on the table. Firstly, we visited her niece Danka, a lovely woman who lived in a house with her son, Lenko. Danka was incredible happy to see Jukan, with whom she had fought the partisan war against the German occupation, from the first day to the last, and so they had plenty to remember. After that, we went to visit the family of Danyitka, Milka's sister. Her son, Sveto, was incredibly rich. He had received a big inheritance from his father, a few houses, and a lot of land. He lived in a big three-storeyed house in Bihach, but half of the rooms were locked. He was wealthy, but despite that, he wore an old suit and a worn shirt. He saved on everything and forced his sister to save as well. They ate very little, and when we got up from their breakfast table, I was always hungry. His sister, Bosa, was much more hospitable, and she gave us sandwiches without her brother knowing. With her, we learnt a new dance, the twist, and she played a recording of a new British group, "The Beatles", of whom we had never heard before.

We travelled to Lipa on a crowded bus. Over time, this road had not gotten any better, and the coach shook badly, but as the road started to climb the mountains, it got worse. At last, we got out onto the plains, and the bus didn't shake as much. We got out at Begovats and walked from there to the Vignevich house. Larisa and I had never been in the mountains before, and we ran around like crazy. Everywhere there were hazelnut bushes growing, and on the slope, wild strawberries were ripening. At last, we came to the house, and Jukan and Milka entered the yard first. Everything here was the same but, at the same time, very different. Before the war, it had been the home of a prosperous peasant, with three houses and a lot of people living there. Life was always in full swing . . . now there was no one in the yard, and only near the doors of the old house did Jukan recognise the hunched figure of old Nana. She saw him and Milka, recognised him, and screamed, 'Hey, Stana, look! Jukitsa has come back.' She hung on Jukan's neck; he lifted her up and realised that she weighed hardly anything.

On her scream, Stana came out, and with her dry, scratchy voice, which had not changed a bit, she said, 'Look what a guest we have here. Jukitsa, what has Russia done to you, you are bald!'

'Yes, none of us have gotten any younger,' he agreed. 'Where are Rade and your children?'

'I'll go and call them, and you, Milka, take them to the new house and drop off their things.' She left, and our parents and grandmother took our things to the new house, and Larisa and I stayed in the courtyard.

We had never been in the country like this before and looked around with astonishment. Under the house were areas for the animals; there was a cowshed and a pigsty under the old house, and under the new house was the lambfold. The smell of manure was so strong, I thought I would vomit. Heaps of manure lay on the ground, and no one seemed to ever clean it up. Everything looked dirty and forgotten, and we tried not to touch anything. A few minutes later, horses came into the yard, followed by Jukan's cousin Rade, who was very tall and already slightly stooped, and his very strongly built son, Ilia, or Ikan as everyone called him. Rade was pleased to see Jukan. They greeted us warmly, and we took our places around the big round table, and Stana brought out rakija and coffee. Meanwhile, the women were making dinner. The cooking was done on an old wood-fired furnace, and the smoke from it rose to the ceiling to where pork legs were smoking. Stana cooked chicken soup and a dish from pasta and cheese. At the same time, she was putting wood in the fire, feeding chickens, and giving salt to the cows, and she never washed her hands. Larisa, my mother, and I were horrified, and we weren't sure that we would be able to eat what she was cooking.

At last, Rade's young son, Sveto, came home. He was also very tall but slim. He could have been called very handsome, and his black eyes burnt brightly. Everyone called him 'Tcrni'—black! He brought home the sheep with his younger sister, Mira. She definitely was not beautiful, with squinty eyes and a voice as rough as her mother's. Soon after that, dinner time arrived, and the adults were eating with obvious pleasure, but Larisa and I sat with squeamish faces. We just managed to eat the soup but didn't touch the pita, a multilayered cottage cheese pie. I didn't like dairy food at all. Rade noticed this and said to Ikan, 'Ikan, go and bring one prshut.' Ikan went out of the room and climbed to the roof. Soon, he came back holding a leg of pork covered in soot. I couldn't begin to imagine how I could eat such dirty food. He gave the prshut to his mother, who began to cut it reluctantly. First, she cleaned the soot from the prshut, and then, holding it to her chest, she began to slice it. After the first slice, I could see the beautiful dark-red meat. When I saw that and smelled it, I immediately knew that this was the meal for me, and from that moment, prshut has been my favourite food.

The men continued to drink rakija, and their voices began to get louder. In this house, everyone was loud, and Klara was equal to them. She didn't know the language, but she successfully used Ukrainian words, and everyone understood her. Soon, it became dark, and they put oil lamps on the table. They didn't have electricity, and everyone went to bed early because village people start to work at sunrise. The men continued to drink, but Klara and the children went to the new house to get ready for bed. Klara worked in almost complete darkness; the one oil lamp was not enough to light up the room. At last, everything was ready, except that the children needed to go to the toilet, but toilets did not exist here! People, like animals, hid in bushes and behind fences. The nights in the mountains were always cold, and it was very uncomfortable for us to go outside and pull down our pants! And for city dwellers like us, wolves and bears seemed to be everywhere, because in Bosnia they are not rare.

But the night sky was incredible here; we felt that the stars were hanging right over us and that you could reach out and touch them. For the first time, I saw the Milky Way, a mass of stars that entirely covered the sky, and I stayed for a long time, amazed at this show. Our beds had been made with thick linen sheets that were cold and damp to the touch, but this feeling lasted just a few minutes, and we fell asleep very quickly. In the morning, I woke up to the sound of bells ringing and saw the sun shining through the window. I stood up and looked out of the window. I saw sheep and cows drinking water from a small pool. I quickly pulled on my clothes and ran outside where the family were gathering. No one was going to work that day, only Stana milked the cows, and Milka and Nana made breakfast. When Larisa came out into the yard, Nana came up to us and gave us a plate of wild strawberries, which she had collected especially for us early that morning, and said, 'Many years ago, I picked strawberries for your father, but I never dreamed that one day I would treat his children.' We couldn't really understand what she was saying, but we thanked her and greedily began to eat the sweet wild berries.

By that time, the men had already had their first little glasses of rakija and coffee, but they were only talking about one thing—about how they would bake a young lamb that day. 'Which lamb?' I wanted to know.

'Come with me, and I'll show you,' Sveto said and led me to a storeroom.

'Don't go!' My mother tried to stop me, but it was too late.

We went into the room, and there in the corner, I saw a long wooden stake with a blood-stained lamb carcass on it. Its mouth was open in a terrible grimace; the end of the stake was sticking out of it. Its eyes seemed to be bursting with the strain. I had never seen anything as dreadful in my life, and I ran out of the storeroom. All the men laughed loudly, and Larisa asked me, 'What did he show you?'

'It's terrible. They killed a lamb and put it on a stake. I don't want to eat it,' I said.

'I will go and have a look too,' Larisa said and went into the room. A minute later, she came back out with an indifferent look on her face. 'That's not so terrible for me!' she said, causing a new wave of laughter.

After breakfast, the men took the lamb and carried it across the valley to the edge of the woods and started to prepare a fire. Larisa, our mother, and I went with them. At the beginning, everyone had to collect wood for the fire, but Rade and Jukan cut out two thick Y-shaped branches that were to hold the stake with the lamb on it. On one side, they lit a fire in a small hole, and soon the fire was burning. Then everyone threw wood onto the fire. They let the fire burn down a bit and then moved the lamb closer to the heat. The stake was constantly rotated by someone, but there were no visible results for a long time. And only in some places did the lamb change colour. Then, finally, the fat began to drip out with a hissing sound. Our appetites began to wake! Jukan and Milan brought mushrooms with big caps from the forest, and they placed these under the dripping fat and then onto the embers. In a few minutes, they were ready, and we all ate them with pleasure; even I did, though I had never had mushrooms before.

Then they used a shovel to rake aside the hot embers, and they put in beautiful pink washed potatoes and covered them again with the embers. At last, after three hours, the lamb was ready and taken from the fire. Rade started to cut the meat from it, and pieces of meat with potatoes were given to everyone. Mother, Larisa, and I had never eaten anything like that, and we loved it. The meat was fragrant and soft, and the potatoes were scattered with salt crystals. The adults had red wine, which was not common in Lipa. After everyone had finished, the rest of the meat was taken home, where we all sat again at the round table. The women ate, and the men again had rakija and coffee and were getting happier. Rade and Jukan remembered cheerful stories from the gloomy war years, and Larisa and I listened to them with interest. Though we didn't understand a lot of what they were saying, everyday our language was getting better. Our mother used Ukrainian words when she had difficulty communicating with anyone. No one noticed that the evening had arrived, and oil lamps were put on the table. Ilia brought out some strange objects and put them on the table, and they started to play. He had three metal glasses, one of which he used to cover a cube, and then he moved the glasses around, and you had to guess where the cube was. This seemingly simple task was deceptive, and the guesses were usually wrong. After that, Rade showed us another game, this one with socks. All these people sitting around the table, who at first sight I had found unlikeable, were now part of my family.

The next day, we all went to mow, and the impression was that the Vignevich family was revived again. For Jukan, who had not done any rural work for many years, it was challenging to keep pace with big Rade and his sons, and even his younger brother, Milan, was better than him. Milan was the initiator of all the jokes, and even gloomy Ikan laughed at them. Every day, there were new adventures for us. The next day, we went to the Mandich house, where Jukan's mother had been born, and Jukan felt right at home here, but our mother, Larisa, and I were treated like exotic fruits, and they called us 'Rusi'. The day after, we went to our relatives in Petrovats and came back to Lipa late at night. It was almost completely dark; only occasionally did we use a lamp. The sky above our heads was covered in stars; just over the horizon was a new moon. And, in addition, thousands of enormous glow-worms shot through the darkness. I had seen glow-worms in Odessa, but they were much smaller, and these ones were moving like meteorites. This fantastic night sky stayed in my memory for my whole life. The road was bumpy, and we travelled slowly. We arrived home at about midnight and went straight to bed.

For us children, the visit to Lipa was like travelling back in time: the absence of electricity and running water, ploughing and harrowing with horse and oxen, and travelling in creaky carts. But, on the other hand, we tried spring water for the first time, a wonderfully tasty drink. We saw wild nature and learnt how to collect berries and nuts. Father showed us the graves of our grandparents and told us about their life. Here, I got the feeling that my roots were growing, and I started to feel like a real Vignevich. However, everything comes to an end, and after one week in Lipa, we went back to Zagreb. On the way, we visited Plitvice Lakes and Postojnski Caves. The lakes were marvellously picturesque, located one above the other, and joined by beautiful waterfalls. The absolutely clear blue water reflected the green mountains, and the clear air created a picture of paradise. The Postojnski Stalactite Cave was so huge that inside there was even a bridge, called the Russian Bridge, in honour of the Russian soldiers who constructed it. The cave was many kilometres long and very deep, with stalactites hanging from the ceiling like different-shaped and coloured icicles.

From Zagreb, we went back to Belgrade, where we were welcomed by my father's cousin Svetko Mandich, who was serving in the police and held the high position of colonel. His second wife, Angelka, was a very beautiful woman but had very poor health. They had two girls together: the very thin Snezhana, with her bright black eyes, and the still very small Biljana. Also living with them was Angelka's son from her first marriage. His name was Radko, and we were the same age. He took me away to meet his friends. They accepted me but often laughed at my language. They took special joy in sending me away to buy matches. They stood not far behind me, watching the reaction of the saleswomen, who sometimes looked at me with surprise, sometimes with indignation. Only later did I realise what association they had with the word 'pichki'! We had quite a good time in Belgrade, and then we went to the eastern border, to Banat Province. Here in the village of Nakovo lived Milka's favourite sister, Marta, with her ten grown-up children.

Before the war, Nakovo had been a German village; but after the war, they had been driven off the land and gone back to Germany. All the houses were solidly built, and each of them had a bathroom and toilet. Here, they didn't have sheep but cows and pigs. The size of the local cows was so big that I could hardly believe it. One cow here gave about twenty litres of milk each day, more than all the Vignevich cows in Lipa altogether. Every one-year-old bull calf weighed about a ton. They planted corn and potatoes, but the most important thing was grape cultivation. Almost every house had a fine white wine, and they mainly drank wine instead of rakija. Life here was similar to the city; the homes had electricity, and in the evenings, the people listened to the radio or watched television. There were a few restaurants in the village, and there in the evenings, they played music and the young people danced.

We stayed in the house of Aunt Marta's son Rade and his wife, Dara, who were so hospitable and wanted us to have everything. Every day we visited other relatives, where again they laid the table with meats, and the main course was usually suckling pig. It was especially tasty in Petar's house, another son of Aunt Marta. Every dinner continued well into the night, becoming a loud party with a lot of wine. And many times they woke up in the morning with a bad headache. Klara wasn't used to having so many loving relatives because most of hers had disappeared during the revolution and the war. And I was most touched by the tears when they stroked my head and said, 'Milan, you are a part of us!' Those words made me feel so warm that I did feel like part of the family.

But here in Yugoslavia, we were not just drinking. George tried to get paid for his war award order, "Spomenitsa". He had to visit the UDBA, where he was met with resentment. In the end, he managed to get only a three-month payment. He also understood that many of his former friends tried to avoid him, not to spoil their own careers. During our stay, my parents managed to sell all the things we had brought from the USSR, and now we had some money to buy clothes that we couldn't even dream of in Odessa: dresses, suits, shorts, trousers, and jeans. We children were especially delighted because now, for the first time in our lives, we had fashionable clothes and didn't need any more second-hand things. But our lives didn't only change visually; if before I tried to look like everyone else, now I felt different, and I enjoyed this feeling.

We went to Yugoslavia the next year too, but this time, we went by sea. George, as an employee of the Black Sea Shipping Company, was entitled to travel for free, but he asked the management to give his family the opportunity to travel by steamship *Adzaria* to Yugoslavia with a discount. For us, the ticket price was hardly more than the price of a train ticket, or you could say, almost nothing. Travel lasted for two weeks, and the ship visited Varna, Istanbul, many of the Greek Islands, Athens, Corfu, Bari, Split, Venice, and Dubrovnik, and all with free food! This cruise was basically for foreign tourists and workers from the embassies. When we were getting ready, we hoped that the trip would be exciting, but it ended up surpassing all our expectations. On board, we had excellent food. On the menu were red and black caviar, large sturgeon and salmon, lobster, crab, and everything that you could think of. On board was a small swimming pool, surrounded by chaise lounges for sunbathing under the hot Mediterranean sun. Such a quality holiday we had never had before in our lives. Every morning we came into a new port, we had breakfast, took some fruit, and got off the ship.

For a start, it was Varna, a city with beaches similar to Odessa beaches, only much cleaner, with walks full of foreign tourists. The next day, we passed the Bosporus and then the suburbs of Istanbul, with its fortresses and minarets, and hundreds of boats crossing between the continents. The traffic was chaotic, and I was surprised that no one collided. We were told, however, that accidents did happen here, and many ships had found their final place at the bottom of the sea. The latest case was a Soviet cargo ship that had run aground and hit the house of a Turkish writer, who, as a result, lost his creative ability and got compensation for that! A few hours later, we came to the small dark-blue Marmara Sea and later through the Dardanelles and arrived at the Ionian Sea. Around us was the unfamiliar hostile capitalist world, from which we were to expect only trouble, but from on board, we couldn't see any horrors and everything looked fine and attractive. At last, we arrived in Athens and went out into the city. From the beginning, we expected provocations from everywhere, but we soon understood that no one cared about us, and we continued to shop around the city and enjoy it. In Greece, it didn't matter where you looked; you could always find a temple, but the Acropolis simply shocked us. It was impossible not to fall in love with it after seeing it all. Later, we visited it many times, and we always found something new.

Italy impressed us no less, especially Venice, with its palaces and cathedrals, with their walls painted by the great masters of the Renaissance, its canals, with hundreds of gondolas with their brightly dressed, singing gondoliers. But it was very expensive to ride on a gondola, so we poor Soviet tourists mostly walked and could seldom afford a cold drink. Dubrovnik was also very beautiful, with its old city inside the fortress. The whole city had kept its one style and looked like paradise. Now we understood how lucky we were to be seeing all this with our own eyes, because none of our friends had been able to go overseas. From that summer, travel became our hobby, and every year we were ready to make another trip. The families of all the Yugoslavian immigrants enjoyed these trips, which allowed our families not only to dress well but also to bring back extra products for sale, make a profit, and very much improve our lives. Our family was not desperate anymore, but we definitely were not rich. The main thing was that we were well dressed and had enough money for food.

The families of the immigrants continued to have close relationships; the children grew up, and by then, I had started to get a sense of the world around us. My friends' parents preferred not to talk about politics, but in my home and in the homes of the other Yugoslav immigrants, these disputes were normal. I listened and developed my own views on politics and couldn't agree with some of the things said at home. Most of all, I was amazed how every one of my father's friends wanted to prove whose land was better. Bosnians praised Bosnia, Slovenians praised Slovenia, Montenegrins, Montenegro . . . why was it crucial for them to prove that his land was best? Why not agree that every land was beautiful and stop arguing about it? For my father, the best people in the world were krajisniks, and I couldn't understand why. I understood that Southern Slavs' blood raged by different rules and saw it myself even more on our trips to Yugoslavia. Here, the local memory was dominated by the long and bloody struggle against the Turks and, more recently, from the Second World War. In the museums, you could see terrible photos of crimes committed by the Ustachi and Germans: mass executions, cutting people's heads off with handsaws, and cutting human hearts out with knives. At the sight of these photos, ordinary people were sick, and it tore at the souls of those who had lived through it. Here, in every family, somebody had lost a life in this terrible war, and the wounds were still very fresh.

People here were very special, mostly very tall, strong, and with burning eyes that you could feel even in your back. The tallest people lived in Dalmatia and Montenegro, and George looked like a dwarf when he was with them. We met many people who were very friendly towards us, and it was a lot of fun to be with them. They could drink a lot, could sing and dance incredibly well, but I always felt that in wartime, these same people could be totally different. Their hot tempers could make them dangerous. All the same, while I was growing older, I felt that I belonged with them.

For our mother, it was more difficult, and not everyone loved her. All of our relatives, especially Milka, felt that she had stolen Jukan from them, and they couldn't forgive her for that. And there was another more important reason . . . it was also critical for them that Klara had been married before and had a son, Dima, from her first marriage. On our first trip, no one even mentioned Dima; only during our second trip George told everyone about him, but still many didn't want to know him. Dima couldn't travel to Yugoslavia because he was in a coded industry producing aviation engines, and going abroad was entirely out of the question. He was under constant observation anyway, but he was an excellent specialist and pretty soon became a group leader. Dima came to Odessa for his holidays, but not every year. By that time, I was grown up and could have some conversations with him. Because he couldn't travel and see the world, our points of view became more and more different. His wife, Galina, didn't make our relationships any easier. In her childhood, she had been spoilt by her parents; her father's high position had made her very arrogant, and her trumpet-like voice turned people away. During the month they spent with us in Odessa in the summer, there were many arguments between Klara and Galina, and they did not have a warm relationship. Klara didn't like her because she thought she was a bad influence on Dima and because she couldn't get pregnant.

In a few years, George's brother, Milan, and his sister, Kosa, started to visit us in Odessa. Indeed, the Black Sea was hard to compare with the Adriatic, but Odessa's sandy beaches were perfect for families with little children. Our annual trips began to bother the OVIR and KGB, and they began to create obstacles for us. It became more difficult to fill the application forms, and the number of documents they requested grew all the time. Sometimes they refused our applications, and we had to go to Kiev or Moscow to lodge a complaint. The higher authorities made the decisions, but we had to lodge the documents with the local branch of the militia, where there were always long queues of people. In Primorsky, the OVIR was ruled by Elena Borisovna, a slightly fat but beautiful woman wearing lieutenant's epaulettes. Her brilliant smile was a deceptive mask; she was able to make you run out of energy just while looking for more and more documents. She didn't have any pity, even to the old or invalid. She could be nicer, but only if you gave her some presents; but in our family, nobody did that, so our documents weren't progressing so well.

The obstacles came not only from the OVIR but from the Yugoslav side as well. On our second trip, George met with the chairman of the Veteran's Resistance Union, whose members were Spomenitsa medal holders. But Jukan remembered well that Ivitsa had joined the partisan movement at the end of 1944, so he didn't have the right to hold "Spomenitsa". When they met, Jukan said to him, 'It's a miracle how you managed to get "Spomenitsa"; I remember when you joined us.'

'Chiko, you have to see your doctor and fix your memory. You forget a lot!' The meeting did not end on a friendly note, and on arriving in Zagreb, Jukan was called to the UDBA office and was given the order to leave Yugoslavia in the next twenty-four hours for breaking the rules of passport control. He had to leave quickly without us, and in the next few years, he wasn't allowed to cross the border. He was removed from the train and returned to the USSR. Despite obstacles, we went on a trip almost every year, and it became the most important event in our lives. Now we were very familiar with Belgrade, Zagreb, Split, Dubrovnik, Budapest, and Venice.

In the next few years, even Lipa changed a lot. On our second visit, they already had electricity, and at night, instead of oil lamps and candles, now they used electric lights. To tell the truth, the mysteriousness of the Lipa evenings disappeared for good. A year later, Rade bought a tractor, and after that, no one used horses for ploughing and harrowing. There was a feeling that everything was getting better and life was becoming more comfortable. But, unexpectedly, the young son, Sveto, decided to move to Zagreb, where he was making quite good money. The truth was that while he was making good money, he spent it even faster, often getting into hellbenders, which quite often ended in fights. However, he never forgot about his family and always came back to Lipa for the most important times: sowing, mowing, and harvesting.

The most important thing missing from the Vignevich farm was children. Ilja was extremely reserved and was not very talkative, and because of that, he hadn't been able to find himself a suitable wife. He'd had a relationship with some women in the past, but all of them had been rejected by Stana, and Ilja, being an obedient son, followed her advice. With the passing of time, it became more and more difficult to find a wife, and Ilja lost his confidence. And Sveto had such a dissolute lifestyle that he never had enough time for a serious relationship. The absence of a successor upset Rade, but he tried not to talk about it. Milan continued to work in the First of May factory, and after a few years, he was given a two-roomed apartment. Kosa gave birth to her second daughter, and they named her Vesna. Kosa's husband's career was successful, and he became the deputy director of the Rade Konchar factory. Kosa held a high post in the town council, and now they had a new car, worthy of their positions.

In Belgrade, things were slowly moving as well. Strina Sofia continued to live in her old house, and her children Sveto and Nada had families. New buildings grew up around them, and people received new apartments with excellent toilets and bathrooms. But Sophia continued to live the same way as twenty years ago . . . but it wasn't her fault. In the same house as them lived two nuns who refused to move into a modern apartment, and the church did not allow anyone to pull down their house. So Sophia's house could not be pulled down. But even though she was living in such cramped conditions, she was always hospitable to our family each visit and never showed that it was hard for her. But we stayed more often with Svetko and Angelka. Their house was much more spacious and their budget more substantial. Svetko and his family started to visit Odessa, where they could enjoy the Black Sea.

Our life in Odessa became more stable, and Mother started to look for a new job. She didn't want to work at Lombard's any longer under the control of the anti-Semite director. And even after he was sacked, she didn't feel well in that place. A new job turned up unexpectedly; she was offered a position as chief accountant for a group of Industrial Enterprises. The director here was Grigoy Ivanovich. He was so polite to Klara that she couldn't refuse the job. He offered her a decent salary and all his confidence. Everyone in the office was friendly and had a united spirit. For the first time, it was a pleasure to go to work. The office was located right in the city centre on Tolstoy Street, very close to Sabornaja Square. There was always plenty of work, but on her lunch breaks, Klara could run around the central shops in search of supplies that were hard to find. In our country, almost everything was hard to find, and you had to really search for things. Sometimes these goods were brought straight to the office, sometimes black or red caviar, sausage or chicken, which were not sold in a shop but taken away to be sold privately. Life in a country of developed socialism was more like a struggle for survival, though we had been promised that we would build a communist country in 1980. But now, very few people remembered Khrushchev's promises, and nobody believed it anymore. Khrushchev had been displaced, and instead of him, there was a triumvirate ruling—Brezhnev, Kosygin, and Podgorny.

Time was flying quickly; we grew up, but after finishing year nine, I remained the smallest in my class, not only of the boys but of the girls as well. It worried me very much, and I quite often cried about it. At last, the school holidays started, and again we went to Yugoslavia, where we spent more than two months. That year, a miracle happened to me . . . I grew as though someone had put yeast inside me! I felt as though I was growing day and night. Firstly, I grew taller than my grandmother Milka, and then I outgrew my mother, and, finally, I outgrew my father and continued to grow! I was delighted. During the holidays, I grew eighteen centimetres, and when we arrived back in Odessa, I found that I was taller than almost everyone in my class. Only one pupil was taller, my best friend, Kostja Pudovkin. But pretty soon, I grew taller than him too. After that, my growth spurt was finished, and I grew slowly to my 184 centimetres. From a timid little boy, I had turned into a tall, skinny, long-haired young man who didn't ignore girls anymore; in fact, I started to develop an interest in them. But my interest wasn't unanswered; the girls started to take an interest in me too. No one treated me as a Russian anymore either; now I was regarded as a half foreigner. This situation made me even more interesting and attractive. Besides that, from our trips abroad, I was slowly developing ideas that were very different from those of the Soviet Union. Now I had difficulty finding a common language with my father. He was anxious because he knew how they punished heterodoxy in our country. That's why he tried to stop me from expressing my political thoughts, even though he often agreed with me.

What he didn't know was that I quite often missed school, pleading my liver illness, and instead of class, my friends and I often went to the cinema. Worse than that, we began to drink and smoke cigarettes. However, what was strange was that my poor school attendance didn't make a big difference in my school results, and my parents only found out about my poor school attendance at the end of the academic year. That year, I graduated and passed the exams for the Odessa

Refrigerating Institute. Larisa had gone into year seven. From the beginning, she had been a strong, independent character, and, consequentially, she was the ringleader in all the school disorders. My parents were quite often called to the school, and the teachers complained about her behaviour. Larisa was more like a boy; after all, she had spent all her spare time with my friends and me.

Our grandmother Zelda began to age considerably after we moved to Odessa, but now, the worst thing was that there were problems with her memory. The first symptoms seemed insignificant. She usually liked to listen to two comedians on the radio, Tarapunku and Shtepsel. They gave her real pleasure. She always waited impatiently for their programme, and while sitting in her chair, she listened carefully, sometimes laughing loudly and even clapping. But gradually we noticed that she listened to them without any emotion, without understanding the humour. Then things began to vanish in the house . . . knives, plugs, scissors. It appeared that Zelda herself was hiding them under a feather blanket. Then it got worse; shoes that disappeared could be found anywhere, even in the refrigerator. She began to forget the names of all her relatives, even her husband and son, and now her life had basically been reduced to meals and sleeping. Now we had to watch her constantly, especially when she turned on the gas and then began to look for matches. We sometimes narrowly missed being blown up. At last, my mother decided that Zelda needed to be placed in a home for people suffering from full dementia, and after a few days, Zelda was taken there.

Klara began to get more letters from America. Her cousin Elsa had found a Russian immigrant who translated her letters into Russian. Klara answered each letter, and shortly they became regular contacts. All her relatives by that time were well off. Oll had houses, cars, and even a holiday apartment in Florida. Oll and Irma had three hotels by this time and began to travel around the world. The idea gradually began to ripen to invite Klara and her family to come for a visit. Firstly, the thought of going to America seemed absolutely improbable but very tempting. I was studying in the institute, so I could not go. Absolutely unexpectedly for all of us, the OVIR authorised for Klara and Larisa to go for a visit, provided that the inviting party buy the tickets. Elsa agreed immediately to buy the tickets, and after a long wait, they flew to the USA. They landed at the enormous noisy airport in New York and were simply amazed at its size. There were so many people around them that they didn't know how they would find Elsa in all this crowd. But Elsa had enlarged a photo of them and pinned it on her chest. She held a poster with their names. Larisa noticed at once and pointed it out to Klara. They ran to her arms.

Elsa appeared to be an easy-going and cheerful woman. She spoke a lot, but they couldn't understand her. Klara didn't speak any English, and Larisa had only learnt a few words, which obviously weren't enough. Then Elsa began to speak to Klara in Yiddish. It helped only a little, as Klara had heard this language just in her early childhood. So they basically communicated with gestures. They went in Elsa's Cadillac across New York, and they saw their first skyscrapers. America amazed them; shops and supermarkets burst with an abundance of goods, restaurants had such a huge number of dishes, and the variety of alcoholic and soft drinks seemed astronomical. There was music playing everywhere, and happy, beautiful people drove by in open cars. Then they went to Philadelphia, where most of Elsa's family lived. They visited different restaurants every day, arriving home late at night but still watching TV. Only when the program ended and, on the screen, appeared the flag and the national anthem played did Elsa get up off the sofa and sing the national anthem, and then they would all go to bed. Klara and Elsa became great friends, and every day it became easier to communicate. Sometimes, Larisa went out with Elsa's sons, and they went to the cinema or dances. Already, within a couple of weeks, Larisa felt at home.

After a few days, they all went to Florida together, where Elsa's husband had bought a new house. For the first time, they met Klara's cousin Oll and his wonderful wife, Irma. Every morning after breakfast, Larisa went with Elsa's sons to the beach, where they would spend the day. Sometimes Klara and Elsa went with them. Larisa felt like a duck in water and was a great success. Her English improved, and every day, Klara lost more control over her. In the evenings, she went to the cinema and sometimes to dances. She began to drink alcohol openly and to smoke. Klara, at first, was indignant, but everyone around them was doing the same thing, and Klara didn't know what to do.

In the meantime, I was at home with my father. My father was not a good cook, and there was not enough food in the house, only bread and milk, and the occasional sausage was a luxury. Life in Bosnia had made him used to simplicity, and I had to look after myself. My life as a first-year student was in full swing. I studied but was very keen on the student hellbenders and card games. Quite often, instead of going to the institute, I stayed at home, and my new friends came over. There was no one to be afraid of; my father was at work all day long. One day, we bought some wine, and the game was in full swing when we heard the doorbell ring. I nervously hid the wine and cards.

'Who could that be?' Vasily asked me.

'No idea, though it could be my mother's brother,' I said, though I knew that my mother's brothers were dead. We hid all the evidence of our gambling, and I went to open the door. On the step, I saw a not-very-tall unfamiliar man who looked a little uncertain. 'Forgive me, but who are you?' I asked him.

'Is this where Klara lives?' he asked.

'Yes!' I answered him.

'Could you call her?' he wanted to know.

'She's not at home. But who are you?' I asked.

'I am her cousin. But where is she?' he said. I was a bit stunned!

'She has gone to visit relatives in America,' I told him.

'To America! And when will she return?' he wanted to know.

'In a month, probably,' I said.

'What a pity! I have come from Tashkent,' the man said with such a sad expression on his face that I felt sorry for him.

'Please come in,' I invited him and went in to see my friends and explained the situation to them. 'Sorry, the game is off for today. I need to talk to my uncle.'

The boys went, and I returned to the kitchen. 'Now I am free, but I have nothing to offer you,' I said. 'Since Mam left, there is nothing in the refrigerator.'

'What is your name?' my visitor asked.

'Milan!'

'What an unusual name. My name is Mishka, but you can call me Uncle Misha.'

'Would you like coffee, Uncle Misha?' I asked him. 'The coffee in this house is very good!'

'Well, well, coffee, yes, please,' Mishka said. I prepared coffee in the 'dzezva', and Uncle Misha watched with interest. 'Who taught you to make coffee like that?' he asked.

'You know my father is Yugoslav?' I explained as I poured the coffee into cups and handed one to him. He took a sip and closed his eyes in pleasure.

'I know nothing about your family. I know only that I last saw Klara in the summer of 1941, and since then, I've spent many years searching for her. I had almost given up, but now I seem to have had some good luck,' he said.

His emotions touched my heart, and I knew that I liked this man. 'Uncle Misha, tell me something about yourself,' I said.

Mishka shrugged his shoulders and said, 'I don't know where to start. I grew up on a German farm in Freiburg with my mother and father. Since childhood, I have spoken three languages, Yiddish, German, and Russian. Your mother was a very young girl when she came to stay with us to escape the famine in Ukraine.'

'Yes, my mother told me something about that,' I said.

'But what your mother probably didn't tell you was the impression that she made in our village. She was an extremely beautiful girl. Everyone looked at her, amazed, and I loved her so much that I could hardly speak. She visited us a few times, and I went to visit her in Odessa. In 1941, I arrived at the Odessa Military College, the war began . . .' And he continued to tell his story, and I sat and listened with interest. For half an hour, he talked about the war with its horrors and about his adventures after the war when he went across Ukraine, searching out those who had cooperated with the fascists in the destruction of the Jews and whom he had killed with his own hands. He was caught by the militia during his execution of a local policeman in Zhitomir and was sentenced to eight years' imprisonment. He served his prison time around Kustanai. After his term ended, he was allowed to leave and live in Tashkent, where he met his future wife, Maria. Over the years, he had tried to find Klara, but he didn't know that she had changed her surname.

He had three days before he had to leave Odessa and promised to return the next day. I promised that I would talk to my father.

My father came home from work at seven o'clock that evening a little bit drunk and went straight to the kitchen to get something to eat. I decided to tell him the news. 'Father, today we were visited by one of Mother's relatives.'

'What kind of relative?' he asked.

'Cousin Misha, whom she hasn't seen for over twenty-five years,' I said.

'Nonsense! Why did he vanish for so long?' George asked.

'He was at war and then in prison for some time after the war,' I told him.

George looked serious and didn't like this news. 'He is a charlatan! I don't trust him, and don't you dare let him into the house. He is simply an adventurer!'

'No, he knows all about Mother's childhood, knew her mother . . .' I tried to intercede, but my father did not want to listen.

'I do not want to see him, and I do not trust him,' Father said.

'Father, this is impossible. He is not telling lies, and he has come here from Tashkent,' I said. 'You should talk to him!'

'Well, we'll see tomorrow,' he said.

The next morning, my father woke up in a good mood and was ready to see the visitor, though he still didn't think that Mishka was speaking the truth. He went to the shop and bought some vodka and some snacks. Uncle Misha came at noon and also bought a bottle of vodka. He also bought some exotic sweets, dried melon, dried apricots, and figs. The conversation was not so easy at first, so I tried to improve the atmosphere. This was made easier with vodka! And after a couple of glasses, they began to exchange military memories. It was interesting for them both to listen to the other's stories. This time, Uncle Misha went into more details about his life. George understood Misha's hardships. By now, they were both decently tipsy, and I was really glad that it had gone so well. The next day was Sunday, and we showed Mishka around Odessa and had a very successful day. He returned to Tashkent in a good mood and with the hope that he would see Klara the next year.

A little later, we had some bad news, though not a surprise. My grandmother Zelda had died in hospital; in the last month, the dementia had completely overtaken her brain, and she couldn't recognise anyone. She was only able to smile or cry, and to eat, though without any enjoyment. She had become very thin, and her face, framed by her grey hair, looked like that of a ghost. She had died in her sleep, ending her torments and the torments of others. Predictions from her early childhood, that if she was patted by the Russian Tsar, she would have luck all her life, had never come true. Happiness had visited her very seldom, and her life had been subjected to heart-rending experiences. She'd had the chance to go with her brothers and sister to America, and there her life would no doubt have been easier. But she chose the other path with her dear David, and she had paid for that with interest! Now, everything had ended, and she was at peace. Neither

my father nor I had any experience in burying a close relative. First of all, we
needed money, but Father had hardly any. Klara and Semyon had more experience
with funerals; they knew the Jewish traditions, and Zelda was buried in a Jewish
cemetery, where the service was conducted by an old rabbi. So, in that way, her
life, which had begun long before the revolution, had ended.

Klara and Larisa arrived home at the end of summer. To get Larisa home
was not easy; her new relatives and acquaintances didn't want to let her go. One
of them, Mr Teplitsky, even sent a car behind her car to the airport just in case
Larisa wanted to run away from her mother. But Klara managed to keep hold of
her, and they arrived at Odessa airport, where Father and I were waiting for them.
What I saw surpassed all my expectations; both Mother and Larisa were very
extravagantly dressed in trousers and bright jackets, and half of their faces were
covered by big sunglasses. Larisa had flared pants with big rectangular cuts from
top to bottom. But what was even more surprising was that Larisa had a cigarette
in her hand and was smoking. But when she came closer to Father, he struck the
cigarette out of her hands, and with a voice that allowed for no argument, he told
her, 'I don't want to see that anymore!' Then he turned to Klara and said, 'How
could you allow her to do that?'

'But what could I do? I lost all control over her, and they are all like that in
America.'

'Well, that was there, and here it will be very different,' George firmly
concluded. Larisa tried to object, but pretty soon she realised that it was hopeless,
and she came over to me. I couldn't believe that my little sister had become a very
beautiful girl. We hugged each other, and I realised that I still loved her very much.

Everyone had called Larisa 'Milaniha' because they knew that she was my
sister. But now she had become an independent person. Now she had different
interests and new admirers. Mother was very excited to be home again, but when
she learnt of her mother's death, she cried for a few days. Then we told her about
her cousin Mishka's visit. She was excited but disappointed that he hadn't waited
for her to come home. But if she couldn't do anything about her mother, she
called Mishka the next week, and after a long conversation, they agreed about
their next meeting. Klara promised him that she would visit them in half a year,
and, meanwhile, we put a stone on Grandmother Zelda's grave and spent all our
available money to do so.

Bad news doesn't usually come alone. Zelda's niece Rahil and her family lived
in Kishinev, and her twin brother, Semyon, lived in Odessa. Despite the distance
between them, they always kept in touch with one another and visited at least once
a year. The year before, Rahil had fallen ill. In the hospital, they discovered that
she had cancer and performed an operation. However, after a while, the cancer

had metastasised, and it was clear that she only had a couple of months to live. Semyon, on the other hand, was always healthy and full of optimism, and we were always grateful to him for what he and his wife, Klara, had done for us when we first came to Odessa. But, unexpectedly, while he was working on some job, he lifted some large item and fell to the ground. He suffered a huge heart attack, and death was instantaneous. Nobody expected such a turn of events, and his wife, Klara, was so upset that everyone thought that she would die as well. For this big, beautiful woman, her husband had been her life support. With him, she had only ever had to look after the house. Her daughter, Asja, and her husband, Uzik, to whom Semyon had given work and had always helped with money, were also in grief. This death upset many people, and relatives from Kishinev decided that they would go to the funeral. But when they got to the station, they got the news that Rahil had also died. So the twins, who had been born just minutes apart, died on the same day, and their souls stayed inseparable. Semyon was buried not far from Zelda, and Rahil was buried in Kishinev.

More relatives died, along with a number of friends from Yugoslavia. One of the first to die was Tihomir Achimovich. He was the one that George liked to play chess with. Tihomir had retired and began to write books, and soon, after a lot of effort, he managed to publish his first book in Russian, *Kosmaets.* He was the only writer in their group, and his wife, Galina, was very proud of his success. Many of their friends began to avoid them, but George and Tihomir regularly visited each other and played chess. They were the only two bald Yugoslavs among all their friends. But George had become bald after an infection brought on by a tick, and his head was smooth; Tihomir's head had a wide bald strip, running from his forehead to the back of his head. He tried to cover this with long hair, which he grew at the sides. This was a labour-intensive operation, and usually the wind was quick to destroy the results, and friends, and often their wives, quite often made a joke of this. Tihomir suddenly found that he had stomach cancer, and it was already too late for surgery. He began to deteriorate rapidly, and he lost weight. But despite this, he and George continued to play chess. In late autumn, Tihomir came to George's place one last time. He was very out of breath when he reached the fifth floor, and it took a while for him to recover. George prepared the coffee and rakija.

'Ziveli,' George said.

'No, Chiko, this toast is not for me anymore. For you, it is to live a long and happy life, but I will not be here tomorrow,' Tihomir said.

'Will you stop talking nonsense? You will still be here.' George was indignant.

'No, Chiko, let's play chess one last time.' They played their game, and then next day, George heard that Tihomir had died. For a long time after that, George had a pleasant feeling that Tihomir had spent his last day with him.

Life went on. My mother and father continued to work, Larissa went to school, and I went to the institute. But I did not study assiduously and spent more time with my friends. Now I had become part of the city life of Odessa. I had heaps of friends, and sometimes I even forgot their names. I had become friends with two boys, children of Yugoslav immigrants, Slava Velich and Slava Buzdum. We spent a lot of time together, trying the patience of the local militia. Visiting restaurants and chasing girls occupied most of our time. Quite often, we got together in the homes of friends, and we spoke about politics. Our views differed strongly from those of the Soviet youth, and, more importantly, we did not try to hide them. My parents knew about this and tried to stop me in every possible way, but I refused to stop. My father often tried to teach me, but these conversations often came to an end in a bitter argument. He wasn't so much against my views but tried to warn me how dangerous it was to speak them openly. He had to confess that all his hopes for the construction of a fair society had not materialised and that the Soviet model of socialism worked only with obvious faults, and hopes for the best had dwindled. However, with his children, he tried not to show his doubts, but all his efforts to make us more careful went like water through sand.

As a result of my busy social life and drinking, I was not ready for my exams. The only way out was to take an academic vacation year because of my ill-health situation. Right after that, I started to get summonses from the Military Recruitment Centre. I stopped opening doors to anyone and told my parents not to accept any letters from the recruitment centre and to tell them that I had gone on a trip. Everything was going well, until one day I made the mistake myself and opened the door to a very handsome, smiling young man.

'Are you Milan Vignevich?' he asked.

'Yes,' I replied.

'Then here is a summons from Voenkomat (Recruitment Office). Please sign up here.' Only then did I realise my mistake, but it was already too late, and I had to go.

In the courtyard at Voenkomat, I came face to face with Slava Velich. 'What are you doing here?' He was surprised to see me.

'I came here because I stupidly accepted a summons from Voenkomat. But how did you get here?' I asked.

'My smart mother accepted the summons and signed for it. That's why I had to come in, but there are two great girls waiting for me in Moscow,' he said.

'I don't know what to do. I have only to avoid it until the beginning of the semester at my institute,' I said.

'Let's see, we'll find something we can do.' Slava tried to calm me. We went into a very crowded room, full of recruits, and only sometimes did an officer come in. We looked entirely different from the others. We were dressed in sheepskin coats, which were bought in Yugoslavia, and looked smart in Odessa. Our hair was so long that it rested on our shoulders. We looked defiant.

Unexpectedly, an officer with epaulettes stopped in front of us. He was a high-ranking Voenkomat officer. 'What a dreadful look!' he screamed at us. 'How dare you come to Voenkomat looking like that. Follow me to my room.' We followed him into a room, in the middle of which was a huge table covered in folders. The colonel went to the table but didn't sit down. He stretched his hands on the table and shouted, 'How dare you come here dressed like that?'

'What's wrong with the way we're dressed?' Slava asked him.

'You could go to a restaurant dressed like that, but not here. And what terrible hairstyles you have. Don't you have enough money to get your hair cut? I'll give you money, then,' he said, pulling out a few notes and putting them on the table in front of us. There were one-, three-, and five-rouble notes. 'Take any note, and go and get your filthy hair cut!' he said.

Then Slava pulled out his wallet, and because he was going to Moscow, it was full of twenty-five- and fifty-rouble notes. 'I agree, but only if you choose one of these notes and come with us, and while we have our hair cut, you can shave off that ugly moustache.'

I couldn't believe my ears, but the colonel seemed to choke. His face turned purple, and, finally, he began to scream like mad. 'Get out of here, you bastards! Out of my sight! I'll show you . . .'

But we didn't hear the rest. We ran out of the room to the corridor and then into the yard and then away onto the street, laughing like idiots. 'What have you done?' I asked him through my laughter. 'Now he will send us to rot somewhere in Siberia.'

'Absolutely the opposite,' Slava said. 'He kicked us out of the room, and we are free to go wherever we want,' Slava disagreed. 'The main thing is not to show up around here. I'm going to Moscow tonight, and they will not see me for a long time.' I understood what he said, and we went to celebrate our successful adventure.

Slava, as he had said, left that night for Moscow and avoided conscription to the army. That same year, he and his father began the process of getting back their Yugoslavian citizenship. But my efforts to avoid conscription turned out to be much harder. I was called again to the Voenkomat and was practically sent to the army without any medical examination. But I decided to fight this to the end; I ran away home, and, thanks to my parents, I was sent for a full medical exam to a hospital, where I used all my skills and imagination to fake liver hepatitis. As a result, I got a deferment of military service, and straight after that, I left for Yugoslavia. When I returned to Odessa, I was enrolled in my second year of education, and the army was no longer a threat to me.

By that time, my political views contradicted Soviet reality. The example of Slava Velich and his father, getting away from Soviet citizenship and receiving Yugoslavian citizenship, attracted me, and I decided to talk to my father about it. I couldn't find a better time than when I came home one night, having been to a party with my friends. My father wasn't exactly sober either. I sat next to him on the sofa and asked him, 'Father, could you please tell me, which land do you love the most?'

'You know perfectly well that there is no better place for me than Lipa,' he answered without hesitation.

'Then why do we live here and not in Yugoslavia?' I asked.

'Because Tito sent us here to study and later called us traitors,' he said.

'But many of your friends returned to Yugoslavia,' I said.

'And what did they achieve? Many of them finished up in Goli Island, and the others, who didn't go to jail, were never trusted and have accomplished nothing in life.'

'But to live in Yugoslavia is still better than living here,' I said and immediately regretted it, because Father became angry as though I had bitten him.

'And why don't you like this land, your motherland?' he asked.

'I don't feel as a Russian anymore but more as a Yugoslav,' I tried to explain. 'Why can the Velich family change their citizenship, but we can't?'

'We'll see how that turns out . . . but I don't want to talk to you anymore.' Father ended the conversation and went to sleep.

And we didn't begin to change our citizenship, though a few years later, life pushed George to take this step. I couldn't do it on my own because I had been born in the USSR and had never lived in Yugoslavia. But the Velich family managed to lose their Soviet citizenship and received Yugoslavian, and so Slava became a foreigner.

⋅⋅✦✦✦✦✦⋅⋅

A few years passed, and Larisa graduated from school, and she was no longer just my shadow. It had been difficult to control her at school, and even my parents found it hard. At school, she got the nickname 'Imported Doll', very similar to mine at the institute. The dean of my faculty called me 'Imported Gold'. So, against our will, the distance between us and the other students was getting wider. It seemed that the surrounding society was rejecting us. After graduating, Larisa decided to go to the university, to the Faculty of Foreign Languages, because she was quite fluent now in English, but in the English exam, she got only three points and didn't make it through. That hurt her self-esteem enormously, and she went to Yugoslavia. There she enrolled at the Zagreb University and began her studies. Everything went well, and she soon found new friends. She became especially close to a girl named Mariana Bedalov, and they became best friends. Mariana was big, loud, and always the centre of attention, particularly when they went out. She loved to visit nightclubs and dancing parties, but she also knew hundreds of folk songs, and when they went to a restaurant, they usually ended up singing with the band. Even in the company of men, she tried to be in the front position, always stating her own points of view; Larisa felt very comfortable in Mariana's company.

After a few months of living with relatives, Larissa began to feel that they didn't want her to stay with them any longer. Mariana asked Larissa to move into her unit, because her parents had moved permanently to Split. Larisa accepted the offer, and now they were together practically all the time. After their first year of education, they decided to go together to Odessa for their holidays. With great difficulty, our father managed to get a permit through OVIR, and in the summer, the two friends came to Odessa. We treated Mariana like a favourite relative, and she felt the same about us. They spent two weeks going to the beaches and restaurants in Odessa, and although the Black Sea is hard to compare with the Adriatic, Mariana was very happy. Meanwhile, Larisa lodged her documents with OVIR to get permission to go to Zagreb for her second year at university, and they told her that her documents would be ready in one month. During this time, George, Larisa, and Mariana decided to go to Moscow and Leningrad. Mariana was simply overwhelmed with this trip and was very happy. They came home in time to go back to Yugoslavia, but Larisa's documents had not arrived, and Mariana had to go back alone.

Larisa was supposed to go to Zagreb a bit later, but as it turned out, she didn't get the documents, and her case was rejected. Nobody expected this, and now Father himself went to the chief OVIR officer. To the question of why Larisa wasn't allowed to go to Yugoslavia, Ivanov responded, 'Our office is not issuing documents for one year.'

'Why not? She is studying at Zagreb University,' George said.

'And how did she get there?' Ivanov asked.

'Easy, she went for a holiday and got into the university!' George answered.

'And you think it's all right that everyone who goes abroad gets enrolled in a university?' Ivanov asked again.

'For me, Yugoslavia is not abroad, it's my motherland,' George explained.

'But your daughter was born in the USSR, and she is a Soviet citizen.' Ivanov was not moved. After a long and unsuccessful argument, George and Larisa decide to go to Kiev and Moscow, where they ran between OVIR and the Ministry of Education. Sometimes they felt that they were getting close to success, but in the end, they realised that they were running around in circles. As a result, they returned home without any success. Larisa swore that she would not stay in this country and that she would run away. By now, Father's patience had run out. On the second day after getting back, he called everyone into the dining room.

'We have a very critical decision to make today,' he began. 'Larisa has decided that she doesn't want to live here anymore. What do you think about that, Milan?'

I had been waiting for such a turn of events for a long time, and so I responded without hesitation, 'I was ready for that when the Veliches submitted their application to change citizenship. Now they are already Yugoslavian citizens,' I said.

'So what? We will start it now,' George said. 'Klara, what do you think about it?'

'Are you asking me? For many years, I have been saying that we need to leave this country.'

'And you will follow me?' George asked her.

'You could do it without me. I have one more son, and you know where he is working,' Klara said.

'But if we change citizenship, he will be in more trouble,' George said.

'It's a very different thing. He has his own life, and you should do what you think is right,' she said.

'So we all agree to start the process, but we need to remember that it could take a long time, and we could all get into trouble,' my father warned us seriously.

'You don't have to frighten us, we are ready for anything,' we answered almost together.

Before applying for Yugoslav citizenship, we firstly had to lose our Soviet citizenship. That evening, we decided to write a letter to the Supreme Soviet of USSR with the request that we lose our Soviet citizenship. Just the idea of doing this sounded criminal, so we needed to write the letter very carefully and skilfully, and it took more than a week. At last, after many alterations, the letter was written with the right balance between our love and respect for the Soviet Union, and a firm wish for George to get back to his home country. The letter was sealed and posted, and now we just had to wait for a response. But the response came, not from Moscow, but, unexpectedly, George was called to the Odessa region Communist Party Committee. Without understanding why, and expecting difficulties, George went to the meeting on the appointed day. He was met by a slender, very neatly dressed man who looked serious but not unfriendly.

'Hello, George Milenovich, please come in and sit down.'

'I don't know why I was called in here,' George said straightaway.

'We need to speak of a serious matter,' the man said. 'Did you write a letter to the Supreme Soviet of USSR?'

'Yes, I sent a letter, but how did you get it?' George asked.

'It was sent to us to find your reason for this' was the reply.

'But why was it sent to you? Didn't I write it to Podgorny by name?' George asked.

'You must realise that he receives hundreds of letters every day, and he couldn't possibly read every one of them. That's why it was sent back to us,' George was told.

'But why send it to you?' George persisted.

'You are a communist, and this is the Regional Party Committee. Let's talk about this,' the man said.

'We sent a letter that we want to lose our Soviet citizenship,' George said.

'Does that mean you are not happy in the USSR? Why doesn't life here suit you?'

'Everything here suits me, but I took Soviet citizenship only temporarily, but now I want to go back to my country, to my mother. Do I have the right to do that?' George asked.

'But you are a member of the Soviet Union Communist Party, and that changes everything.' The secretary began to apply pressure.

'But I am a member of the Yugoslav Communist Party as well, and I fought all the Second Word War against the German occupation,' George said.

'We know, and no one wants to understate your war efforts. But you have lived in the USSR for twenty years, your children were born here, and they are Soviet citizens,' he said.

'Yes, they are my children, and my motherland is theirs too,' George insisted.

'Maybe someone hurt you, and that's why you have decided to leave?' the secretary went on.

'Yes, I did have a reason, when my daughter was not allowed to go back to the university in Zagreb, where she was studying,' George said.

'But, George Milenovich, OVIR can't let everyone go overseas to study,' the secretary continued.

'For me, Yugoslavia is not a foreign country, and that's why I want to go back. But in doing this, I don't want to offend the Soviet people, who have treated us as real brothers.' George tried to be respectful.

This conversation lasted at least ten minutes, but it became clear that there was no way to change George's mind. The party secretary stood up, went to George, and said, 'I feel sorry that I was not able to change your mind. But it was a pleasure to talk to you. You can go home now, and we will discuss the situation and let you know the results.' The conversation was finished, and they said goodbye to one another. A few days later, George was told that the first thing he needed to do was resign from the Soviet Communist Party, and only after that could he apply to lose his Soviet citizenship. We did everything that they told us to do and waited for an answer.

Meanwhile, there were quite a few changes in our lives. Larissa was very angry with what had happened to her; she became easily irritated and often came home very late. By that time, I wasn't close to her any longer, and we had big arguments. Larisa wasn't happy that I was using our family relationship to put pressure on her, and we drifted further and further apart. At the same time, my life had changed as well. I started to go out with a girl, Valentina, whom I had known for many years. We used to go to the same school, and I knew almost all of her friends. At school, I had been almost a head shorter than her, but now I had outgrown her, and I became the subject of her interest. Up to that time, I'd had no interest in a long-term relationship, and wild parties with my friends hadn't helped to find anyone. But Valentina was a very determined girl and began to appear more and more in my life. For a while, I would go out with her but usually end up picking up one of her friends, and this hurt her.

That year, she graduated from university, and on that evening, she was to have a graduation party at a restaurant. But in the middle of the day, she went to Dolphin Beach, where we met. We spent a couple of hours in the café Voloshka, celebrating this important occasion, and in the end, she invited me to her graduation party, and I accepted. That evening, we danced and drank a lot, and after the party, we walked home together, often stopping to kiss. But when we were walking through the park, we fell down on the grass, and from that time, we began to develop a serious relationship, though I was not sure that I could have one. At the same time, Larisa started going out with another partner, a boy called Eric, with the nickname Katsap. He wasn't handsome at all; neither did he have a great body. He had curly hair and a mean face, and no one could understand how he had managed to attract Larisa's attention, but we slowly began to understand. Eric had been born into a large and unusual family; the majority of them were in involved in different private businesses, which were very dangerous in the USSR. On the other hand, they had plenty of money. Eric loved to go out and party and was familiar with many underworld figures. He loved to drink a lot, and he especially liked to smoke marijuana and got Larisa to join him.

I loved to drink as well, but I didn't like marijuana and had only tried hashish a few times. I didn't approve of Larisa's new habit. I didn't ever tell our parents, but there was no need to. My father from the start hadn't liked Eric and did his best to break up the relationship. But my mother liked him very much and was sure that the only reason that George didn't like him was he was Jewish. But she loved Eric because he was Jewish. Opinions in our house were divided, and we often argued about it. If our father was still trying to stick to his pro-communist ideology, our mother was no longer able to believe in it any longer and was leaning towards Israel. I always felt Serbian, and my mother was often offended. 'How can you say that when, by blood, you are half Jewish?'

'I'm not rejecting your blood,' I said, 'but you don't know your ancestors and hardly follow any traditions, so I don't feel Jewish. But look how many relatives I have in Yugoslavia, and from them, I know my roots. I have their surname, and that's why I feel like a part of them.' Mother was disappointed, but deep in her heart, she understood me. I couldn't blame her either. She had been born in a country where to know and remember your family history was not always safe, and sometimes it was easier to forget. During my childhood, I had tried to be the same as everyone else, but with time, I had drifted more and more away from the surrounding reality. I tried to be loyal to communist ideals but felt disappointed with insufficient freedom and a deprived lifestyle.

In the middle of autumn, Valentina and I decided that we would start our own new family. First, we had to talk to Valentina's parents about it. That wasn't easy, because the stories going about my adventurous lifestyle were much greater than they were in reality. Yes, I loved to go out and I enjoyed drinking, but rumours were going around that I was a dirty, drug-addicted womaniser, and these rumours got back to Valentina's parents. Occasionally, when walking with their best friend, the academic Bogatsky and his wife, they would pass by my long-haired friends and me at one of our drinking parties. They were disgusted that such young people had no respect for Soviet values, and when they found out about our plans, they refused to even talk about the subject. But Valentina was a very strong personality and would not allow anyone else to decide her future. She loved me so much that the question was, would we have a wedding party, or would she go with me without their permission? Her parents had only one choice—to agree, and after that, I went to visit them and to ask for the hand of their daughter in marriage. They gave their permission without any enthusiasm, and after that, we sat around the table, opened a bottle of champagne, and drank it. So the meeting ended successfully, and the next day, we came to talk to my parents, which was much easier. I had only to introduce my future wife. My parents had no objections, just one question—how were we planning to survive financially? We couldn't give them a clear answer, because at that time, only Valentina was working, and her salary was only ninety-six roubles a month. This would last at the most for one week, but in half a year, I would graduate from the institute and get my first job. Meanwhile, we needed our parents' support.

Next, our parents had to meet and decide when and where to have the party. After only one meeting, it was clear that our parents were incompatible. The relationship between Klara and Edward was particularly tricky, because all his life, Edward had been anti-Semitic, and this was shown in unpredictable situations. Klara was extremely sensitive on that subject, and every time it came up, it usually ended in a big quarrel. Valentina and I tried all the time to smooth the situation, and thanks to our efforts, the wedding plans were going quite well. We wanted a small wedding, but our parents changed all that. The Ivanovskys wanted to invite all their very important friends, my mother invited all her Odessa relatives, and after that, my father wanted all his Yugoslav friends and then decided to invite our relatives from Yugoslavia. Dima and Galina were coming from Ufa, and the rest were my and Valentina's friends. The number of guests grew to 100, and the amount of money needed grew as well.

The wedding was taking place in "Zemchuzina", a restaurant in Arcadia, one of the most popular places in Odessa in summer. But our wedding was in the middle of winter, and that day, it was snowing. My uncle Milan and his wife, Anchi, and Aunt Kosa and Uncle Nicola arrived from Yugoslavia. They saved me by bringing me a wedding suit from Zagreb, which fitted me perfectly. The suit had been made by my mother's tailor friend and was so badly made that I was ready to kill the tailor. But in the end, everything worked out, and on the way to ZAGS, the marriage registration office, I was happy with the way I looked. Valentina wore a short white dress and a white hat, which looked quite strange on a cold winter day. The ceremony was very solemn, and a lot of people witnessed it. The crowd was very mixed: professors from university and their families, military officers and their wives, my father's best friends, Yugoslavian immigrants, relatives from both sides, Valentina's girlfriends, and my long-haired friends. Everything went quite well in spite of the constant friction between our parents.

Straight after the ceremony, everyone went to the restaurant. Snow was falling non-stop, and in spite of our wish to go directly to the restaurant, we had to walk the last 500 metres. It was especially difficult for the women in high heels; they often slipped and fell over. We arrived at the restaurant at five o'clock, and the guests were supposed to arrive at six. The restaurant looked great, but inside it was incredibly cold, and the heaters did not fix the problem. People started to warm themselves with alcohol. After a few drinks, people started to feel much better. The snow was getting even heavier, and it was harder for guests to get to the restaurant because they had to walk longer distances. But inside, it was getting more comfortable; human bodies warmed it up. Then the music began, and it got better still. At last, the guests took their places at the tables. Toasts were drunk, and vodka and champagne flowed. Then guests started shouting, 'Gorko!' and Valentina and I had to stand up and kiss, while the guests counted how long every kiss lasted. I had the feeling that this was not happening to me, that I was just watching it from the sidelines.

After that, people started to dance, and this went on late into the night, and the restaurant became hot! Unexpectedly, Milan Ribar decided to sing for us. He was entirely drunk and unsteady on his feet, but in spite of that, he did really well. The musicians spontaneously accompanied him. He sang a Serbian song; he did it so beautifully that everyone became quiet, and when he had finished, the guests applauded him for a long time. George was happy and did his best to make sure that everyone had everything that they wanted. He paid particular attention to his brother, Milan, and sister, Kosa, because they had come all the way from Zagreb. Klara, like a true accountant, watched that all the food was put out on the tables and that they wouldn't be overcharged, because that was common in Odessa restaurants. But everything went smoothly, and guests stayed late into the night. Valentina and I left first in a car filled with flowers brought by guests. We went to our unit, rented for us by our parents for half a year. The next morning, we left for our honeymoon trip to Leningrad, where we spent one excellent week. After that, we had to get back to the challenges of everyday life.

We had to survive on a very limited income, but we still loved to go out. Odessa is a very unusual city, where it's important to make friends and to share everything you have with them, and then they share everything with you. Valentina and I did that easily, so we were usually the centre of any party. We never had enough money, so we often ate at our parents' house. At the beginning of our married life, Valentina hardly knew how to cook anything, and often we ate sausage and canned food. Not many people thought that our marriage would last more than a couple of months, but in spite of all the predictions, we lived happily.

After our marriage, life didn't stop. Soon, Larisa told our parents that she wanted to marry Eric, and that was a big shock to our father. The reason was not just that she wanted to marry him but that, with his family, they wanted to immigrate to Israel. But immigrating to Israel was just on paper; the true target for immigration was Australia, where one of their relatives was already living. My father had nothing against Jews, but as a result of Soviet propaganda, he didn't like Israel and was simply furious at Larisa's decision.

'How could you do this now?' my father asked her. 'We just lodged the documents to change our citizenship. Wait a bit, and everything will change!'

'No, it's not clear how long all this will take or what decision they will reach. But I don't want to live in this country any longer,' Larisa said.

'That means that the only reason that you want to get married is so you can leave the country?' George tried to make it clear.

'No, I love Eric, but my desire to leave is playing a big part in this,' she answered.

'But doesn't it worry you that people will think we are traitors?' George kept going.

'What difference does it make to you? You are trying to get out of this country too,' Larisa said.

'No, it is totally different. We are trying to get to my motherland. Yugoslavia is a socialist country, and I am a communist, but you just want to put us to shame,' George said.

At that point, our mother could not stay out of the conversation. Like a torpedo, she attacked all father's reasoning. 'Have you forgotten that I am a Jew, and Israel is my motherland?'

'Don't speak nonsense. What kind of motherland is Israel for you? You have never even been there,' George said sarcastically.

'Don't laugh about it. For every Jew, Israel is the historical motherland,' she answered.

'What kind of Jew are you if you can't speak the language and don't follow any of the traditions? You are a Soviet citizen, and you need to clear your head of all this rubbish,' George said.

'It doesn't matter whether you agree with me or not. I will go anyway,' Larisa warned them.

'Then you will go without my agreement,' George said and left the balcony.

But Klara whispered in Larisa's ear, 'Whatever you do, don't rush. I will try and make him change his mind. Try not to make him angry.'

In the evening, I came home and took Father's side. I was sure that Larisa would jeopardise our plan of moving to Yugoslavia, which we had started mainly for her. Now, Mother had to fight both of us, but she was doing it very successfully, and the more she argued, the more we knew we would not be able to change her mind.

'Isn't it better just to agree than to lose her?' She made her point.

'Have you ever thought of the problems Dima will have? He is working on a secret enterprise, and this will ultimately ruin his career.' I tried to convince her.

'I was thinking about that. You ruined his career anyway when you lodged the forms to drop Soviet citizenship, and why does Larisa have to care about his career and not about her own good?' That kind of argument lasted for many days, and in the end, Klara managed to convince George.

After that, our parents had to meet with Eric's parents, Sasha and Manja, who were quite lovely people. Sasha was the head of the family, and his duty was to look after the family's well-being. He had done it very well, and his family had not known any hardship and was even quite well off, like the rest of the Krimotats. Now, all the Krimotats decided to immigrate. In that year, practically any Jew was allowed to go to Israel if they wished. Many were leaving, but they were treated by others as traitors, and George was not happy that his daughter was marrying one of them. After meeting with Eric's parents, he gave up, and they started to prepare for the wedding. After our wedding, our family budget was practically broken, and my parents had hardly any money. From the other side, the Krimotat family was in a hurry to immigrate and couldn't afford to waste time. So, practically, all the money was paid by the Krimotat family, and our parents managed to provide only 2,000 roubles. The wedding happened in May, in a big clubhouse, and they had plenty of guests. The majority of the guests were from the Krimotat's side, and because of that, the music was mainly Jewish. Klara was pleased, but deep in his soul, George was hurt, though he didn't allow it to show. Larisa was pleased with the wedding, and straight after, they lodged their forms for immigration. The newly married couple went to live in our apartment, and they had a room with windows facing Lenin Park.

Valentina and I continued to live in the rented unit, but it was challenging. By that time, I had graduated from the institute and, with great difficulty, managed to avoid being sent to a village school. I was allowed to find a job for myself, only because Valentina had a job at the Odessa University. In a few months, the owners of the unit came back from a business trip, and we had to move in with our parents. Now there were three families living in our unit, and Valentina and I slept on a sofa in the middle of the lounge room. There was no question of privacy. Larisa, Eric, Mother, and Father all went through our room in the middle of the night to go to the toilet. We couldn't complain, though, because the situation was not supposed to last for long and was changing quickly. Larisa's and Eric's papers were processed without delay. In that year, thousands of Jewish families were permitted to go to Israel. Thousands of people were leaving because they were tired of waiting for the promised bright future. They'd had enough from a country where any business activity was treated as criminal and people were jailed for views or actions deemed disloyal.

The procedure to get a visa was quite often speeded up by bribes, which became quite normal in Soviet offices, including OVIR. The first to leave from the country was Eric's brother, Alik. As expected, he didn't go to Israel but stayed in Rome, waiting for permission to go to Australia. In a couple of months, Eric and Larisa got permission too, and they quickly prepared for travel. The mood at home was very sombre, because we didn't know when we would see her again, but no one wanted to show any emotion. Larisa herself looked very calm and happy. As usual, we saw them off from Odessa Central Station, on the well-known train to Lvov. Only when we were on the platform did we realise that we were probably seeing her for the last time. George and Klara were openly crying, I was crying myself, even Valentina was crying, but Larisa was holding up much better, only shedding a few tears. We hugged her, but even that couldn't move her, and suddenly the train whistle sounded and the train began to move. Eric and Larisa jumped onto the step, and the train began to pick up speed. We ran after the train a bit longer until it disappeared, and after that, we walked back together to Eric's parents. His parents did not have to cry; they were to follow them in a few months' time. Just a couple of days later, Larisa and Eric met with Alik in Rome and lodged the documents to immigrate to Australia. About half a year later, they disembarked from the plane in Sydney, where they would start their new lives.

+ + ◆ ◆ + + +

Our family stayed at home, waiting for news from Moscow. Valentina and I moved into the room where Larissa and Eric had lived, and now we had some privacy. This privacy was quite limited, though, because when my mother wanted to talk to us, she called us out loudly to the lounge room. Just after Larisa's departure, we received the answer from the Supreme Soviet of the USSR, to say that my father and I were allowed to leave Soviet citizenship and stay in the USSR as stateless people. We were given a light-brown certificate, 'Permit to live in USSR for a stateless person', instead of the red passport. From that moment, we began a new life as half-foreigners. I couldn't work out what it really meant. Now I had to look for a new job and found it in "Chernomorneeproekt", which was located just in front of our block of units. I was taken as an engineer in the geological research laboratory, with a salary of ninety-six roubles. This money was just enough to keep us from dying. So my work career began. I would wake up twenty minutes before starting work, wash and clean my teeth, eat a sandwich, and run to work. Our laboratory was for improving geological research. My job was to make electronic devices to measure soil resistance and to record data from the measuring instruments. In the laboratory, we produced new machines for geological research and then took them for field testing.

Just at that time, our institute was doing geological research on Grigorjevsky bay, for the future port Uzniy and an ammonia plant. The head of our laboratory was Shpikov Alexnader Grgorjevich, a highly intelligent man. His father had worked with my mother years before. Shpikov treated me quite well but sometimes had problems with my behaviour. The director of our institute was the former communist party secretary Voronin. He was an unbelievably rough and rude person, and just his appearance was enough to create panic among the workers. Soon, I realised that as a stateless person, this gave me the chance to behave differently, more independently, and without being frightened. Voronin told Shpikov to pay attention to how his workers looked and dressed. Another problem was that as a stateless person, I was not allowed to travel more than fifty kilometres from Odessa. But in spite of everything, in those three years, I made many friends there, and I was especially close to Sasha Knobelman, who was very witty, and Semyon Peisahovich, who was red-haired and always funny. The scientists in the "Chernomorneeproekt' were well organised when it came to drinking from lunch break until evening, and Valentina was not very happy about it. But the drinking culture at her job in the chemistry faculty in Odessa University was even rougher. All the male scientists drank hard, because there was always a freely available supply of pure alcohol.

In spite of all these difficulties, our young family survived. The best moments in our lives were at holiday time, when we travelled to Yugoslavia, sometimes by ship, sometimes by train. Our relatives in Yugoslavia fell in love with Valentina, even my grandmother, who thought now she would become a great-grandmother. But we weren't in a rush to have children; we had hardly any money, but thanks to our trips, we were able to dress well. In Odessa, we were surrounded by friends. My old friends Ura and Lelik, Kostja and Gena, Vadik and Poldik, and Ruslan and Slavik didn't fit in with our married lifestyle and were pushed aside. I met them on my own. Now we spent more time with married couples Vova and Zenja Kompaneets, Sasha and Ira Boronetskie, Valera and Lena Parovini, and our new friends Sasha and Tamara Degtjarev and Zenja and Sveta Kovali. But there were hundreds of other friends with whom we spent time. Our life in Odessa was anything but dull. Our friends were divided into winter and summer friends. We spent the cold winter months indoors, and the summer we spent on Dolphin Beach with friends for whom sea, sand, sunshine, and champagne were most important. Odessa is a resort city, and the beaches were most important, and I felt that this was my motherland.

But no matter how much I loved it, I was waiting for just one thing—to get Yugoslavian citizenship and to get away. We had lodged our documents for Yugoslavian citizenship, and like the Velich family, we were expecting a positive result, but the results were disappointing. After one year of waiting, our application was rejected. The reason for that was that George had not been loyal to the government of Yugoslavia. It seemed that in the twenty years since Tito's death, nothing had changed. My application was rejected because I hadn't been born in Yugoslavia and had never lived there permanently. This blow was entirely unexpected; we were both in shock and didn't know what to do next. My father was afraid that he had dragged me into a difficult situation.

'What do you think we should do now, Milan?' my father asked.

'I don't even know what to say to you,' I answered.

'Maybe you will ask for your Soviet citizenship back. You are a young man and need some stability in your life,' he said.

'What are you talking about? Will you apply to get your Soviet citizenship back?' I asked.

'No, I'll try to fight my case, and in the end, I will win,' he said.

'Then I will fight with you,' I said.

'You and your wife should have children, and for that, you need stability,' he said.

'No, Father, to ask them to give us back our citizenship would be stupid. Even if they do give it back to us, they will never forgive us for rejecting it. I think it's better to stick together and keep fighting for Yugoslavian citizenship.'

Father hugged me tightly and said, 'I feel sorry that I've involved you in this difficult situation, but if you stick with me, we will lodge an appeal in the Supreme Court. But, first of all, you have to speak with Valentina.' And I did. She was very disappointed with my decision.

'You are only thinking about yourself. Did you ever think about me?' she asked.

'We will continue to live as before,' I said.

'And what if I don't want to live like that anymore?' she asked.

'What can I say? I can't stop you, but I can't give up my fight. You must do what is right for you,' I said.

'But I love you,' Valentina said.

'If you love me, then let's continue to live as we did before, and maybe I will get citizenship,' I said. And we started to wait for results again.

+ + + + + +

Klara was very happy with her job, where everyone from the ordinary workers to the very top, including the director, respected and loved her, and the working conditions in the factory were good. Now she had an opportunity to go and meet Mishka. She took a short holiday, bought a ticket, and went to Tashkent, where Mishka met her as a true sister. His wife, Lena, a large blonde woman, was glad to see her as well. Together they walked around, showing Klara Tashkent, which had changed a lot since the war. They remembered pre-war years, when they were very young and all their relatives had been alive. They also had so much to tell each other about the years after the war and what had happened to them.

Mishka had no children and felt quite isolated because all his relatives had been killed. The terrible war years and the years when he had killed those who had cooperated with Germans and killed Jews, years in jail, and life on restrictions had all helped to make Mishka into a strange man. He looked normal, but he was different; Klara felt sorry for him and tried to cheer him up. With these confused feelings, Klara returned home.

This wasn't the only thing that worried her, but Dima and Galina as well. Galina was continually putting pressure on Dima and dominated the home. They had already been married a long time but still didn't have children. Unexpectedly, great news came from Perm that Galina was pregnant and going to Ufa to her parents' house to give birth. Sometime later, the news arrived that she had given birth to a son and named him Janka. And though no one loved her for her terrible temper, everyone was happy for them. Klara decided immediately to buy a ticket and visit her new grandson. Dima and Galina adored Janka and spent all their free time with him. Everything was done according to a very popular American writer, Dr Spock, and they believed in a great future for Janka. He was a big healthy baby, with flushed cheeks, surrounded by his parents' attention.

Dima and Galina continued to work at the same aircraft factory where Dima was treated with great respect as a very knowledgeable engineer. He participated in all the new plane test flights and worked with the best pilots. From early childhood, he had dreamed of becoming a test pilot, but because he was colour-blind, that was not possible. But now, close contact with these brave and skilful people gave him real pleasure. The test flights were not always successful, and one of them was even deadly. He was often called to other test flight airfields when an accident happened, and he had to find the reason why. Dima did his job well, and once he travelled back home aboard the personal plane of the Marshal of Aviation. Every opportunity they had, they came to Odessa for the summer, and that year they came with Janka. Klara ran around with her grandson, praising his good health and rosy cheeks and his refusal to get out of the water. Janka was able to stay in the water all day without feeling cold. Only one thing upset everyone . . . Janka hardly ever spoke. He was silent all the time, but as proof to everyone that he wasn't dumb, he said just one thing, 'Give me!' I played a lot with him, and we both had fun. Galina was like a mother hen, protecting her firstborn, though she never cooked and just gave Klara instructions. There was always the feeling of electricity in the air. At last, after one month, they went back home, leaving Klara totally exhausted.

After another month, news came from Perm that Janka had started to speak, not just words but long sentences. He even remembered that he had an uncle Milan in Odessa and a cat called Antoshka. Everyone was happy with this news, but soon other news arrived from Perm, completely contradicting the first news: Dima was divorced from Galina, and, more amazingly, he was marrying a girl called Natasha. We didn't know how to react; no one particularly liked Galina because of

272

her complicated character, but they had a son! The news kept coming, and in the next letter, Dima explained that Janka wasn't their true son but had been adopted. Dima had promised that he would not forget about Janka and would continue to support him financially. Klara was furious that she had not been told the truth. She lost interest in Janka, and George practically never expressed his feelings about it all. I had the opinion that it's not fair to give up on the child. Galina didn't give up easily, though, and was constantly causing strife for Dima and Natasha. But Natasha wasn't a little girl, and she could stand up for herself, and in the end, Galina gave up. Now they lived in Natasha's mother's house, with Natasha's daughter, Julka, and Klara was angry that no one had discussed it with her.

George continued to work at the same factory with his friends Ribar, Velich, and Janesh. Though Velich had received Yugoslavian citizenship, he continued to live in Odessa. His son, Slava, had enrolled at Belgrade University and now came to Odessa for his holidays to have fun with us and have a spree with the local girls. I couldn't join him on these adventures anymore, but Valentina and I met him from time to time in restaurants, though we were always short of money. To live at the time of developed socialism was not easy . . . not only were people paid miserable wages, but also it was hard to buy anything. The shops often sold poor-quality goods; the vegetables and potatoes were occasionally rotten; the fruit and berries were not fresh. Milk was available in shops only in the morning, but kefir and ryazhenka were even more scarce. Sausages didn't smell like meat, and the meat itself was so badly cut that most of it was just bones. The better products were usually sold from the back of the shops. In Odessa, the majority of people bought food from the marketplace, which was more costly but of better quality. In the market, I had a butcher friend who sold me meat for five roubles per kilogram. It was expensive, but you could make a decent meal from it. To get to the market, we had to get a trolley bus and carry back heavy carrier bags. In the winter, it was even worse, and my hands would turn blue carrying the bags. But what a pleasure it was to sit around the dinner table. Valentina and me, we only bought one sofa and one "Belarus radio" in all our years in Odessa. Everyone lived like that, so no one felt different.

Soon, Valentina changed her university job for a job in the Physics-Chemical Institute, which was part of the Ukrainian Academy, and the director there was a long-time family friend, Alexander Bogatsky. The majority of her friends moved with her. The job here was much more interesting; the institute was located in a new building with a modern laboratory, and she was paid ten roubles more. I had to change jobs as well; my boss Shpikov began to disapprove of my behaviour because I openly disagreed with the Soviet invasion of Afghanistan. The last straw was that I quit my Komsomol membership. After that, I had a big argument with Shpikov, and I went to look for a job at the Astronomic Observatory. I went with my friend from work, Semyon Peisahovich. At the observatory, he had a good friend of his mother's, Professor Uri Romanov. They had two vacant positions;

we were sure that Semyon would get one of the positions, the only question was if I would get the other. But the academic Tsesevich said that he already had a Czechoslovakian man, and one Serb would not be a problem. But he couldn't employ Semyon, because in the university there was a limit on the percentage of Jewish people in the workforce, and it was already too high at the observatory. Professor Romanov didn't know how to break this news to Semyon, but he had already figured it out. I was shocked by that news and decided to leave with Semyon, but he stopped me. 'Don't be stupid. It's you that has problems with Shpikov, and you need to stay here. I don't have this problem at work.'

He made me stay, and I got the job. I was employed in a group in Ljonja Paulin, where they built telescopes, and I had to look after the electronic parts. In the group, there were another two engineers, Vasily Melnichenko and Uri Bobovich, and one toolmaker, Kolja, with amazingly skilful hands, but he was a hopeless alcoholic. I got used to the new place pretty quickly and found plenty of new friends. The observatory was located just opposite the entrance to the stadium, where our team, the "Chernomorets", played, and we never missed a match. Before every game, there was the essential alcoholic preparation, and only after that did we go to the stadium. In summer, the majority of people took a couple of hours of break to go to the beach . . . it was quite a good life. But the most exciting part of the work was the business trips to different parts of the enormous USSR: the Urals, Altay, and the Caucus Mountains, where we installed our telescopes.

That year, Valentina and I decided it was time to make a baby, and we tried to do it while we were on the ship going to Yugoslavia, where we felt most comfortable. For that reason, we avoided alcohol and regularly made love. We didn't have long to wait for the results; just two months after our trip, we knew that Valentina was pregnant. This news had the effect of fireworks in the Vignevich and Ivanovsky families. George and Klara waited impatiently for the arrival of their grandchild, and life was given a new meaning for everyone. Valentina carried the baby quite easily, and it was difficult to see any changes until the seventh month. We expected the birth to be a difficult one, because I was Rhesus positive and Valentina was negative. All Valentina's family came to help, and she was to give birth in the Medical Institute surrounded by the best professors. The day before giving birth, we were at a party at Professor Zubkov's family house, and Valentina was even dancing. She was taken straight from the party to the hospital, though I asked her to hold on, because on that day, the World Championship Football had started and Brazil was playing Holland. When we arrived at the hospital, Valentina was taken in, and I was left to wait under the windows. But after a couple of hours, I decided that no one needed me, and I went to watch the football.

Valentina's labour was long and painful, and only on the next day did she give birth to a boy, fifty-one centimetres long and 3.6 kilos. We named him Phillip.

George and Klara were very happy, and I, as all proud fathers do, went away to do the most important Russian job—to drink with my friends to the birth of my son. I have to admit that I had plenty of friends, and the celebrations lasted well into the night. In the morning, I was utterly wrecked! Valentina showed me my son through the window. He looked so tiny, with a beautiful nose. All of us were excited, and straight after that, I had to run to the shop to buy a baby bed, because Valentina wouldn't allow anything to be bought before the birth. At last, everything was ready for Valentina and Phillip to come home, but instead they went to the Ivanovsky home, where her mother could help her. I had to move to Tairova Prospect as well, but I couldn't get used to it, and I quite often ran back to my parents' house.

Practically nothing had changed in our house; we were still waiting for good news about our citizenship, but nothing came. None of the other Yugoslav families had followed our example and had kept their Soviet citizenship. By that time, they had learnt more Russian habits and had gotten used to drinking vodka. Especially good at that was Slavak Stojanovich, a huge Montenegrin man who drank vodka with enthusiasm and was also keen to start affairs with pretty women. No less than him, Kolja Gruich also loved to drink and tell stories about his adventures and his close relationship with the KGB. But his lifestyle caused a massive stroke, and the party animal was gone. Soon after that, Borja Dragishich died. He was the youngest of the immigrants; he was very handsome and hardly ever drank. It seemed that he would have a long and healthy life, but suddenly they found he had cancer, and it was already too big and too late to do surgery. As a result, he died quickly in a couple of months.

The next thing to happen was a huge scandal that shocked everyone in the Yugoslav immigrants' society. One day, Milan Ribar came home unexpectedly and found his wife, Kapa, in bed with Slavko Stojanovich. Milan loved his beautiful wife and was furious. He really wanted to kill Slavko, but the huge Stojanovich was a lot stronger than the slim Milan. As it came out, this relationship had already been going for quite a while, and it brought out heated debates between everyone who knew them. All the women blamed Kapa and called her a prostitute. The men didn't know what to say, but the majority blamed Slavko. George was in a most difficult situation, because in the last year he had become very close to Slavko and often spent time with him after work, but with the Ribar family, we were practically relatives during all the years in the Soviet Union. George tried to calm Milan, but he didn't want to listen and demanded a divorce. In a conversation with Slavko, George expressed his disgust at Slavko's dirty affair with the wife of one of his best friends. Ribar exchanged their two-roomed flat for two one-roomed flats, and Milan began to live alone. Slavko was kicked out of his home by his wife and moved to live in their dacha in Arcadia. Many friends closed their doors to him, and he started to spend more time with friends from work at the Polytechnic Institute. As opposed to that, Ribar visited us a lot more often; it seemed that he appreciated more our mother's cooking and orderly house. And he often said as much to George.

Our mother managed everything very well. She spent long hours at work, and then she ran around the shops and then did the cooking at night. On weekends, she cleaned the house and did the washing. Now with two of her children grown up and out of the house, and only me at home, she kept worrying about all of us. Most of all, she wanted to be closer to Larisa, who was living in Australia. There was little chance that she would see Larisa again because of the terrible Tatiana Michalovna's said to her at OVIR, that she would never see her douther again, but Klara refused to concede that. Our mother gave the impression that she was a weak and vulnerable person, and she quite often complained about her life and poor health. But her weaknesses were deceiving. If anyone tried to threaten or hurt her family, she would show unbelievable resistance and force. She reminded us of a wild lioness at these times. It was impossible to make her shut up and admit defeat. Now the image of her enemy was wholly associated with OVIR, which was trying to break up her family, and that became her battleground.

Four years after Larisa's departure, George decided to try to visit her in Australia, and she sent him an invitation. It was clear the OVIR would not allow George and Klara to go together, but it would be difficult to stop George, and he lodged all the documents himself. And they did let him. They bought the ticket for the flight from Moscow to Sydney with a stop in Singapore. The price of the ticket was very high, and Larisa bought the return ticket. The big problem was that George didn't speak English at all and had to rely on imitation and mimic. But in spite of his language problems, George got to Sydney with very few difficulties. At the airport, Larisa met him, but he hardly recognised his daughter because of her dark suntan and changed hairstyle. It was only when she rushed at him did he recognise her.

'My dear daddy! At last we are together again,' she said. 'You thought that we would never see one another again.'

'It's true, I did think that, but now I can see that the planet is not so big,' he replied.

'You are right, and you will see that Mother will come here as well. Let's take your luggage and get out of the airport.' They walked out of the airport and to the car park. They put the luggage in the boot, and George opened the door, but Larissa stopped him. 'Do you want to drive the car?' she asked him. Only then did he realise that he was trying to get into the driver's seat, because in Australia they drive on the left-hand side of the road. Larisa sat behind the wheel, and off they went. They went slowly round the bends, and George could not believe that his daughter was driving the car. There were one- or two-storey buildings along the road, with palm and plane trees, and unfamiliar birds and parrots flew in the sky.

After a fifteen-minute drive, the car made a final turn, and there in front of them was the great Pacific Ocean. 'Here is our Bondi Beach,' Larisa said.

'We'll swim here every day.' After that, they went home and took the luggage into the room. Larisa made coffee and took a bottle of slivovica, bought just for the occasion, from the cupboard. They sat around the table, had a shot of slivovica, and started to talk, feeling as though they had not been apart for four years. George spent three months in Australia and got used to the 'take it easy' lifestyle. This was his first chance to live in a truly capitalist country and had to expect that there would be some surprises. The abundance of goods in the shops was incredible, but that was not what amazed him most. All his adult life, he had been exposed to socialist ideas that only socialism would allow people to live in a socially just society, where everyone has everything that they need and no one would be exploited. But long years of building communism hadn't brought the future any closer, and George realised that theory was entirely different to reality. The time of prosperity hadn't arrived, and real life was full of hatred, hierocracy, and lies. Here in 'cruel capitalism', everything looked different. No one looked in desperate need; the people were kind and smiling. He was trying to see the very poor people, but he couldn't see any. He saw a poorly dressed young man, but he was just a "hippy".

Sometimes, George felt that he could live in Australia: the people dressed very modestly, and the best way to dress was in shorts and T-shirts. All life in Bondi was around the beach. People rode on surfboards, and George swam in the ocean as well as watched how people surfed. Because of the big waves, he couldn't go deep into the water and swam mainly near the beach. But on weekends, he went with Larisa to swim on the harbour beaches, where the waves were smaller, and they were more picturesque. Larisa and Eric both worked in the mornings, and George was alone. Quite often, Eric's parents, Sasha and Manja, visited him. They were very kind to him and tried to entertain him. Also, he met Asja and Uzik, with their son, Shurik, who had emigrated from Odessa to Australia and had started their new life there. George remembered their last days in Odessa.

After Asja's father, Semyon, had died, his wife, Klara, had not known how to live. To help her find a reason, she was advised to marry Uzik's father, who by that time had lost his wife. For Klara, this idea seemed completely absurd, but her children insisted that it would be better for her, and so she agreed. But this marriage didn't last long. Klara told them all that Semyon called her every night, and soon after, the doctors found that she had cancer so advanced that there was nothing to be done. The cancer simply consumed her body; a large woman with very fat arms and legs changed into a skinny, old, tired woman in just a few months. She died quickly and was buried next to her husband, and everything ended as it should have. After that, her family and other relatives from Kishinev decided to immigrate to Israel. They all received invitations and started to prepare their documents, but Asja's daughter, Larisa, chose not to go because she had different plans. By that time, she had married a nice Jewish boy, Osik, who loved her madly and loved her relatives as well, even our Vignevich family. Very soon,

Larisa gave birth to a little girl, Anja, and Asja became a grandmother before she was thirty-eight years old. After that, the young couple moved to Moscow, where Osik had a great job, and immigration wasn't in his plans. They decided not to go now but to join the family afterwards.

Uzik, Asja, and Shurik left from Odessa railway station, and many friends and relatives went, including our family, to say goodbye. The farewells were spoiled by Shurik and his beloved school girlfriend. There were rivers of tears and screams from parents as they tried to pull them apart. Nobody was able to say goodbye properly. The train moved away, accompanied by screams worthy of a Shakespeare tragedy. They arrived in Vienna and started to wait for permission to go to Australia. Klara asked Larisa to send them an invitation, and after that, everything went smoothly. In a few months, they were met by Larisa at Sydney Airport. They couldn't stay with Larissa because she didn't have enough room for them, so they stayed with Eric's parents. After that, they were supported by a Jewish welfare group; they started to receive unemployment benefits and rented their flat. Uzik didn't need any help; he had very skilful hands and plenty of self-confidence, you could even say impudence. He quickly found a job as a panel beater and started to get very good money. Asja didn't have a job and did the housekeeping, and Shurik found a job in a jewellery store. After one year, Uzik opened his own panel beating shop on the very prestigious Oxford Street.

A couple of years later, they bought their first house in Fairfield, a suburb in southern Sydney. A few weeks after George's arrival in Sydney, Larisa called Asja and Uzik and told them that my father was with them, and they came to see him the next day. Larisa prepared dinner, they had a few shots of vodka, and Uzik, as usual, became very loud and started to tell anecdotes. Then he began to sing, and after that, they played a few chess games, which almost resulted in a fight. Before they left, Uzik invited George to his house and to stay for the weekend. Uzik had a big home, with three bedrooms, two toilets, and two bathrooms. There was a big dining room, a garage, and even a swimming pool. George couldn't believe that Uzik had achieved so much in just a few years and was even a little envious. It seemed that in this wild capitalism, people lived much better, and he started to think that maybe he could achieve this as well.

In the Warshavsky family, it was clear who the king was, and Uzik sat on his throne very steadily. He made all the money, and when he came home, Asja tried to do everything to please him. At home, there was always plenty of food and alcohol, and Uzik refused to eat without a bottle of vodka on the table. With George there, the bottles were emptied very quickly. After that, they began their political debates, and in these, Uzik became very loud. Asja and Shurik suffered during these discussions. Shurik was very loud but entirely inoffensive. In spite of his warm welcome, George was happy to get back to his daughter's house, where there were no disagreements at all. He had no feeling now that they lived on the opposite side of the world, and he was sure that they would meet again. He fell in love with Australia, and he brought his feelings back with him when he returned to Odessa. At home, he faced many questions, and most of them came from me. He couldn't answer all the questions, but he found the best answer. 'I think I could stay and live over there!' and that answer pleased everybody.

But we had to continue our Supreme Court case; though in the Court of Bosnia Herzegovina, we were getting negative answers. It became clear that everything was decided in the same place. Every year, we had less and less hope, but the thought of getting our Soviet citizenship back was even less appealing. As people without citizenship, we were protected by the Red Cross, a very respected organisation but entirely without power. It helped that we didn't have to lodge our documents at OVIR anymore but with the Red Cross, where we didn't have to suffer the humiliations of the OVIR. But to receive documents, we still had to go there. To apply for Soviet citizenship again would mean we would lose any chance of overseas trips, but our family couldn't live without our holidays in Yugoslavia. About a year later, I decided to try my luck to visit Australia and asked Larissa to send me an invitation. Larissa didn't waste any time and sent me a letter very quickly. I lodged my documents with the Red Cross, and OVIR, through gritted teeth, accepted them. Now I just had to wait.

But if everything was not going the way we wanted in our lives, Milan Ribar's life went downhill altogether. It seemed that after his separation from Kapa, his life started to improve. But then disaster struck again. His son, Nikolay—everyone called him Nika—was a handsome young man. One night, he took his girlfriend home and was walking back home alone. Someone came from behind him and hit him. He fell to the ground, lost consciousness, and was robbed. When he regained consciousness, he walked home. At home, a very scared Kapa washed the blood from his head and tried to find out what had happened. Nika couldn't explain it very well, and in the end, he asked to be left alone because he wanted to sleep. Early in the morning, he was still asleep. Kapa called Milan to tell him what had happened, and Milan came almost immediately, but Nika still wouldn't wake up. They tried throughout the day but without success, and in the evening, they decided to call an ambulance. They took him to the hospital, where Kapa and Milan sat next to him all night, but he didn't recover consciousness and died practically in their hands. The doctors told him that in cases like that, they should not have let Nika sleep but to go straight to the hospital. But no one had known that before. Nika lost his life, and the person responsible was never found.

His death in one day turned Kapa from a beautiful woman into and old woman; she turned grey, her eyes didn't shine anymore, and her voice became scratchy. She didn't want to live anymore and wanted to be buried with Nika. Friends held her arms when his coffin was placed in the ground because she wanted to jump in with it. Milan was holding up a bit better, but he looked terrible as well. He had always been tall and lean, you could almost say elegant, but now his cheeks had shrunk, and he was hunchbacked. His eyes often looked as though they were full of tears, and he walked as though nothing interested him. For the funeral, all the Yugoslavian immigrants came, not only from Odessa but from Kiev and Moscow as well. Such a tragedy had never struck them before, and they all tried to support Milan as best they could.

Only Gioko Negovan was closer to him than our family, and after the funeral, Ribar spent a lot of time at our home. Ribar had to talk out all that was in his heart, and my father did his best to listen and understand him and, when it was necessary, to drink a bottle of vodka. One evening, Ribar, George, and I were out on the balcony, smoking. Suddenly, Ribar asked, 'Do you remember, Jukitca, when we were partisans, sleeping on the forest floor, when the fierce ants were eating our bodies?'

'Of course, I remember those parasites,' George said.

'I think it would have been better for me if they had eaten me alive than to come to this godforsaken country, the USSR,' he said. These words struck pain in my heart, because Ribar was like a second father to me. It didn't matter that he had a daughter, Lena, and a granddaughter; the stress of Nika's death was too big for him, and life lost all colour for him.

His life ended in the same tragic manner. Once after a late night of drinking, he brought home a young prostitute. It wasn't clear whether he had fallen asleep or they'd had an argument, but in the morning, he was found in his bed with a fractured skull. Next to his body lay the murder weapon, a heavy crystal ashtray. Some money was stolen and a few valuable items. The neighbours had seen the girl, but she was never found. At his funeral, there were practically the same people as had been to Nika's funeral. Everyone felt not just sad but angry as well. Father and son were killed in almost the same way; both died from a blow to the head, and this cruelty shocked everyone. The wish to find and punish those responsible was very strong, but in a few months, it was almost forgotten. I had the idea to write on the gravestone 'The Ribars don't live here anymore', but that's gone as well.

During the long years of fighting with OVIR, my nervous system was exhausted, and I developed the very unpleasant Raynaud's syndrome. It had all started when I was fourteen years old and went for a winter holiday to visit Dima in Ufa, where we spent a lot of time skiing. On one day, it was very cold, minus twenty-five degrees. When I had lived in Ufa as a boy, I was used to these temperatures, but after years in Odessa, my body forgot how to behave in such temperatures. We went too far from the station that day, and when I started to feel cold, I was ashamed to tell my brother. Dima was so involved in his skiing that he didn't notice. When I told him, it was already too late; my hands and feet were frozen, and I could hardly walk. Dima and his friends got scared and started to rub my hands and feet with snow. The pain became even worse, and they rushed me to the station. It took a long time to get home, and as soon as we arrived, they prepared a hot bath for me, and I slowly began to feel better. But after that, I began to feel cold a lot faster than other people. For a long time, I didn't pay any attention to that, but when I grew older and began to drink and smoke, my symptoms became more severe. My relations with OVIR and UDBA weren't making it any easier. By that time, I recognised that my problem was getting worse . . . my hands and feet were getting colder faster; sometimes they turned blue and occasionally as white as a sheet. The most difficult time was in the observatory workshop, where there was no heating.

One day in late autumn, we came out on a break to have a beer in a stall at the entrance to Shevchenko Park. Here, we met my good friend Slava Jamkovoy. He saw me struggling and said, 'Milan, show me, what is the matter with your hands?' I must say that Slava was a good doctor, and I showed him my hands. 'This colour is wrong. What are you doing about it?' he asked.

'What's wrong with them?' I asked him.

'Your blood vessels are working poorly, and it most likely means that you have Raynaud's syndrome,' he explained.

'And what could happen?' I asked him.

'You could lose your hands and legs before you turn forty,' he said.

I lost my breath at this horrible thought, and my friends from work got scared as well. 'So, what do I have to do?' I asked.

'First of all, we will do some investigations, and then we'll decide what to do. But one thing I can definitely tell you, you have to quit smoking. That is damaging the blood vessels the most.'

That dark prediction scared me a lot, and I took it very seriously. Slava organised for me to have all the tests done in his clinic, and his diagnosis was completely correct. There was no remedy for this mostly female disease. I had a few physiotherapeutic sessions and was advised to avoid the cold. But the continuingly difficult situation with our citizenship made my hands look dark purple. At last, I was permitted to go to Australia; everything went smoothly, though my level of English was close to zero.

At the airport, I was met by Larisa, and she was so happy and cheerful. But not the beautiful weather or the amazing views could take away my sad mood. Only on the fourth day did I realise that I was seeing everything in black and white. I forced myself to shake off this inexplicably sad mood, and I began to see the world in full colour again. Now I tried to smile more, and Australia was the ideal place to do this. Here, almost every one smiled and lived with a positive outlook. Slowly I learnt to do this as well. Swimming in the warm ocean, driving around the amazing city, with its Harbour Bridge and new Opera House, which had been built in a stunning modern style, helped me to be more relaxed and balanced.

I decided to extend my visa and try to make some money. Larisa and I went together to the Russian embassy, located in Woollahra, in a five storeyed building, behind a tall steel fence. Inside the embassy, there were photographs of life in the victorious socialist country and portraits of our communist leaders and, of course, Leonid Illyich Brezhnev. I explained the reason for my visit and was told to wait in the foyer. Finally, a man dressed in a black suit came out to see me. 'Give me your passport and application,' he said. I gave him my documents, he looked at them and said, 'What is this? I haven't seen such a document in all my life. I'll have to go and consult with someone.' He left, and I continued to study the photographs around the walls. I didn't have to wait long. Soon, he came back and said, 'Look, you are not a Soviet citizen. You can stay here as long as you want.'

'No, I want to extend my visa for six months,' I said.

'Then I will take your documents and request for a visa extension, and you can come again in a few days.' We said goodbye and drove back home. In my head, I kept hearing the words that I had been told, that I could stay in Australia as long as I wanted. That meant that OVIR didn't have the right to hold me, and my head started to spin.

After my visa was extended, I found a job in Katie's factory, where Eric was working. I was involved in packaging and loading the trucks with the products that were to go to the shops. The job wasn't all that easy, but here, for the first time, I was being paid a good money and could buy a lot of things if I wanted to. I was getting paid in cash and had practically nothing that I needed, so my savings were growing fast. Half a year went quickly, but in that time, I got used to this easy and logical lifestyle. In my free time, I decided to read Solzhenitsyn, about whom I had heard only negative reviews from the Soviet press. Now I read his book "Arhipelag Gulag" and was totally shocked. I didn't have any doubt that what he wrote was the truth, and this truth upset me so badly that I didn't know how to go and live in that country again. I shared my thoughts with Larissa.

'But why do you have to go? Stay here,' she said. 'In the Soviet embassy, they told you that you are not a Soviet citizen, and for them, it's not important if you stay here or go back.'

'Yes, I could stay, but it's possible that they will not allow Valja and Phillip to come here,' I said.

'No, I don't believe that even they would do that, but I don't want to persuade you—you have to decide for yourself.'

'I know for sure that I don't want to live there, but I also know that I can't afford to lose Valja and Phillip. I think I must go back and apply for immigration to Australia from home.'

'Do as you wish, and I will send you an invitation anytime you ask me,' Larisa said.

'Great! I will talk to Valja, and if she agrees, I will send you a letter, which will end with the words "Do it!"' So we agreed on everything.

My stay in Australia for half a year had made me enough money to buy a ticket for a ship going from Perth to Singapore. I also bought clothes and presents for everybody in Odessa. For Valja, I bought a little diamond ring, about which she had always dreamed, and to make money in Odessa, I bought two beautiful, powerful portable tape recorders, unlike anything I had seen before. I was going back full of energy and the will to start a new life. The trip on board the ship was excellent. For the first time in my life, I had money and felt calm and comfortable. After that, I had to fly from Singapore to Moscow, and it was there that I had some trouble. I found that my luggage was twenty kilos heavier than allowed, and I had to throw away half of my things, and I had to carry the tape recorders as hand luggage. At last, we landed in Moscow. At the border, the guard ripped off a piece of the return visa from my Russian passport, which had been issued by the Russian embassy in Sydney, and I was allowed to get into the airport, where I was met by my father and Valentina. Half a year apart from each other had put a strain on my relationship with Valentina, and when we arrived in Odessa, little Phillip didn't recognise me at all. He tried to smile at every passing man, and only when I stretched my arms out to him did he run into my grasp. Mother was thrilled to see me, and she said that I had become a real man. She asked questions non-stop, and that annoyed Valentina, who demanded that, as her husband, I should be paying more attention to her. But it was not easy for her to be angry for long, because I had bought her the gift of a beautiful diamond ring. We were left alone only when it was time for bed.

'Can you believe how quickly I got used to Australia, and, you know, I think I could stay over there forever. I just don't know how to live here anymore,' I confessed.

'If you felt like that, why didn't you stay there?' Valentina asked angrily.

'I couldn't do that, because of you and Phillip,' I said.

'Couldn't you do it all from Sydney?' she asked.

'What if they wouldn't let you come to Sydney? They told me that nobody could hold me here now, but are you ready to go now?' I asked.

'Yes, I'm ready now,' she said.

'It's a pity I didn't know that, but now I will write to Larisa and get her to send an invitation letter,' I said.

After that, I went to OVIR to exchange my documents, where I was given some bad news. Tatiana Michalovna took my documents and went out of the room. When she came back, she said to me, 'Comrade Vignevich, our chief officer wants to see you. Follow me, please.' I obediently followed her to a room where I was met not by Ivanov but by another officer, who began straightaway.

'Comrade Vignevich, we gave permission for you to go to Australia for one month. How is it that you only came back after half a year?' he asked.

'I extended my visa in the Russian embassy in Sydney,' I answered.

'Why isn't it shown on your passport, then?' he asked.

'Because they glued this extension of my visa to the page, and the border guard at Sheremetyevo Airport ripped it off,' I explained.

'But there is nothing to see in your passport. How do we know you are telling the truth?' he persisted.

'You could call Sheremetyevo Airport and ask them. No one would allow me into the country with an expired visa,' I reasoned.

'No, we will not call anyone. You have to prove it, so you make the call,' he said.

'You know perfectly well that no one will talk to me,' I tried again.

'Why? You can try,' he suggested.

'I don't have to do anything! I did everything properly. You could find out from the embassy in Sydney,' I said.

'Do as you want, but remember that if you can't prove it with documents, we can punish you,' he answered me.

'And how will you do that?' I wanted to know.

'We will not permit you to travel for three years,' he told me, and the audience was over.

Now I had to learn to live in the USSR again, but I could not work out what to do. My mind was absolutely fixed on moving to Australia. Now that Valentina was ready to go, I had to talk to my parents. I did not think there would be too many obstacles, because after my father's trip, he had told us that he would happily live in Australia. The next day at lunch, I told my parents, 'Mama, Papa, we have decided to move to Australia.'

'That's great,' my mother replied. She now could see the possibility to reunite the family. She was so enthusiastic because she had long dreamed of living in a place where life was not a constant struggle, and Australia seemed the perfect destination. 'What do you think, George?' she asked him.

George was silent for a short time but then said, 'No, I'm not going to Australia!'

'Why not?' we all asked him almost simultaneously.

'Because all my life, I have been a communist and have been supporting socialism. I can't go after that and beg for a handout from capitalism,' he said.

'Why beg for a handout?' I asked him. 'We will find jobs, and life will be beautiful and comfortable,' I said.

'Yes, you should go. I don't want to stop you. But your mother and I will stay here,' he said.

'Did you ask me?' Klara almost screamed. 'I want to go as well!'

'If you wish, you could go with them, but I will stay here,' he said uncompromisingly.

'How could I go without you? We are tied by the same rope, so I will have to stay here with you. But our children should go, and they will be together,' she said.

'What are you talking about, Klara Davidovna?' Valja interrupted her. 'I'm sure they will never let us out of the country.'

'No, they can't do that,' I disagreed. 'They can make it difficult, but they can't stop us, and if we lodge the documents together, nobody will be able to stop us. Please, Father, change your mind,' I pleaded.

'I don't have to think anymore. I've decided to continue to wait for Yugoslavian citizenship. What about you, don't you want to go to Yugoslavia anymore?' George asked.

'Why? I do want that, but we have been waiting now for seven years. How much longer will we have to wait, and will they ever allow us at all? I could get old waiting for that,' I said.

'Then let's wait for an answer from the court, and then you should start,' he said. And we waited, but not for long, and the answer was negative.

Before lodging the papers for immigration to Australia, I decided to visit my grandmother in Yugoslavia one last time and to show her Phillip, her great-grandson, because by now she was very sick, and this was possibly our last chance to see her. She was an old, uneducated peasant woman who always wore a black dress and a black scarf on her head. But in spite of that, her natural sense of humour and her simple and robust peasant logic helped her understand and solve difficult situations and even to support others. We had become much closer in recent years, especially the year of the Moscow Olympics, when Valentina's and my passports and all our money were stolen in Dubrovnik. I spent about two weeks with grandmother, and our relationship became much stronger. I didn't have the money for going out, and we often spent our evenings together. From her, I found out a lot about the Mandich and Vignevich families. At that time, there was a film on television about Nikola Tesla, the most famous Yugoslav and world scientist. Grandmother watched the movie and then said, 'I know all about him. He's one of our relatives.'

At first, I didn't believe her, but slowly it became clear that she was telling the truth. As it turned out, Nikola's mother was the sister of Milka's grandmother, so Nikola and her father were first cousins and even went to the same school. This news struck everyone because it was a great honour to have such a relative. I realised that she had unique knowledge hidden in her memory, and I started to ask questions about her father. She spoke about him without enthusiasm; she didn't remember him well; he had died when she was just a little girl. He had gone to Banja-Luka markets and had seen policemen beating protesting students. He tried to stop them, but they abused him. Then he told them that Austrian pigs were no better than Turkish dogs, and he was arrested for that. They accused him of insulting the Austrian Crown, and he needed to publicly apologise for that or he would be executed. But Toma Mandich was a well-respected Chetnik who was well known for his fights against the Turks. He had risked his life, not once but many times, and he wasn't scared this time either. He refused to apologise and was executed, and Milka never saw him again. No one could believe that he had died when it would have been so easy to avoid it, and Milka was hurt that he decided to stand up for his views without thinking about his children, who were left orphans.

For me, these stories were revelations. To have in your family tree one of the most famous physicists in the world, the only man who had been allowed to sit in Edison's armchair, was an honour, but for me, what was more interesting was my stubborn grandfather. I was attracted to him, because for him, it was more important to die than to apologise or change his mind, and that happened very rarely. In the Soviet Union, I was surrounded by people who didn't want to express their political views at all. Long, cruel years of the Stalin regime had killed in people the wish to speak out about the system. That's why, for me, I was very happy to know that the blood of this proud man was running through my veins.

But Milka knew the history not only of the Mandich family but of the Vignevich family as well. She could recall everything that she had heard about the family. Now she told me about the time when they lived in Montenegro, were baptised, and built the first church of St. Vasily, and he had become the saint of our family. After that was the Turkish invasion and the battle of Kosovo Fields, and the Vignevich men took part in that battle. After that were the long years of Turkish occupation; the Vignevich family always had problems because of their refusal to obey orders. But the Turks never forgave disobedience, and punishment was severe, and in the end, the Vignevich men ran to the Adriatic Islands and became pirates. They did that for a long time but then got in trouble with the Venetians and had to go back to Bosnia and settle near Mazin. She remembered almost every family member from that time. But our close family was started by Jukan's grandfather, Juech, who went to America in search of gold. In this gold rush, he had managed to make a lot of money and to buy land from a local Beg and to build a new house where he settled with his big family.

From all these stories, I reached the conclusion that my ancestors had always hated injustice and had always been rebellious. And if the Mandiches were more educated, the Vigneviches were more rough and ready to resist, which was why nobody wanted to fight them. 'Your father is the same,' Milka told me. 'I was always afraid that this rebellious spirit would wake up in him too. And I was right, he left me, and, in the end, he finished up in cold and faraway Russia.'

'I can't blame him for that,' I said. 'Because of that, I was born.' We spent about a week in such conversations, and she remains in my memory like that. Thanks to her, I started to feel even closer to the Vignevich family. Now I wanted to bring my son to show her, but OVIR refused to issue me a visa, giving the reason that I had overstayed my time in Australia.

It became very clear that my relationship with OVIR had reached the next level of open warfare, and this struggle was going to be very difficult. We decided to lodge our documents for a permanent move to Australia. Before that, Valentina left her job, so she didn't need a reference from work, and I got a new position as a lighting engineer in the Odessa Musical Comedy Theatre, where the rules were not as rigid as at the university. We were preparing for a big struggle, and my father was to play a significant role in defending us, because, without him, the KGB would easily make short work of us. Even without that, the militia was always watching us. Quite often they visited our neighbours and asked them questions about what was happening in our house and who visited us. On our floor, just opposite us, there lived the Tischenko family. The head of the family, Zhora, had spent some time in jail and loved to drink alcohol, so he often had brawls and fought with his wife, Valja. They had two sons: the older one was Igor, who had sworn in 'Mat' (dirty Russian slang) from early childhood; and his younger but no less rough brother was Serjoga. From early childhood, they showed advanced criminal tendencies, and were first sent to a children's colony, and later had spent time in jail. But as neighbours, they seldom created any problems for us and were quite respectful. The militia often visited them and asked them questions about us, but what they didn't know was that after these visits, Valja came and told my parents everything. There was such mistrust at the beginning, but with time, we got used to it.

And if the attitude of the KGB and OVIR made us uncomfortable, the attitude of the ordinary Soviet people towards us was excellent. In my student years, I was used to often being arrested for an identity check, and after several hours, when the evening had been spoiled, they would let me go home. But with time, their attitude towards us was continually getting worse and worse. One evening, Valentina and I were walking home from a party, arguing about whether we should call in to our friends Ira and Sasha Boronetsky to pick up a forgotten umbrella. At that moment, a motorbike with two militiamen on it stopped next to us.

'What's happening here?' one of them asked.

'Why are you bothering us? Nobody called you here,' Valentina said. She was a little tipsy because I had picked her up from a friend's party. I hadn't had a drink at all, and I tried to calm Valja down. But for the 'ments', that was enough already. They got off their bike and came closer.

'Look how clever you are! You start a loud argument and don't allow normal people to sleep. Let's go to the militia headquarters,' one of them said and grabbed her by the elbow.

'Please don't try to resist,' I begged her, but she didn't want to obey; she pulled away her arm and pushed the officer.

'You have no right to touch me. Leave us alone!' she yelled.

'I will show you our rights!' the officer screamed, and he punched Valentina, and she fell to the ground.

At that moment, blood rushed to my head; I lost control and screamed, 'What are you doing!' and hit the officer twice, and he fell to the ground. To hit militia officer was an extremely rare event, and for a moment, there was silence. But after that, it was like a tornado started. The two ments started to hit me from both sides.

287

I managed, like a boxer, to get into a tight defensive position, and thanks to that, I came out with minimum damage. After that, they called for a second militia bike, and we were taken to the local militia headquarters. Here, they placed us in separate rooms, but before that, I was beaten by the same ments once again. I only managed to stop them by screaming that I was not a Soviet citizen. After that, they stopped. I couldn't see Valentina, but I could hear her crying, complaining about pain in her shoulder and demanding to be allowed to go home.

After that, they began to fill in the arrest formalities and continually threatened me with at least two years' jail sentence for striking a militiaman on duty. But in spite of the enormous pressure, we refused to sign the confession and were taken to spend the night in the jail for preliminary detention. Next morning, we were to appear in court. We had to sleep in the common room, on a wooden 'narah'. Valentina was in with prostitutes and thieves, and I was in with alcoholics and hooligans. At first, they tried to bother me, but I pretended that I didn't understand them and crawled into a corner. In the morning, they brought us back to the militia headquarters and started the questioning again. I continued to resist and insisted that I did not accept any guilt and that I would not sign any confession. Also, I said that officers had tortured and abused us all night, and I insisted that the officers apologise for that. In response, they laughed at me, saying that I would serve two years in jail for striking an officer on duty. I said that I had only hit the officer after he had hit my wife. It became clear that our arguments were reaching a dead end, and the officer decided to call our parents. Valentina's father was afraid to dirty his name and refused to come, but my father and mother arrived immediately and started negotiations.

They were told the militia's version of events and were told that Valentina and I had to apologise and, in that case, we would only have to pay a fine, and we would be allowed to go home. My mother was told that she had to make Valentina and me accept guilt. When Klara saw me in sitting on a chair in the corridor in such a dreadful condition, she ran to me and said, 'Milanchik, what's wrong with you? Do you feel all right?'

'I feel like shit,' I admitted.

'How did you manage to get so drunk yesterday that you started a drunken brawl and that you even hit a militiaman?'

'And you believe them? Yesterday, I didn't drink at all. They humiliated us, and now you accuse me?' I said angrily.

'No, I trust you, but it's impossible that they arrested you without any reason at all. And they are even angrier at Valentina than with you,' she answered.

'I don't want to listen to what these bastards are telling you about us,' I told her.

'Don't listen if you don't want to, but I made a deal with them. You just have to apologise and then you will just have to pay a small fine,' Klara said.

'Are you out of your mind? They were the ones breaking the law. I'm not prepared to forgive them.' I was absolutely confident and ready to go, but when Valentina found out that I was ready to go to court with the militia, she categorically rejected it!

'Last night, I went through such shit, and I am so exhausted that I don't want to spend another second here. Let's agree with everything, or I will die!' she said.

After that, there was nothing left for me to do except to agree with her, but later I couldn't forgive myself for that. The court hearing left us feeling shamed. The judge called us 'debauchers' and ordered us to pay twenty-five roubles each. Then we were allowed to go home. We felt abused and exhausted and went to our room to sleep. But even here we were not left alone, and our local militia officer came for a visit. He rang the bell, and when George opened the door, he tried to get in. But, here, my father ran out of patience; he stopped the officer with his hand and asked, 'Where do you think you are going?'

'I came to find out what our offenders are doing,' he said.

'You will come to my place only when I call you,' George replied angrily and forcefully pushed the officer away. The ment were not used to such treatment, but this time he swallowed it up and left. After this, daily life in USSR became impossible, not just for me but for Valentina as well.

✦✦✦✦✦

A few months later, we had a call from Milan in Zagreb. He told us that my grandmother Milka had been taken to hospital in a critical condition and that George should go immediately. The next day, he received a telegram from the hospital, where grandmother's condition was explained. OVIR got the documents ready in two days. The same day, George bought tickets and packed his luggage and took the train to Kiev. That evening, his brother called to say that Milka had died that morning. The funeral was to be held in two days in her dear Lipa, where she had been born, grew up, and lived most of her life. But George didn't know this, and after arriving in Kiev early in the morning, he went to the Yugoslav embassy. Here, he was met as coldly as usual, but when they found out that he was going to visit his dying mother, he was given a visa immediately. Now, he just had to buy a ticket for the Moscow-Belgrade train. As usual, it was packed, but by using his professional skills, and with great difficulty, he made it, and that evening. he departed for Belgrade.

All the way to the border, he was worried because he had been turned back so many times. This time, he decided not to give up but to get through, no matter what the cost. He couldn't fall asleep because of his worrying thoughts, but in the short moments when he did fall asleep, he had dreadful nightmares. In the morning, they arrived at the Carpathian Mountains and then to the border city of Chop. Here, they spent about three hours and then went on to Budapest, where they spent another four hours. Jukan decided not to get out and stayed on the train. He sat in the dark carriage, thinking about his mother. He loved her more than anyone else in this world. When he had been a child, he had promised her that he would never leave her. But fate had decided differently, and now he lived in USSR and only occasionally had been able to visit her. He was hoping to see her while she was still alive, to hug her and apologise, but he didn't know that her soul was already far away.

After that, for a couple of hours, the train rushed to the Yugoslavian border, going so fast that it felt sometimes as if they were flying. Before the border, Hungarian officials entered the train to check passports, and then came the Yugoslavians. George recognised the face of the officer who had taken him off the train last time and hadn't allowed him to enter Yugoslavia, and Jukan got ready for a fight.

'Your documents, please,' the frontier guard said and smiled when he had them. 'Ah, it's you, Comrade Vignevich. We've known one another now for a long time! What is the purpose of your visit now?'

'Unfortunately, the purpose is not nice. My mother in on her deathbed in hospital, and I'm rushing, hoping to see her alive. Here is the telegram,' George said.

The border guard read it and got off the train with the promise to be right back. He came back with a bright smile on his face. 'You can continue your trip,' he said, opening the passport and stamping it.

'Thank you,' George said. 'To be honest, I doubted that I would be successful.'

'How could we stop you under these circumstances?' the border guard made a hopeless gesture. 'I have nothing personally against you, you know. We simply have directives for every situation,' he confessed.

George arrived in Belgrade early in the morning and bought the first available ticket to Zagreb. He had a couple of hours to wait and decided to call his brother, Milan. But, strangely, no one picked up the phone at the other end. Then he decided to call Kosa, but again no one answered. Finally, he spoke to Kosa's daughter, Sanja. From her, he discovered that his mother was already dead. In spite of having really expected this news, his legs gave way and he sat down on the floor. She told him that the funeral would take place the next day in Lipa. George left the telephone box, sat on a bench, put his luggage down on the ground, and cried. He sat there for about four hours, not paying attention to what was going on around him, and only when he heard the announcement for the train to Zagreb did he go to the platform. It didn't matter how hard he had tried; he still arrived too late for the funeral. He got to the grave only the following day. The small village cemetery was located on the top of the hill, not far from the forest. From here was a fantastic view of the surrounding landscape where she had spent almost all of her life. Virtually opposite the grave was the Mandich house, where she had been born and had spent her young years. Further down across the plain was the

Vignevich house, to where she had been taken by her husband, Mile. With him, she had spent many happy years and had given birth to four children.

Jukan sat at the edge of her grave and apologised for being late. Tears ran down his face, but in his soul, he was at peace. His mother had lived a long and difficult life, and now she was at rest between her relatives. The view from her grave was so fantastic that it was hard to imagine anything better . . . it was unbelievably quiet and calm. On this land, many people had lived with their big families, but now there were only old people, and in the Vignevich house, only Sveto and his mother, Stana, remained, and Jukan went to visit them. They were happy to see him and brought out some rakija. They drank and remembered Milka, who was the soul of this house.

+++++

The struggle to get permission to immigrate to Australia was even harder than I had imagined. The next four years turned out to be the hardest. Our house reminded military headquarters that we were continually considering our next plan of action. At first, when we had lodged our documents, we were sure that they would let us go. OVIR had its own set of rules, but we were not about to give up. Now, Valentina was no less determined than I was. She didn't work anymore, and it was very difficult to survive on one income. At the theatre, I was paid a little more money, but it was still not enough. As a result of this very stressful situation, the blood circulation in my hands and legs was getting worse, and now they were always blue and sometimes completely white. Many doctors advised me to move to a warmer climate, and I realised that I could use this as my primary reason for immigration to Australia. I had meetings with the chief MVD officer of the Odessa region, but with no significant results. My trips to Kiev and Moscow didn't bring any results either, and I was growing bitter. I was no longer the cheerful long-haired man who was easily distracted and confused, but a person with growing experience of the struggle with the KGB. To talk to them was a difficult business. They could easily distract you and take the conversation to a different topic. Quite often I blamed myself for losing track of the topic and starting to talk about something else. But over time, I was getting stronger, and it was harder for them to distract me.

Very often I was able to prove my case, but even then, they were able to find an excuse. 'Yes, maybe you are right, but we have our rights,' they would say.

'What are your rights? Show me them,' I would demand angrily.

'We can't show them to you, but, believe us, we have them' was the reply that didn't tolerate any objections.

My mother saw how I was struggling and pushed George to take some action. He went to the Red Cross, KGB, and the Ministry of Foreign Affairs, but all without success. In spite of that, he tried again and again, though he hated the idea that I would leave him. On the contrary, my mother had a secret wish that her children would reunite in Australia and that she would probably join them there, though she said nothing of this to George.

Life continued to go on, and we had to satisfy our everyday needs. George and Klara didn't work anymore and had to live on their pensions, though Klara had the right to work for a couple of months each year. Valentina and I were struggling too, but the two tape recorders that I had bought in Australia were sold for 3,500 roubles each, and that helped. It was a lot of money, but it was disappearing quickly. Now the centre of attention in the family as our son, Phillip. He was growing quickly and had been playing tennis since he was five years old. He didn't have far to go; the tennis courts were very close, just across the fence of the stadium. Valja wasn't working, and she could spend all day with him. He gave us plenty of hope; he was hitting forehands and backhands and trained with pleasure. Now he had plenty of friends who played tennis with him. His best friend was Gija, the son of a very famous world champion shot-put thrower, Nunu Abashidze.

George worshipped his grandson and was fearful that, in the near future, he would lose him. Dima, meanwhile, had married Natasha, and soon she gave birth to a son. They named him Roma. A year later, they arrived in Odessa for a holiday with Natasha's daughter from her first marriage. Our three-roomed apartment was turned into a hotel. There was food being cooked in the kitchen all day, and there was always someone in the bathroom or clothes being washed. In the evenings, there was always wine on the table, and practically everyone, except Mother and the children, smoked. As usual, we got into political debates. Dima had never been overseas, and because he was working in the defence industry, he was a patriot. On the other hand, I had been travelling overseas since I was a child. Also I was not a Soviet citizen and was critical of the totalitarian Soviet system. In these debates, Father was between us, and these arguments were loud and heated, but we were always happy to see each other in the morning. Dima never understood my desire to leave the USSR and considered it a betrayal.

Klara tried to keep in contact with Mishka, who still lived in Tashkent, but because of the distance, it was hard to keep a warm relationship. She lost almost all contact with her relatives in America. After Larisa had left, there was no one who could read and write in English, and communications ended. Elsa sent a letter once a year, and Klara responded in Russian. Elsa took the letters to a translator, and it wasn't easy, but thanks to that, we knew that there had been a few dreadful events in her life. In the one year, he husband and son had both died of brain cancer. This event hit her very hard, but she had tried to keep her spirits up. Then she met another man, married him, and moved from Philadelphia to New Jersey. Oll and Irma were hardly working anymore and mostly travelled the world. Usually, they travelled on luxury boats through exotic countries. Their children had already grown up and had their own much bigger businesses.

In the summer of 1983, Oll and Irma were to visit Odessa on board a luxury vessel, and they wrote to Klara that we could meet them at the port. We found out exactly when they would arrive in Odessa, and Mother applied for permission to meet her relatives. It was a rule in the Soviet Union to ask permission for everything. Finally, we were allowed to meet them on the sea terminal premises. At the expected time, George and Klara and Valentina and I arrived for our meeting. We saw the huge sea liner, moored at the pier, as big as the sea terminal itself. All the approaches to the ship had been barricaded by frontier guards. We had to wait an hour before we were allowed to go up to the second floor and sit down in a small room. Irma and Oll came out of the ship down the gangway and came into the same room but through the other side. We embraced and kissed each other and sat on chairs that were standing along the walls. We wanted to say a lot to each other, but it wasn't easy. Our guests spoke English and Yiddish; Klara spoke a little Yiddish, but it was of little help. Thanks to my time in Australia, I could speak a little English, but it still wasn't enough, and we mostly communicated through our hands. It was enough to express our warm feelings. So we exchanged our feelings and gifts, and after an hour, we were told by the frontier guard that our meeting was over. Our American guests left, and we stayed with our problems.

But it wasn't just them that had left. The closest of Valentina's friends were Ljalja Rud, Natasha Jashnicova, and Valja Krukova. Ljalja and Natasha were openly dreaming of marrying a foreigner and leaving the country, while Valja seemed to be a very ordinary Soviet girl who had graduated from school and her institute with a red diploma. Her father was an army officer and a Soviet patriot. She read a lot, studied foreign languages, English and French, and I always felt sorry for her that she would never have the chance to use them. And suddenly the news arrived, out of the blue, surprising everyone, that she was marrying a West German man, Marcus, a computer teacher, and that after the wedding, they would move to Germany. He was much older than her but was a very open and kindnatured man. After the marriage, they did leave for Germany but visited Odessa at least once a year, and we had a big picnic party for them, with a heap of meat and smoked mackerel. After that, Natasha found an Italian husband, and Ljalja found a Danish man, and both moved abroad.

We were happy for them, but, at the same time, I felt that it wasn't fair that I had been trying to get out of the country for more than ten years, but they had a much easier time. Our documents were going around in circles, and every time we seemed to be back at the starting point. But in a month's time, my residency was supposed to expire, and as usual, every three years, I was supposed to apply for renewing it. But this time, I decided not to do that. I was called in to the regional police office, where I met with the even more obese Elena Borisovna. During the last few years, she had been steadily trying to ruin my life, and in spite of her beautiful face, in my brain I thought of her as a toad.

'How are you, Comrade Vignevich? Have you forgotten that your residency permit is about to expire?' she asked.

'Really, so what am I supposed to do?' I asked.

'You have to fill in the form and ask for permission to extend your residency,' she told me.

'No, I don't want to do that. On the contrary, I want you to let me leave this country.'

This answer surprised Elena Borisovna very much. Her face became red, and she choked a little. 'You are always confusing things,' she said. 'Departure from the USSR is one thing, and living in a country without permission is another you could find yourself with a criminal sentence.' She tried to intimidate me.

'No, I refuse to do this, because these two actions contradict each other. But if the law says it has to be done, then take my documents and stamp them but without my request, and I will put my green certificate of permanent residency on the table.'

Elena Borisovna wasn't ready for such a turn of events and didn't know what to say. 'You know, Vignevich, I've tried to convince you. Now I will send you to regional OVIR and let them talk to you, but remember that I have warned you,' she said, and the meeting ended on that note. I left and started to wait with the family to see how the situation would develop. My mother tried to support me and quite often tried to start a conversation on a different subject, but her loud voice and constant panic made me even more nervous. She forced my father to go to the Red Cross to ask them to support me.

My father was far less talkative, but I always felt his support. He was a well-respected person, and thanks to him, I could behave more freely with the KGB; without him, they would speak to me more rudely. Meanwhile, Valentina was getting used to my constant struggle with the KGB and was ready for more resolute action. She bolstered my confidence; little Phillip understood very little of what was going on, but he was also very excited. In the last years, I had become so used to this constant battle with the authorities that I wasn't scared anymore. Frequent meetings with high officers from OVIR and MVD and occasional trips to Kiev and Moscow had taught me a lot. I wasn't a naïve, easily distracted little boy anymore. Now I was able to control the conversations and not get distracted by OVIR officers. Even very high officials had a problem to prove their case. For a long time, they had humiliated me, but I had learnt from them and now was ready for a decisive fight. I also felt that if you decide to have a fight, do it at a time most suitable for you, and now was the right time for me. I felt confident in my fight with this brutal organisation. Every man has one most important fight in his life, and I was trying to lift my spirits: 'If you know that you are fighting against evil, make sure you win. If each of us wins his little battles, the world will get better.'

I was called to regional OVIR and met by a small but far more treacherous Tatiana Michalovna, and she began the attack straightaway. She said almost the same things but in a more threatening manner. She couldn't convince me and finally took me to her boss's room, where Ivanov started the attack himself.

'You are a young man, and you don't understand what troubles you can get into,' he said.

'No, I well realise what kind of power you have, but I refuse to submit any longer. I'm sick, and if I don't leave the USSR, I face the risk of becoming an invalid,' I answered him.

'Then extend your permanent residency, and after that, apply for departure,' he told me.

'No, I refuse to do these two contradictory actions. Don't even try to persuade me,' I said.

'Then you will go to jail for breaking the rules of staying in the country without the correct documents,' he argued.

'Then arrest me right now because I will not make this request. If you can do it without my application, then here are my documents,' I said confidently. Now more than ever, I was confident that this was the right time and I would never get a better chance. The way the OVIR employees were acting told me that they were out of their comfort zone and didn't know what to do. The skirmish had begun and was now raised to the highest level.

I continued to work and occasionally visited OVIR. At home, we were constantly discussing the plan, and everyone supported me. But after the first fine arrived, the confident mood began to vanish, and the women started to doubt my chances. My mother began to question if this risky game was worth it. In those days, I grew thin, and my hands became even bluer. Sometimes I felt a pain in my heart. Valentina saw all that, and her mood changed, but this time I had decided not to give in and to fight to the end, because I had seen that the OVIR employees were very uncertain as well. Then the second fine arrived. And now the MDV had only one step, and I was ready for that too. I had a strong feeling that they were only bluffing, exceeding their rights, and, at the last minute, they would meet my demands. But we still had two steps to reach this critical point. It was all looking like a game of chess: the officials made their move and then I had to work out my move and then it was time for the officials to make another move. The end of the game was coming fast, and I knew I had to make my last move, which was quite frightening. I was ready for the move, but I wasn't supported at home anymore.

Father tried to give advice. 'I can understand you, my son, but it's getting dangerous, and they could ruin the rest of your life,' he said.

'Dad, I was prepared for that a long time ago. And I don't want to give in,' I answered, shrugged my shoulders, and fell silent.

But at that moment, my mother joined in with her loud voice, and she talked through her tears. 'My dear son Milanchik, send them to hell and don't deal with them. These bastards will ruin your life. I beg you, don't risk it all. Write what they want and don't risk your future.' She grabbed my hands and pressed them against her chest.

Frightened by the loud voices, little Philipok started to cry and scream, 'I don't want it like that!'

At that moment, Valentina joined in the conversation. She started to speak with the tone that I was most afraid of. 'Why are you only talking about yourself? Did you think about us? Do you think it will help your son if you go to jail? And I don't want that as well. So you decide now to be with us or continue your battled with OVIR without us.'

That threat definitely broke me down, and I was compelled to agree that the next day I would go to OVIR and do what they demanded of me. I did that the next morning, and I saw the signs of relief on the faces of OVIR officials. I had the impression that they were in deep trouble, but I could only suspect it. My mood was down, and I didn't want to talk to anyone. My father felt guilty because he knew that if we had submitted our documents together, OVIR wouldn't have been able to stop us. But the officials were feeling relieved, and Tatiana Michalovna even suggested that we resubmit our documents for Yugoslavia.

Meanwhile in the country, there were changes happening quickly. The Politburo of the Communist Party of USSR looked like an old people's home, and the majority of them were mad. But, suddenly, one after another, they started to depart this world for a better one! Mourning marches were played on the television more and more often, and, finally, Leonid Illyich Brezhnev died. In his last years, he quite often lost his place in his speeches, and even his false teeth! Everyone knew that he wouldn't last long. On the radio and television, there were many speeches about what a great leader of all the working classes he had been. The impression was that the world would not be able to keep turning after this dreadful loss, but everything turned out quite the opposite way. Brezhnev died and was immediately forgotten by the world. He was succeeded by Andropov, with his big promises for the future, which never became true because of his illness and sudden death. After him came the even more fragile Chernenko, who almost immediately died as well. Again, on the television, they played mourning music, but now people were openly laughing about their decrepit leaders.

At last, the change arrived. Unexpectedly, the younger and good-looking Gorbachev arrived, and the country felt that there was a hope of substantial change. He started with a fight against alcohol, which frightened a vast number of booze lovers, and after that, perestroika started. The first shoots of freedom began to show, and after long years of communist dogma, glasnost arrived. I submitted my documents for a trip to Yugoslavia, this time by myself, and I had decided that if they let me go this time, I would not come back. Everybody in my family knew that, and even Valentina supported me. In OVIR, they also suspected it, and Tatiana Michalovna told me, when she gave me my documents, 'Don't even think about not coming back. Remember, we will not allow your wife and child out of the country.' The farewell at the train station was like a funeral; no one knew when we would see one another again, and only Phillip was in an excited mood, expecting presents on my return.

At Zagreb, I was met at the station by Larisa, who had come from Australia to help me at the Australian embassy, and we were planning to go to Belgrade the next day. At the embassy, we found an unexpected obstacle; my documents for permanent residency were in Moscow, and they would need at least a couple of weeks to get them to Belgrade. The other problem was that with my existing documents, I had no rights to leave Yugoslavia to go to another country. The only way was for me to get the status of a refugee, and to do that, I had to go to the United Nations office in Belgrade. I was very uncomfortable with the very frosty attitude of the officials. They were not touched by the story of my long fight with the KGB. From the Australian embassy, we went by taxi to the United Nations office, where again we had to fill out forms and to wait in a long queue in a corridor. The majority of the people were from Eastern Europe who had arrived in Yugoslavia as tourists and had decided to claim political asylum. There were also people who had swum across the Danube River from Hungary and Romania. Each of them had a heartbreaking story to tell, which would make an ordinary person cry, but the officials here had been hardened by many tales like that, and they were used to other people's grief and pain.

Finally, our number came, and from the room, a very handsome man came out and presented himself as Comrade Klarich. He listened to us with a smile on his face and finally gave us his view on the situation . . . that I must reject my documents and take refugee status. That should take a couple of months, and I should move to a refugee camp, where I would live and do all the necessary medical tests.

'Must I live in a refugee camp?' I asked.

'Where else would you live?' Dr Klarich asked me.

'I could live for a few weeks with my relatives, and that would give you time to look through my papers,' I said.

'I don't mind your doing that,' he said.

'The most important thing is that you'll work with his documents and not leave them lying on a shelf,' Larisa added.

'Don't worry about that, I'll do the best I can,' he reassured us. In the end, we checked all the details again and left.

The next day, we returned to Zagreb, where, for three days, we walked around the city, visiting different bars and restaurants. We had a great time, but then Larisa had to leave to meet her husband, John, and continue their holidays in Italy. I stayed with my uncle Milan and decided to go to Lipa to help Sveto, who was now the only man living in the house, with his mother, Stana. He had to do everything himself, but he didn't have enough time to graze the cattle and sheep, so we would help him to build enclosures for them. I had never been involved in agricultural work before and only now understood how difficult it was. It was already October, and in the Bosnian mountains, snow often fell at that time. Every morning, after a light breakfast, we went out on the planes, where we drove stakes into the ground and stretched barbed wire between them. By the end of the day, we were exhausted and came back to the house for dinner, which Stana had prepared for us. Her cooking skills hadn't improved at all, but the main thing was that it wasn't hygienic, and I could hardly eat it; the exception was prshut and potato, which was better than any I had tried anywhere else. After that, we drank rakija and talked.

In the last years, Sveto had changed a lot. About seven years ago, he had still been a handsome young man with dark hair, cheerful and healthy. Now he was a skinny, grey-haired, and toothless old man. Very little was left of his cheerful nature; now it had been replaced by inexplicable rage. He had never found a wife and had few friends locally. Everywhere around him were only old people, but in the surrounding Muslim villages, there were plenty of young men. It worried him very much. The Mandich house was half empty as well, and the whole district looked quite depressing. We slept in the first room in the new house, where a wood-fired oven was located, but the heat from it wasn't enough to warm the room adequately, and we had to lie down in a cold bed and heat it up with our bodies. From Lipa, I came back to Zagreb in a good mood and stayed another two weeks in my uncle's house. But pretty soon I began to feel that my uncle's wife, Anchi, wasn't happy anymore with my presence, and I decided that it was time to go back to Belgrade.

From the train station, I went straight to see Dr Klarich, but when I got there, I had some unpleasant news. In spite of his promises, no one had touched my documents at all in my absence.

'But why didn't you do anything?' I asked indignantly.

'How could we do anything without your signature, and how could we do a medical examination without your presence?' he asked.

'Why didn't you tell me this a month ago? I wouldn't have gone anywhere.' I couldn't calm myself down.

'You just messed it all up yourself,' Dr Klarich concluded. There was no point in arguing with him, and I had to start again. I handed over my documents to him, and he gave me a certificate of a refugee. I picked up my luggage and took a bus to the refugee camp on the outskirts of Belgrade, not far from Avala Obelisk.

Here, I was settled into a room with a young Romanian man who had run away from Ceausescu's regime by swimming the Danube with a friend. The Romanian man's room was not clean, and the strong smell of the male body sweat was present, and I could hardly stand it. Then I went to the dining room, where I was placed around a table with a couple from Czechoslovakia and a man called Peter from Hungary. He simply hated the Soviet Union and continuously used foul language when talking about it. I have to admit that the atmosphere was very unhappy, and I was supposed to live here for a couple of months. By that time, I would be as smelly and unhappy. In the evening, I drank alcohol with the Romanians, telling stories about our lives and dreaming about a better future.

The next morning, I woke up in a terrible mood, and after breakfast, I went to the United Nations Office. Here they told me that I would have to spend from three months to a year in the refugee camp. During this time, they would consider my case, and in the meantime, I would have to pass all the medical examinations. Only after that they would decide which country to send me to. Most likely it would be the USA, Canada, Germany, or Australia. My wish was only to go to Australia, but they couldn't promise that. Now I had faced two difficult choices: to stay in the refugee camp far away from my family, with no guarantees that I would get to Australia, or to give up and go back to Odessa. The second choice was an admission of defeat, but I would be with my family. Before I made my final decision, I went again to the Australian embassy to find out if they had received any of my documents. The result was even more depressing; in all this time, they had not managed to move any paperwork from Moscow to Belgrade, and this was the final straw. On the same day, I asked for all my documents back, and in the evening, I took the train back to Odessa.

At home, everyone was surprised and happy to see me. For my father, it was as if life had returned; my mother was trying everything to improve my mood, but it was difficult. Valentina suggested that I take back my Soviet citizenship, but I flatly refused. I returned to my job in the theatre, and no one found out what I had done in Yugoslavia on my holiday. But, again, life showed itself to be unpredictable. Gorbachev's reforms gained speed, and glasnost opened people's eyes to the recent past. Old authorities started to disappear, and new ideas were born. Not everyone loved it, and some people resisted the changes. New times began in OVIR as well. Unexpectedly, I was called to a meeting with the chief OVIR officer, and he started with a straightforward question.

'Well, Comrade Vignevich, do you still have a wish to immigrate to Australia?'

'Yes, I do,' I answered confidently.

'Then you should lodge your documents again, and I think that this time the answer will be positive.' And this time, everything went smoothly. Practically without any questions, they accepted our documents and made their decision in a couple of months.

The same people who for many years had only tried to make things difficult for us were now smiling and trying to give the impression that they were trying to help us. But I knew it wasn't true, and they would prefer to harm us. But as it turned out, we still had one more obstacle to overcome. We had to get written permission from all our relatives and a signed declaration that they had no financial claims on us. My parents signed it on the same day; Valentina's parents did as well but with grim and unhappy faces. But her brother, Seryoga, refused to do it. Everyone knew that he was influenced by his wife, Galina, a very selfish and unpleasant woman. All our efforts to talk to Seryoga were in vain. Some of my friends suggested that we use physical pressure, but I categorically refused to do that. I decided to do it differently.

Early in the morning, I went to the Ivanivsky's apartment, where I had calculated that Galina would be on her own, just with her little daughter. I knocked at the door.

'Who is that?' Galina said as she opened the door.

'I have to speak with you,' I said.

'What about?' she asked.

'Seryoga is refusing to sign our documents, and I feel that you are the influence,' I said.

'Nonsense,' she denied. 'I have nothing to do with that. But why should he sign your papers if it could ruin his career?'

'What career are you talking about? I have to assure you that to sign the papers is in your best interest, because then we will be far away from here. If you do not sign them tomorrow, Valentina and I will move in to this apartment and take one room. I know your plans well! You have decided to divide this apartment between you and Valentina's parents, but, trust me, we will destroy your plans. That's why you need to sign those papers by tomorrow, otherwise we will move in. Do you understand me clearly?' It was clear that she did understand me! She was so angry that her eyes filled with tears, but she said nothing. Next day, Seryoga came and signed the papers, and now all the formalities were done, and we just had to wait.

Tatiana Michalovna gave us the wonderful news and the international passports for Valentina and me. Now the road to Australia was open, but we weren't very excited. By that time, great changes were being made in our country, and the feeling of freedom and hope was in the air. We had waited for this all our lives, and now, when they were starting to happen, we were leaving the country. Valentina had her doubts as well.

'Maybe we should stay?' she asked. 'We are not so young anymore. It may be hard to make a new start.'

But after a short time thinking, I said, 'I've spent so much of my life fighting for the right to leave this country, and it would be very stupid now to stay. No, those changes are not for us. Let the others enjoy them. We will pack our things and go,' I answered. After that, I went to Moscow to the Australian embassy to get our visas. Here, I met a few unexpected difficulties because six years had passed since I had been given permission to go to Australia. In the beginning, the embassy officials couldn't find any documents at all, but eventually they put a visa in our passports, and I went back home.

One week before we were due to leave, my brother, Dima, arrived from Ufa with his son, Roma. In the evenings, we drank wine in the kitchen and discussed difficult political subjects. Dima could never understand my wish to leave the USSR, and now we had our last chance to talk about it.

'Tell me, why do you want to leave the country that has looked after you and educated you?' he said.

'Don't talk nonsense. That wasn't the country that did that, it was my parents,' I told him.

'Your mother was born here, and you grew up here. This is your motherland,' he added.

'My father's motherland is Yugoslavia, and I've always felt different, and with the years, that difference just kept getting bigger,' I explained.

'I would be ashamed to leave my country,' Dima kept pushing.

'And you don't have to leave your country, so don't worry,' I said to calm him. We went to bed tired and drunk! But these debates didn't spoil our relationship.

As usual, we left from Central Railway Station. All our relatives and heaps of friends came to say goodbye. Practically everyone was crying, assuming that we were seeing each other for the last time. I felt as though I was dying here, to be born again in another place, but not knowing what to expect.

＋◆＋◆◆＋◆

After we had gone, Klara and George were left alone. Their usually noisy apartment was almost silent, and the silence was dreadful. George began to avoid home. He and Klara began to walk a lot in the parks, and in summer, George spent most of the day on the beach. The sea helped to get rid of his melancholy, and the sound of the waves distracted him from his sad thoughts. Besides that, there were plenty of my friends on Dolphin Beach, and they always came to ask about news from Australia. Klara sometimes went to the beach too, but it was harder for her. Since she had broken her foot, now she limped, and over time, it was getting worse. She mostly involved herself with housekeeping, running around the shops, preparing the food, and doing the washing. In the evenings, they sat around the television and talked about the children.

'What kind of life is it without children?' George complained.

'That's why we were supposed to go with them,' Klara said.

'Yes, maybe you're right!' George conceded.

'I'm always right,' Klara said. 'If not for your stubbornness, we would live now with our children in Sydney, and they wouldn't have wasted so much time and energy to get away.' George had to agree because he knew that it was the truth.

But he knew what he wanted—to return to his Bosnia, and now with even more determination, he decided to get Yugoslavian citizenship.

He lodged all the documents again, this time on his own. After my departure, he didn't want to stay in this foreign country, though so many of his friends were still here. More than anyone else, he visited Milan Kalafatich, who was already very old and hardly moved at all, but his brain still worked well, and he was able to play chess and discuss the important news at the same time. Quite often, Tule Milich joined them; by now, he was old too but refused to stop. George often met with Dmitry Velich, who was thinking about moving to Germany, where his son, Slavik, lived. The Janesh and Boich families were still alive, and Chuk sometimes came. Occasionally, he met Slavko Stojanovich, who was isolated because no one could forgive him for how he had spoiled Milan Ribar's life. Slavko remained a cheerful boozer and womaniser, but now George didn't like his dirty jokes anymore. So George and Klara weren't lonely, but they hated their half-empty apartment. They often talked to us on the phone, but these conversations always ended in tears.

Meanwhile, in Australia, we were doing quite well. At the airport, Larisa met us, but for the first few weeks, we had to move in with Asja and Uzik, who, by that time, had bought a house in Bondi, one of the most prestigious suburbs in Sydney. Larisa had split up with her second husband, John, and now lived with her friend and was leaving for Hong Kong to work in IGM. At first, we were a little frightened, but we quickly realised that we could rely only on ourselves. With the help of Larisa's husband, we found a unit to rent not far from the beautiful Coogee Beach. In the beginning, we studied English at a college, but in a few months, I found a job as an electrician on a construction site and began to earn very decent money. I didn't want Valentina to look for additional income from unskilled jobs and to search for a career in chemistry, and after a few months, she found a job in the University. Our financial situation improved every day. Little Phillip went to school and was soon speaking English. Our unit was located not far from the tennis courts, and Phillip began to take lessons with a private trainer. Everything seemed to be going well, except for the deep feeling of nostalgia that Valentina couldn't shake off. Sydney airport was not far away, and the planes flying over our heads only deepened Valentina's unhappiness.

One day, as we were walking along our beautiful Coogee Beach, I said to Valentina, 'Believe me, one day you will love this beach no less than our favourite Dolphin Beach.'

But Valentina strongly disagreed. 'Trust me, it will never happen. I will never love this beach as much as Dolphin.' There was only one way to beat this disease, and that was to go back to Odessa and see it again. By that time in the USSR, many changes had happened. People had the opportunity to travel overseas, and those who had left the country were able to revisit it. But before going back to Odessa, we decided to invite my parents to come to us. We sent them an invitation, and

OVIR didn't put any obstacles in front of them. It was difficult to describe Klara's feelings when she received her foreign passport from Tatiana Michalovna, who had promised her years ago that she would never again see her children. At Sydney airport, we all met them: Valja, Phillip, Larissa, and me. We were all crying, but this time they were tears of joy. George couldn't let go of his grandson, Phillip. We went from the airport in my Ford Cortina, which I had bought just a month before their arrival. Never in their lives had they had a car, and now it was a real surprise for them to see that, after only a year in Australia, I had managed to buy one.

I took them to Larisa's place, which she had rented just for their arrival in Coogee. Here, there was enough room for three people, and my parents had their bedroom with the window facing the courts where Phillip was coached and played tennis. On the right side of the courts, they could see a wide strip of Coogee Beach. They thought they were living in paradise. Every morning, they spent at least a couple of hours on the beach. Valentina and I were busy during the weekdays, but on the weekends, we spent time with them. During her years in Australia, Larisa had almost forgotten how to communicate with her parents, but now she did it with great pleasure. Deep in her heart, Klara began to hope that they, too, would be able to move to Australia, but there was one huge obstacle in their way. Because of their age, they wouldn't be able to come to Australia on an independent immigration visa; they wouldn't score enough points. The only way was for Larisa and me to invite them for family reunification, but in this case, we had to pay a lot of money, and neither Larisa nor I had that sort of money. More than that, Dima was still living in Ufa with his family, and she didn't want to leave him behind.

They had to return to Odessa, where the financial situation was getting even worse. To make it easier for them, we bought them two personal computers, which they would be able to sell when they got home, even though they didn't know anything about computers. This plan was very successful; at that time, computers hardly existed in USSR, while many institutes and enterprises needed them. With Dima's help, they managed to sell them for a huge amount of money such that they had only dreamed of. And they made another smart step; they managed to privatise their flat offered by the government, and for a few thousand roubles, they now owned their unit. Practically straight after that, a terrible inflation followed, which destroyed all their savings, like the savings of millions of other pensioners.

Valentina, Phillip, and I visited Odessa a few months later, thanks to an invitation sent to us from Valentina's parents. On the way, we visited Ljalja Rud in Denmark, and Valentina Krukova in Germany, totally surprising them that after only a year and half, we were able to afford this trip. Ljalja lived in a large house full of antique furniture and artefacts, with a big courtyard, tennis courts, and a swimming pool. Together with her famous husband, Ture, we travelled around the country and visited the palace where, according to Shakespeare, the well-known Prince Hamlet lived. We stayed with them for a week and then went to Germany, where we received a no less warm welcome from Valentina Krukova and her husband, Markus. He was a really warm and hospitable owner, which was very unusual for Germans. We drove along the Rhine River with them, tried plenty of tasty food, and drank litres of German wine. When it was time for us to leave for the Soviet Union, Valentina and I both felt a bit tired.

In the airport at Kiev, we had to wait in a queue for the very long customs formalities, but at last we passed the border and went to the station. The train was to leave in a couple of hours. We found a place on a bench in the waiting room, and I decided to take Phillip to the toilet. But the closer we got to the toilet, the awful smell got stronger, and Phillip refused to go in. After the hygienically clean restrooms of Australia, even for me the smell was revolting, but for a child, it was too much, and he told me that he would wait and use the toilet on the train. But the toilet on the train was also awful, and the poor boy had to suffer until we got to Odessa to the Ivanovksy home.

When we had left USSR a year and a half ago, the country was beginning to feel that changes for the better were on their way, but the situation was now much worse, and already many people couldn't make ends meet. One of our best friends, Sasha Boronetsky, who had been well off and had lent me money for our tickets to Australia, was now simply struggling for his existence. I had paid back his loan in less than half a year. But now, his car, "Ziguli", was in dreadful condition, and he couldn't even buy a battery for it. I gladly used the opportunity and bought him a battery, but there was nothing else I could do for him.

Our holiday turned out to be very demanding on our health; at every meeting with friends, there was a lot of alcohol consumed. It was like a carnival; emotions were overwhelming, and my strength was wearing away. When we finally got to the airport, I could hardly stand on my feet, and it took a long time after our return to Sydney before I felt myself again.

After our departure, Klara and George's mood went down sharply. Knowing that they would probably end their lives separated from their children was devastating. After spending just a few months with us in Sydney, they understood what happiness is and how difficult it would be for them to achieve that. Meanwhile, life in the Soviet Union was falling to pieces. It had become impossible for George and Klara to exist on their pensions, and only the money from the computer sales made life a bit easier. Fewer friends were still alive, and their health was getting worse. One day, Kalafatich died. He and George had spent a lot of time together over the last year, and George was very sad.

But life sometimes had some pleasant surprises. Unexpectedly, the answer from the Yugoslavian Supreme Court arrived; his case had been overruled, and now George was allowed to become a Yugoslavian citizen. All that he had fought for over all those years had now become true, but it came a bit late for George now that his son had gone to Australia. He decided to go ahead at any rate, and in USSR, the first signs of disorder began to appear. At first, disobedience began in the Baltic republics; they didn't want to live under Moscow rule and demanded independence. After that, a revolution began in Georgia, and then there was the coup in Moscow. Gorbachev was removed from power, and a group of conspirators tried to turn history back. Their rule didn't last for long; ordinary people who had already tasted freedom rose against them. At the front of the people's movement stepped up the cleverest of all, Boris Yeltsin. People stood in front of tanks, and the army refused to take part in any suppression. In a couple of weeks, all the organisers of the coup had been arrested and condemned. Gorbachev returned to Moscow, but he didn't have the same powers as before. Then Yeltsin, as the Russian President, declared independence, and the rest of the republics became independent by accident, and Gorbachev became president of nothing. Ukraine became independent and fell into chaos; factories closed down, people lost their jobs, inflation hit, and the new currency, 'kupons', was so hopeless that people used them in packs. The only way to make money was to travel to other countries and bring back some products to sell at the markets.

In Ufa, life began to derail as well. The aviation industry where Dima worked had lost its financial support, and it became a challenge to survive. Dima now seemed to forget how he had criticised me when I was planning to leave the motherland and immigrate to Australia. Now he decided to immigrate to Australia, and he asked me to send him an invitation. I was surprised after all his criticisms, but I gladly sent him all the documents he needed and the invitation. But Dima couldn't use the invitation because I would have to pay a lot of money, which I didn't have. So he submitted his documents for independent immigration. Now everything depended on the number of points they could accumulate, and their not-so-young age was the main obstacle. Only their young children were able to improve the situation.

If I was pleasantly surprised by Dima's request, the call from Valentina's mother simply revolted me. Dianna Vasiljevna asked Valentina to send an invitation to her brother, Seryoga, his wife, Galina, and their daughter, Lena.

'Mama, how could they ask that? Don't you remember that they wouldn't give us permission to leave USSR and immigrate to Australia?' Valentina asked.

'Of course, I remember, but, believe me, if you will not help him, he will die here from alcoholism,' Dianna Vasiljevna said.

'Why should I have to worry about that?' Valentina asked.

'Because he is your brother and he is my son. I'm asking you to help him, and they will never do any harm to you,' she said.

'OK, Mama. I have to talk to Milan,' Valentina said and put down the telephone. 'Did you hear everything? You know what she is asking?' she said to me.

'I guess so,' I replied.

'And what do you think about it?'

'I'm asking you,' she said.

I was silent for a few minutes, trying to find the words. 'I can't believe what impudence they have to ask us for an invitation when they refused to sign the papers for us for our immigration,' I said.

'I will never forgive them for that as well. But it's not them asking us, it's my mother, and the second thing is that he is my brother,' she said.

'I know that he is your brother, and you have to decide, but, believe me, if you do invite them, they will hurt us again, and not just once,' I said.

We discussed this problem for a few days, but, finally, Valja decided she couldn't refuse her mother's request and started to fill out the forms for immigration. She sent them to Odessa, and now we just had to wait. Seryoga and Galina were much younger than Dima and Natasha, and with their young daughter, they had a much better chance to get to Australia. What amazed me was that Dima obtained his permit in less than a year, and they started to get ready for their trip. Klara was delighted that her dream that all her children would be together would come true, though unfortunately without her. It was much easier for her to see Dima's family leave because he had already lived away from her for more than twenty years, not like me. We were still so close that every conversation ended in tears.

After Dima's departure, George went to Yugoslavia to collect his new passport. By this time, Yugoslavia, too, had started to fall to pieces. George never could forget how Tito had sent them to study in USSR and how they had been forgotten after the fallout with Stalin. But he had to admit that during Tito's time, Yugoslavia was quite a happy and united socialist country. Now tensions between the different nationalities became obvious. George didn't like it at all. As usual, after his arrival, he went with his brother, Milan, to visit Lipa and to visit their mother's tomb, which now had a marble slab. In the family house, there was just the one man, Svetko, and he had changed so much, he was hardly recognisable. The tall and powerfully built man had turned into a toothless, crooked old person. Now he was drinking excessively, which wasn't surprising . . . everywhere around him was almost completely desolate. The majority of the people had left the land, and only old people stayed.

On that day, however, three of his friends from Vrtoch came to visit him, and they sat around the table. There was plenty of rakija, and a heated conversation was going on about politics, and the arguments got louder. They argued about the country falling apart, blaming the Croats but mostly the Muslims.

'They threaten that they will take away our Bosnia!' Svetko screamed angrily. 'I would rather die than let them do that.'

'They are rising everywhere from here to Kosovo!' his friend Kojo supported him. 'They are terrorising our men and raping our women! For how long can we tolerate that? We should have already begun to fight back and make them bleed!'

Such speeches made even hot-headed Jukan indignant. 'Hey, boys! I think you are trying to act too quickly. Better to try and solve this one peacefully. If you let the nationalistic genie out, you will never be able to get it back in the bottle. I went through the last war, when all our similar emotions were allowed to come out, and you know how much blood was spilled. But even at that time, we did manage to keep our patience.'

'That was then,' Svetko interrupted him. 'Now it's all different. There are only old people left in our villages, and there are plenty of young ones in their villages. They think they will finish with us. But you know that it's better not to make a Serb angry! I remember that you fought in the last war and have a great deal of experience. I remember you telling us that you had enough ammunition hidden away to arm a division. Stay with us, and you can be our commander.'

Svetko's friends supported him, loudly agreeing, and Jukan was pleasantly surprised that they still remembered him. But he also remembered the terrifying days of war, and he didn't want to participate in the next round of madness. 'No, boys, it's not my war. I don't want to see any more blood. If you decide to do it, then do it without me,' he said.

'Yes, Jukita, you are getting old if you don't want to stay with us in this fight. Maybe you've simply forgotten how much trouble those Turks brought to our family,' concluded Svetko. After that, they didn't speak on any serious subject anymore; they just drank! In the morning, Jukan and Milan got into the car and drove back to Zagreb. On the way, they discussed last night's difficult conversation, and Jukan was sure that this country was falling apart.

But the business part of his trip was going well. He was issued a passport; they promised him a pension and that he would get a flat either in Sarajevo or Banja Luka. Now he had to act quickly. He had to go back to Odessa, sell the apartment, and return to Yugoslavia with Klara. He didn't want to stay in Odessa under any circumstances. When he arrived back, he explained the difficult situation in Yugoslavia and asked, 'What do you think? Should we go?'

'And what will we do if war does break out?' she asked.

'Then as a last resort, we will become refugees and seek asylum in Australia,' he said.

This idea definitely convinced Klara, and now, heart-warming thoughts returned, that they might get together again with their children. They decided to sell the flat. Since they had redeemed it from the state, the price of the unit had grown at least tenfold, and now it was worth quite decent money. The area they lived in was one of the most prestigious in Odessa, but it was in the usual five-storeyed apartment, built in the time of Khrushchev. It was very close to Dolphin Beach, and many people dreamed of living there.

The unit was bought by a very pretty young girl who was a beach lover. She paid them all the money up front, and what was more important was that she allowed Klara and George to live in the apartment for as long as it took for their immigration papers to be ready. I took about two months, in which time they sold everything they could and managed to send most of the money to my account in Australia, leaving a smaller amount for their daily needs. Then they said goodbye to all their friends, this time forever, and left for Yugoslavia. They felt like gypsies; they didn't have a house anymore and had no idea of where to go.

At this time, in Bosnia, the real war started, and the bloodiest fights were around Bihach. Any hope of going to Bosnia disappeared, and they decided to go to Zagreb and stay with Milan and Anchi. Here, they lodged their application for refugee status. But it wasn't possible to stay for long at Milan's house. His wife, Anchi, was annoyed by their presence, and it wasn't hard to work out why . . . they lived in a small unit with their two grown-up children, Martina and Igor. The unit was too small even for them. Their financial situation was always hard, and Anchi demonstrated this in every possible way to Klara. Klara felt this irritation deeply, and it began to affect her health. She didn't feel well, and then she caught the flu.

They decided to go to Belgrade and spend a few days with Strina Sofia. By that time, she was really very old, but as before, she was very hospitable. To stay with her was impossible because of lack of space. More than that, the house was freezing, and Klara started to cough. From here, they went to the Red Cross and told them what had happened to them and what a desperate situation they were in now. They asked for political asylum in Australia. They were promised that everything that could be done would be done, but they would have to wait at least a couple of months. Klara and George decided then to go to Banat, where George's cousin Rade lived, to spend some time with them. Rade's wife, Dora, was a very charming and hospitable woman who had always been pleased to see them. The trip to Veliko Selo by bus was quite exhausting. Here, winter had already begun, and it was terribly cold. Klara indeed had the flu; she had a high temperature and could hardly stand. They had to walk from the bus; George carried both bags, and Klara was limping behind him. She often had to stop to take a rest, and she groaned loudly.

'Klara, please make an effort and concentrate. It's only a few hundred metres away,' he said.

But Klara had run out of energy, and there was nothing left for her to concentrate with. 'Oi, George, believe me, I will not survive this and will probably never see my children again,' she told him. George picked up the bags again and continued to walk to the Radko house. Now it was only about ten metres away. When he reached the gate, he turned around and saw Klara lying face down on the road. He threw down the bags, ran back, and tried to lift her. But her body had become almost lifeless and was very heavy. It took him a while to drag her body and prop it up against the fence; after that, he ran to the Radko house. He opened the gate, ran into the yard, and saw Dara with a bucket of water in her hands.

'Dara, do you recognise me?' he called.

'Jukita, what are you doing here?' she was amazed.

'Dara, I will tell you everything later, but could you help me carry Klara? She has fallen down almost in front of your house, and I don't know if she's alive or not,' George said.

'Oh, God, help us!' she screamed and ran with George out of the gate. Together they carried the now unconscious Klara into the house and laid her on the sofa in the lounge room. Dara acted as though she were a nurse in a battlefield. The house was warm, and they began to remove Klara's wet winter clothes. Then she took a wet towel, wiped Klara's face, and put a towel on her forehead.

Klara took a deep breath and opened her eyes. 'Where am I?' she asked.

'You're with relatives,' Dara reassured her. 'We will fix you very quickly.' Dara took total control, and she worked quickly. George had run out of energy and was happy to follow Dara's confident actions. She washed Klara and put dry clothes on her. After that, she made her drink milk and honey. Klara was drinking and coughing and had a blank look in her eyes. Dara took her temperature, and it was 39.2 degrees. 'We have to get her to bed,' Dara said. 'Help me carry her to our bedroom.' In spite of George's arguments, she insisted that they sleep in her bedroom. Her hospitality was limitless, and she did everything possible to get Klara back on her feet. When Radko came home, she found work for him to do as well. For the first time since they had left Odessa, Klara and George were able to relax and sleep well. In the morning, Klara was feeling much better, though she had hardly any memories of the previous day. Dara brought her a cup of tea and some cheese pita. At first, Klara refused to eat, and then without any real desire, she bit off a little piece but gradually ate it all. After that, she felt much better and tried to stand up, but Dara said she must stay in bed at least another day. Like an obedient child, Klara did as she was told and fell asleep again.

Now George had enough time to visit another cousin, Peter, who lived on the other side of the village. He went with Radko, and on the way, George told him everything that had happened to them lately, how they had sold everything in Odessa and how now they were waiting for political asylum. Radko listened with interest and then suggested that until they had positive news, they should stay at his place. George gladly accepted his offer, tears running down his face. Now that they had a roof over their heads, he could feel more relaxed and could take in what was happening around him. The news from everywhere was scary. Everywhere, nationalists had grabbed power: Milosevic, Tudjman, and Izetbegovic. They infected everyone with their hatred, and people went mad and got involved in a bloody turmoil. In front of George's eyes, the country that he had fought for in the Second World War was now falling to pieces. He couldn't believe that it could happen in the middle of Europe in the twentieth century. But he knew that once it started, it would be a vicious war. He had no wish to get involved, and the only way was to run away.

When Klara was feeling a bit better, George went to Belgrade. Now, the United Nations office was crowded. The longer the war went on, the more refugees were arriving in Belgrade, and everyone had his own story of tragedy and grief. George was met by a young brunette with a tired face who was bored with hearing about other people's grief. Their documents were not ready, but George explained the situation with their homelessness and his wife's illness. The woman listened attentively, but it was clear that the story did not touch her. However, she promised to try and accelerate the process, and she did. George and Klara had to go to Belgrade as soon as Klara was well enough. With this good news, George went back to Banat, where he found Klara slowing walking around the room. The good news raised her spirits immediately, and she even began to smile for the first time since they had left Odessa. Dara and Radko continued to care about her as if she was their own daughter, and the results slowly showed. Klara walked much more confidently, though she still limped. She didn't know how to thank them and could only say, 'Dara, I know for sure had it not been for you, I would never have survived. I will be grateful to you for the rest of my days and will never forget you.'

'Stop it, Klara. You know that had you been in my place, you would have done the same thing,' Dara interrupted her.

'No, darling, you gave me your own bed when others didn't even want to give me a place in a corner. You, Dara, are simply a saint!'

Klara began to walk more confidently, though she still limped. Her cough gradually eased, and her face got a healthy colour back. At last, they decided it was time to go back to Belgrade. At their departure from the bus station, everyone was crying because they felt that they would never see one another again. They went straight to the Red Cross on their arrival, and everything now moved at a steady pace, without any obstacles. Their documents were all ready for them, and they were settled in a hotel until their departure for Australia. They got their visas from the Australian embassy and passed their medical examinations. Now it wasn't difficult to wait because Klara knew for sure that she would soon see her children again, and that was the best compensation for the many long years of struggle against the authorities. She had won this unequal struggle, she who was born in the uncertain years of revolution. She had lived through famine, war and evacuation, the sorrow of anti-Semitism, and hard economic times.

Meanwhile, far away in Australia, we were making good progress, and now we were firmly on our feet. Valentina and I were both working, and Phillip was studying at high school. We had good relations with Larisa, but we didn't visit each other often. Now we had many friends, but in this new life, we had learnt to rely only on ourselves. Then, suddenly, everything began to change. Dima arrived first, with his wife, Natasha, daughter, Julia, and son, Roma. I was incredibly happy to see them, and after meeting them at the airport, I took them back to our home. After many years of living in Sydney, in an English-speaking environment, Philip's Russian language was not very good, and I hoped that Roma would help him to remember it. But my hopes evaporated in a few months when they started to speak to each other only in English. Of course, it was too crowded with seven of us in our apartment, but, fortunately, it didn't last for long. In a few weeks, we managed to rent a two-bedroomed apartment for the Miroshnik family. Almost as soon as they had gone, we got new guests; Valentina's brother arrived with his daughter, Lenochka, but wife stayed behind in Odessa. I never forgot the kind of trouble that Seryoga had given us, and so I wasn't all that happy to see him, but I tried not to show it. They stayed with us for a little while and needed a lot of help, but, at last, we found a separate apartment for them, and they started their own life. Even after everyone had moved away, we still had to help them, because they didn't have private cars, and I had to go shopping with them and take them to their homes. Now we had quite a big family, and every Friday night we got together to celebrate the end of the week.

So many people waited for Klara and George when they arrived in Sydney. After checking their passports and a short customs inspection, they came out at the arrival terminal and were hugged by all their children. Larisa and I were amazed at how old our parents had become. Mother moved as though she were an invalid, and Father had lost a lot of weight and the confidence had gone from his eyes.

'Thank you, God, that you allowed us to meet again one more time,' Klara said through her tears.

'Don't worry, Mama, you will live with us for a long time, and we will have the chance to argue with you many times,' I said, trying to cheer her.

'No, children, with God's help, I will not last more than a year.' She brushed aside the suggestion.

From the airport, we drove to Larisa's home, a big apartment in Double Bay. Here, we had dinner and drank some alcohol. After our first glasses, the atmosphere became more cheerful and very warm. At that moment, George and Klara felt that they had lived their lives for a good reason and that their long struggle was now finished with their long-awaited victory. We didn't stay long at the table, because after their flight, our parents were very tired and they wanted to go to bed. The next day, Larisa took her parents to the ocean. The day was terrific; there was not a single cloud in the sky, and the ocean shone like a huge mirror, reflecting the bright sunshine. At that moment, George started to write in his mind a letter to his grandmother Marija.

Dear Baka,

Your prediction was right, and the Black Sea was not able to stop me. Now I'm standing on the edge of the Pacific Ocean, and, apparently, I will stay here for good.

Farewell, your naughty grandson,
Jukitca.

The End